ABENGONI

F I R S T   C A L L I N G

Copyright © 2014
MVmedia, LLC

Published 2014

All Rights Reserved.

This story is a work of fiction. Any references to real events, persons and locales are intended only to give the fiction a sense of reality and authenticity. Any resemblance to actual persons, living or dead is entirely coincidental.

ISBN Number: 978-0-9960167-9-7

Cover art by Julie Dillon
Cover Design by Uraeus
Layout/Design by Uraeus
Edited by Rebecca Kyle

Manufactured in the United States of America

First Edition

ANOTHER CALLING

Generally speaking, there are two major types of fantasy fiction: heroic and epic. Heroic fantasy – also known as "sword and sorcery" – focuses on the exploits of a single, larger-than-life character. The literary archetype for heroic fantasy is Conan the Barbarian, created back in the 1930s by the late Robert E. Howard. Epic – also referred to as "high" (but not on drugs) fantasy – paints on a broader canvas, with numerous characters interacting in multiple storylines. J.R.R. Tolkein's *Lord of the Rings* trilogy is the ur-text of modern epic fantasy, and George R.R. Martin's *Game of Thrones* saga is its present-day exemplar.

When I began writing my stories in the early 1970s about Imaro, a black warrior whose adventures take place in an alternate-world Africa I call Nyumbani, I was enthusiastically following in the footsteps of Howard. His fiction captivated me when I was a young man, and I consciously wrote the Imaro tales in the tradition he established. *Lord of the Rings* was another influence, but it took a while for me to develop a set of storylines that would fit into a broader fictional scope. Indeed, more than 20 years would pass between the creation of the "Howardian" Imaro and the conception of a subsequent, "Tolkeinian" series.

At that time, another alternate vision of Africa sprang from the depths of my imagination. The name for this new other-Africa was Abengoni. And instead of the travails and triumphs of one central character, as in Imaro, the Abengoni saga would involve a broad spectrum of contact between two cultures – one black, one white. *First Calling* is the initial volume of that saga.

It's not just the content of these two creations that is different, however. Imaro was born not solely from my enjoyment of heroic-fantasy fiction, but also from dissatisfaction. My love of the genre was tempered by discomfort with the racist depictions of black people and Africa that were found far too often in its stories. I wanted to promote positive portrayals of

ABENGONI
F I R S T   C A L L I N G

A Novel By

Charles R. Saunders

MVMEDIA

Fayetteville, Georgia

blacks, and present mythic and folkloric visions of Africa that would counter the "jungle stories" stereotypes. I wanted to show that African mythology, culture and history were as valid as the Celtic and other European traditions on which much of modern fantasy is based. To the extent that whites were depicted at all in Imaro's milieu of Nyumbani, they were foes, not friends.

For Abengoni, a different creative drumbeat thrummed in my mind. What if there were another Earth in which people from parallel versions of Europe and Africa encountered each other on an equal basis, rather than fictionally reprising the racism and colonialism that have for centuries wracked the so-called "Dark Continent" of the world we know? What if European and African folkloric traditions could be integrated within the context of an epic fantasy saga, rather than remain at racial loggerheads?

The Abengoni series is my answer to those questions. It was conceived and written in a spirit of amity rather than anger. Yes, the people of different races within the pages of *First Calling* are aware of their surface differences, such as skin tone and nose width. They are not color-blind. But they do not attach the suite of negative stereotypes to those differences that have led to the bigotry, discrimination, segregation and apartheid that have plagued our world for far too long. The distorting lens of racism does not exist in Abengoni.

Wow, what a concept ...

As I mentioned earlier, Howard and Tolkein were my primary literary influences. But there have been non-literary influences in my work that have been just as strong.

When I was writing Imaro, I often felt as though I were channeling the spirit of Malcolm X – the spirit of rebellion.

When I was writing Abengoni, I felt as though I were channeling the spirit of Dr. Martin Luther King, Jr. – the spirit of reconciliation.

Both spirits are vital components of my creativity today. My spirit of rebellion has been on display in my work for 40 years, in the Imaro stories and the tales of Dossouye, my black Amazon warrior. In *First Calling,* the time for reconciliation is here.

-- Charles R. Saunders

Dedicated to: Milton, Vickie, Brandon and Alana Davis --
My Sword-and-Soul Family

PART ONE
BEYOND THE STORM

CHAPTER ONE
THE SHADOW OF A SHIP

1

Suspended inside a transparent bubble of air beneath the surface of the harbor of Khambawe, Jewel City of what was once the Matile Mala Empire, Tiyana was visible only as a slender silhouette. On this, the day that marked the First Calling ceremony, Tiyana would serve as the Vessel of the Jagasti who was the Sea Goddess: Nama-kwah, the Dancer-on-the-Waves. Although Tiyana was the daughter of Jass Gebrem, the Leba, the One to Whom All Gods Spoke, at First Calling, her lofty lineage held little meaning compared to the distinction of being the one who would absorb Nama-kwah's essence and, for only the most fleeting of moments, *become* the Goddess for those who witnessed the rites.

Even so, however, Tiyana knew she was nothing more than a substitute for the Jagasti she served. Centuries had passed since Nama-kwah herself had last answered First Calling, the ceremony that expressed the Matile people's gratitude for the long rains that nourished lands parched by a harsh dry season. The rite had become a vestige of a time in the distant past when Nama-kwah and the other Jagasti were strong and the Matile Mala Empire ruled half of the sea-bounded continent of Abengoni, and dominated the remainder.

In those long-gone days, Nama-kwah had guided fleets of Matile ships across the wide sea-ways of the world to trade with lands far to the north and east, and in return brought goods-laden vessels from those lands to Matile Mala. Now, the harbor held only fishing boats and a small number of war galleys. The latter were maintained to guard against raids by marauders from the Shattered Isles, home of the Uloans, whose feud with the Matile mainland dated back to ancient times and was ultimately responsible for the downfall of both peoples, and for the withdrawal of the Jagasti to their unreachable Realms.

Strains of music from the docks that abutted the harbor filtered through the water to Tiyana's ears. Drumming mimicked the rhythmic roll of the sea; fluting echoed the skirl of sea-birds; sweet singing Called to Nama-kwah without any need for words ... the singing reminded Tiyana of the story of how Etiya's song had called the Jagasti to save the Matiles' ancestors from the serpent, Adwe.

As she listened to the water-muffled music, Tiyana breathed slowly and shallowly, to conserve the limited amount of air allotted to her inside the bubble. Like her father, she possessed the power of *ashuma*, the once-potent sorcery practiced by the Vessels of the Jagasti. Her command of those skills did not match that of the Leba. However, her *ashuma* was sufficient to conjure the air-bubble and suspend it in the water until the time came for her to perform the final phase of First Calling.

Apprehensive thoughts crept into Tiyana's mind as she gripped the Mask of Nama-kwah tightly in her hands. This would be only her third performance of the ritual. Even so, her previous Callings had been flawless.

Yet this time, something was wrong.

During her two earlier Callings, she had sensed Nama-kwah's presence. She had felt the Goddess reaching to her from the beyond farthest depths of the sea, and heard her voice speaking within her mind. And when Tiyana placed the Mask over her head, she had *become* Nama-kwah, Dancer on the Waves, a transformation that imbued her with unmatched awe and joy for the brief time it lasted.

But this time she felt ... nothing. She heard ... nothing. And as she gazed through her bubble at the deep water surrounding her, she saw ... nothing.

At her other Callings, Nama-kwah's Children – luminous fish of multifarious shapes, sizes and colors that appeared only during the ceremony – had surrounded her; another blessing from the Goddess. On this day, however, the waters were empty. Even the ordinary fish had vanished. It was as though Nama-kwah and her Children had decided to shun the Calling – and the Matile people as well.

Where are you, High One?

Tiyana asked that question in her thoughts time and again. But she received no reply from the goddess. And the longer the silence lasted, the more uncertain she became. The uncertainty grew as it fed upon itself.

So ominous was the portent that Tiyana was tempted to lift her bubble to the surface and beg her father to halt the ceremony. But that thought passed as quickly as it came. On this day, Jass Gebrem was far beyond being her father. He was the Leba, the highest religious authority in the land. Tiyana knew that a mere absence of fish in the water, Nama-kwah's Children or otherwise, would be far from an adequate reason to ask him to end First Calling. But it would probably be sufficient to end her service as a Vessel.

Then the music and singing paused – a cue Tiyana quickly heeded, despite her misgivings. She fitted the Mask carefully over her head, then peered through its eye-slits. And, as she had feared, she felt no answering touch from the Goddess, even though Nama-kwah's face overlaid her own in a perfect fit. She wore the Mask, but she was still only Tiyana, not the Nama-kwah/Tiyana she had been in the earlier Callings.

Tiyana had practiced *ashuma* many times without Nama-kwah, but she had never before performed First Calling in the Goddess's absence. Now she would have to dance alone before the massed populace of the Jewel City, and others who had come from elsewhere to attend the ceremony … alone before her fellow Amiyas … alone before her father.

And she was afraid.

But she had no choice. If she were not to appear during the pause in the music … she did not even want to think about the consequences of such a sacrilege.

Tiyana uncurled her body, stretching the air-bubble to its limit. Slowly, her *ashuma* lifted her toward the surface. Empty water swirled past her. Fears filled the empty space where the Goddess should have been.

Where are you? she asked a final time, hoping against hope to hear an answer from Nama-kwah, to feel even a slight hint of her presence.

Nothing ....

2

Above the surface, sunlight glinted faintly through waves of vapor that shifted in discernible patterns, like a tapestry fashioned in the air. As the mist moved, the Degen Jassi, the glittering aristocracy of Matile Mala, gazed at the surface of the harbor from the section of the docks set aside for them. Seated on a gallery of stone benches polished smooth by the backsides of countless generations of ancestors, the lords and ladies of the Degen Jassi watched, and waited for Tiyana to begin her performance.

Gossamer wisps of mist swirled and eddied around their sandal-shod feet, and they tightened their brightly-striped mantles, or *chammas*, against a slight chill soon to be banished by the sun. Color combinations signified rank: only the Emperor, Dardar Alemeyu, could wear the royal black and gold. The *chammas* draped the men's tunics and trousers of bleached cotton; and the women's bodies, for *chammas* were the only garments Matile women wore, leaving one or both shoulders bare. The men decorated their trousers, called *senafil*, with strips of shells and beads sewn into the fabric.

The Emperor sat on a stone seat mounted on a dais that lifted him above the rest of the aristocracy. His white beard framed narrow, ascetic features over which dark skin stretched taut and only lightly wrinkled, despite his age. His hooded eyes stared far into the distance, beyond the place where Tiyana would rise from the water. His head tilted at a slight angle, as though the crown of kingship weighed heavily upon him. Yet Alemeyu's title of Emperor was more symbolic than real; the present borders of Matile Mala encompassed only a fraction of the territory his people once held across the northern half of Abengoni.

Dardar Alemeyu's Empress, Issa, sat at his side. Beneath her crown, her hair was beaded with gold and silver, and her royal *chamma* was striped like a sunset in crimson, gold, and orange. Although the jewelry looped around her neck and arms had been handed down through countless generations of Empresses, each piece looked as though it had been crafted only the day before the ceremony.

Decades younger than the Emperor, Issa had only recently taken the place of her barren predecessor, whom Alemeyu had set aside after too many childless years. She, too, had yet to produce an heir to carry on a royal line that counted its years of tenure on the throne in the thousands. Issa was not alone in suspecting the fault lay within the Emperor rather than herself. But she wisely kept that belief to herself.

If Dardar Alemeyu died childless, the throne would pass to his nephew, Jass Eshana, the Dejezmek, or commander of what remained of the Matile armies. Eshana was the son of the Emperor's sister. Next in the line of succession was ... Gebrem, his first cousin, the son of Alemeyu's father's brother, who had been Leba before him.

To have either man follow him on the throne was the last thing Alemeyu wanted – he was determined that the dynasty would be continued through him. And so he continued his fruitless efforts to extend his ancient line efforts with wife after wife, while the Degen Jassi and others shook their heads in pity, and at times contempt, behind his royal back.

At the Emperor's other side, a tame cheetah sat immobile as a spotted sculpture. The weak sunlight glinted from the jewels on the collar that encircled the great cat's neck. At times, Alemeyu thought the beast, which he named Makah, was his most loyal courtier. Almost unconsciously, he stroked Makah's fur as he waited for Gebrem's daughter to appear above the waves.

Like the rest of the people gathered at the Khambawe docks, the Degen Jassi were dark of hue, with skin shades ranging from ebony to cinnamon. The hair of men and women alike was worked into rows of braids: for some people thick, others tiny; some short; others long; the men's mostly unadorned, the women's bedecked with colorful shells and beads and intricately-carved ornaments of ivory and amber, silver and gold. The stripes on their *chammas* spanned the spectrum of colors; the garments underneath were mostly white cotton. Some of the Degen Jassi were young; others old. Family resemblances stamped by many generations of ruling-class endogamy were clearly discernable.

Behind the benches of the Degen Jassi stood a row of attenuated statues that at first glance resembled a sculptor's unfinished products. Their arms had no hands; their legs, no feet. The eyes of the statues were little more than indentations gouged into the slate-gray surface of their faces.

Noses and mouths were afterthoughts, and their narrow bodies, standing several times the height of a human, were smooth and sexless.

These were the Ishimbi, and legends spoke of a time when the Jagasti themselves breathed life into the shapes of stone in times of need, and the Ishimbi walked and struck down the Matiles' enemies. But no one now alive could remember the last time the Ishimbi had moved from their places.

Ranks of soldiers clad in carapace-like cuirasses of hardened leather and armed with huge, curved swords occupied the space between the Degen Jassi and the crowd of commoners who had come to witness First Calling before commencing their daily toils in the city that spread in precincts of flat-roofed houses and towering obelisks behind them.

Jass Eshana, a stalwart man of middle years, stood at their head. His helmet was crested with hair from the mane of a lion he had slain, and he wore a leopard-skin *chamma* over his armor. The role of the Dejezmek's soldiers was strictly ceremonial. As the Degen Jassi well knew, the ordinary people of Khambawe were no more likely to rise against their ruling class than were the inanimate Ishimbi. Without the prestige and power of the Degen Jassi, the rest of the Matile would lose the scant standing they had left in the land they once ruled.

Behind the Degen Jassi, two separate groups sat on elaborately carved wooden stools. One of those groups was the Imba Jassi, rulers of the agricultural lands on the fringes of Matile that were once powerful kingdoms in their own right. Their garments were less elaborate than those of their urban cousins: solid-colored lengths of cloth knotted about their waists and shoulder-shawls, called *harai*, that bared most of their upper bodies. Their hair grew bushy and unbraided, and their weapons were their only ornaments. On their faces, they wore expressions of habitual ferocity, for they were the ones who had to directly face the threats to the frontiers of Matile territory. Their hard eyes showed their disdain for the soft decadence of city life.

The people the Imba Jassi ruled were part of the Empire in name only, the same way the Mala was an empire in name only. Direct governance from Khambawe was a thing of the distant past. Yet the historical and blood ties that connected them to the Empire remained strong, and they always attended First Calling, even though they no longer arrived laden with items of tribute for the Emperor.

The other guests were neither Matile nor human. They were emissaries from the hidden land of the Tokoloshe – the kingdom of the dwarves. Robes of gray, black and brown swathed the squat bodies of the half-dozen Tokoloshe delegated to attend the ceremony. Their faces were wide, dark, broad-featured slabs of hard flesh surrounded by manes and beards of frizzy black hair. Each of them wore a pendant of polished granite around his neck; the Tokoloshe valued simple stones far more than they did the precious metals and gems humans so avidly craved.

For years beyond counting, the Matile had maintained an alliance with the Tokoloshe kingdom, forged as a matter of necessity against their common enemies. It had continued long after those enemies had been vanquished, and the Tokoloshe were still welcome guests at Matile rites such as First Calling. But no human had ever visited the Tokoloshes' underground homeland. No one even knew where it was.

As a sign of respect, Matile craftsmen had made the emissaries stools low enough to accommodate their short legs. The six emissaries sat silent and motionless as the rocks they revered.

There were no seats for the rest of the crowd: a brightly-clad throng of merchants, craftsmen, jewelers, dyers, incense-makers, stone-cutters, silversmiths, menial laborers and market-women who had roused their children early to witness First Calling. Still, their vantage point was better than that of the throngs of ragged slum-dwellers who hovered at the periphery of the crowd, hoping to catch a glimpse of Tiyana's dance.

On a weathered platform carved with sorcerous symbols, one man stood apart from the rest, even the Emperor. This man was black-bearded, of middle years and stature, ordinary in appearance save for the saffron-and-white *chamma* that swathed his lean body, and the piercing power of his dark-eyed gaze.

This was Jass Gebrem, the One to Whom All Jagasti Spoke; the Leba, or supreme priest, of the Empire. Gebrem stood second in rank only to Dardar Alemeyu, but had influence that in at least one way exceeded that of the Emperor who, for all his royal prerogatives, could not communicate directly with the Jagasti.

Master of the few arcane arts that remained to the Matile people after the devastation wrought by the Storm Wars, Gebrem was the one who controlled the Calling. In his right hand, he held the *abi*: a long, flattened silver rod upon which the symbols of all the Jagasti were carved. The *abi* served as a focal point for the *ashuma* power he wielded.

So far, the ceremony had passed as it should. The drummers, arrayed on a wharf that jutted into the harbor, kept their hands motionless above the cowhide covers of their tall, cylindrical instruments. Behind them, other music-makers held long wooden flutes called *imbiltas* between their lips.

As well, the wharf held four young women who were so similar in appearance that they all seemed to be duplicates of each other. They wore long, ivory-colored *chammas* that left their slender brown shoulders bare, and head-cloths of the same hue that trailed down to the backs of their ankles.

These were the Callers of Nama-kwah, whose wordless song had filtered down to Tiyana. They were a four-birth; double-twins, an event so rare among the Matile that scholars and sooth-sayers were still debating its true significance. Among another people, the four sisters might have been put to death soon after they were born. The Matile, however, generally considered their birth as a miracle, a sign that the Jagasti had not totally forgotten them.

Jass Gebrem raised the *abi*, then lowered it. The time had come for Tiyana – and Nama-kwah – to appear.

3

The moment Tiyana broke through the surface in a shower of flying spray, the drums, *imbiltas* and Callers joined a new song – a song of welcome and rejoicing. This song was the true First Calling: the summoning of a new season, a reiteration of hope for the future; and echo of songs sung long ago by Etiya, whom the Jagasti first heard in the Beforetime.

The music of the Calling wafted out to sea and sky, and the mist followed the Callers' voices, gliding away from the docks and returning to the sea that spawned it. The listeners swayed, eyes closed, captured by the evocative harmonies. Even the taciturn Tokoloshe were impressed by what they heard, though they made no outward demonstration of their reactions.

The drumming muffled the slap of waves against a battered hull. The flutes drowned out the sigh of the breeze through tattered sails. The singing hid the creak of weakened timbers.

And an overwhelming will worked magic that masked the approach of strangers through the mist in the harbor....

Tiyana paused on the water, standing on its surface as though it were solid ground. Mist flowed in translucent streams around her body, which was clad only in threads of silver spun fine as the strands of a spider's web. Tiny, perfectly cut diamonds decorated the strands. Her frame was slender and long-limbed, and her skin was dark as night.

The silver Mask of Nama-kwah showed features of serene, otherworldly beauty to which mortals might aspire, but could never hope to attain. Layers of lacquered scales hung like beaded braids from the back of the Mask to a point well below its wearer's shoulders.

Tiyana held her pose a moment longer.

Where are you? she asked for the last time.

There was no reply from Nama-kwah.

Mustering her determination, Tiyana thrust her fears into the background of her mind. And she began to dance on the waves.

Nama-kwah dwelled in her own Realm, an ocean-beyond-the-ocean in the world-beyond-the world. She had withdrawn from her worshippers after the Storm Wars, much of which had been fought in her part of the Beyond World. The after-effects of the war plagued her even now, and she had every reason to retreat completely to her Realm, and leave the mortals in the Beyond World to live out their short lives. Yet once in every tenth or twelfth human generation, a Vessel would be born with whom Nama-kwah could speak from afar. On the time scale of immortality, the Vessels flickered briefly, then died, like candles in a rainstorm. Still, Nama-kwah cherished the contact, even though the Jagasti had long ago vowed to remain apart from a world that the misuse of their power had changed too much.

Yet now the sense of danger she felt was so great, so potent, yet it was a danger she could not define ... and she was going to have to give up even her limited access to her latest Vessel. There was the need for a warning before she finally abandoned the contact.

Nama-kwah moved her silver-scaled limbs through water that shone from within rather than above. And she reached outward from her Realm.

Tiyana moved her body with practiced ease as the music of the Calling embraced her. She spun and whirled as though weightless, and her feet hardly raised a ripple on the harbor's surface. The soft sunlight of morning turned the filaments of her costume into strands of silver fire and the diamonds into tiny stars.

Beneath the Mask, Tiyana's brow furrowed in deep and desperate concentration. The Goddess had always guided her movements in the past;

now she was alone as she had never been before. One misstep, even the slightest imperfection, and she would have to answer not only to Nama-kwah, but also to her father, whom she loved and feared in equal measure, and to whom she had devoted her life after her mother died several years before. Her parents had borne no other children; all of Gebrem's hopes for the future rested on her slim shoulders.

For all the attention Tiyana focused on her movements, however, discerning eyes could detect that all was not right with her dance. Her movements were graceful, but there were also slight moments of hesitation, of doubt. And those moments dispelled the illusion that it was Nama-kwah herself dancing on the waves, rather than her vessel.

Issa turned to Dardar Alemeyu.

"What is wrong with her?" she asked. Her concern was genuine; Tiyana was only a few years younger than she, and the two women had long been friends.

The Emperor shrugged, and Issa looked away.

Alemeyu wished Tiyana no harm. But he had despised her father as long as the two had known each other, which was all their lives, and that sentiment was heartily reciprocated. If the deficiencies in Tiyana's performance continued, Jass Gebrem's prestige would be sharply diminished. And that would please the Emperor.

At Alemeyu's side, Makah began to growl ... a low, almost inaudible rumble. The cheetah remained motionless, but her growling continued. No one other than Alemeyu noticed. And Alemeyu saw no significance in the sound.

In the harbor, Tiyana continued her dance, struggling to maintain her focus on staying above the surface. Then Nama-kwah spoke to her in a voice that was not loud; only a whisper that was the barest shade of sound.

Danger ...

That single word cost Tiyana her concentration. The *ashuma* that held her aloft vanished like smoke. The substance of her air bubble disintegrated with a loud, popping noise. With a cry of consternation and a loud, ignominious splash, she fell into the harbor.

The moment Tiyana sank beneath the surface, the music halted abruptly. The Callers stood open-mouthed; drummers' hands hung motionless; flutes remained silent. Soldiers shifted their weapons, and a low murmur of dismay ran through the crowd, carrying even to the people who were too far in the back to have seen Tiyana's fall, but could still understand the alarm they heard.

Only the Ishimbi statues remained unmoved by the unprecedented calamity that had compromised the ceremony.

Jass Gebrem's face contorted in anger and mortification as he stood on his platform, hand clenched tightly around the *abi*.

How could she do this to me? he raged silently.

The Leba leaned forward and peered through the mist in search for a sign of his daughter, concern and anger warring inside him. When Tiyana's masked face broke water, the Leba opened his mouth to berate her – then snapped it shut when he saw the shadow looming in the mist directly behind her. It was the prow of a ship – a ship far larger than any seacraft that was moored in the harbor ....

Nama-kwah never waited to determine whether or not her Vessel had received the warning she sent. Already, she could sense the coming of a menace unlike any she had known since the days of the Storm Wars.

She shook her head, and scaled tresses swirled through the water. What was to come would be a matter for the people of the Beyond World. It could not be controlled by her ... not without the other Jagasti, who had no interest in intervention.

Turning away, Nama-kwah swam deeper into the border between the ocean of Khambawe and the Ocean-beyond-the-ocean, with a horde of her Children trailing in a luminous wake. She did not look back.

CHAPTER TWO

PEOPLE FROM THE PAST

1

Tiyana had only a moment to consider the full measure of the mortification her fall had caused before she became aware that something large was behind her. She turned, and a small cry trapped itself between her lips and the Mask when she saw the huge, dark bulk looming out of the mist and bearing down on her.

Then she dove and kicked frantically out of the way, barely in time to prevent herself from being trapped against its bow. A moment later, the slow-moving ship passed her. Then it collided with the unyielding docks of Khambawe. The shock of the impact stunned her momentarily, and she drifted toward the bottom of the harbor before snapping awake, then swimming upward, her lungs desperate for air.

On the docks, the loud crunch of wood against stone broke the spell of shock that had held the crowd speechless and motionless. At the sight of the strange ship, the musicians and Callers had stood frozen in place, as had Jass Gebrem. And the Degen Jassi and soldiers and the rest of the watchers could only stare wide-eyed and incredulous as the outlines of the intruding seacraft grew clearer in the thinning mist.

Then a shout rose from the crowd:

"*Uloans*!"

The murmurs grew louder, more panic-stricken.

Jass Eshana was the first to heed the cry that named the Matiles' worst enemies. The Dejezmek barked a series of orders to his troops, who swiftly formed a barrier of leather and steel between the dock and the Degen Jassi. He also dispatched a runner through the milling, confused crowd to call for reinforcements. The circumstances had become so unsettled that even the normally imperturbable Tokoloshe had risen from their stools. They stood apart in a tight knot, whispering in their rumbling language through their thick beards.

In the meantime, the Leba made his way to the Emperor, who greeted him with an accusing glare and harsh words.

"What is this?" Dardar Alemeyu demanded. "Where is your *ashuma*? How could you not have known this was coming?"

Makah was still at Alemeyu's side. The low rumble continued to issue from the cheetah's throat, and its tail twitched in a counterpoint to the Emperor's demands.

Jass Gebrem did not answer immediately. He held the *abi* in both hands, using it as a focal point for his concentration. He was questing, using arcane senses shaped by years of study and sacrifice, to probe the strange ship. Although he could wield only a fragment of the *ashuma* his ancestors once commanded, that small amount was sufficient to tell him what he needed to know – and to frighten him, though he refused to show it, especially in front of Alemeyu.

While the Leba worked his arts, Jass Eshana ordered his troops to move forward to repel an anticipated onslaught from the Uloans. But no horde of scarred, shrieking madmen emerged from the huge, stricken ship. Only broken planks caught on the stone edge of the dock prevented the seacraft from sinking.

On closer inspection, it became clear to the soldiers that this was no ship that had ever been made by any Uloans. The islanders' craft were low and lean, powered by banks of oars as well as sails. This ship was twice the size of the largest Uloan raider the Matile had ever seen, and no oars protruded from its sides. Its sails – at least what was left of them – were also different: canvas rectangles stacked high on tall masts like sheets strung from tree branches. Uloan sails, by contrast, were triangular in shape, like the fins of sharks.

Yet the lines of the intruder were not unfamiliar, even though the last Matile to have seen anything similar to them had long since gone to the grave.

"I asked you a question, Gebrem," the Emperor said, a dangerous, sword-like sharpness edging into his tone.

"Actually, you asked three," Jass Gebrem retorted.

He considered his next words carefully, as he always did when he knew his cousin was angry. Alemeyu's frown cut deeper lines into his face as he waited for Gebrem's reply.

"A powerful type of *ashuma* is at work here," the Leba said at last. "I do not recognize or understand it. But it is not Uloan, as we can plainly see even without the aid of *ashuma*."

"Powerful?" the Emperor said skeptically.

"Extremely. It ... obscured my senses while I conducted First Calling. Had my own *ashuma* not been distracted ..."

"Excuses explain nothing," Dardar Alemeyu snapped. "What is this ship? Who is on it, if it does not belong to the Uloans?"

"I believe it is a ship of the Fidi – the people of the Lands Beyond the Storm," Jass Gebrem said slowly, ignoring the exclamations of disbelief that arose from the Degen Jassi within earshot. He held up a hand to forestall the skepticism the listeners expressed.

"We have both seen images of ships like this drawn in old books and inscribed in stone, and woven into the tapestries that hang the Palace," Jass Gebrem reminded the Emperor. "And we have heard the stories told to us over the generations. It is true that there are some differences in this ship from the ones in our books and tapestries. But then one would expect that, considering all the years that have passed since the time of the Storm Wars."

"If it is from the Fidi, why is it here now?" Dardar Alemeyu demanded. "And how could it have survived the storms?"

Jass Gebrem did not reply immediately, because he could not even begin to understand how any ship could have remained intact amid the vast maelstrom that raged constantly off the northern coast of Abengoni – perpetual storms that were the legacy of ancient animosities, tempests that had long isolated Abengoni from the rest of the world.

Unless it was ashuma, he thought uneasily.

Then Issa broke in on the conversation.

"What of Tiyana? She was in the path of the ship."

The sudden thought of his daughter's body crushed between ship and stone overrode the Leba's initial fury at what he had at first thought to be her unforgivable bungling of the Calling. He turned to the Emperor.

"We will learn soon enough who it is that wields the *ashuma* on the ship, and who it is that sails on it," he said. "But now, I must see to my daughter."

Before Dardar Alemeyu could respond to the Leba's less-than-respectful tone, a stir rustled through the crowd. Gebrem turned and saw Tiyana climbing on to the dock not far from the wrecked ship.

For the briefest of moments, it appeared that Nama-kwah herself had risen from the waters, to walk again among the Matile, the people who were the favored of the Jagasti. Then the moment passed, and it was clear that it was not the goddess, but her Vessel, naked save for the dripping Mask and silver strands of her costume, who approached Jass Gebrem, then knelt contritely before him.

The Leba reached down and gently removed the Mask from Tiyana's face. Her features bore a remarkable resemblance to those of the Goddess, but on a mortal level rather than the plane of divine flawlessness. And the look of entreaty that infused her dark eyes as she gazed up at her father could be nothing other than totally, vulnerably human.

She knew she was not to blame for the ruined Calling. But she also knew an Amiya could not make excuses. Her father had told her that time and again since she became old enough to understand the words. She bowed her head and awaited his judgment.

Gently, the Leba laid his fingers under Tiyana's chin and lifted her face until her eyes looked into his.

"You were not the reason the Dance on the Waves was defiled, my daughter," Jass Gebrem said softly. "It was *that*."

He gestured toward the ship that leaned against the dock like a beached leviathan.

Tiyana nodded gratefully. As she rose to her feet, Jass Gebrem turned once again to the Emperor.

"The storm has sent us this ship, Mesfin. Something must now be done. The decision is yours," he said. "What is your will?"

The Emperor gave the Leba a hard glare, similar to the ones that had often passed between them when they were boys: Alemeyu the elder by a few years, each well aware of what the other's position would be once they became men. Gebrem had smoothly passed the responsibility back to him. The Leba's intonation of the word "Mesfin," which was an honorific meaning "Majesty," grated on Alemeyu's nerves; he knew Gebrem considered him an unworthy occupant for the Lion Throne. Gebrem had, however, spoken the truth, even though Alemeyu was loath to acknowledge it. The Emperor had to make a decision, and make it quickly.

Then a voice that sounded like boulders grinding together interrupted Alemeyu's dark thoughts.

"May I speak, Mesfin?"

Alemeyu looked down. The speaker was Bulamalayo, the ranking member of the Tokoloshe delegation. At any other time, his request would have been a serious breach of Court protocol: at First Calling, the Tokoloshes' role was to quietly observe and be impressed by the glorious association between the Matile and the Jagasti, regardless of whether that connection remained intact now.

But this was not any other time.

Far from it ...

"You may speak, Bulamalayo," Alemeyu said.

"Our magic did not detect this strange ship, either," Bulamalayo said. "But then, we are too close to the sea."

Gebrem nodded his understanding. All Tokoloshe were born with magic, but its source lay deep within the earth. The farther they strayed from that source, the weaker their sorcery became. And for them, the water of the sea was as inimical as air was to a fish.

"Nonetheless, the ship's arrival could affect the interests of Tokoloshe as well as the Matile," the emissary continued. "If you board it, we wish to join you."

Dardar Alemeyu considered for a moment. Like many Matile, he considered the Tokoloshe a furtive, secretive people, not always to be trusted. Still, their continued alliance with the Matile was vital, given the menaces that beset the former empire from all sides.

"Agreed," he said to Bulamalayo, who inclined his massive head in acknowledgement.

Turning to Gebrem, Alemeyu said: "Let us see, Leba, what your Calling has summoned."

Gebrem held his peace. Inside, he seethed. Alemeyu had adroitly passed the responsibility back to him for whatever might occur next.

2

At Dardar Alemeyu's command, Jass Eshana organized the boarding of the ship. A ramp was brought from a nearby Matile ship and positioned against the damaged hull. One company of soldiers acted as a human barrier to keep a growing crowd at bay; another formed a cordon around the Emperor, the Degen Jassi and the Tokoloshe. The rest joined their commander's boarding party. Fortunately, the rumor that the ship was Uloan had been dispelled; the panic was gone and the crowd was mostly curiosity-seekers who pushed forward to get a better glimpse of the intruder. The word "Fidi" rustled through the crowd like a leaf borne on a breeze.

Eshana looked to the Emperor, who responded with a slight nod. Then, the Dejezmek ordered his troops to ascend the ramp. A moment before reaching its upper end, Eshana stopped short, forcing the others behind him to do the same.

Is this an Uloan trick? he asked himself, even though he doubted that the islanders were capable of such subtlety. Still, he wondered.

Could the Islanders have copied the design of the ships from the Lands Beyond the Storm to serve as a distraction? Could they even now be lying in wait to ambush him and his men, then swarm into the city?

That was unlikely ... yet still possible. With the Uloans, anything treacherous was possible.

"Draw weapons," Eshana ordered. With a sinister, snicking sound, fifty long, curved blades slid as one from their leather sheaths. Then, one by one, Eshana and his troops dropped down to the deck of the ship and out of sight of those who waited on the dock.

Several moments passed before the Dejezmek reappeared. An uncertain expression crossed his face before he spoke.

"You may come aboard, Emperor," he said. "It is ... safe."

He returned to the deck without saying more, as though any further words were trapped in his throat, unable to emerge.

The Emperor exchanged puzzled glances with Issa and Jass Gebrem. Then the Degen Jassi, along with a still-damp Tiyana and the Tokoloshe emissaries, made their way up the ramp and joined the soldiers on the deck. And their eyes widened as they stared at a scene that combined horror and history in equal measures.

It took only a single glance to confirm that the people who lay scattered across the deck were not Uloans. The Uloans were similar in appearance to the Matile; indeed, the ancestors of the islanders had migrated from Matile Mala ages ago, and there had been much contact between the two peoples before the Storm Wars split them apart forever. And even after centuries of estrangement, they remained the same race, if not the same people.

The occupants of the ship, however, were pale in color, the skins of some of them almost white as salt, while others' had been darkened by the sun or reddened by the wind. Their hair grew in many different colors. Some had black hair, like that of the Matile, Uloans, and all the other races of Abengoni. But the locks of others were otter-brown or fox-red or a tawny yellow, like the color of a lion's hide, or blades of grass during the dry season.

As well, many had sharp features, which to Matile eyes looked as though they had been cut too thin. Their noses were like beaks; their brows protruding; their lips thin lines. Yet for all those surface differences, most of the people on the deck were clearly human. There were others, however, who just as clearly were not ....

These were short, wide-set individuals with thick, chest-length beards and hairy hands. At first, as well as second glance, they looked like paler versions of the Tokoloshe. At the sight of them, Bulamalayo and the other emissaries spoke excitedly among themselves in their own rumbling language; in the distant past, ships that came from the Fidi lands had never included people who appeared so similar to them.

The wet, bedraggled clothing most of the strangers wore was not dissimilar to that of the Matile – tunics and trousers, but no *chammas*. Some, however, were swathed in robes of varying shades of blue that were somewhat like the Matile over-garment. Most the clothing was worse for wear, with abundant patches and mends.

Those among the soldiers and Degen Jassi who had read antique texts and perused dusty pictures remembered that the Fidis' homeland was so distant the seasons changed during their voyages to Matile Mala. Before the Storm Wars had ripped Uloa and Matile asunder and spawned the typhoons that ravaged the northern seas, a long-distance trade had been established with the Fidi. The Matile had coined their name for the others from that of the foreigners' main nation, Fiadol, whose seafarers knew no fear.

It was the Fidi who had initiated the contact, exploring seas far beyond any they or anyone else had known before. Once trade relations were established, ships from Matile and Uloa sailed northward and brought back tales of huge cities and strange people, unicorns and dragons, trees with leaves that changed color every year, and a cold season that turned raindrops into bits of white powder that covered the ground like a pale, chilly blanket.

The Fidi ships brought cargoes of linen and wool and wine, for neither flax nor grapes grew in Matile Mala, and sheep were unknown. In return, the Matile sent the jewels for which the city was renowned, along with, gold, silver, elephant tusks and *kef*, a red fruit whose twin seeds could be brewed into a strong, stimulating drink.

What the Fidi prized above all else, however, were the craft works produced by the Matile and Uloans alike: necklaces, bracelets and hair ornaments, as well as sculptures in ivory, wood and precious stone, all highly valued by collectors throughout the Fidi lands. Matile works adorned the homes of kings and merchants who paid prices that made the sailors' voyages more than worthwhile.

Some Fidi had remained in Matile, intermarrying with the local population. And some Matile had sojourned in the Fidi lands as well, some eventually returning, others staying and making new lives in a strange land. For several generations, the two lands had enjoyed a profitable, albeit long-distance, association.

Then the catastrophic Storm Wars severed those bonds, and memories of the Fidi lands, like the splendor of the Matile Mala Empire, subsided into the shadows of the past. As the centuries passed, no one in what was left of the Empire expected to see ships from Fiadol again. The land from which they came was lost on the other side of the storm, and so were the Fidi themselves ... until now.

The Fidi lay scattered like straws on the deck of their ship, appearing more dead than alive. Dark bruises and blood spots mottled pale skin; the limbs of some were bent at unnatural angles; clothing hung in tatters from gaunt frames. Those who were breathing seemed to be clinging to consciousness by only the slenderest of threads. They looked as though they had endured an ordeal no one among the Matile could begin to imagine.

The ship had fared little better than those aboard it. Its sails and rigging were torn, and many planks on the deck were broken. A crack ran through one of the masts; it looked as though it could topple at any moment. As the shallow waves of the harbor pushed the ship's broken hull against the dock, wood rubbed against stone with a sound like a low moan of pain. Even to Eshana's unpracticed eye, the vessel looked as though only a miracle had saved it from sinking long before it reached Khambawe's harbor.

Jass Eshana saw no danger on this derelict ship; only tragedy.

"Sheath swords," the Dejezmek commanded.

The soldiers immediately obeyed.

"Are they all dead?" the Emperor asked as the soldiers returned their weapons to scabbards tipped with silver.

Eshana knelt and touched the throat of the Fidi lying closest to him, a young, yellow-haired woman wearing loose breeches, an open shirt and a short, straight sword at her side. A faint pulsation fluttered against his fingers.

"This one isn't," he said.

The Emperor's face remained expressionless. No one could tell whether Alemeyu considered that to be good or bad news. Eshana looked at the Emperor for further instructions.

"Give them all the help they need," Alemeyu said.

"See to it," Eshana told his troops.

Then the commander noticed a hatchway that led below the deck, and pointed toward it.

"And see if there are any more down there," he added.

The soldiers hurried to carry out the Dejezmek's orders. Their weapons were not necessary now, but the raw healing skills some of them had acquired on the battlefield could be of some use to these strangers.

Then Bulamalayo entered the proceedings.

"We wish to assist the ones who are – like us," he said.

The Tokoloshe emissary was telling, not asking. Although the Emperor noted the breach of protocol, he only nodded. Precedent and custom meant little now. He had a feeling that the coming of the Fidi was a portent of a change to come. And he wasn't certain he was ready for change of any kind.

3

In the meantime, Tiyana and Jass Gebrem had turned their attention to a lone figure slumped against the ship's mainmast. It was a man swathed in a deep-blue mantle. His head was inclined forward, hiding his features. His knees were drawn up to his chest; it appeared that he could topple onto his side at any moment.

Then the Fidi straightened, rose to his feet, swayed for a moment, then stood fully erect.

An ambience of power emanated from the man, and both Gebrem and Tiyana recognized it as the source of the magic that had disrupted their *ashuma* during First Calling. They drew back in alarm, marshalling their *ashuma* for protection if necessary. Then they moved forward again.

No one else had noticed that the blue-clad Fidi was standing: another indication of the power that was beckoning – or compelling – Gebrem and his daughter to come closer. When they did, they saw a man well beyond his middle years, with a mane of white hair that began past his forehead and ended below his shoulders. Yet it was fatigue more than age that had etched the lines that scored a narrow face that was clean-shaven, save for a tuft of white beard that pointed downward from his chin.

His eyes were his most prominent feature – eyes the color of the gray clouds that brought the Long Rains to Abengoni. Those eyes stared straight into Gebrem's, as though the Fidi were reading the Leba's thoughts....

Tiyana touched her father's arm and gave him a questioning glance. Then her grip tightened, for the Fidi was reaching beneath the folds of his robe. Before Gebrem or Tiyana could react, the Fidi's hand re-emerged. In it, he held a small, dark sculpture – a replica of the Ishimbi statues that lined the dock. Tiyana and Gebrem exchanged a look of astonishment.

The Fidi essayed a small smile. And he opened his mouth, as though about to speak. Then he swayed, as if the cost of his effort to rise had caught up with him. His mouth closed, and a moment later so did his eyes. And he slowly slid forward, his legs no longer capable of holding him upright.

Without thinking, Tiyana reached out and caught the Fidi. Beneath his robe, the man was sturdier than he appeared. But Tiyana was strong enough to manage his weight. Holding him close enough to feel his faltering heartbeat, she gently lowered him to the deck.

Now the Emperor and the Degen Jassi approached the mainmast. Before they reached Gebrem and Tiyana, one of Eshana's soldiers emerged from the hatchway. A grim expression marked his face as he reported to Eshana.

"Are there any Fidi down there?" Eshana asked.

"Yes," the soldier replied.

"Are any alive?"

"Some."

As the Degen Jassi murmured to each other, the Emperor appeared lost in thought – or dreams of long-dead days of glory, when Fidi ships came regularly to Khambawe's docks. Only Issa dared to interrupt his reverie.

"We cannot allow these people to die, Alemeyu," she said.

The Emperor looked at her, but said nothing.

The Leba spoke then.

"The Fidi must have braved the Sea of Storms for a compelling reason," he said. "We must learn why it is that they have risked so much to come here."

Dardar Alemeyu considered Gebrem's words and found no hidden agenda or disguised duplicity within them. He conveyed that evaluation to the Leba by means of a curt nod. Then he turned to Eshana.

"The Fidi will need food, water, and healers," he said. "They are too weak to be moved from the ship; whatever they require to survive must be brought here to them. See to it."

The Dejezmek touched his fingertips to his brow in salute to Alemeyu. Then he snapped rapid a series of orders to his troops. As the men hastened to carry out the Emperor's wishes, Jass Gebrem gazed thoughtfully at the Ishimbi replica the Fidi still clutched in his hand.

During his boyhood studies, Gebrem had read about the replica.

It was one of a set carved more than five centuries ago for a Fidi merchant-lord who had been fascinated by the originals. According to legend, the sculptor, whose name Gebrem could not remember, had sailed on a Matile ship to the Fidi lands to deliver the replicas personally. Then the Storm Wars struck, and the sculptor never returned.

Jass Gebrem looked down at the sorcerer, whose head rested comfortably in Tiyana's lap.

You, my friend, I, myself, will heal, he promised silently.

On the dock where it had been left behind, the Emperor's cheetah, Makah, continued to growl.

CHAPTER THREE

QUESTIONS

1

From the shining splendor of Gebbi Senafa – the Imperial Palace – to the sad squalor of its slums, the Jewel City buzzed with activity, the source of which was the arrival of the visitors from the Fidi lands. After the Emperor had reached his decision on the Fidis' fate, he and the rest of the Degen Jassi – all except the Leba, Gebrem – departed from the ship. Jass Eshana's soldiers used sturdy ropes to secure the crippled vessel to the dock, preventing it from breaking up and sinking.

Once the ship was stable, other Matile ascended the ramp. Some carried painted, earthenware pots of *kef*, and others had baskets of *injerra*, the flat disks of bread eaten throughout the Matile Mala. Still others brought steaming bowls of *wat*, a spicy stew that seared the tongue like fire.

Healers came as well – men and women garbed in unadorned *chammas*. They carried their herbs and talismans in leather pouches, and their surgical implements rested, like swords, in scabbards. With the healers came the Keepers of the Dead, who were laden with bundles of fragrant leaves that would mask the odor of the Fidi who had not survived their long voyage. Later, they would prepare the foreigners' bodies for burial.

As the day passed, throngs of curiosity-seekers came to the docks to catch a glimpse of the strange ship. Guards posted by Jass Eshana refused to allow any of the gawkers aboard, and eventually the crowds diminished. But the gossip did not. A storm of rumors swept from the high-class *kef*-houses to the seedy slum taverns called *talla-beits*; from the market squares to the jewelers' shops; from weapon-makers' forges to thieves' dens.

Why did they come here? was the question all asked, wherever they were.

No one knew. Nonetheless, most people speculated.

Some thought the Fidi were escaping from some unknown calamity in their homeland – perhaps Storm Wars of their own. Others believed the foreigners were the harbingers of an invasion. But the most frequent conjecture was that Nama-kwah herself had brought the Fidi to Khambawe, for reasons known only to her Amiya, Tiyana, who would soon reveal the Goddess's purpose to all.

2

In the Beit Amiya – the House of Vessels – the low-roofed, many-chambered building in which the Vessels of the Jagasti dwelled, Tiyana stood beside a rectangular pool of clear water. The pool lay at the center of an inner courtyard surrounded by the plain, white-washed walls of the building. Flat stone benches lined the sides of the pool, and flowering shrubs splashed the courtyard with color. Its water welled from a spring sacred to Ateti, the Jagasti who was the Goddess of lakes and rivers.

At Tiyana's side, a *shamasha* – a servant-girl recruited from Khambawe's sprawling slums – used nimble fingers to undo the tiny clasps that held the strands of her costume together. Clad only in a length of plain white cloth knotted around her waist, the *shamasha* worked carefully. Tiyana had forgotten the girl's name; in the Beit Amiya, *shamashas* came and went like shadows. In the eyes of the Amiyas, the *shamashas* were little more than slaves. This one was younger than most, with narrow hips and a chest still flat as a boy's.

One by one, the diamond-studded filaments fell away until Tiyana was naked. Holding the scanty costume as though it were a spiderweb, the *shamasha* laid it into a lacquered box no larger than her fist. The Mask of the Goddess had already been returned to its place in the temple common to all the Jagasti. By the time the girl turned back to Tiyana, the Amiya had already slipped into the pool and submerged herself.

She stayed under long enough to allow the fresh, spring-fed water of the pool to dissolve the salty rime of the sea. But she could not wash away the misgivings that had begun well before she saw the shadowy bulk of the Fidi ship looming over her.

Nama-kwah had warned her of impending danger. Was the Goddess telling her the threat lay in the coming of the Fidi? Tiyana doubted that. She was not a scholar, but based on what she had learned of bygone times, she knew Fidi had never presented any hazard to the Matile. They were nothing more than strangers from an unimaginably distant land, strangers who until now had been nearly forgotten.

Yet the goddess had given Tiyana her one-word warning at almost the exact moment of the Fidis' arrival …

Tiyana tried once again to contact Nama-kwah. But the silence from the Goddess was so emphatic that she wondered if she would ever hear the Jagasti's voice again. That possibility was too terrible to contemplate, so she stopped thinking about it.

Abruptly, Tiyana kicked her legs, propelling herself back to the surface. She used no *ashuma* this time; the magic power was far too precious to waste on such mundane matters as bathing.

For a long moment, Tiyana floated face-up on the surface of the pool, allowing the fully risen sun to beat down on her bare skin and burn away her many misgivings. Then she swam to the side of the pool and climbed out of the water. She was refreshed in body, but still troubled in spirit.

The *shamasha* handed her a *chamma* striped with the green and blue colors of the sea – Nama-kwah's colors. After draping the garment loosely over one shoulder, Tiyana dismissed the girl with a curt gesture. As the *shamasha* quietly disappeared into the shrubs, Tiyana sat down on one of the benches and gazed at the pool, as though the answers she was seeking could be found in its depths.

"Tiyana."

Startled, Tiyana turned in the direction of the voice she had heard. She smiled when she recognized the man and woman coming toward her.

The woman, whose name was Yemeya, was one of the four Callers who had sung in the ceremony. She had removed her long headcloth, and sunlight glinted from the ornaments of amber and gold woven into her thick braids. With Yemeya was Keshu, Amiya of Halasha, the Jagasti of iron, the blacksmith's craft, and war. Keshu wore white cotton trousers decorated with strips of shells. Above the waist, he wore only bands of leather ornaments across his broad, muscular chest. His dark face was solid and broad-featured, as though forged by the god he served, and his hair was braided into dozens of short, unadorned spikes.

"You looked as though you were still dancing on the waves," Yemeya said as they drew closer.

Tiyana raked a hand through her short hair, which had been cropped close to her scalp to accommodate the Mask of Nama-kwah. Now, she would allow her hair to grow until the time for First Calling came again.

"Maybe I was," she said. "And, I hope, more successfully."

They all shared a chuckle at that bit of self-deprecation.

"Well, Tiyana, no one in Khambawe should be happier than you that the Fidi ship came here today," Keshu boomed as he sat beside her on the bench. With easy familiarity, Yemeya sat by Tiyana's other side, bracketing her, but not close enough to crowd her.

"Why do you say that?" Tiyana asked.

"You couldn't have asked for a better excuse to explain away the mess you made of your Calling."

Tiyana stared at him speechlessly and open-mouthed for a moment. Then she began to laugh. Keshu and Yemeya joined her, and they rocked and hugged each other until the mirth finally let them go. They would savor this moment of levity while they could. Only in the courtyard of their House were the Amiyas and others, such as the Callers, able to allow such a break from the disciplines to which they had dedicated themselves since childhood.

"Can you imagine how it would have been if that ship had come during one of *my* Callings?" Keshu said when he could speak again.

That started a fresh wave of laughter, for the Calling of Halasha involved the handling of fire and molten metal in an extremely dangerous manner. When the mirth subsided once again, Yemeya asked a serious question.

"Tiyana – what happened out there?"

Tiyana did not answer immediately. Keshu and Yemeya were her best friends, and ordinarily she would never have hesitated to confide in them. This time, however, she sensed that she could share Nama-kwah's cryptic warning with only one other – her father.

"That is for the Goddess to say, not I," she finally told her friends.

Yemeya and Keshu both nodded their understanding. Then they each clasped one of Tiyana's hands. Keshu carefully concealed his emotions as he felt Tiyana's hand in his, for his feelings toward her extended far beyond friendship. And he could not let her know of those emotions.

Not now – not ever.

As the Amiyas and the Caller sat silently gazing into the pool, the angle of the sun's rays turned the water blood-red. If that change of color was a portent, it went unnoticed.

3

As night's darkness settled over Khambawe, and the Moon Stars illuminated the sky, Jass Gebrem continued his healing of the white-haired Fidi. Soldiers had carried the unconscious man into a cabin below the deck of the ship. A probe by his *ashuma* told him the cabin belonged to the Fidi. After the man had been placed on a bed, Gebrem ordered the soldiers out, indicating that he was not to be disturbed.

Sitting on a chair of a design unlike that of anything made in the Matile lands, Gebrem used his *ashuma* to examine the Fidi. The *abi* served as his focal point as he probed. He found neither illness nor injury as his arcane senses delved beneath the stranger's robe, and beneath his skin. Despite the whiteness of the Fidi's hair and the lines that time and troubles had cut into his face, Gebrem quickly realized that the foreigner's vitality was more than a match for that of a much younger man.

But that vigor, uncommon though it was, had been depleted to its limit – or, perhaps, beyond. The toll exacted by the sorcery the man had exerted to convey his ship through the Sea of Storms had left him sorely debilitated; he was close to death despite the magic that imbued him.

Gebrem realized that the stranger needed a regeneration of his source of magical strength more urgently than any relief that could be provided for his body. Until that source was replenished, food, water and physical healing would be of secondary importance.

As he concentrated on the Fidi's innermost essence, Gebrem could sense that the man had already begun a process of self-healing. Without external assistance, however, the course of his recovery would last many days, perhaps even weeks, with a strong possibility of failure. Gebrem's *ashuma* could accelerate the speed and intensity of the stranger's healing, and enhance the likelihood of success.

Closing his eyes and grasping the *abi* in both hands, Gebrem visualized the Fidi's essence as a candle-flame wavering weakly in the darkness of a night in which the Moon Stars were obscured by thick clouds. As he concentrated the power of his *ashuma*, the flame began to grow brighter and stronger, driving the darkness away. Gebrem quickly realized that the Fidi's own strength was increasing, adding further fuel to the internal blaze.

Suddenly the stranger's volition roused, and Gebrem felt as though he were astride a runaway *quagga*, with the reins flying out of his reach. The candle-flame he envisioned grew blindingly bright, like a new sun invading a midnight sky. The sheer power of the burst was alarming. But Gebrem refused to break the contact, however dangerous it might be. He could feel the Fidi reaching out to him, just as he had during their first encounter on the deck of the strangers' battered ship ...

A soft knock sounded at the door of the cabin, breaking Gebrem's concentration. His eyes flew open, and the *abi* nearly fell from his hands. Angrily, the Leba rose and pulled the door open. Jass Eshana was there, unperturbed by the anger in Gebrem's eyes.

"Do my words mean nothing to you?" Gebrem raged. "I explicitly said I was not to be disturbed."

"Your explicit words mean a great deal, Leba," the Dejezmek returned calmly. "But not as much as Alemeyu's."

Gebrem scowled as Eshana continued.

"The Emperor has requested our immediate presence at the Gebbi Senafa. Not just us – all the Degen Jassi, and the Imba Jassi as well."

Gebrem replied to the summoning to the palace with a sharp nod of assent, followed by a dismissive gesture. If Gebrem's abruptness affronted Eshana, the Dejezmek didn't show it as he withdrew from the cabin, closing the door behind him.

Then Gebrem turned back to the Fidi, half-expecting him to have regained consciousness and be looking at him. But the stranger's eyes remained closed, and he inhaled and exhaled in the slow rhythm of deep slumber. Gebrem probed lightly with his *ashuma* and found that the Fidi's flame continued to burn brightly. There was little more the Leba could do now; he could only wait until the Fidi recovered on his own. And he seemed well on his way to doing so.

Still carrying the *abi*, Gebrem departed. He was determined to return to the Fidi's side as soon as he could – which would be as soon as the Emperor allowed, and who knew when that would be?

Moments after the cabin door closed, the Fidi opened his eyes.

4

Leather reins rested easily in Jass Eshana's hands as he guided his two-wheeled *gharri*, a light chariot, through the tree-lined streets of Khambawe. The well-trained team of *quaggas* – large, horse-like animals with faint stripes on their hindquarters – responded instantly to the slightest nuance of command, enabling Eshana to divide his attention between the route he was travelling and the drone of the voice of Gebrem, who was standing beside him. As usual, Gebrem was complaining about the Emperor.

Street torches set at regular intervals splashed light on the intricate facades of the houses the *gharri* passed. Most of the houses were single-storied and flat-roofed, with exteriors painted in the colors of the gems for which the city of Khambawe had gained renown and of the flowers that grew in stone pots beside the doors. From time to time, the *gharri* was engulfed by the shadows cast by the towering obelisks that commemorated the greatness of bygone times.

Clattering behind Eshana and Gebrem came an escort of soldiers in *gharris* of their own. Unlike the city's meaner districts, where hyenas and beggars fought over refuse and gangs of thieves called *tsotsis* ruled the night, the streets the two Jassi travelled were safe. Even here, however, it was never wise to be out alone after dark; hence the armed escort.

"He has not changed, and he never will," Gebrem grumbled. "Even when we were boys, he would alter the rules in the middle of a game when he was losing...."

Eshana nodded non-committally. He had heard words like these far too many times in the past. Why the Leba had long ago chosen him as an unwilling confidant, he would never know; the two kinsmen had never been particularly close in other matters. But Eshana listened nonetheless, because for reasons of his own he, too, bore little love for the Emperor.

"He'd say, '*I* will be Emperor one day and *you* won't, Gebbie," the

Leba mocked. "Emperor of *what*? Matile Mala is barely a speck of what it used to be – and even that speck is getting smaller."

The *gharri* reached the circle of *woira* trees that surrounded the Gebbi Senafa. Thick-limbed and sturdy-boled, the *woiras* stood like giant sentinels sheltering the seat of the Matile Mala Empire's power. A smoothly paved road led through a gap in the trees, and in the distance the lights of the palace glittered like a swarm of stars. For all its significance, however, the palace was not a towering structure. The spire atop its conical roof barely topped the crowns of the trees. Yet even the darkness of night could not cloak its splendor.

Light from the Moon Stars cast a diffuse glow from the Gebbi Senafa's silvered exterior. Its gates and octagonal walls glittered with jewels: the wealth of a vainglorious empire on display. Successive Emperors had augmented the splendor on the walls as they received tribute from all parts of Abengoni. Alemeyu, however, had added little during his reign.

The palace gates hung wide open, and the entrance soon swallowed the *gharri* that held Gebrem and Eshana as they turned their discussion to what they might find it necessary to say at the council of the court. Servants took the reins of their *quaggas* as the Jassi stepped out of their *gharri*. The soldiers stayed where they were; they would be needed to escort the Leba back to the Fidi ship when the council with the Emperor was finished.

5

Ordinarily, the Degen Chamber of the Palace swarmed with servants, soldiers and supplicants. Of the multitudinous rooms and chambers in the imperial house, only the Degen Chamber was accessible to the common citizens of the Jewel City. There, the nobility of Matile Mala sat in council and judgment: deciding petitions and grievances, dispensing justice and determining the direction of the empire, all accompanied by rigid protocols that had long ago outlived their original purpose and meaning.

For this night's council, though, pomp had been set aside. Only the eldest of the Jassi could recall a similar unscheduled gathering of the Degen Jassi, never mind one that included the Imba Jassi – but not the Tokoloshe, who were closeted in a conference of their own. That extraordinary council had occurred nearly a century before, when the Uloans had mounted a massive surprise attack that nearly overwhelmed Khambawe.

One ship from a remote land hardly constituted a similar invasion. Still, the sudden arrival of the Fidi after a centuries-long absence demanded immediate attention.

As the latecomers filed into the huge, torch-lit chamber, the tapestries that covered its walls stirred with their passing, lending an illusion of motion to the scenes from Matile history and mythology woven into the fabric of the hangings. The people were depicted as round-faced, large-eyed caricatures, a convention that remained unaltered over the millennia that had passed since its beginning.

On this night, Dardar Alemeyu eschewed the Lion Throne that stood atop a high dais in the middle of the chamber. Instead, he and Issa joined the assembled Jassi – Degen and Imba alike – at a broad, circular table made from the hard wood of an ebony tree.

Gebrem and Eshana were among the last to arrive. As he sat down on an intricately carved stool, Gebrem sensed a sharp glance from the Emperor. The Leba looked at Alemeyu, then looked away. If Alemeyu wanted to take him to task for his tardiness, so be it ....

When the last of the Jassi arrived, Alemeyu spoke without the formalities that usually opened a session of the Degen. And he came directly to the point of the meeting.

"The past has paid us a visit," he said. "A forgotten people have returned."

He paused, and looked around the table, meeting the eyes of each Jass in turn before speaking again.

"Why did the Fidi come here?" the Emperor asked. "And what should we do about them?"

Silence greeted his questions. Gebrem felt Alemeyu's eyes on him again. He knew the Emperor was waiting to hear from him, not anyone else. Gebrem spoke without looking at Alemeyu.

"It is obvious, Mesfin, that they have come here for a purpose that is of utmost importance to them," Gebrem said. "Why else would they have risked their lives by sailing on the Sea of Storms? My counsel is that we should treat them as honored guests while we learn what that purpose is."

"But they interrupted your Calling," the Emperor said. "And they nearly killed your daughter."

"Do you suggest they intended those things, Mesfin?" Gebrem asked.

This time he met Alemeyu's gaze.

The Emperor paused before replying.

"I am *suggesting* that the timing of their arrival may not have been coincidental. I am *suggesting* that the white-haired one – the one who held the Ishimbi statue in his hand – possesses *ashuma* of a power far superior your own; otherwise you would have detected the coming of his ship. I am *suggesting* a person who wields such power could be dangerous to our Empire."

Gebrem's brows lowered in reaction to the sting of the Emperor's barb about the weakness of his *ashuma*. But before he could retort, a new voice cut in.

"Do we kill all the Fidi now? Or do we kill only the white-haired one, the one who's got the power?"

Gebrem and several others winced. The new speaker was an Imba Jass named Hirute, a woman who ruled a collection of farming villages close to the land of the Thabas, the hill-dwelling tribesmen who constantly encroached on Matile territory. Her *harai*, slung loosely over her breasts, still carried some of the dust of her long journey to the capital for the First Calling ceremony.

"The Thabas are troublesome, like weeds," Hirute continued. "If these Fidi, too, are weeds, we should pull them up before they, too, become trouble."

Although the Imba Jass's lack of tact grated on the sensitivities of some of the more sophisticated Degen Jassi, her sentiments were understandable. The Uloans were a threat to the capital and other coastal areas; they seldom ventured far inland, and they had never struck deeply enough to harm the frontier Matile. For them, the more immediate threat was raids from the Thaba tribes that came as regularly as the rainy season.

In the days when the Empire's power was at its height, the Thabas had been forced into slavery, laboring in Matile fields and mines. Although they had long ago freed themselves from the Matile yoke, their hunger for vengeance for their earlier captivity remained unabated, and their attacks were ceaseless.

Now, the Thabas and Uloans were slowly closing like the jaws of a trap on the ragged remnants of the Matile Mala Empire. If the Fidi represented yet another source of danger, the days of the Matile people could well be done ....

The Emperor looked at Gebrem. Although the two had known each other all their lives, the Leba gathered nothing from Alemeyu's gaze. Had the Emperor already decided the Fidis' fate? And if so, would Gebrem suffer if his counsel did not coincide with whatever it was Alemeyu already had in mind?

Gebrem spoke – not to Alemeyu, but to Jass Hirute, who looked as though she wasn't particularly impressed by either the Leba or the Emperor.

"I would understand your feelings if there were not outlanders, but Uloans – or Thabas – on that ship," he said. "In that case, this council would not have been necessary. We would have taken the appropriate action."

Hirute nodded. Then she narrowed her eyes and waited for the Leba to continue.

"The Fidi were never our enemies," Gebrem said. "History tells us their ships came only to trade. Can any of you think of a single time the Fidi did harm to any Matile?"

Neither Hirute nor anyone else answered him. If they remembered the Fidi at all, they remembered that relations between the Matile Empire and the distant country from which the Fidi came had been better than those with some neighboring parts of Abengoni. A number of Fidi had even settled in Matile lands, where they were welcomed, although their bloodlines had long since been absorbed into the general population. On rare occasions, a Matile child was born with lighter hair or skin, or strangely colored eyes. Such infants were called "Children of the Sea." But no one in the chamber could recall the last time they had heard of such a birth in Khambawe or other parts of the Mala.

Hirute spoke again.

"We have changed a great deal since those days, Mesfin. They may have changed, too."

Jass Eshana broke in.

"This – power – that brought them here could be put to use against the Uloans and the Thabas. I would say that is a good reason to keep our visitors alive. Perhaps we can learn something useful from them."

Although the words came from Eshana's mouth, the thoughts echoed those of Gebrem, which he had mentioned during the *gharri*-ride to the Palace. Had the Leba spoken them, however, the Emperor would have likely dismissed them as self-serving, even though they were not.

Now, all Gebrem had to say was, "I agree."

After a long pause, Alemeyu said: "So do I."

Eshana and Gebrem avoided exchanging a glance, and waited for the Emperor to render his final decision.

"The Fidi are your responsibility, Leba," the Emperor said sternly to Gebrem. "See to it."

The Leba nodded acknowledgement of Alemeyu's decree. And with that, the council ended.

CHAPTER FOUR

UNDERCURRENTS

1

Legends claimed that the Tokoloshes' embassy in Khambawe had been raised in a single day and night, centuries ago when the Matile made their alliance with the dwarven race to prevent the possibility of a conflict that would have proved destructive to both sides. Limned by the bright glow of the Moon Stars, the building's squat, bulky proportions mimicked those of its inhabitants. Rock monoliths of uneven height surrounded it like a circle of giant, broken teeth.

The edifice was a windowless rectangle of gray stone, seamless save for a single entrance that was so low a human would have had to bend almost double to pass through it. But in all the long history of the alliance, no human had ever been invited into the Tokoloshe embassy, which occupied an isolated section of the city. Although it was nominally under the Emperor's rule, the embassy was treated as though it were Tokoloshe territory. And the Tokoloshe needed no guards to enforce their disconnection from the rest of Khambawe.

Its immediate surroundings were barren of houses, commerce, or even ordinary street traffic. No one, not even the *tsotsi* gangs that infested the city's slums, ventured near the featureless stone block. It was as though the Tokoloshes had taken a small portion of their hidden kingdom and planted it into Matile soil.

Inside, the main chamber of the embassy was lit by a single, head-sized ball of phosphorescence suspended in pitch darkness. Its pale, albescent illumination picked out the faces of the Tokoloshe envoys who had been present at First Calling, along with many others who had not attended the ceremony. Their broad visages were devoid of expression, and their deep-set eyes were fixed on the ball of light as though it held the secrets of life and death. They were waiting for the ball to change from a simple source of illumination to ... something else.

And now, that waiting was to be rewarded.

Slowly, a shape began to form in the midst of the glow. Features coalesced, and a face took shape, as though sketched by the hand of an unseen artist. Finally, the transformation of the glowing ball was complete. Surrounded by a nimbus of luminescence, the head of an aged Tokoloshe floated bodilessly in the darkness of the chamber. No one spoke. But all regarded the head with great reverence.

Then words issued from the simulacrum, although its lips remained motionless.

What is your message?

The words were spoken in a sibilant hiss that was totally unlike the grating growls of the Tokoloshe who replied – Rumundulu, the true head of the embassy. He had remained in the background during First Calling – present, but far from Bulamalayo's side. It suited the Tokoloshes' purposes to allow the Matile to believe Bulamalayo was their chief envoy. Much of who they were and what they did remained enigmatic to the Tokoloshes' hosts, even as their long-time alliance continued.

"A ship has come – from the Fidi Lands," Rumundulu said.

A long moment passed before the simulacrum spoke again.

I know you would not lie, it said at last. *You would never dare to do so. But how could a ship from there have survived the Sea of Storms?*

Rumundulu took no umbrage at the pointed nature of the question. For he was speaking to his ruler, Mungulutu, the King of Stone, First among all the Tokoloshe. Even among the long-lived Tokoloshe, Mungulutu was ancient, his lifetime spanning that of many human generations. And for almost as long as Mungulutu had lived, he had wielded absolute power over all Tokoloshe, wherever they were.

"The Fidi are led by a sorcerer of great potency," Rumundulu replied. "I could sense his strength, even though he was weakened and near death."

Mungulutu's simulacrum remained silent, as if he anticipated that Rumundulu would have more to say. And he was right.

"That is not all," Rumundulu said.

Mungulutu waited.

"On the ship, there were Fidi who were ... like us."

The simulacrum's eyes widened, and his mouth dropped open in amazement. None of the Tokoloshe could recall ever before seeing such an expression on their ruler's face. It was as though a lion had opened its jaws to speak instead of roar.

Mungulutu quickly regained his dignity, and the lines of his face returned to the stern glare they had assumed before. When he spoke again, his voice had a sharp edge, like a sword.

Like us? In what way?

"In every way, except for the color of their skin," Rumundulu replied. "This I saw with my own eyes."

This time, Mungulutu's silence stretched over several heartbeats. Rumundulu knew what the Stone King was thinking, for he had been harboring similar thoughts ever since the Fidi ship had come. Although the Tokoloshe had never traded directly with the Fidi as the Matile had, they had known of the people from across the sea during the time before the Storm Wars. And never before had a Fidi ship's crew or passengers included Dwarvenkind.

As far as the Tokoloshe knew, there were no others like them in the rest of Abengoni. The Kidogo, the pygmies who dwelt in the vast forests to the south of the Thaba lands, were undersized humans, not dwarves. And during the time when Matile ships plied far seas, the Tokoloshe had heard of no others like them elsewhere in the world.

That had been alarming, because the Tokoloshe were waning, even as their magic remained strong. With each passing generation, fewer Tokoloshe infants were born. More of their territory above and below the ground was falling into disuse. It was as though their time was passing, like that of the Matile Mala Empire with which they had so long been linked. But that was a possibility they refused to accept. And now ... if there were indeed other dwarven in the world, then the long-lived Tokoloshes' chances for survival would be significantly enhanced.

You must make contact with them, Mungulutu said.

"That will be difficult," Rumundulu said. "The Matile have placed the ship under close guard, and will allow no one to approach it."

He paused, knowing that was not what the Stone King wanted to hear. He knew what he was expected to say next, so he said it.

"But the task will be done."

See that it is, Mungulutu said curtly.

With that, his simulacrum faded, as though the same artist who created it was now effacing his work. Then the ball of light that had held it winked out of existence, plunging the chamber into pitch darkness. But that darkness lasted only a moment. Rumundulu spoke a single, guttural syllable – and flames erupted from sconces set in the walls, bathing the chamber in a lava-red glow. This light was more natural, although a human would still have considered the chamber to be oppressively gloomy.

The chamber had been carved to resemble the interior of a cave. Stalactites and stalagmites ended only inches from each other, like interrupted pillars in the world above. The floor was an uneven carpet of stone, and the ceiling hung oppressively low.

Benches carved directly out of the cavern's walls were the chamber's only furnishings. The Tokoloshe who sat on them looked expectantly at Rumundulu. Only Mungulutu held higher authority than the embassy head, and the Tokoloshe always deferred to highest authority available. Now, that was Rumundulu. Rumundulu did not discuss his plans or seek counsel. He spoke tersely, knowing his words would be obeyed.

"We wait," he told his people.
"We plan."
"Then, we act."

2

Jass Hirute took a long swallow from her cup of *talla*, the grain ale nearly all Matile drank copiously, whether they lived in the cities or the countryside. The cup was a piece of stained ceramic that had passed through hundreds of hands before hers. Its condition was in keeping with its surroundings, which were at best seedy; and at worst, squalid.

Hirute and several other Imba Jassi were drinking in a *talla-beit* located in one of the less-savory districts of Khambawe. Those who dubbed Khambawe the "Jewel City" had apparently never visited this area. It was not as dangerous as the Maim, which was the lair of most of the city's predatory *tsotsis*. But it was still a place in which only the brave or foolish ventured out alone at night.

Hirute considered herself more than sufficiently brave, at least in comparison with soft-handed city-dwellers. But she was far from foolish …

in the borderlands, the foolish did not survive very long. That was why she had gone to the *talla-beit* in the company of two of her neighboring Imba Jassi – Jass Tsege and Jass Fetiwi – as well as armed men and women from the retinues of all three Jassi. Together, the rural-dwellers had taken over a large section of the *talla-beit*, much to the displeasure of several displaced local drinkers.

Despite their resentment, the locals offered only angry glares at the intruders. The rural-dwellers' weapons – large, sharp knives that were the next-best thing to swords – were prominently displayed on the tables. And their willingness to use those weapons at the slightest provocation was well-known.

Hirute took another pull of *talla*, emptying her cup. Then she spoke, her voice barely rising above the din of the *talla-beit*.

"I don't trust them," she muttered.

"Don't trust who?" Jass Tsege asked.

He was a burly, blunt-speaking man who had been a friend of Jass Hirute's late husband, who had died fighting one of many incursions from the Thaba tribes.

"These newcomers," she replied. "These Fidi."

Tsege only grunted noncommittally. It was Jass Fetiwi who asked the obvious question.

"Why not?"

Hirute's brows contracted at the sound of Fetiwi's voice. He was the opposite of Tsege – a slender, devious-looking man who had an annoying habit of mimicking the aristocratic mannerisms of the Degen Jassi despite his contemporaries' clearly expressed contempt for his – and the Degen Jassis' – pretensions.

Fetiwi's territory adjoined that of Hirute. Almost since the day Hirute's husband, Jass Kassa, had died, Fetiwi had been pressing Hirute to become his wife and join her territory to his. Hirute had no interest in such a union, and she had always let her neighbor know that. But Fetiwi refused to be discouraged.

For all that, though, Fetiwi's question was a good one.

"We don't know why they're here," she finally replied. "We don't know what they want from us."

"Well, we won't know that until the Leba spends some more time with them," Fetiwi said.

Hirute gave him a pitying glance.

"We'll know what the Leba decides he wants us to know," she said. "And we'll only know even that when he wants us to know it."

"And when he does, it probably won't be much," said Tsege.

"It never is," Hirute agreed. "The city people only pay attention to us during these useless ceremonies. We keep asking them for help against the Thabas, but nothing ever comes. If it weren't for tradition and the Jagasti, there'd be no reason for us to come here at all."

Tsege snorted derisively.

"And for some of us, even the Jagasti aren't a good enough reason not to stay home," he said.

There was a moment of uneasy silence before anyone else spoke.

"You're talking about Jass Shebeshi," Hirute said quietly.

Shebeshi was the Jass of Imbesh, a territory located in the remotest part of the remaining Matile lands. He had not come to First Calling with the others. Not only did Shebeshi refuse to participate in the nominally obligatory rites and ceremonies conducted in the capital; he also defied convention – and by most standards, common sense – by attempting to expand his lands into those held by the Thabas.

Thus far, Jass Shebeshi's ambitions had not brought any consequences from either the Thabas or the Emperor. And the longer the rebel Jass went unscathed, the more significant his defiance became. It was even rumored that he had stolen some cattle from the Thabas – an act of near-suicidal recklessness on the frontier, akin to pilfering gold from the Emperor's treasure house, for the Thabas valued their cattle above all else.

"You know, Shebeshi just might have the right idea," Fetiwi mused. "If more of us joined up with him, and with each other, we could leave this so-called Empire behind and start something better on our own."

He was looking directly at Hirute as he spoke, and in his eyes, the hidden meaning of his words was clear. Hirute's response was harsh.

"If Shebeshi sticks his fool head out too far, he's going to get it chopped right off his shoulders," she said. "As for me, I'm not 'joining' anybody for any reason. The Thabas haven't bothered us since I avenged Kassa's death, and we get along just fine on our own."

Hirute held Fetiwi's gaze. A flash of anger – and perhaps something more – flickered in Fetiwi's eyes before he looked away.

Hirute drained her cup of *talla*, then held it up to be refilled by the young girl who was serving the Imba Jassis' table. When her cup brimmed once again, Hirute took another long swallow, then wiped her lips with the back of her hand, then wiped her hand on her *chamma*.

"I don't trust these outsiders," she reiterated. "I'll be glad when we're out of here, and that can't be too soon."

The others drank to her sentiment.

3

The Fidi were not the only outsiders in Khambawe. There were others, of whom the Matile were totally unaware. Their existence was the best-kept secret in the city. And the price for any betrayal of that secret would be paid in blood ...

On the seacoast, far from the lights of the Khambawe, a lone fishing-boat rested at anchor. It was indistinguishable from the many other craft that harvested the huge shoals of fish that swam close to the shore. Its owner, known to fellow fishermen as Sehaye, claimed to have come from Akara, a tiny island off the eastern mainland that had been considered remote and inconsequential even at the height of the Matiles' power.

If others wondered what had caused Sehaye to venture so far from his homeland, they kept their questions to themselves. They had their own nets to mind, and little reason to cast any lines of curiosity into the life of a loner. Sehaye was polite but taciturn, speaking only when spoken to. His catches were neither larger nor smaller than usual. No one knew how he spent the meager profits he earned; he had neither family nor friends nor any known vices. He was seldom, if ever, the topic of gossip on the wharves. There were many more-interesting people to talk about.

Had they known the truth about Sehaye, however, the Matile fishermen would have burned his boat and sent him to the bottom of the sea tied to his own anchor. For the island he came from was not Akara, and it was not located to the east, but to the west. He was an Uloan, from the Shattered Isles that lay beyond the mist. As a spy, he angled for information that would help his people gain their revenge against the mainlanders. This night, he had news to send that he knew would create a furor on his home islands.

A scrawny, dark-skinned, narrow-faced man with a tangle of short, undecorated braids sprouting on his head, Sehaye sat near the stern of his boat. He was carefully stuffing a small tube of wood down the gullet of something that, at first glance, looked like a motionless fish. But the light of the Moon

Stars showed that the object he held in his hands was nothing at all like an ordinary piscine. Its body was scale-less; viscid, as though created from some repellent internal organ rather than nurtured by any natural process. Its fins tapered at odd angles, and its eyes resembled flat pieces of stone stuck into the substance of its head, as a child decorates a model molded from clay.

The construct was called a *gede*, and it was a product of the Uloans' peculiar version of *ashuma*, a version that had long ago deviated well beyond the type of magic practiced by the mainlanders.

A grimace of distaste crossed Sehaye's face as he completed his task. No matter how many times he had sent such messages to the Uloas, he could not accustom himself to the touch of the *gede's* skin. He had brought two of the constructs with him when he came to the mainland and, as the *huangi* – the master-sorcerers of the Islands – had instructed, he had placed them in a stagnant pool near his small house. No matter how many times Sehaye pulled a *gede* from the foul-smelling water, there were always two of them waiting for him when he returned.

He reached over the side of his boat and gingerly placed the loathsome construct into the water. It sank like a stone beneath the surface – then came to sudden, sorcerous life, rising and shooting away far more swiftly than any natural fish could swim. Its path led to the Shattered Isles; its unpleasant wake remained long after its body had swum out of sight.

In the tube was Sehaye's written account of the coming of the Fidi. He knew no harm would come to the thing he had sent to his masters; even the most ferocious predators in the sea would swim far away to avoid it.

He watched its path as it disappeared in the darkness. Then he retired to the sleeping-mat laid out below the deck. He did not plan on losing sleep wondering what the *huangi* would do with the information he had sent them. Once they decided, they would let him know, and he would do whatever they told him.

In his own way, Sehaye was just as much a construct as the *gede*. That did not bother him. He was working toward Retribution Time, when the Uloans would return from the islands and destroy the mainlanders. And now he believed that time would come sooner than he had previously thought.

When it came, he would be happy, for he had become weary of living among the arrogant, decadent Matile. He longed for the day when he could slice his fish-knife through the bellies of the idlers who lounged at the wharfs.

Soon come, he told himself. *It soon come ...*

CHAPTER FIVE

TSOTSIS

1

Khambawe had been a city in crisis long before the Fidis' ship appeared in its harbor. Like a fruit rotting from the inside, the Jewel City's shining surface was pleasing to the eye, but masked the decay rotting at its core. And the corruption was spreading, slowly and inexorably.

Even at the height of its past splendors, Khambawe's streets had been infested with thieves, and the honest people in its districts of destitution had labored, borrowed, and begged to maintain their existence, only to fall victim to those who preferred to pilfer what others worked hard to obtain.

Then, in the wake of the Storm Wars, much of Khambawe, as well as many other cities in the Matile Mala Empire, had quickly succumbed to ruin and neglect. Some of the areas torn apart by war had been repaired only indifferently; others, not at all. As the Empire's decline accelerated, so did the advent of lawlessness in the crumbling inner precincts of its ravaged cities.

Children whose parents and other older relatives had died in the wars grew up unattended in an environment that rapidly become almost feral in its sheer harshness and brutality. For safety, the children banded together in gangs; for survival, they stole whatever they could find. They began to call themselves *tsotsis* – the unwanted ones. Their lives were short and fierce, and they were as deadly to each other as they were to outsiders.

At the time when the *tsotsis* had been most vulnerable – the time when the gangs were first forming even as the Matile as a whole were struggling to piece their society together again – the city's authorities had been too weak and distracted to give the incipient problem the attention it needed. Now, it was much too late to begin such intervention. Even an army would have had difficulty in dislodging the *tsotsis* from their lairs. And Khambawe's army was not available for such a task – not when there was still the danger of attacks from the Uloans.

Few were the outsiders who dared to enter the *tsotsis'* grim realm without a specific purpose – usually one that involved dishonest intentions on their own part. Fewer still were those who returned alive to tell of their experiences. But the *tsotsis* themselves were far from confined to the parts of the city they claimed as their own. Like predators in the wilderness, the gangs prowled Khambawe with impunity, robbing individuals as well as mercantile establishments, abducting the rich and holding them for exorbitant ransoms, and trafficking in gambling, prostitution, and a narcotic leaf called *khat*. They had even managed to infiltrate elements of Khambawe' society that would have been beyond their grasp had the *tsotsis* not become masters of disguise and deception.

If the *tsotsis* had ever become united, they, not the Emperor and the Degen Jassi, would have ruled the streets of all Khambawe, not just their own areas. But savage, long-term blood feuds among the various gangs, which called themselves "sets," prevented even the contemplation of such a mutually beneficial alliance. The sets had long ago divided the core of Khambawe into warring fiefdoms with boundaries that shifted like sand in the wind. Their territorial wars were like those of the Thabas in the southern hill country, and every night, the hyenas and wild dogs that infested the streets fed on the *tsotsis'* casualties.

And of all the bloody, blighted districts over which the *tsotsi* sets battled each other and reigned supreme, none was more violent and dangerous than the one called The Maim …

2

The *shamasha* girl who had removed Tiyana's First Calling costume possessed a name. But she had ensured that no one within the Beit Amiya knew what it was: Kalisha. It was a name that had been bestowed upon her by a long-forgotten mother on the day she was born. And that mother had given Kalisha precious little else once the child was weaned from her breast.

In the Beit Amiya Kalisha, like the other female servants who ministered to the needs of the Vessels, was addressed primarily as "you, *shamasha*" or "you, girl." And she did not encourage her employers to learn what her name was; or, indeed, anything else about her.

For Kalisha's name was not the sole secret she kept. She was only playing a role as a *shamasha*, hired like so many others who flocked at the entrance of the Beit Amiya, hoping to gain not only employment, but also a respite from the difficult life of the streets of the poorer parts of Khambawe.

Yet Kalisha was not just any child of the streets. She was a *tsotsi*.

Had Tiyana or anyone else in the Beit Amiya known of Kalisha's affiliation with the thieves and murderers who were beyond even the reach of the Jagasti, she would have been banished from the premises of the House, if not slain outright. Officially, the *tsotsis* were conceded only the parts of Khambawe that no one else wanted. The rest of the city was supposed to be off-limits to them, but the reality of the *tsotsi* problem was far different from the fabrications the Degen Jassi desperately wanted Khambawe's populace to believe.

The *tsotsis* had little difficulty penetrating the more respectable parts of the city whenever they wanted, and not only to pilfer and plunder. Often, like Kalisha, they posed as servants and menial laborers, roles through which they could gather information and plan future robberies. The *tsotsi* sets called such masquerading "fronting." Kalisha knew of several other *tsotsis* from sets other than her own who were fronting within the walls of the Beit Amiya. But she had better wit than to let them know she knew who they were. She was certain the others knew about her as well. An unspoken truce held among the *tsotsis* fronting in the Beit Amiya. They knew it was to their mutual benefit not to pursue their sets' rivalries under the noses of the Amiyas.

Kalisha was well outside her place of employment now, slipping like a shadow between buildings and through alleys in which no one else from the Beit Amiya would ever willingly go. Her only garment was a scrap of black cloth twisted around her slender hips. A small, sharp knife nestled snugly between the cloth and her skin. When she slipped into the pools of darkness that lay beyond the reach of the Moon Stars, Kalisha was all but invisible. And when she emerged again into the light of the Moon Stars, she moved so quickly she could hardly be seen.

Anyone watching her would have considered the route she took circuitous and without any conscious purpose. But there was a method to her meandering course; it was not as random as it appeared.

Kalisha never duplicated her path on the clandestine trips she took to the Maim. Nor did she allow the same number of days or weeks to pass between such journeys. One of the few pieces of advice her mother had given her was these words: "Predictable *tsotsi* be dead *tsotsi*." She never thought of her mother much anymore; not since she had died in a skirmish between her set and another.

Now, Kalisha skittered through the city's meanest streets like a spider, never spending more than a moment in any lighted area. The closer she came to the Maim, the fewer of those spots she found. The buildings she passed became shabbier, the streets narrower, the smell of urine and rotting garbage stronger, the scuttle of rats' feet louder. No trees or flowers grew here.

Tsotsi-set symbols – patterns of slanted slash marks decipherable only other *tsotsis* – were scratched into the walls of some of the houses. They were messages of hate and defiance, territorial markers, challenges, insults. No one bothered to try to eradicate the symbols anymore, for they would only be replaced almost as soon as they were erased.

It was becoming quieter now. Only the occasional scurry of a rat broke the silence; Kalisha herself moved almost without a sound.

Thus far, Kalisha had encountered no one. Only fools – or other *tsotsis* – revealed themselves in the streets this close to the Maim, especially at night. In the corners of her eyes, she had detected a few flickers of movement in the shadows and assumed that whoever made them was also on *tsotsi* business. She did not want – or need – to know more than that.

As she passed a half-fallen wreck that might once have been a shop, Kalisha heard growls and the sound of snapping bones. The noises were coming from the direction where she needed to go, and so she continued. She fought down a spike of fear when she drew close enough to see what was making the horrible clamor, even though she had already suspected what it was.

A hyena was tearing at a nearly naked corpse – the remains of a luckless victim of the *tsotsis*, stripped of everything valuable and dumped in the street. In the time before the Storm Wars, hyenas never dared to venture near Matile cities. Now, they were as numerous as the packs of dogs with which they sometimes competed. As they did in the wilderness, hyenas disposed of the dead in the neglected parts of Khambawe.

The hyena raised its head and glared at Kalisha, who kept her distance. Blood dripped from its massive jaws and speckled its mangy fur. Kalisha stared back at the beast. She kept her hand on the hilt of her dagger. She had no illusions concerning the effect the weapon would have if the hyena chose to attack her. But she also knew she would soon be dead if she betrayed any sign of fear.

As well, there was the chance that this beast was more than a hyena. It could be an *irimu*, a creature of legend that was human by day and turned into a hyena at night. Kalisha had scoffed at the legend, thinking it was nothing but a tale for children. Now, she could not be so certain it wasn't.

The hyena stared at her a while longer before uttering a series of high-pitched yips that sounded like demented human laughter. Then the scavenger returned to its grisly repast, and Kalisha moved on, still uncertain whether or not she had, indeed, encountered an *irimu*.

She was even warier now, constantly on the lookout for danger that walked on four feet – or two. But nothing else accosted her before she reached her destination, which lay at the hostile heart of the Maim.

3

Eventually, Kalisha reached an opening between two buildings that leaned against each other so precariously only their proximity to each other prevented them from collapsing into the street. From the far side of the opening, she heard the welcome sound of drumming.

Kalisha squeezed into the opening, and darkness of the space between the walls swallowed her. Moments later, she emerged into a courtyard, beyond which stood a tumbledown *aderash* – a mansion that had in the distant past belonged to a Jass. Now it housed a notable of a different kind.

As she crossed the courtyard, Kalisha's posture straightened, and her eyes no longer flickered back and forth, searching for danger. As well, her gaze lost the studied impression of vacancy she and other servants, fronting or not, affected in the Beit Amiya. Here, in the Maim, she was not just another *shamasha* among people who believed they were her superiors. Here, she was an equal.

A single *tsotsi* stood at the entrance to the broken building. He was a lean young man clad only in a black leather *senafil* studded with silver. His head was shaved except for a strip of braids that hung from the middle of his scalp. Both his hands were wrapped around the shaft of his *tirss*: a fearsome-looking weapon that sprouted tines like the sharp fangs of a carnivore. That, indeed, was what the name meant: "teeth." The weapon was designed not only to kill, but to inflict grievous pain as well. At the sight of Kalisha, the *tsotsi's* hands clenched on the hilt of his *tirss*.

Kalisha made a swift sign with her own hands. The guard relaxed, shifted his weapon aside, and motioned her to enter the building. He knew Kalisha well. But if she had not given the proper sign, he would have killed her where she stood. So would the other guards hidden on the roof and in the shadows. Rivalries among the various sets was as unrelenting as any among the tribes and nations of Abengoni, and to be unprepared for trouble in the Maim was to be prepared for death.

The interior of the *aderash* belied its ruined exterior. Light from dozens of torches flickered on finely woven tapestries, intricately carved furniture, multi-patterned carpets. Treasures looted from the rest of Khambawe lay scattered in careless heaps in various locations on the floor.

Scores of *tsotsis* filled the room. Many danced to the sensuous beat of a trio of male drummers accompanied by a woman shaking a beaded rattle. Others sat and stared with glazed eyes as they chewed leaves of *khat* or quaffed potent *talla* ale. Children – some barely old enough to walk – scurried underfoot. There were no older people; life was short in the *tsotsi* domain, and those who survived beyond their twenties usually departed from the Maim, preferring to disguise their origins and live the rest of their lives in safer places.

The dancers called greetings to Kalisha as she worked her way toward a huge pile of loot in the middle of the room.

"Amiya-girl," they said, laughing, referring to her position and her place of employment.

Kalisha only nodded and kept going until she reached her destination.

At the top of the jumble of jewelry and cloth sat Jass Mofo, leader of the Ashaki *tsotsis*, one of the most powerful sets in the Maim. Like most *tsotsis*, he was lean and sinewy. Braids decorated with beads of silver and gold hung from his half-shaven head. A thin mustache and goatee framed his full-lipped mouth, and he gazed at Kalisha with hawk-like eyes. His clothes were those of a Jass, and he wore them with far greater panache than many of Emperor Alemeyu's courtiers. A sword rested at his side, within easy reach.

Mofo was not alone in his perch. At his other side, on a slightly lower level of the pile, sat a young woman not many years older than Kalisha. Her skin was a deep, lustrous umber, and her face combined innocence and lasciviousness in equal measure. Her hair was a mass of beaded braids that clicked together as she moved her head in rhythm with the drumbeats.

The white-and-gold-striped *chamma* she wore was pulled down to her waist, leaving her upper body bare, save for a jewelled necklace. Mofo's hand cupped one of her small, round breasts, his fingers fondling the nipple. As the woman chewed a leaf of *khat*, her eyes looked through, not at, Kalisha.

This was Kimbi, Jass Mofo's consort of the moment. Like her predecessors, her tenure would last until he tired of her or got her pregnant, whichever came first. In either case, she would no longer be his responsibility.

"What you done got for me now, Amiya-girl?" Mofo asked Kalisha.

In response, Kalisha dug into the cloth at her waist and pulled out a tiny leather pouch. She upended it, and a small link of silver dropped into the palm of her hand. She held the shining bit of metal up to Mofo's gaze.

"This from the costume Tiyana be wearin' for First Calling," she said in the rough dialect of the Maim, a speech pattern the youth gangs had developed during their bitter isolation.

"I take it out and weave the chain back like it been," she continued. "They never be knowin' what I done."

She tossed the link up to Mofo, who lifted his hand from Kimbi's breast and caught the piece of silver in an easy, deft motion. He gave it a quick appraisal. Then he laughed.

"You just the best, Amiya-girl," he said. "You my luck."

His laugh broke through Kimbi's *khat*-induced torpor. She stared hard at Kalisha for a moment, then dismissed her as too young to be of concern. She closed her eyes and leaned her head against Mofo's knee. Then she took his hand and placed it back on her breast. Mofo was not distracted; his attention remained on Kalisha.

"I can be give you, *hmm*, twenty hands of *khat* for this," Mofo said to Kalisha. "Heard?"

Kalisha nodded. He was her Jass; if he had offered her only one hand of *khat*, she would have taken it. Among the *tsotsis*, twenty hands of the leaf was worth a fortune.

"Want some now?" he asked, teeth flashing in a grin.

"No," Kalisha replied, even though she would have liked nothing better than to chew the plant's leaves and sway to the drums along with the others. But she had to get back to the Beit Amiya before dawn, and to attempt do so with her mind numbed by *khat* would be to invite disaster.

She knew Mofo had just given her a test. His slight nod indicated that she had passed it to his satisfaction.

"We put it in your stash, for when you want it," he said. "You go on back now, Amiya-girl. And keep you eye on the strange ones who come on the boat. Heard?"

Kalisha did not wonder how Mofo knew about the arrival of the Fidi. Sooner or later, the *tsotsis* learned everything of importance that happened in Khambawe. Nor did she question his interest in them, for he was her Jass and his words meant more to her than the Leba's or the Emperor's.

"Heard," she acknowledged.

She nodded to Mofo, then turned to depart from the *aderash*. The other *tsotsis* said farewell to her as she made her way past the guard. But her mind was on Kimbi, not the others. She was determined that one day, when she was old enough, she would take Kimbi's place at Jass Mofo's side – if she and he both managed somehow to stay alive until then.

Chapter Six

Awakenings

1

The morning after the meeting of the Degen and Imba Jassi, Gebrem and Tiyana returned to the Fidis' ship. Some of the foreigners had awakened, and were being fed and ministered to by healers and their *shamashas*. Of those who woke, some blinked in disbelief, as if they were having trouble coming to grips with the reality that they were still alive. The ones who had regained more of their senses stared in curiosity at the Leba and his daughter, who paid little attention to them as they made their way toward the cabin of the sorcerer, the white-haired man of power.

The father and daughter had talked earlier, after the end of the meeting in the Gebbi Senafa; and after hearing what had transpired at the council, Tiyana had insisted on participating in the healing and questioning of the blue-robed Fidi. Gebrem was not certain that task would be safe for her. He wondered if her *ashuma* was strong enough to withstand the powerful flare of the Fidi's spirit.

"He came during my Calling," Tiyana argued when her father voiced his misgivings. "It's as though the Fidi were the ones I Called, not Nama-kwah. I feel responsible that he and his people have come among us. And you, Father, have always taught me to live up to my responsibilities."

Gebrem could have ordered her to stay behind, and she would have had no choice other than to comply. He did not do so, however, because his own feelings about the coming of the Fidi echoed hers. He, too, felt accountable for their arrival, because as Leba, all aspects of the First Calling ceremony were his responsibility – even those that he did not undertake directly. And now, he and his daughter would share the accountability for this unknown man who carried an ancient Matile artifact as though it were a talisman.

As they made their way to the Fidi's cabin, Tiyana carried a tray of food and a flask of *kef*. Ordinarily, that would have been a task for a *shamasha*. But Gebrem had earlier relayed orders that no one other than himself and Tiyana would be allowed to enter the cabin. He was confident the Emperor would not countermand him this time. There was no reason for him to do so. But sometimes, Alemeyu did things for no rationale Gebrem could discern, and Gebrem had long since given up trying to comprehend his cousin's motives.

When they opened the cabin door, Gebrem and Tiyana were surprised to find the Fidi sitting up in his bed. The man's eyes were clear, and his face had lost its death-like pallor. A smile lifted the corners of his mouth when he saw who it was that was entering the cabin. The Ishimbi figure that had eased the initial apprehensions the Matile had experienced lay near him on the bed.

As the two Matile approached the bed, the Fidi spoke to them.

"Greetings to you, my friends. My name is Kyroun ni Channar," he said. "Please accept my sincere gratitude. My people and I owe you our lives. We are deeply indebted to you."

Tiyana nearly dropped the wooden tray she was carrying, and Gebrem's mouth fell open in astonishment. The Fidi was speaking fluently in the language of the Matile – yet, at the same time, he was not. Gebrem and Tiyana's ears heard a language they could not comprehend, presumably the Fidi's native tongue. But in their minds, they were hearing Matile words.

The incongruity between the unintelligible sounds they heard and the words their minds understood was disorienting, if not frightening. It was yet another manifestation of this man's sorcerous power. Because the extent of that power was still unknown, Gebrem was only a moment away from calling the guards.

Then Kyroun reached out to steady the tray that teetered precariously in Tiyana's hands. His gaze held hers for a moment, then shifted to Gebrem. The unfamiliar gray color of the stranger's eyes was disconcerting. Looking into them was like gazing at storm clouds roiling in the sky moments before thunder would begin to peal and lightning flashed.

Despite Kyroun's still-obvious weariness, a deep well of strength showed clearly in his eyes. But there was something else in those gray depths that forestalled Gebrem's impulse to call the guards.

It was sense of urgency – a *need*, like that of a man about to die of thirst in a desert.

"The Spell of Tongues is a simple one, Jass Gebrem – Amiya Tiyana," Kyroun said, ending the short, tense silence.

"The sounds of human speech are infinite, yet the essence of the meaning of speech is universal. The Spell of Tongues distills that essential meaning from the sounds, thus rendering my speech intelligible to you, and yours to me."

"You ... know our names," Gebrem said while Tiyana surrendered the tray to Kyroun. "What 'spell' explains that?"

He remembered the brightness of the flame inside the Fidi ... he remembered how that blaze had nearly consumed him ....

Still struggling with his uneasiness, Gebrem sat down in the same chair he had occupied when he had healed the Fidi. He looked at Kyroun, waiting for an answer to his question.

Kyroun smiled – another quick upturn of his thin lips, sufficient to reassure Gebrem, if not Tiyana. Her father had told her of his experiences during his healing of the stranger, and she could not ignore the notion that the Fidi's power was the reason Nama-kwah had conveyed her message of danger during First Calling. But she had not mentioned that thought to Gebrem. For all she knew, the Fidi could just as easily have come to warn of the same danger that Nama-kwah had, whatever it might be. Yet her reservations remained.

"Your names, I know, but little more than that, Jass Gebrem," Kyroun said. "At the moment my life-light was flickering to its end, my mind touched yours, and I learned the name of the one who rekindled it – and, as well, I learned the name of the one he holds dearest."

He smiled at Tiyana, who lowered her gaze and looked away.

"I cannot count the days that have passed since I last smelled good food, let alone tasted it," Kyroun said.

"I am sorry ...Kyroun. Please eat," Gebrem said. "There will be more than enough time for talk."

He motioned for Tiyana to pass the tray to the Fidi. Kyroun took the tray from her hands, then ate heartily, using the *injerra* to scoop up the *wat* as though he had done so all his life. He also sipped the hot *kef* carefully without choking, unlike most of the Fidi outside the cabin, who had tried to gulp it down as though it were merely colored water the first time they drank it, then suffered the consequences when its bitter taste burned their throats.

While Kyroun ate, Tiyana sat on one of the other chairs in the cabin. Sunlight streamed through the open porthole, illuminating the bed, chairs and desk crowded into the small room. A map was unfurled across the top of the desk. Gebrem walked over to the desk and peered down at the chart. On it, he recognized the outline of Abengoni's northern coast – and the boundaries of the old Matile Mala Empire. When he gave it a closer look, he saw that the map showed cities that no longer existed because they had been obliterated in the Storm Wars.

A sense of sadness for what the Matile had lost assailed him, but he willed that feeling away. He needed to concentrate on understanding how – and why – the Fidi had braved the Sea of Storms to come to Khambawe.

"They still talk about this drink in my country, even though no one has tasted it for centuries," Kyroun remarked as he swallowed more *kef*. "We never could get the beans to grow, even in the hottest climates."

A polite silence followed while Kyroun finished his repast. When the last of it was gone, Tiyana spoke quickly and bluntly, broaching a topic Gebrem would have approached with greater subtlety.

"You and your people have taken an incredible risk to come to us through the Sea of Storms. Why?"

Gebrem opened his mouth to admonish her, but then closed it without speaking. Tiyana's own life had almost been lost during First Calling; she had a right to know the reason why the Fidis' ship had nearly crushed her against the wharf.

Kyroun locked eyes with her. The creaking of the ship's timbers was the only sound to be heard in the cabin as the clash of gazes intensified, with Tiyana refusing to yield despite the strange color of the Fidi's eyes and the power that lay within their depths. Then Kyroun smiled broadly, deepening the lines on his face.

"It was you," he said softly.

Tiyana gave him a quizzical look.

"When it seemed that we would never reach land; that the wind and waves would defeat us and send us to the bottom of the sea, your magic shone like a beacon, guiding us to safety," Kyroun explained. "I knew as long as I concentrated on the source of that magic, we had a chance to survive. And so we did. You, Tiyana, are the one who saved our lives."

The sincere warmth and gratitude that shone in Kyroun's eyes as he spoke was almost enough to cause Tiyana to forget that his ship had come close to killing her the day before.

Almost, but not quite.

"As for the question you ask, the answer is simple," Kyroun added. Then he paused, as though he were preparing himself for the reaction his next words were certain to elicit.

"I have come home," he said.

2

Water splashed over the face of Pel Muldure, captain of the *White Gull*. Wetness entered his mouth and crept into his nostrils.

Drowning ... wind shredding the sails ... waves smashing, rocking, destroying....

Muldure's dark eyes snapped open as the water dripped down his neck and shoulders. Sunlight dazzled his vision and he blinked rapidly, as though he had been in darkness for a long time.

Drowning....

With a hoarse outcry, Muldure sat up, flailing his arms as though struggling to stay afloat in a whirlpool that was sucking him down. He heard a sharp intake of breath close by. Then he felt the hard deck of his ship beneath him, swaying gently. Relief filled him. He was not drowning. His ship had not sunk. He had reached his destination, which was all any sailor could ask from the gods of the sea.

Muldure continued to blink until his vision cleared. Endless days of dark-gray skies alternating with the black of starless nights had left him unaccustomed to the sight of sunlight. He looked down at himself. The brocaded captain's vest that was his pride and joy was now reduced to shreds. A length of cloth covered with unfamiliar designs covered his legs, hiding his boots and sea-breeches, which he was certain would be in equal disrepair.

Automatically, he reached for the cutlass that always hung at his side. Its scabbard was empty. Had he lost his weapon? Or had it been taken from him?

Then he looked up – and saw a face hovering above his own, a face covered by skin darker than any he had ever seen before. It was a young woman's face: narrow, framed with braids of hair bedecked with multicolored beads. Startled eyes stared into his. Then white teeth flashed in a tentative smile.

He examined the woman more closely. Her neck was slender, as were the shoulders her garment left partly bare. The rest of her body was wrapped in a single length of plain, white cloth. She was kneeling beside him. In her hand, she held a damp, dripping rag.

Drowning....

Muldure grinned ruefully, reflecting on how grotesquely a dream could magnify a few drops of water. In response, the dark woman's smile broadened, and she appeared to relax. Then Muldure spoke to her, expressing in a single word the question foremost on his mind. It was a word that was not to be found in his own language, but one that had started him on his voyage through the Sea of Storms.

"Ma-teel?" he said in a tentative tone.

The smile on the woman's lips abruptly changed to a gaping circle of surprise. Had she not shot out a hand to balance herself, she would have toppled backward onto the deck. As it was, water splashed out of the vessel she was holding.

Before either she or Muldure could react further, a loud laugh cut through the air. Muldure turned his head and his gaze met a familiar pair of eyes: sky-blue beneath a tousled mass of yellow hair cut raggedly to shoulder length. The face in which the eyes were set was heart-shaped, with an upturned nose and a generous mouth. It was not a beautiful face, but it was not a plain one, either.

Her name was Lyann, and she was Muldure's first mate on the *White Gull*, the finest ship ever to sail from the docks of Angless, chief port of Fiadol. But then, in Muldure's opinion, all the ships he had ever helmed had been the best for a time – until ill-fortune took command away from him.

"About time you made it back the land of the living, Captain," Lyann said. Her bantering tone couldn't quite mask an underlying sense of relief.

Muldure could only nod; his throat felt as though he had swallowed sandpaper, and it seemed that every muscle in his body was being hit with hammers.

Hands on breeches-clad hips, Lyann looked down at him. Above-average in height, her lean body had been hardened by nearly a decade of life at sea. Her tanned skin had not yet acquired the leathery look of a longtime seafarer. The time when it would, however, would not be much longer in arriving.

The wooden buttons of her white linen shirt were undone and its tails were knotted over her flat, smooth-muscled stomach. The scabbard belted at her side was, like his, empty. But Muldure was still too disoriented to worry much about being weaponless in a strange land.

Still grinning, Lyann made a drinking motion with one hand. For a moment, Muldure was puzzled. Then he realized her gesture had not been directed toward him.

In response to Lyann's signal, the dark woman at Muldure's side, having recovered her composure, offered him water in a black earthenware cup. He took the cup in his hands, raised it to his lips, and drank. The water was cool and sweet, as though flavored with fruit. It soon smoothed the roughness in his throat.

He smiled his thanks to the woman. She spoke to him in a torrent of syllables that meant nothing to him. Even though he couldn't understand her, though, the reaction she showed when he spoke the word "Ma-teel" told him all he needed to know.

Against overwhelming odds, the *White Gull* had arrived at its improbable destination ... Ma-teel, the almost-mythical Land Beyond the Sun, a place that over the centuries had become more legendary than real after all contact with it had been mysteriously lost.

"You plan on getting up anytime soon, or do you intend to spend the rest of your life sitting on your arse?" Lyann demanded, breaking into his thoughts.

"I'll get up," Muldure said. "No telling what might happen to this ship with *you* in charge."

Lyann laughed. Then she extended her hand. Muldure took it, and with her help he made it to his feet. As he stood, dizziness assailed him, and every bruise on his body throbbed in painful protest. He willed some stiffness into his legs and managed to remain upright.

He was only a few inches taller than Lyann, with a frame spare and sinewy as whipcord. Endurance, not size, was his strong suit. He could outwork and outfight sea-dogs twice his size and half his age, and outsmart the rest. A thick, drooping black mustache framed his mouth. Only the thinning black hair pulled back from his forehead and his rough, permanently-browned skin betrayed the many years he had spent on ships that sailed from the Ice Isles to the Moondragon Sea, working his way up from cabin-boy to captain at an age younger than most.

And then he had worked his way back down again ... and back up ...

and back down, a cycle he seemed doomed to repeat itself until he died.

Muldure's heart sank as he surveyed the deck and realized the extent of the damage the *White Gull* had sustained. Broken planking; holes in the hull; stone dockwork piercing the bow; a web of ropes securing the ship to the wharf – at first, and second, and even third glance, the ship appeared to be beyond any hope of salvaging.

And the condition of its passengers and crew was only slightly more heartening. Some were on their feet and moving about, and when they saw him they waved and called out greetings, which he returned. Others lay injured, tended and fed by dark-skinned men and women – Ma-teel – like the one who had given him water. Still others – far too many others – were simply ... gone. He did not have to speculate on the significance of their absence.

Muldure also noticed that, as always, the Almovaads – the Believers – had separated themselves from the ship's crew. He scowled for a moment. He had never thought the Believers were his betters, although he was certain many of them were convinced otherwise. Now, after nearly going to the bottom of the sea, where differences in belief and station meant nothing, here they were, keeping themselves apart again.

He also noticed that no one – passenger and crew alike – retained their weapons. That observation was now beginning to increase his sense of unease. Had they come all this way only to fall into captivity?

He turned to Lyann.

"Are we under guard?" he asked.

"Yes, but in a very polite way," she replied. "There's soldiers all over the docks. These people have given us everything we need. But they won't let anybody off the ship."

"What about the ones who didn't survive?" Muldure asked.

Lyann shook her head. A sad expression crossed her face.

"They took the dead off the ship," she said.

"And what about ... *him*?"

"He's in your cabin, as always," Lyann replied. The grin was gone from her face.

"He's alive," she added.

Muldure said nothing more, but he was certain Lyann knew what he was thinking as he glanced in the direction of his cabin, which he had sometimes shared with her before it was taken from him.

He brought us through the storms, just as he said he would, Muldure thought. *But the cost ... gods above and below, the cost ....*

"He's not alone in there," Lyann said. "He's getting special help from what looks to be important people."

"What else would you expect?" Muldure said.

They exchanged a long look that combined apprehension and distaste. Then Lyann took Muldure by the arm and led him toward the other survivors, who raised cups of water and other drinks to celebrate their captain's recovery. He gave the cabin a final glance before he joined the others.

3

It took a moment for Gebrem and Tiyana to digest what Kyroun had told them. The Fidi remained silent, waiting for the others to speak first.

"Home?" Gebrem finally repeated incredulously. "Here? How can that be? I do not understand."

In response, Kyroun reached over to his side and pushed the Ishimbi statue closer to Gebrem.

"This item has been in my family for many generations," he said.

Gebrem reached out to touch it, then hesitated, and looked at the Fidi.

"May I?" he asked.

Kyroun nodded.

Gebrem ran a finger across the smooth, basalt surface of the carving. It was as though he were touching a piece of his country's history, a history that he had only recently relearned.

"Only one set of these was ever made," the Leba mused. "Yekunu, greatest of all Matile sculptors, carved five Ishimbi replicas for a Fidi merchant lord named Hulett Jull, and he accepted Hulett Jull's invitation to accompany him – and them – to the Fidi Lands.

"That was more than 500 years ago."

Gebrem had uncovered that piece of information in one of the many tomes on the Fidi he had studied long into the night after the Emperor had made the strangers his responsibility. He was certain he now knew more about the newcomers than anyone else in Khambawe – especially the Emperor.

"You are right," Kyroun said. "And this is the last of them."

He paused before continuing.

"The forebear who passed it down to me was Yekunu," he said.

Gebrem and Tiyana looked at him, trying to find a sign of Matile ancestry in his appearance – a hint of wideness at his nose or lips, a dark undercast to his skin. There was no such sign. But then, the passage of time had also erased most of the few strains of Fidi blood among the Matile who had such ancestry.

Kyroun was aware of their scrutiny, but he continued to talk. The dissonant effect of the sound of his speech and the meaning of his words was beginning to ease. It was beginning to seem as though he were actually speaking Matile, rather than his own language.

"After the Storm Wars left him stranded, Yekunu stayed for a time with Hulett, and he was honored in the kingdom of Fiadol," Kyroun recounted. "But he became restless, and eventually he departed from Fiadol. Hulett Jull gave him one of the Ishimbi statuettes as a parting gift, to remind him of his lost homeland.

"For many years, Yekunu travelled across Cym Dinath, our continent, which is large enough to hold more than two of yours. His sculptures earned him both a living and a reputation that has lasted to this day. In time, though, he grew weary of wandering.

"He finally settled in Lumaron, a kingdom far to the east of Fiadol, on the edge of the Geron Shi Desert. There, he married into a clan of artisans and began a family of his own. And the Ishimbi statuette was passed from descendant to descendant to keep the memory of Yekunu's long-lost homeland alive. My father bequeathed it to me on his deathbed."

Gebrem and Tiyana remained silent for a moment, reflecting on what Kyroun had said thus far. They were intrigued by the saga of Yekunu, and the survival of the memory of the Matile in Kyroun's faraway land. But there were further questions that needed to be answered.

Tiyana spoke first. Her words betrayed the lingering suspicions the stranger's warmth toward her had only partially allayed.

"That explains why you have the Ishimbi statuette. But it does not explain why you are here."

"Tiyana ...." Gebrem began, a tone of warning in his voice.

"She has a right to remain suspicious, Jass Gebrem," Kyroun

interjected. "So do you."

"I am not necessarily suspicious," Gebrem said diplomatically. "Merely ... curious."

"Just so," Kyroun said with a smile and a nod.

"I could spend hours – days – answering the questions both of you have," the Fidi continued. "And, of course, I have questions of my own. But there is a better way for us to learn the answers we each seek. It is called In-Seeing. Through In-Seeing, I can show you how and why my people and I have come here. And I, in turn, can learn what has become of my distant ancestor's homeland in the many years that have passed since he left it."

"How do we accomplish this 'In-Seeing'?" Gebrem asked.

"It is simple. Just hold my hands, and I will do the rest."

Kyroun extended his hands. Gebrem took one of them without hesitation. But Tiyana held back for a moment.

She looked at Kyroun's outstretched hand. Never before had she seen such skin. She could discern a tracery of blue veins on the top of his hand. Among the Matile, only the faintest hint of blue could be seen under the lightest-brown skins of the few whose distant Fidi ancestry still showed. Tiyana had no idea what color her veins were, and she hadn't even thought about it until now.

Kyroun's hand also featured a number of tiny brown flecks, like spatters from an artist's paintbrush. *Perhaps they are his legacy from Yekunu*, Tiyana thought.

Then she took his hand. And the In-Seeing began.

CHAPTER SEVEN

WHAT KYROUN SAW

Behind his closed eyes, Kyroun beheld the past in which Jass Gebrem, Tiyana and most other Matile believed, and the present they now endured. It was a weave of images gleaned from dusty tomes and ancient legends; stories carved in sculptures, woven in tapestries, sung in songs – all of it filtered through a mental prism that rendered the Matiles' history as half-truth, half-dream, beginning with the legend of Etiya ...

Long ago, in the Beforetime, the land called Abengoni was encircled by the coils of an enormous serpent called Adwe. The people of Abengoni could not live on the land; Adwe enveloped all, and even the sun could not penetrate the darkness cast by the serpent's vast bulk. Not only did Adwe refuse to allow people to dwell on the surface of Abengoni; the serpent demanded tribute from them as well. So impoverished were the people of Abengoni that all they could offer Adwe in return for their miserable existence was the lives of their first-born children when they reached adult age.

The people lived in darkness and despair, even as they longed for the time before Adwe had tightened his coils around their world. They remembered the sky and the sun, the grass and the trees, the sea and the rivers, the abundance of animals. Yet even as Adwe blotted out those memories, the yearning for what they once had did not die among the people; and as time passed, they planned ways to get it back.

Singly, or in small, determined groups, the people sought ways to slay Adwe, or, at least, to escape the oppressive presence of the serpent's bulk. All their schemes ended in their deaths. They would not be the only ones who died. When Adwe became angry, he would twist his coils, and that twisting would mercilessly shake Abengoni, and the guilty and innocent alike would die.

Whether he twisted or remained quiescent, Adwe continued to demand sacrifices, and the people descended further into hopelessness.

One day, a young woman named Etiya was chosen to be the sacrifice. And this time, the sorrow was even deeper than usual when the sacrifices were made, for Etiya was a singer, and the strains of her sweet voice provided the only hint of brightness in the gloomy netherworld to which Adwe had relegated them.

When the time came for her to be sacrificed, Etiya went willingly to the place from which Adwe would claim her, as he had countless of others before her. Resistance had by then become unthinkable. Yet Etiya was determined not to die meekly and quietly. She would sing one last song before the serpent took her.

And when Adwe came, his unimaginable bulk filling the horizon, Etiya sang. The words of her song bespoke hope and defiance, and the melody reached down to where her people huddled in their endless darkness and misery. If for only a moment, Etiya's song lifted them from the bleak depths into which their spirits had fallen.

Adwe paid no attention to the song. The serpent cared nothing for either bravery or beauty, both of which were abundant in Etiya. But her song extended far beyond Adwe, and even beyond Abengoni itself. Etiya's song travelled to the Realms of a pantheon of deities called the Jagasti. Although the Jagasti knew nothing of Abengoni, they hearkened well to the words of the song. And as the deities listened, they took pity on the singer of the song and her beleaguered people, and they decided to come to their aid.

The moment before Adwe was about to devour Etiya and silence her song, the Jagasti came down from their Realms and fell upon the gigantic serpent. Wielding weapons of sunfire and lightning, sky-iron and storm wind, they slew Adwe and cut his body into a myriad of pieces. Then they took those pieces and flung them high above Abengoni, where they became the Moon Stars, luminous clusters of light that would shine far brighter than any other star in the night sky.

When they were done with Adwe, the Jagasti released Etiya and her people from their imprisonment, and showed them how they could best reclaim the world the serpent had stolen from them. The Jagasti remained among the people for a time, until they longed for their own Realms and returned there.

Etiya continued to sing for the rest of her life. Her people took the name "Matile" – the "restored ones." And the Matile made the Jagasti their gods and goddesses, and continued to sing to them long after Etiya's life ended.

Kyroun then saw the time after the demise of Adwe, when the Matile were simple farmers and herders who had only recently ended ages of wandering, hunting teeming hordes of wildlife and gathering abundant fruits across the northern rim of Abengoni.

During that ancient time, the Matile's claim to the land had been fiercely disputed by beings of human shape but inhuman nature – brutal, man-eating ogres called Zimwe and the enigmatic Tokoloshe, who were not then allied with humankind.

The fierce battles among the foes soaked the land with blood. No race could hold sway for long; their advantages – the size and ferocity of the Zimwe, the sorcerous talents of the Tokoloshe, the sheer numbers and dogged determination of the Matile – always offset each other and led to more conflict and bloodshed.

It was the discovery of a different kind of magic that eventually allowed the Matile to prevail over their foes: *ashuma*, a direct link to the power of the Jagasti, who had remained apart in their Realms beyond the boundaries of the mortals' world since they had rescued the people of Abengoni from Adwe.

Kyroun saw the face of the first Matile to wield *ashuma*, and heard his name: Jaussa, an ocher-daubed, befeathered shaman who stared in fear and wonder at the eldritch energy that glowed brightly in his outstretched hands, consuming them even as he watched.

When later Matile shamans learned to harness that awesome power, they used it to drive the Zimwe into a wasteland far to the east. The Tokoloshe, realizing that their own sorcery was no match for *ashuma*, wisely made an alliance with the Matile and retreated to their underground domains. The great animal herds grudgingly retreated from plains that became farmland, and orchards replaced vast forests.

Freed from the constant struggle to survive, the Matile learned to build in stone rather than straw; to record their thoughts in written symbols; to fully explore the power of the gift for which Jaussa had paid with his hands; to walk with the Jagasti, who had decided that the Matile were once again worthy of their company, long after they had first heard Etiya's song...

Akpema of the sun, Nama-kwah of the sea, Alamak of the stars, Ufashwe of the wind, Halasha of iron, and many others ....

Kyroun saw magnificent cities begin to rise throughout the north of Abengoni, glittering like stars in a midnight sky. Their names whispered in his mind: Khambawe, Tesseni, Aglada, Jimmar, Ibela and dozens more. Each of those cities was the capital of its own kingdom. With the menace of the Zimwe and competition from the Tokoloshe gone, the Matile kingdoms ultimately became bitter rivals, incessantly warring against each other, conquering, overthrowing, re-conquering and overthrowing again.

First Khambawe would hold sway over the others, then Tesseni, then Aglada, then Jimmar, then Khambawe again in a never-ending cycle of battle and bloodshed. Finally Dardar Issuri, warrior-king of Khambawe, was able to conquer the other city-states one by one, finally melding the whole of the north into a vast empire and siring the dynasty that continued to rule until this day.

Kyroun saw Gebrem and Tiyana's image of Issuri in his mind: a huge, dark lion of a man, braided hair flying as he mowed his enemies down in battle after battle. Legends whispered that Issuri was the son of Akpema, God of the Sun, and the *ashuma* of the Jagasti had flowed in his veins along with his blood.

The newly-united Matile kingdoms became the mightiest empire Abengoni had ever known. At the Matile Mala Empire's pinnacle, the people of Khambawe and the other cities had lived lives of unimaginable luxury. Their land was fertile and rich in precious metals and stones, which they crafted into exquisite jewelry and art objects. Their armies, aided by the power of *ashuma*, were invincible. Only distance limited the reach of their conquests.

Those acquisitions began in the south, where a hilly landscape marched ever upward, finally forming an escarpment of mountains that marked the division between the north and south of Abengoni. This vast hill country was called Thaba, as were the large, brawny people who dwelt there. The Thaba people were scattered tribes of farmers and nomadic herders who had long ago shunned the changing ways of their lowland neighbors, and had since been left to themselves – until the ambition of Issuri's heirs sent mighty armies into the hills to place the contentious tribes firmly under the new Empire's heel.

The Matile built no cities in the Thaba country. But the people there chafed under the rule of the northerners, who enslaved them and carried them off at will, unwittingly emulating the depredations of the serpent Adwe. In their own land, Thaba slaves worked the rich reefs of diamonds and gold that honeycombed their hills. Others groaned under the Matile lash on the farms of the lowlands and performed the tasks at which the *shamashas* would later toil in the cities.

Stubbornly, the Thabas resisted Matile rule, and their warriors sometimes managed isolated victories over Empire troops. But the magic of their *inyangas* – diviners – proved no match for the might of *ashuma*, and the Thaba rebellions inevitably ended in defeat, with the Matile inflicting increasingly cruel reprisals. Resentment grew like a rancorous tumor in the Thaba hills, but the Matile were blind in their arrogance, and did not deign to notice the hatred. Besides, the Matile had long since shifted their hunger for hegemony to other places.

A parched desert covered much of the territory to the south and west of the Thaba country. This sun-blasted landscape was called the Khumba Khourou, or Great Thirstland. The Khumba Khourou was inhabited by the Kwa'manga, a small-statured, golden-brown people who had long ago learned the secrets of survival in an arid land.

Relations between the Matile and the Kwa'manga were peaceful, though the Matile considered themselves superior to the smaller people despite the fact that the Kwa'manga were born magic-users. However, the desert-dwellers employed their talents only to help them survive their chosen environment and to defend themselves. The Empire left the Kwa'manga alone; there was no glory to be gained in dominating a desert.

The sea, though, was another matter.

Almost by accident, the Matile had discovered new territory when a storm blew a fishing boat off course, pushing it to the vicinity of a chain of large islands located just beyond the horizon of the seacoast. The fishermen found no humans on the islands, only giant birds, huge-eyed, monkey-like creatures, and semi-animate plant life. After the fishermen made their way home and told their tale other, more adventurous, Matile colonized the islands.

They called their new home the Uloas – the god-gifts. Although they maintained close ties of trade and kinship with the mainland, subsequent generations of Uloans gradually developed their own, separate way of life.

As their power grew, Matile from both the mainland and the Uloas explored the rest of their huge island-continent, sending out flotillas of ships filled with soldiers and trade goods, as well as overland expeditions.

South of the Khumba Khourou, Matile explorers found an extensive savanna called the Mbali-pana. Mostly flat grassland, the savanna also featured scattered groves of trees as well as circular depressions that were once the craters of volcanoes, and deep gorges cut by ancient rivers that had long since run dry.

On the Mbali-pana, immense herds of animals – many of which did not exist elsewhere on the continent – roamed freely, sharing abundant pasturage with cattle-herding nomads and hunters. Collectively, the savanna tribes called themselves the Ole-kisongo – the People of the Spear.

Although their warriors were ferocious in battle, the Ole-kisongo were not the true guardians of the Mbali-pana. Soon enough, the Matile explorers had learned of the Wakyambi, an Elven race with a magical affinity for their land. Like the Elven of the Fidi lands, the Wakyambi were far more long-lived than humans. Their darker color and long, tufted tails distinguished them from their kin in other parts of the world.

The Wakyambi greeted the Matile explorers peacefully, and took them to their home – a single, anomalous mountain peak called Kiti ya Ngai, or Seat of the Gods. Because of the flatness of the rest of the land, Kiti ya Ngai was visible for scores of miles.

There, the Wakyambi demonstrated their extraordinary power to control the beasts of the wild. In times of need, the Wakyambi could assemble a mighty animal army, which, along with the loyal Ole-kisongo, was more than capable of dealing with any threat to the Mbali-pana. Although they were confident that their *ashuma* was a match for the Wakyambis' animal sorcery, the Matile saw nothing in the endless savanna that was worth the sacrifices such a conflict would surely bring. They also found that despite the opulence of their empire, they possessed nothing either the Wakyambi or the Ole-Kisongo wanted or needed.

Wiser if not wealthier, the Matile explorers returned to their ships and sailed farther southward, watching the coastline slowly transform from savanna to an enormous belt of rain forest that stretched across the waist of the continent. The region was called the Mashambani-m'ti, or Land of Endless Trees.

The explorers found that foliage grew so thick and close to the shoreline that harbors to the Mashambani-m'ti were virtually nonexistent. But several rivers flowed from the rain forest into the ocean, and the Matile proceeded to sail their ships up the greatest of those streams, called the Luango.

Along the banks of the Luango, the explorers encountered a wide variety of cultures, ranging from the simple hunting-and-gathering lifestyle of the Kidogo pygmies to the sophisticated riverine kingdoms of Mukondo, Usisi, Bashoga, and Nyayembe, among others. The other rain-forest inhabitants were taller than the Kidogo, but still below-average compared to the Matile and the Thabas. Their skin was of sable to ebony hue, and collectively they were known as the Bashombe people.

The many rivers and tributaries that wound among the ranks of trees provided the main avenues for transportation and communication in the Mashambani-m'ti. Stone was rare in this region, so wood and thatch constituted the primary building materials. And Bashombe weavers and woodworkers achieved a degree of artistry stonemasons in other lands would envy.

The Matile explorers were received warmly by the river kingdoms, each seeking its own advantage from the contact. Demonstrations of the power of *ashuma* awed the Bashombe sorcerers, called *ngangas*, and the explorers were treated almost as gods.

Bashombe dignitaries accompanied the explorers when they set sail homeward, to see for themselves the wonders of the Matile Empire. Trading posts were soon established near the mouth of the Luango. The trading posts became colonies, and Matile influence spread throughout the Mashambani-m'ti.

When asked what lay to the south of their land, the Bashombe said there was only the Jhagga, an uninhabited, noxious swampland. Their curiosity aroused, the Matile sent another expedition southward to see what, if anything, lay beyond the Jhagga.

The Jhagga turned out to be worse than the Bashombe had ever imagined – a foul place, teeming with nightmarish creatures. South of the swampland, however, the explorers found more hospitable territory – a rocky, semi-arid steppe interspersed with stands of forest and patches of grassland. It was truly land's end, the southernmost tip of Abengoni. Its inhabitants called it the Kashai.

The people of the Kashai grew to unusual height – well over seven feet in many cases. Their physiques were slender rather than bulky, and they were very dark-skinned. These elongated people, known as the Ikuya, lived in settlements varying in size from villages to small cities. Some of the Ikuya choose to follow a nomadic way of life, grazing their herds on the modest plains.

The Ikuya generally lived in peace with each other, but they were perpetually at war with the *irimu*, remnants of a shape-shifting race that had inhabited much of Abengoni before the arrival of humans. Although the *irimu* possessed the power to transform into lions and leopards, and hyenas, the ancient humans were able to wrest the land from them and drive them into remote areas. Scattered remnants of *irimu* survived as far north as the Thaba hills and even the Matile Mala, but the Kashai was their home and last stronghold.

From there, the shape-changers had mounted reprisal raids on the Ikuya. When the Matile landed in the Kashai, they were greeted with great alarm and consternation from the Ikuya, who had become so isolated they believed they were the only humans in the world. They thought the Matile were *irimu* who had developed a new guise that mimicked humanity, and the Matile could do nothing to disabuse them of that delusional belief.

The Ikuya attacked in force, and the explorers were lucky to escape with their lives. Later, in their intransigent arrogance, the Matile returned in force and built a fortress-city called Buhari at edge of the sea, and they defended it at all costs from the Ikuya, who were as determined to destroy it as they were the *irimu*.

Sailing around the bottom of the continent, other explorers headed north, reaching the eastern side of the Mashambani-m'ti, where they received a warm welcome from the local Bashombe, who had heard of them long before they had arrived.

Further northward, the explorers found an escarpment that formed a great plateau called the Gundagumu, a beautiful land of meadows, lakes, rivers, valleys, forest, and rolling hills. This fruitful territory supported a number of kingdoms and city-states that were constantly at war with each other over land and resources. Prominent kingdoms included Chiminuhwa, Vengaye, Mbiri, Inyangana, and Kadishwene. They all welcomed contact with the Matile.

The Matile learned that the dwellers of the Gundugumu were called the Changami. In appearance, the Changami were an odd amalgam, combining the large stature of the Thabas, the features of the Matile, and the golden-brown skin coloring of the Kwa'manga.

In the Changami, with their warring kingdoms and rapidly developing civilization, the Matile were reminded of themselves as they had been before Dardar Issuri had unified their region. Were the kingdoms of the Gundugumu to become similarly united, they could one day pose a threat to the Matile Mala Empire.

The Degen Jassi of the time contemplated a war of conquest, but dismissed the idea. With the aid of *ashuma*, the Matile would have won such a war in the end. But the cost of maintaining direct dominance over the Gundugumu would have offset the benefits of the victory.

Instead, the Matile chose a subtler method of control. They encouraged the rivalries among the Changami kingdoms, playing one side against the other to ensure that they would never coalesce into an empire. The strategy proved successful; the kingdoms' strife intensified even as the Matile influence grew stronger.

This was the Matile Mala Empire at its peak. With the exceptions of the Mbali-pana plains, and the desert to the south, Matile control had spread throughout Abengoni. And Matile ships plied the seas of the rest of the world, establishing trade that further enriched the Empire. Not only did they sail west to the lands of the Fidi; they also ventured to the east, where they discovered Itsekiri, a sister continent of dark-skinned people; a land of deserts dotted with oases and pierced by mountains. The people of Itsekiri were not seafarers, but they welcomed trade and other contact with the Matile.

As time passed, however, the Matiles' golden age began to show inevitable signs of tarnish. And it was the Uloans who lit the spark that eventually set a mighty Empire ablaze.

The rulers of the islands grew restless within the Empire, and their discontent provided fertile ground for the intrigues of one of the Jagasti – Legaba, God of the Underworld. Long-shunned by worshippers of the other Jagasti, and even by those gods and goddesses themselves, Legaba took full advantage of the islanders' resentment of rule from afar.

Kyroun saw Legaba as a shadow whispering into the ear of an island Jass who sat on a throne flanked by plants that moved in the absence of wind ....

Encouraged by Legaba and his minions from the underground, the Uloans proclaimed their independence from the Matile Empire. The Emperor of the time, Dardar Tesfaru, could not allow such secession to stand. If the islands succeeded in breaking away from the Empire, what would prevent other regions from doing the same?

Thus began the Storm Wars, a conflict that intensified from one generation to the next. The Uloan sorcerers' *ashuma* matched that of the mainlanders, and huge battles unleashed awesome destruction on land and sea. The Jagasti themselves joined the fray, seeking to destroy the outcast Legaba, whose very existence had become an affront to them.

In the final, apocalyptic battle, the sorcerers' *ashuma* careened out of their control, and even the control of the Jagasti. On the mainland, entire cities were incinerated in blazes of eldritch fire. And the Uloan islands were ravaged, nearly half their land-mass swallowed by the sea.

Yet for all the destruction the war wrought on the lands of the Matile and Uloans alike, it was the sea that suffered the worst cataclysm. There, the runaway *ashuma* had thrust the elements of wind and water into an eternal war of their own, a conflict that created incessant storms off the northern rim of Abengoni. Those storms effectively isolated the sea-bound continent from the rest of the world.

The major battles between the Matile and the Uloans ended then; not through any definitive victory or defeat for either side, but because both were too devastated to fight any longer. Their civilization lay in ruins, and the number of dead was beyond counting. Yet the enmity between the rivals remained even as they set about the grim task of salvaging of lands from which even the Jagasti had retreated.

However, the misfortune of the Matile was not yet done. In the aftermath of the Storm Wars, the enslaved Thabas threw off their yokes and rose up against their weakened masters. Their blood-soaked, vengeful revolt came close to wiping out the Matile who had managed to survive the wars.

The Thabas who lived in the cities returned to their ancestral hills, where they joined their long-lost tribesmen in the eradication of all Matile outposts in their country. Especially vicious was the revolt in the mines, which were destroyed with the former overlords trapped inside. The Thabas despised diamonds and gold, and the mines they once worked were sealed and cursed by the newly empowered *inyangas*.

Over the ensuing years, the Thabas raided what was left of Matile Mala with impunity, taking cattle and women as they please. They also hunted the game animals that roamed through the rubble of deserted Matile cities. The old days of Matile domination became a bitter memory to the Thabas, and their frequent raids and skirmishes were a way of obliterating that memory in blood.

Much of the landscape of the former Matile Empire had been permanently altered by the rampant *ashuma*. As time passed, the lands to the east became known as the Nangi Kihunu – the Monstrous Land. Herds of beasts – some altered by the effects of uncontrolled *ashuma* – reclaimed the wasteland, as did the Zimwe and such fearsome offshoots as the *izingogo*, humanoid quadrupeds that hunted in packs and hated all other living beings; the *igikoko*, eaters of carrion and corpses; and the *makishi*, malevolent giants that dwelt in the most remote, desolate areas of the Nangi Kihunu.

The decline of the Matile Empire affected the rest of Abengoni as well. The Matile colonies in the Mashambani-m'ti were abandoned; their people either made their way back to their beleaguered homeland or stayed behind to be dominated and absorbed by the more vigorous Bashombe kingdoms. In the Gundugumu lands, Matile embassies and trading posts were abandoned. And in the Kashai, the Ikuya finally razed Buhari and scattered its inhabitants.

Throughout the continent, the once-great Empire was shunned, and the very name Matile became a murmur of myth. And in the sister-continent to the east, Itsekiri, it became even less than that.

Penned into the northwestern horn of Abengoni, the Matile remnant managed to survive. They rebuilt what they could, and reclaimed a small measure of the *ashuma* they once commanded. The Jagasti did not abandon them completely, but their involvement had diminished. And the Matile were constantly beset by the Uloans' ceaseless quest for revenge. And to the south, a mighty Thaba *nkosi*, or chieftain, named Tshakane was uniting scattered clans and tribes, forging them into a spear aimed at the remaining Matile lands ....

That was what Kyroun saw. Almost all of it was true, in one way or another.

CHAPTER EIGHT

What Gebrem and Tiyana Saw

While the minds of Gebrem and Tiyana wove their patchwork dreams of Matile history, Kyroun fashioned his own carefully prepared Seeing for them. Instead of showing them the entirety of Cym Dinath, the great landmass that held his homeland, Kyroun provided only glimpses, scenes that verified legends passed down since the time the Fidi regularly visited Abengoni.

Tiyana and Gebrem saw a land covered in white, where fur-clad hunters pursued herds of shaggy elephants ....

They saw endless forests of trees with tiny needles instead of leaves on their boughs ....

They saw a range of mountains with peaks higher than the Seat of the Gods ....

They saw teeming cities scattered across the Dinathian lands; some as magnificent as Khambawe had once been, others so squalid their obliteration would have been a blessing ....

They saw a vast desert called the Bashoob, speckled with oases, that separated west from east ....

And on the eastern edge of that sea of sand, they saw Lumaron, a city of delicate spires and tree-shaded streets, a link between the nomadic tribes of the Bashoob and the ancient, powerful kingdoms of the far east. This was the city that Yekunu, the Matile sculptor, had made his home.

Then Kyroun showed them his life ....

Gebrem and Tiyana saw him as a slim, dark-haired boy, a youngest child pampered by a family that had accumulated wealth for generations as artists and artisans. Young Kyroun's brothers and sisters inherited their share of the talent that ran in their family, the legacy of Yekunu. But nothing of that wellspring of creativity had ever touched young Kyroun.

His hands could not create anything of beauty. The floor of the family's studios became littered with the debris of statuettes he had broken in disappointment over his lack of ability. He could sense the pity in the eyes of his family when they looked at the pieces he had not destroyed, and that pity gave him greater hurt than any harsh words or blows could have inflicted.

As he grew into lonely adolescence, Kyroun discovered an outlet for his frustration and disappointment – fighting.

Balled into fists or clenched around the hilt of a sword or the narrow end of a cudgel, Kyroun's hands discovered the aptitude that had eluded them in the studio. He soon became the terror of Lumaron's streets, bursting into a berserker's fury at the slightest provocation. Only the high standing of his family kept the brooding, belligerent youth away from prison or the gallows as he wreaked havoc throughout the city during the course of his growth into manhood. More than one Lumaronian believed that Kyroun's life was headed inexorably toward a quick and violent end.

Then Kyroun's father, Channar ni Abdu, died suddenly, leaving the family's studios to the older children. To the surprise and chagrin of his brothers and sisters, however, it was the rebellious Kyroun who received the most precious heirloom of all – the Ishimbi statuette that was the legacy of their long-dead ancestor from a faraway, half-forgotten land. Kyroun himself had been shocked by the gesture; his relations with his father had grown distant as the years passed.

Still, he kept the statuette, and earned the enmity of his eldest brother, a renowned sculptor who believed the Ishimbi rightfully belonged to him.

Realizing he no longer had any place in the life of his family, Kyroun departed Lumaron, joining a company of sellswords headed for the fractious lands of the east. Ten years passed before he returned.

Kyroun was just past the end of his adolescence when he left Lumaron; he came back a hard-eyed, battle-scarred man of the sword. Of his time among the warring nations of the east he said nothing, not even to his family. Some whispered that he had been an assassin; other rumors spoke of terrible deeds that caused even the bloodthirsty Easterners to drive him from their midst.

If he had accumulated any wealth in his years of warfare, he kept it well-hidden. His horse – which to Gebrem and Tiyana looked like some strange, stripe-less breed of *quagga* – and weapons were all he possessed when he rode again through Lumaron's gates.

Kyroun's reckless youth had long since passed. No longer was he inclined to lash out at anyone he believed affronted him. Still, he could not find a niche in Lumaron, a city that preferred to create wealth rather than wage warfare. Soon he departed again. This time, he headed west, his sword hired to help protect a trade caravan headed across the Bashoob to the oasis kingdom of Pashtar.

There, he nearly met his end.

A rival merchant had betrayed route of the caravan to a bandit chieftain who awaited their coming like a desert lion crouching patiently amidst the dunes. The ambush was swift and merciless. Kyroun and his fellow sell-swords fought valiantly, but the bandits' numbers were overwhelming, and he went down, bleeding from a dozen wounds.

After gathering the caravan's goods and camels – beasts totally alien to the eyes of Tiyana and Gebrem – the bandits departed, leaving the merchants and sellswords for dead. And dead they were – all except Kyroun.

Vision blurred, blood soaking his garments, Kyroun staggered to his feet. Around him, corpses lay strewn like chaff in the sand. He swayed, about to fall, about to join his comrades in death ....

Then a light blazed in front of him, nearly blinding him. Kyroun blinked and rubbed a bloody hand across his eyes. And then he saw the light coalesce into a human-like form that towered high above him, tall though he was.

At first he thought it was a *djinn*, a desert devil, come to collect his soul in recompense for his many sins. Then the glowing apparition spoke to Kyroun in his mind in a tone that tolled like a great bell.

I am Almovaar, the apparition announced.

Kyroun shook his head in disbelief. Almovaar was a god worshipped above all others in ancient days when Lumaron was only a small trading town. Then, as the town grew into a thriving city, foreign deities gained ascendance and eventually Almovaar was relegated to the background, then nearly forgotten and, by some, shunned. Yet Kyroun, having studied history as a youth, knew who this old god was.

"What does a dead god want with a dying man?" Kyroun demanded. He was beyond any fear of affronting a deity.

I offer you life – for a price, Almovaar said to Kyroun.

Kyroun remained silent. For all he knew, this vision was nothing more than an illusion, a hallucination that preceded death. Still, he did not want to die.

"What is the price?"

Be my Seer, Kyroun ni Channar. Bring me worshippers. Rebuild my temple. Restore my name among the people.

Kyroun's reaction surprised him. Purpose suddenly kindled in his benighted soul. The emptiness he had known since the day he became bitterly aware that he could not create art like the rest of his family was suddenly filled. He realized he could, indeed, do what the god asked of him.

"I am yours," he told the deity.

As I have always known, said Almovaar.

Then the god reached out a lambent hand and touched Kyroun. And Kyroun's mortal wounds healed instantly, and his near-death weariness vanished, to be replaced by preternatural vigor.

As the revived Kyroun stretched his arms in wonder, the apparition of Almovaar began to fade. Before he disappeared completely, Almovaar whispered three names in his mind. And when he heard them, Kyroun knew he had received yet another gift from his new god.

Kyroun knew he would have to leave Lumaron again. But before he departed from his homeland for the second time, two men died horrible, inexplicable deaths. One was the leader of the bandits who had ambushed the caravan. The other was the merchant in Lumaron who had arranged the betrayal. Theirs were the first two names Almovaar had spoken to Kyroun.

Now Kyroun's path led northward, across the vast steppes that abutted the Bashoob, toward the towering Rafja Mountains, where the legendary sorcerers of Yaghan made their home.

Yaghan was the third name Almovaar had spoken. Kyroun realized he would need to learn the wisdom the Yaghans offered in order to make best use of the power necessary to restore Almovaar's status in Lumaron. He knew Almovaar could give him the magic. But he also knew he needed to earn the right to use it.

Many had made the arduous pilgrimage to the Yaghan's stronghold, a paradise in the midst of harsh mountain peaks. But only a few survived, for the Yaghans had laid many traps and obstacles along the way to weed out the unworthy.

Kyroun survived all the Yaghan's lethal tests. When he finally arrived at the warm land their magic had created from rocks, ice and snow, the Yaghans welcomed him as a pupil. For the next twenty years, he delved into arcane mysteries and learned how to handle sources of power only the most elite among sorcerers dared to tap – and his mastery eventually exceeded their own.

Finally, the Yaghans told Kyroun he had learned all they could teach him. And he finally understood that it was in sorcery, rather than art or arms, that his true talent lay. When he made his way back down the Rafjas, none of the perils that had confronted him during his ascent appeared. There was no need for them.

Once again, Kyroun returned to the city of his birth – this time as a seer rather than a man of war. Many of his old acquaintances failed to recognize him. And to his family, which had continued to prosper, he was a stranger in more ways than he had been before.

Soon after his arrival, Kyroun rebuilt the long-abandoned Temple of Almovaar and gathered the few in Lumaron who remembered the city's first god. Then he began to preach in the streets and the market squares, seeking new worshippers as he had promised Almovaar in the desert.

At first, he made scant headway, for the veneration of the newer deities had become firmly ensconced. And none of Kyroun's family ever set foot in the new Temple of Almovaar.

Then Kyroun began to perform miracles. Utilizing the knowledge he had acquired from the Yaghans, he healed the sick and made the maimed whole. He turned desiccated land into lush fields. He made barren women fecund. He destroyed an army sent by a steppe-lord to pillage a border city that was loyal to Lumaron.

New worshippers soon filled the Temple of Almovaar. Those who felt forsaken by Lumaron's other gods returned to the older deity. People of the Shadim, a mysterious race of wanderers from the east who were looked upon with suspicion by westerners, also responded to Kyroun's preachings. Even a group of Dwarvenkind, who normally were disdained by much of humankind, listened to Kyroun's sermons and became Almovaads – Believers – because their own gods had not saved them from the cave-in that had destroyed their underground home, and Kyroun offered them protection from those who felt threatened by the Dwarvenkind's very existence as they wandered through lands alien to them.

He even counted among his followers a lone Elven woman, an

exile from her people who refused to disclose her reasons for joining the Almovaads. It was enough for Kyroun that someone from the most elusive of all the races of Cym Dinath would choose to join his cause. He suspected that the woman possessed qualities she kept hidden from him. In due time, he would learn what they were.

As the ascendance of the Almovaads increased, so did the jealousies of the other gods' priests. They could not oppose Kyroun openly, for he had gained the favor of Lumaron's rulers. Instead, they plotted in secret, pooling their resentment and their resources for a swift, sudden strike.

But Almovaar warned Kyroun of what was to come. The deity spoke to him through the medium of Ishimbi statuette the Seer kept with him at all times.

These people are unworthy of you or me, Kyroun, Almovaar said. I see now that our destiny lies in a place far from here.

"What is this place?" Kyroun asked.

Your true homeland.

"But *this* is my homeland," Kyroun protested.

No. Your family forsakes you. And even now, those who serve other gods are coming to slay you. You and I are not wanted or needed here. You and I are needed in the home of the one who made this object.

Kyroun shook his head in disbelief. Family history had told him Yekunu had been forever separated from his faraway homeland by storms that never ceased. Yet now his god was telling him that was where he needed to go.

The Seer's hesitation lasted less than a moment. Almovaar had not yet failed him yet. And he would not fail Almovaar.

"We will go," he said to the sculpture in his hands, even as Almovaar's presence faded yet again.

When the mob the rival priests had incited arrived, bent on destroying the Temple of Almovaar, it stopped short in fear and astonishment.

What stood before them was not the restored, resplendent house of the elder god. Instead, they saw the temple as it had been before the Seer Kyroun had returned from his time among the Yaghans – crumbling, deserted, spider-haunted.

Of Kyroun and the Almovaad congregation, there was not even the slightest of signs ...

Kyroun had gathered his remaining followers at the edge of the Bashoob. There, he told them of the new mission Almovaar had revealed: a journey to a place that no longer existed on maps of the known world.

He offered them a choice. They could join him in his quest for the lost homeland of his ancestor. Or they could go elsewhere – anywhere other than Lumaron, where the Almovaads were clearly no longer welcome. For himself, the choice was inevitable and irrevocable.

"I will go to Matile, as Almovaar commands," Kyroun told them. "Almovaar will protect us from the storms. If necessary, I will go to Matile alone."

Only a small fraction of the Believers refused to follow their Seer when he began to walk westward across the Bashoob. The rest – a congregation numbering nearly a thousand – joined him on the long journey to Fiadol, greatest of the seafaring kingdoms in Cym Dinath.

Along the way, additional Believers had deserted, frightened by the prospect of sailing into the teeth of an endless storm. But others – outsiders who listened to the sermons Kyroun preached whenever the Almovaads stopped to rest – became Believers and took the places of those who had fallen away, so that in the end their numbers became larger than ever.

Finally they reached Fiadol, a swaggering coastal city laden with the wealth of the world gained through trade. There, Kyroun searched for a ship-captain willing to undertake a seemingly suicidal voyage into the Sea of Storms, an area even the most foolhardy seamen shunned.

With the treasure his sect had accumulated and taken from Lumaron, Kyroun could have purchased an entire fleet. But none of Fiadol's captains was willing to sail into a maelstrom of wind and rain that had no known end, regardless of the Seer's repeated assurances of protection from his obscure god.

"For all you know, this Ma-teel place of yours could be nothing more than a bunch of washed-out ruins," one grizzled sea-dog told him. "It might even be under water by now."

Kyroun knew that was not true. He also knew Matile was better-remembered in Fiadol than the skeptical captain had indicated. But all he could offer for veracity was the Ishimbi statuette and the word of Almovaar, neither of which meant much to a non-Believer. Even demonstrations of his hard-won skills at weather-control magic failed to impress the seafarers. But they did bring down the disapproval of Fiadol's established priesthood, whose members warned him to cease his encroachments on their sphere of influence.

It seemed Kyroun's voyage had ended before it could ever

begin. Some of his followers even began to question the wisdom of his determination to find the lost land of his distant ancestor.

Then one of the Believers found Pel Muldure, a captain who was down on his luck and landbound. Lured by a promise of wealth, Muldure had undertaken a privateering venture that had gone awry. Disavowed by the Fiadolian noble who had hired him, Muldure had been judged harshly by the seamen's tribunal, losing both his ship and captaincy credentials for his troubles.

The latter he had regained after a period of penance, and the payment of a large fine. But no one was willing to hire his services, and he became a fixture at the drinking dives that dotted Fiadol's wharf district, much to the despair of the few friends he had left.

"I will buy the ships we need," Kyroun told Muldure when they met at the encampment the Seer had established for his followers. "Almovaar will protect us on our voyage. And when word of your feat of seamanship spreads across the world, those who now disdain you will speak your name in tones of wonder."

"You say your god can get a ship to this lost land," Muldure said. "Can he bring us back here?"

"Do you really *want* to come back here?" Kyroun countered.

Muldure considered. He believed Kyroun was a madman and his proposed voyage an invitation to suicide. Yet without a deck under his feet and a tiller in his hands, he might as well be dead anyway.

Pel Muldure accepted Kyroun's offer. He had nothing to lose. Neither did the crews he assembled for the two ships Kyroun's gold bought. Some of them were old friends, such as Lyann, who had suffered for their loyalty to him; others were dockside drifters and miscreants who, like him, were unable to find other employment.

When the ships, the *White Gull* and the *Swordfish*, set sail from Fiadol's crowded harbor, the other captains provided a derisive sendoff. "Voyage of fools," they called the venture. They did not expect to see either Muldure or the Almovaads again.

Months passed before the *White Gull* and *Swordfish* came within sight of the Sea of Storms. At first, it appeared as a faint gray smudge stretching from one end of the horizon to the other. Day by day it grew, consuming the sky as the Almovaads drew closer, the Seer sailing in the *White Gull*, the *Swordfish* trailing in its wake. Then the storm engulfed them, and the thaumaturgy Kyroun had learned from the Yaghans was put to its ultimate test.

He constructed a protective barrier around both ships, an unseen shield strong enough to prevent the warring elements of wind and water from wreaking their havoc. At the same time, he conjured a ghost-wind that propelled the *White Gull* and *Swordfish* forward, ever forward, in the direction in which old maps indicated Matile lay.

To perform either task would have been a remarkable feat of sorcery. To do both simultaneously, unceasingly – the Almovaads' awe of their Seer increased ten-fold. Even the ship's crew – of whom only a few had become Believers – began to respect him as the days in the storm passed.

More than that, they began to fear him ....

Still, Kyroun was only mortal, a flesh-and blood conduit through which the power of Almovaar flowed. Soon enough, the conduit corroded. Kyroun's weakening was imperceptible at first. However, as the days in the storm dragged into weeks, the strain on the Seer became more noticeable. And the disquiet among Believers and non-Believers alike grew with each buffet of wind and wave against the ship's hulls.

When the last of Kyroun's strength ebbed away, the thwarted elementals lashed at the *White Gull* and *Swordfish* with a vengeful fury, nearly tearing both ships apart. But Kyroun managed to summon a final gust of ghost-wind that pushed the *White Gull* out of the storm, even as he and the others who remained alive lost consciousness. But he did not have enough strength left to save the *Swordfish*. The Elven woman had been on that ship. Kyroun had preferred that she sail with him, but she had insisted on a different arrangement, and he had not argued with her. Now, she was lost, as were all the others on the doomed ship.

But he could not regret that loss. He could not do anything more as the *White Gull* drifted with the tide until it struck the docks of Khambawe.

"And now I am home," Kyroun said, ending his story.

He then released the hands of Gebrem and Tiyana, and the In-Seeing came to an end.

CHAPTER NINE

Contemplations

1

The original surfaces of the rooms, halls and chambers of the Gebbi Senafa had not been visible for centuries. Layer upon layer of paint, gilding, sculptures, tapestries and furnishings had provided a thick patina of opulence to the interior of the palace. And this was only the latest of the royal dwellings, an earlier one having been abandoned long ago.

In only one small room of the Gebbi Senafa did the walls remain bare of ornamentation. Unlike the other rooms of the palace, this one had no formal designation. Its sole function was to serve as a sanctum for Matile monarchs at times when they needed solitude.

Dardar Agaw, the Emperor who had salvaged the remnants of the Matile Mala at the end of the Storm Wars, had been the one who set aside this austere chamber. According to his writings, which his successors had studied with varying degrees of diligence, Agaw had needed a place in which he could be free, even for a short time, from the entreaties and machinations of his courtiers and advisers. The tactic had proven successful for Agaw, at least in terms of his reign as Emperor. History credited him with preventing a complete collapse of the Matile people in the wake of the disaster that had befallen them.

Now, Dardar Alemeyu was the one who sat on Agaw's plain, granite bench – the only furnishing his predecessor had permitted in the chamber. The decision Alemeyu pondered was not nearly as momentous as the ones with which his distant ancestor had been burdened. Agaw's meditations had shaped the future of the Matile. Alemeyu's task was only to consider the fate of the Fidi.

The room in which he sat was small, little more than a cubicle. Its walls were made of granite slabs, featureless save for scratch marks that were all that remained of the decorations Dardar Agaw had ordered to be removed. The overall effect of the chamber was more reminiscent of a prison cell than an Emperor's refuge. But sometimes, Agaw had written, the entire palace was a prison for the one who sat on the Lion Throne. There were times when Alemeyu agreed wholeheartedly with his predecessor's view.

A single candle provided the only illumination in the windowless room. It cast a weak, wavering light on the Emperor's face as he sat on the hard, stone surface of Agaw's bench. The bench was much less comfortable than the Lion Throne. But comfort was the last consideration on Dardar Alemeyu's mind.

The Emperor was not wearing his crown. Still, the black-and-gold *chamma* that swathed his body symbolized his rank, and his inescapable responsibility.

He had come to Agaw's sanctum soon after a meeting with the Leba and his daughter in the Chamber of Audiences, with only his palace guards in attendance. As he sat with his hands clasped beneath his white beard, Alemeyu remembered what had been said after Gebrem and Tiyana had told him what had happened during their latest encounter with the Fidi sorcerer.

For a long time after the two had finished their tale, Alemeyu had looked at them without speaking. Then he asked a single question.

"Do you believe what this man has told you?"

"Yes," Gebrem answered without hesitation.

Alemeyu turned his gaze to Tiyana.

"So do I," she said.

"Why?" Alemeyu asked them both.

An uncomfortable span of silence followed the Emperor's question, as though the Leba and his daughter were struggling with knowledge that was easier to understand than to articulate. Amply aware of the limited patience reflected in the Emperor's hard-eyed gaze, Gebrem tried to formulate an answer that would enlighten, not irritate, the irascible monarch.

"We touched the Fidi at a level beneath what the eyes can see," the Leba said. "And when mind touches mind, Emperor, there can be no deception."

Tiyana nodded agreement.

"The Fidis' ship nearly killed me, Mesfin," she said. "That gives me more reason as anyone to be suspicious of them. But I saw the same honesty inside the sorcerer that my father did."

"So you trust him, then?" the Emperor asked.

"I ... distrust him less."

Alemeyu willed a smile from reaching from his lips. Despite the long-standing tension between him and Gebrem, he sometimes wished Tiyana were his daughter, not his cousin's. This girl had the makings of an Empress ...

He pushed that thought aside and hardened his voice. But his thrust was directed more at Gebrem than Tiyana.

"But you have said this man has great *ashuma* power. How do you know he is not using that power to deceive you into accepting his tale?"

Gebrem and Tiyana looked at each other. There was only one honest answer they could provide, and Gebrem gave it.

"We do not know, Mesfin," he said through tightly compressed lips.

"Just so," Alemeyu said.

He waited a moment before continuing. It was a moment similar to many in the two men's lives: yet another opportunity for Alemeyu to reassert his superiority over his younger cousin, the son of his father's brother. He remembered that the relationship between his father and his uncle was not dissimilar to the one he now endured with Gebrem.

Perhaps it will always be so, between an Emperor and a Leba, he mused.

"I must think on this matter in solitude," Alemeyu said. "Wait here."

And with that, he left Tiyana and Gebrem in the Audience Chamber.

Before he had departed from the chamber, Alemeyu already knew what his decision would be. However, Gebrem needed to be reminded – yet again – that he was not the Emperor. The Leba's leading role in the interlude with the Fidi might well have inflated his perception of his status. A long wait in the Audience Chamber would remind Gebrem of his true place, which was several levels below that of the occupant of the Lion Throne.

Now, Dardar Alemeyu looked at the candle burning in Agaw's sanctum. The Emperor had used the time to think about many other matters, including whether or not it was time to put Issa aside and find another woman to give birth to the next Emperor or Empress. When the candle was finished, he would tell Gebrem and Tiyana what he had in mind for the Fidi.

2

In Kyroun's cabin on the *White Gull*, a gathering of another kind was taking place. With the Seer was a group of other blue-clad Almovaads – Acolytes and Adepts. These were the Believers who had demonstrated an aptitude for sorcery. The others remained outside the cabin.

More than two dozen Almovaads were crowded into a space that could comfortably accommodate less than half that number. However, any discomfort they might have experienced meant nothing, because they were in Oneness, a mystic communion that encompassed much more than the In-Seeing Kyroun had shared with Gebrem and Tiyana.

There was no need for a contact of hands in Oneness. The Almovaads in the cabin had progressed far enough to work their sorcery independently. Yet they were not independent now. They were One with their Seer … and One with Almovaar. Although their bodies were crammed together in a small space, Oneness set their minds free in a space that seemed limitless; an expanse of pale, blue light like an early-morning sky reflected in clear water. The Almovaads' thoughts rippled across the surface of that space.

The Matile are determining our fate now, Kyroun told them. His thoughts, though voiceless, were as clear as the ice in the Northlands of Cym Dinath.

Their Emperor will make the decision.

Can you not look into the Emperor's mind and be aware of what he will decide?

That thought came from Eimos, a young Acolyte who harbored ambitions of becoming an Adept. But he was impatient – too much so for Kyroun to allow him to advance to the practice of a higher level of sorcery before gaining sufficient control over his impulses.

I can, the Seer said. *But I choose not to.*

Why not? the Acolyte asked.

Kyroun did not reply. His silence was a test, an opportunity for

Eimos and the others to learn a lesson.

But Eimos was not the one who broke the silence. It was Byallis, a young woman whose raw talent did not match that of Eimos. She was, however, his superior in discipline, which was why she had ascended to Adept status and he had not.

If you entered his mind, you would be tempted to influence his thoughts, Byallis said. *And for reasons of your own, you do not wish to do that.*

Precisely, Kyroun said. His approval of Byallis's insight purled across the Oneness like a wave caressing a shoreline.

The Emperor and his people must welcome us of their own free will, the Seer explained in response to the unspoken question that stirred the Oneness. *And they must come to Almovaar the same way all of you did.*

What if they do not accept us? Eimos asked.

Again, Kyroun did not answer directly. Instead, he lifted a tiny portion of the veil that divided the Oneness from the pure presence of Almovaar. The glimpse of that presence shot through the Oneness like the first ray of sunlight after the passing of a storm. The essence of their god touched them all, and once again, the Acolytes and Adepts were grateful that they had been granted even a minuscule fragment of Almovaar's potency.

Hopefully, it will not come to that, Kyroun said. *For now, though, we must await the Emperor's decision.*

So. We nearly die in the water, only to leave our fate in the hands of a stranger instead of our Seer. Almovaar gives us power. Why do we hesitate to use it?

The new speaker was Ruk, a stolid Acolyte from the Northlands. Ruk seldom said much, either in or outside the Oneness. When he did, his words tended to be as subtle as a blow from a quarterstaff.

What we do is Almovaar's will, Ruk, Kyroun said firmly. The Northerner was a good man, especially in a fight. But, as with Eimos, Kyroun did not feel he could trust Ruk with the amount of sorcerous power an Adept could wield. Control of impulses was not Ruk's strong point.

There was no need for further discussion after that. The Oneness ended, and after they had taken the time they needed to return to the world outside their communion, the Almovaads began to file out of Kyroun's cabin.

Eimos, a slender, rakish-looking, black-haired man, stepped aside to allow Byallis to precede him through the door. Byallis cast him a sidelong glance as she passed him. The smile on Eimos's face was innocent enough. But it didn't reach as far as his eyes, which were a shade of blue that was startling in his swarthy-skinned face. And as soon as she was gone, his smile disappeared.

Byallis was a plump woman with curly brown hair that cascaded below her shoulders. Kyroun's hopes for her were high. But even in the Oneness, he was careful to conceal his approval. It was best not to encourage rivalries by directly acknowledging favorites. The Seer could never have shielded his ships from the storm if internecine struggles among the Adepts and Acolytes had distracted his concentration during the dangerous voyage.

Ruk was one of the last to leave. A huge, hard-looking man whose head was topped with a shock of straw-colored hair, the Northlander cast a questioning glance in Kyroun's direction. He looked as though he belonged on a battlefield rather than in a religious order.

The Seer spoke to him with his mouth rather than his mind.

"Keep watch, my friend," he said. "Keep very vigilant watch."

Ruk responded with a short nod. Then he left the cabin, and the Seer was alone, except for Ulrithana, a Shadimish Adept who was his closest confidant save for his second-in command, a man named Ferroun ni Tamiz. He wished Ferroun were with him now. Although he had no sorcerous ability, Ferroun was the perfect administrator, and he would have been able to defuse the tension that was now building among some of the Adepts. And that would have freed Kyroun to concentrate on rebuilding his strength, which he felt certain he would need no matter what the Emperor decided concerning the fate of the newcomers.

But he had assigned Ferroun to the second ship, the *Swordfish*. And the *Swordfish* was now at the bottom of the sea.

Kyroun closed his eyes and let out a long, slow sigh – the only outward sign he would allow himself to express of the weariness that assailed him. When he opened his eyes, he saw Ulrithana looking at him calmly, with the far-seeing gaze of her people. The Shadimish woman was not much taller than the Dwarven. Her body seemed lost in the expanse of her voluminous blue robe. Her features were finely drawn, and her eyes had the characteristic Eastern fold that caused them to appear to be slanted at an oblique angle.

"You miss Ferroun," Ulrithana said.

"Yes," Kyroun acknowledged. "And I miss everyone else on the

Swordfish. We need them here. But I could not save them."

"You did what you could," Ulrithana said. "Almovaar could ask no more."

Kyroun nodded. He knew Ulrithana held little love for Ferroun; she considered him a rival, even though he could never become an Adept.

"I must rest now," he said.

Ulrithana nodded in turn, and left the cabin. Her stiff-backed posture was the only indication that she was less than pleased to be departing.

Kyroun sighed again. He knew Ulrithana wanted to remain with him, to lie with him on his narrow bed. But he was far too distracted to enjoy her company. He closed his eyes and lay down on the bed. Using the Ishimbi statue as his focal point, he willed the weariness from his muscles and bones, emptying himself of human frailty so that the strength of Almovaar could flow into him like water into a cup. For, like the Amiyas, he, too, was a Vessel.

3

No one saw the furtive figure that slipped quietly over the side of the *White Gull* and scurried into the shelter of the shadows on the dock. Not the ship's crew who, had they noticed his departure, would have merely looked the other way and let him be gone. Not the Matile guards, who were not expecting any of the newcomers to attempt to leave the ship. Not the self-righteous Almovaad Acolytes and Adepts, who were absorbed in their Oneness with Kyroun and their god to notice whether or not the miserable ship was still afloat.

Indeed, if anyone on the *White Gull* had reason to miss the presence of Athir Rin, they would never admit it.

Catching his breath, Athir leaned against the wall of a dockside building. He allowed the smells, the sounds, the *feel* of this new city to seep into his skin.

Athir was a small, wiry man with pinched features, close-cropped, sandy hair with a small tail trailing past the nape of his neck, and a stubbly beard. His pale eyes shifted constantly, as though they were searching for the nearest escape route.

Like a persistent bit of flotsam, Athir Rin had washed up in nearly every seaport in Cym Dinath. He was a bandit and bilker by trade, and a sailor by necessity. A ship sailing away from a dock was the best way he knew to escape death or dismemberment at the hands of those whose laws he flouted and pockets he lightened.

That was how he had become a member of the *White Gull's* crew. He had stolen jewels from a merchant in Fiadol, but had not been able to fence them quickly enough in the city's underground market. Cutting his losses, Athir had lost himself in Fiadol's teeming wharf district before the merchant's private men-at-arms could catch up with him, never mind the city guard.

Eventually, he had heard about the Almovaads and their Voyage of the Doomed. And he knew he stood a better chance for survival on their mad venture into the Sea of Storms than he would if he remained much longer in Fiadol.

Desperate to fill out his crew, Pel Muldure had agreed to take Athir on board despite his notoriety in sailors' circles. In docks throughout Cym Dinath, Athir Rin was known as the "Ship's Rat." Despite that cognomen, however, Athir was a good seaman. He had to be; otherwise he would have been thrown overboard from most of the ships on which he had sailed.

When the Seer's protection finally failed and the storms struck, Athir had barely managed to live through the ferocious battering of wind and wave. Now, he had made landfall and he was alive. By Athir's lights, that meant he owed nothing more to Muldure, or to the Seer, whom he had initially considered a madman, but now grudgingly respected. Even so, Athir could never become a Believer. The only deity he acknowledged was the god of chance.

He gazed out at the dark streets of Khambawe. He looked nothing like a Matile, but he knew he could find ways to blend in with the seamier elements of the populace. Athir had done so many times before, in places where he would have seemed as out-of-place as a hawk in a henhouse.

The Ship's Rat cast a final glance at the broken hulk of the *White Gull* and the people on board who were oblivious of his departure.

"So long, suckers," he muttered before disappearing into the darkness of his newest rat-hole.

4

Gebrem and Tiyana sat alone in the Chamber of Audiences, save for the ornately armored Emperor's Guards. The presence of the guardsmen was only a formality; many generations had passed since the last time blood had been spilled in the Palace. As the Empire waned, its people clung ever-closer to the symbols of their previous glories, and of all those symbols, none stood higher than the Emperor.

Palace *shamashas* had placed cups of *kef* on the low table at which the Leba and his daughter were seated. Gebrem raised his cup to his lips, sipped slowly, and gazed at Tiyana through the faint wisps that rose from the hot liquid.

Tiyana noticed the concern showing in his eyes.

"What troubles you, Father?" she asked.

Gebrem smiled fleetingly as he placed his cup back on the table.

"I was remembering when the Fidi's ship crashed into the dock after you fell into the water," he said. "I thought I had lost you."

Tiyana gave his hand a quick squeeze. She had been a small child when her mother, Membiri, died from a disease neither healers nor *ashuma* could cure. Gebrem and Membiri had no other children, and the Leba had never married again after his wife's death. Being Leba was Gebrem's duty; being father to Tiyana was his life.

An unspoken message passed between them as Gebrem took another sip of *kef*. They both knew the flawed First Calling no longer mattered; the coming of the Fidi was of much greater significance – perhaps greater than anything that had happened to the Matile since the Storm Wars ended.

"The Emperor is taking a long time to decide," Tiyana said.

Gebrem grimaced and shook his head.

"Alemeyu decided before he went into Agaw's Chamber," he said.

"Then why – "

Tiyana broke off as she realized the answer to the question she no longer needed to ask. By forcing her and Gebrem to wait, Alemeyu was asserting his authority. But she still didn't understand why he needed to do so. Was he not the Emperor? She decided not to ask Gebrem to explain Alemeyu's motives. Her father had a tendency to become rancorous whenever he talked about his exalted cousin.

"What do you think he decided?" she asked instead.

Gebrem shrugged.

"Alemeyu has always been difficult to predict," he said. "But I don't see any reason to keep the Fidis captive. Do you?"

Tiyana thought for a moment, thinking of the sliver of doubt that still remained in her mind; the single word Nama-kwah had spoken to her.

"No," she finally said.

Danger ...

"For now," she added.

Gebrem was about to respond to her equivocation when a stirring among the guards signalled the Emperor's return to the Audience Chamber. When he came into sight, Dardar Alemeyu was shrouded in shadows, and his face betrayed no emotion.

As Gebrem and Tiyana rose to their feet, Alemeyu strode wordlessly toward the Lion Throne and settled into its seat. Without his crown and other regal trappings, he seemed diminished by the grandeur of the huge throne. But there was no lessening of the authority in his voice when he spoke.

"I have made my decision," he said.

He paused, staring hard at Gebrem and Tiyana in turn. He allowed the silence to stretch uncomfortably before he continued.

"The Fidi have come from afar to be among us. We will grant them that wish. They will abide here as our honored guests."

That was what Gebrem wanted to hear, although he allowed none of his gratification to show. However, the Emperor's next words soured that moment of satisfaction.

"You, Leba, saved the life of the Fidis' sorcerer, this Kyroun. What Kyroun does – or does not do – is your responsibility."

Again, Gebrem concealed his true reaction. He did not yet know the true extent of the Seer's sorcerous power. And he did not know what he would – or could – do once he did learn.

"As you wish, Mesfin," was all Gebrem could say.

CHAPTER TEN
SEHAYE'S MESSAGE

1

Like pieces of a broken necklace, the Uloan Islands lay strewn across the sea west of Abengoni. In the time before the Storm Wars, the Uloans' homeland had been a magnificent archipelago, a gem of the ocean that matched the splendors of Khambawe, the Jewel City of the mainland. There were islands large and small, bordered with beaches of white and gold sand, clothed in verdant mantles of semi-animate vegetation called *mwiti*, and crowned with cratered hills – remnants of volcanoes that had long been dormant, but never dead. Flowers grew in rampant profusion throughout the archipelago and the animal life, which was different from that of the mainland, was as docile as though it had been domesticated long before the first humans had set foot on the islands. Birds of brilliant plumage flew like jewels through forest and sky, singing songs of welcome.

The descendants of the original settlers from the mainland had built beautiful towns and cities of coral, tamed the islands' animals and moving plants, and cultivated soil that was so fertile that farmers' crops could grow almost unattended. One crop, sweetcane, grew only in the Uloas, and traders from the islands carried it to the mainland and eventually to other parts of the world, including Fiadol, even as the mainlanders traded crafts and *kef*.

For centuries, peace and prosperity had reigned in the Uloas, so much so that they became known far and wide as the "Happy Isles." But the Uloans were not satisfied with their contentment for long, even though others who visited their islands always went away envious of the way of life the Uloans had developed.

Yet the Uloans, in turn, coveted the continent-spanning influence of the Matile Mala Empire. Embers of ambition for greater dominance eventually flared into flames of jealousy and hatred against the mainland, which continued to consider the islands part of the Empire and demanded tribute along with the trade between them. And those flames eventually grew into a conflagration that would consume not only the islands, but also the mainland, which had long since ceased to be the Motherland in the minds of the islanders.

The land from which their ancestors had come was now seen as an impediment to the Uloans' overweening aspirations, an obstacle that needed to be removed. The Uloans' dreams of a destiny of dominance over the mainland had been planted and patiently nurtured by the renegade god Legaba, who was using the Uloans as tools in his schemes against his fellow Jagasti, who had made him an outcast after an altercation that had shaken their Realms. The Uloans were willing accomplices of the Spider God, and the disastrous results of their subsequent course of action were as much their responsibility as Legaba's.

The Storm Wars were the culmination of combined human and divine arrogance, and in the end arcane forces were unleashed that went beyond even the Jagastis' control. And when the cataclysmic conflict called the Storm Wars finally ended, the Uloas were no longer idyllic dreamlands. Smaller islands, and parts of the larger ones, had been swallowed by the sea. The sleeping volcanoes had awakened, burying cities in mounds of lava and ash. The sands of the white and gold beaches turned red as the blood that had been spilled during the Storm Wars. And the island's unique, semi-animate plant life, the *mwiti*, had become ... restless.

Few Uloans had survived the appalling carnage the Storm Wars had wrought. Those who still lived continued to maintain their loyalty to Legaba, even though the Spider God's promises of empire had failed disastrously. For Legaba was all they had left, because they had long since abandoned the worship of the other Jagasti who had been revered by the Matile and Uloans alike. And as the decades after the Storm Wars became centuries, the Uloans had grown farther apart from their Mainland kin. Their customs changed, as did their speech and even their appearance, until the blood and cultural ties that once bound them disappeared almost completely.

And as the Uloans gradually rebuilt what they could of their broken realm, a singular purpose drove them onward as the centuries crawled forward. That goal was Retribution Time. One day, a day the Uloans believed would soon come even as the years dragged by, the mainlanders would pay for the destruction they wrought upon the islanders. Retribution Time …

And now, Sehaye's *gede* was on its way to the Shattered Isles.

2

On a dark, overcast morning, the *gede* washed up on the crimson beach of Jayaya, the largest remaining island of the Uloas. After the wave that carried it onto the shore retreated, the *gede* continued to slide across the incarnadine sand, hitching its gelatinous body forward like an inchworm and leaving a glistening, foul-smelling track of ooze behind it.

When it had travelled far enough away from the water to prevent another wave from taking it back to sea, the sorcerous construct stopped moving. And it waited to be picked up: its task completed, its semblance of life gone.

The green of the foliage that grew beyond the red sand was so bright the plants appeared to glow even on a sunless day. Pink and yellow *mwiti* flowers grew amidst the grass, and multicolored *mwiti* fruits festooned the branches of the trees that abounded in the background. But the plant life was far from ordinary, for the petals of the flowers opened and closed like fingers, and the fruits pulsated like beating hearts. The grass moved like ocean waves, yet there was no breeze blowing to stir its blades.

Then the grass moved in a different way, impelled by a volition other than its own. And a serpentine form emerged and wriggled onto the sand. It was dark green and about four feet in length. Despite the surface resemblance to the ophidian-kind, however, it was not a snake. It was an *ubia*-vine, a *mwiti*-plant that was capable of independent motion. *Ubias* could not move quickly enough to be dangerous to people or animals mobile enough to evade them. However, a stationary object like the *gede* was another matter.

Small leaves sprouted at random intervals on the narrow tube that constituted the *ubia's* body. There was no discernable head at its anterior; only a mouth-like stoma encircled with thorn-like barbs. Its tail end was pointed like a spike.

The *ubia*-vine moved closer to the *gede*, which remained inert. When the vine reached its quarry, its mouth fastened onto the *gede*'s side, and the barbs began their work, cutting into the viscous flesh and channeling the pieces into the *ubia*'s gullet. The lapping waves drowned out the sound of the *ubia*'s cutting and chewing.

The lifeless *gede* had no defense against the *ubia*'s determined assault. Its poisonous flesh and sorcerous aura had protected it well from the predators of the sea as it swam from the mainland. But those defenses had no effect on the predatory plant life of the islands, which had been altered by the uncontrolled magic unleashed during the Storm Wars. And with its charge completed, the *gede* was now only an inert lump of tissue, and it could do nothing to save itself as the *ubia* burrowed its way ever-deeper into the construct's motionless form.

Soon the barbs reached the wooden tube ... and sank into it.

Then footsteps rustled in the bright-green, waving grass. And an Uloan stepped onto the beach. The grass-blades pressed down by his feet sprang upright – and continued to move long after they were standing straight again.

The Uloan, whose name was Bujiji, uttered an exclamation of dismay and rushed to the *gede*. He reached down and ripped the *ubia* from its prey, easily avoiding the teeth-laden mouth that whipped toward him. He cut the vine in half with the long, broad-bladed knife he carried, then hurled the pieces into the sea. The severed sections of the *ubia* continued to thrash as they sank beneath the surface.

Muttering bitter curses, Bujiji reached deep into the *gede*'s mouth. Despite grimacing in disgust at the touch of the construct's gelatinous substance, he closed his fingers around the message tube. Then he yanked the tube out, pulling pieces of the *gede* with it. At the sight of the marks the *ubia*'s mouth-barbs had made on the wood, he cursed again. He knew those marks would soon make trouble for him – trouble he could not avoid.

As the Uloan turned and strode away from the beach, the torn *gede* lay in the sand, dead eyes staring up at the gray sky. Within moments of Bujiji's departure, another *ubia* came out of the grass and wriggled toward the construct to finish the meal the other had begun.

3

As he strode through the seaside forest, Bujiji glared again at the marks on the message tube. Those marks were clear evidence of his late arrival at the beach, and the near-disaster his tardiness had caused. Bujiji had only himself to blame for whatever happened next. Jass Imbiah had told him the *gede* would be waiting for him to pick up, but he had stayed too long with Awiwi, his current love, before going to the beach to retrieve the message the construct brought.

It was worth it to I, Bujiji thought, remembering the sensation of Awiwi's sweat-slicked skin sliding against his as they made love. *Well worth it.*

The *ubia*-vine had not broken the tube; the message inside remained intact. That was the most important thing. Bujiji knew Jass Imbiah would berate him, and that would be an ordeal, never mind the far worse punishments the woman who was the ruler of Jayaya, and first among the Jassi of the other islands, was capable of inflicting. Those other punishments were not likely to happen … he hoped.

"It was still worth it to I," he said aloud, not caring that there was no one close enough to hear him.

Bujiji was a sturdy, sienna-skinned man of medium height. His only garments were a multicolored cloth knotted around his lean waist with ends that hung halfway to his knees, and a pair of leather boots that warded off the grasping strands of grass that adhered persistently, and painfully, to whatever flesh they touched. His knife, which he had sheathed again, bumped against his hip as he walked into the *mwiti*-forest.

In contrast to spies like Sehaye, Bujiji could never pass unnoticed on the mainland. His head was shaved, and he allowed no hair to grow on his face. His scalp was covered with lines of raised scars that stretched from the beginning of his forehead to the nape of his neck, giving the effect of a spiderweb. A series of straight, vertical lines were incised into the rest of his face.

His upper body was decorated with a stylized spider-cicatrice. The outline of the spider's bulbous thorax had been carved into the middle of his chest, and its eight legs reached across his entire torso, meeting in the middle of his back, as though the arachnid had trapped him in a lethal embrace.

The scarification patterns were symbolic of Legaba, the only god the Uloans acknowledged, considering all the other Jagasti to be Mainlanders' devils. All but a few Islanders wore his holy image on their skin, and gladly bore the pain of its incision during their coming-of-age ceremonies.

Bujiji thought about the spy who had sent the message from the Mainland. He did not know the identity of the man or woman; those who were to be sent to the Mainland were singled out at a young age and isolated from the rest of the islands' populace until the time came for them to go across the sea. Of necessity, informants were left blank-skinned, like the Matile.

And for that, Bujiji pitied the spies, regardless of their value to the ultimate cause of Retribution Time. He was glad that he had not fit the specifications that would have placed him in their ranks.

Without conscious thought, the Uloan ducked away from an *ubia* vine that had extended itself from an overhanging tree limb. The sweet scent of the clenching flowers tickled his nostrils. He ignored the smell. If the petals of those flowers ever touched his skin, they would fasten onto it like the waving grass, and they were even more difficult to tear away. Yet if they were not removed, they would cling until all the blood had been leeched from his body.

As he trotted through the weaving grass and towering trees, Bujiji passed charred, twisted ruins caught in the embrace of encroaching *mwiti* trees – remnants of the destruction the Storm Wars had wrought. Bujiji paid the relics no heed. The Dying Time was part of the far-distant past. And Retribution Time – the time when vengeance would be wrought against the Mainlanders – belonged to an unknowable future that would soon come, however long "soon" proved to be.

Then a chittering sound from a nearby tree caught his attention. Bujiji looked up, and saw a vaguely manlike shape capering in the branches. The creature pointed at him and its screeches sounded like imprecations.

"Hush, *munkimun*," Bujiji said. "You got no quarrel with I."

Unlike on the Mainland, there were no true monkeys in the islands. But the swarms of long-armed, long-tailed arboreal creatures the first settlers had encountered when they arrived bore a strong resemblance to the simians they had left behind. However, the islands' tree-dwellers had huge, round eyes, and the ears that jutted from their heads resembled those of a cat more than they did a monkey or ape. The creatures were lemurs, distant relations of monkeykind that had mostly died out on the Mainland ages ago.

Even on the islands, there were few *munkimun* left now. And whenever one of them saw a human, it would scream out its grievances over the ravages of the Storm Wars, and their displacement from the home that was theirs before the humans cleared parts of the forest to build their own dwellings.

Bujiji listened to the *munkimun's* imprecations a few moments longer. Then he found a fruit – one that did not pulsate – and tossed it to the arboreal creature, which caught it deftly and began to chew on it. And he continued his journey away from the beach without having to hear anything more from the lemur.

Soon there were no more ruins to be seen. The grass no longer moved, nor did the fruits on the trees pulsate. Bujiji was now back among the flat-roofed coral houses of Ompong, the capital city of Jayaya and the last outpost of the Uloans' former splendor in the time when they were truly the Happy Isles.

Bujiji greeted the other spider-scarred people he passed. As they returned his calls and waves, the other Uloans cast a wary glance toward the damp tube in his hand. Their eyes were sharp enough to see the marks the *ubia's* teeth had made, and they knew what would waiting for Bujiji when he delivered the spy's message to Jass Imbiah. After he passed, they sucked their teeth and shook their heads in sympathy even as they thanked Legaba that they were not in Bujiji's boots.

Jass Imbiah will not be too vexed with I, he tried to reassure himself as the notched tube pressed hard against his palm. *At least I catched the message before that* ubia *did ...*

Jass Imbiah held the message tube in her slender hands. She sat on an ivory throne in her palace of pink coral. The ivory from which the throne was carved had been brought over from the Mainland in ancient days; no Uloan had seen an elephant since the days before the Storm Wars, when travel and trade between the Mainland and the islands had been frequent.

Although Jass Imbiah had lived for a long time, her true age was impossible to guess from her appearance. Her body was swathed in a voluminous *chamma* of red and green stripes, and a cap of silver decorated with a carved spiderweb covered her head; only her face and hands could be seen. Her fingernails jutted like talons. And every visible inch of her umber skin was covered with small scars cut in the shape of spiders, making the usual indications of age difficult to discern.

Six heavily muscled guards flanked Jass Imbiah's throne, three to each side. Their hands rested on the hilts of huge, curved swords that could lop off a man's head at a single stroke. Thick, v-shaped incisions marked their chests, and rows of spider-scars lined their arms. Thin lines resembling whiskers were cut into their cheeks. They wore headgear of dry yellow grass that simulated the mane of a lion – a beast that, like the elephant, no Uloan had seen in centuries. Yet those animals of the Mainland continued to serve as powerful symbols in the Islanders' memories, and a connection to ancestors far away in time.

Also present were *huangi*, the priests and priestesses who wielded the dark *ashuma* of Legaba. They were clad in costumes made from the radiant plumage of birds that lived nowhere other than on the Uloas. For all the brightness of their garments, the expressions on the faces of the *huangi* were forbidding in their severity. Like Jass Imbiah, their bodies were covered with spider-scars.

Bujiji was on his knees before Jass Imbiah's throne. His gaze followed her as she looked at the barb-marks on the tube. Beads of sweat slid down the scars on Bujiji's face. Now, he was beginning to regret the extra time he had spent with Awiwi, despite the pleasure that dalliance had given him.

"You bring I this tube with the mark of the *ubia* on it," she said. "What these marks mean?"

"Them mean I and I almost not catch the tube in time," Bujiji answered truthfully, with not even a thought of prevaricating. "But I still catched it before the *ubia* can. The message inside not harmed."

That was all he could say in his own defense. Now, he could only wait for Jass Imbiah to proclaim his punishment.

But Jass Imbiah said nothing about punishment. Instead, she slid one long fingernail down the side of the tube. Her nail left only a slight scratch on the wood. Yet the tube split open like a dry reed.

She pulled Sehaye's message out, unrolled it and read it. First, her eyes widened. Then, they narrowed. Then, her brow furrowed in a scowl, and the corners of her mouth turned downward.

"Them mainland blankskin find they a new ally," she murmured, more to herself than to Bujiji or the guards. "An ally who come from far, far away."

She paused and reread the message. When she spoke again, she still seemed to be thinking aloud.

"I and I must ..."

Jass Imbiah's body stiffened as she broke off in mid-sentence. Abruptly, she shot up from her throne, her feet lifting from the ground before she caught her balance and began to pace the floor in front of her throne. Her movements were stiff and disjointed, as though she was no longer in control of her limbs. Her eyes rolled up, showing only bloodshot white crescents.

The others in the chamber looked on wide-eyed, for they knew that Legaba was now *riding* – possessing – Jass Imbiah. And they trembled inside, for even though Legaba was their one god, he was could be vengeful, spiteful – and unpredictable.

With a sudden twist of her limbs that seemed to wrench her body in several directions at once, Jass Imbiah tore off her *chamma*. Her naked form was lean, cadaverous, androgynous, ageless. Spider-scars covered her from head to foot. And on her skin, the spiders were moving ...

When Jass Imbiah spoke again, Bujiji and the guards covered their ears and collapsed to the floor in awe and agony, even as they realized that Legaba was riding Imbiah, who was his Vessel. Her voice was no longer that of a woman, or even a human being. It was Legaba's voice: a voice that roared mightily through the palace and into the streets of Ompong, and from there across the whole of Jayaya and to all the Shattered Isles.

RETRIBUTION TIME! the Uloans' god cried again and again through the fraying vocal cords of his Vessel.

RETRIBUTION TIME! RETRIBUTION TIME! RETRIBUTION TIME!

Throughout the islands, the Uloans heard the revelatory message of their god. Some people shouted in ecstasy and repeated the cry of the revenge that they and their ancestors had long hoped would "soon come." Others wept in trepidation. All knew that the destiny for which they had waited so long had finally arrived. All knew that their lives had changed from this day; and that the lives of some would be lost when the Uloans gained their revenge for the evil the Mainlanders had done to what were once the Happy Isles.

4

Much later, alone in her chamber in Ompong, Jass Imbiah gathered her strength, which had been sorely depleted during Legaba's violent possession of her body. The only light came from a ring of candles mounted in the skulls of mainlanders who had been slain in battles of the past. The dim light of the candles wavered on her scarred face as she mouthed words of power handed down from her ancestors. Her muscles ached, and her throat felt as though it had been ripped inside out. She concentrated on healing herself.

Among the Uloans, Jass Imbiah's position was a combination of Emperor and Leba. Other Jasses ruled on other islands, but only Imbiah had the ability to withstand being ridden by the Spider God. Still, her power over the other Jasses had been more symbolic than real – until now.

Until Retribution Time ...

Even as one part of Jass Imbiah's mind focused on the healing process, another ruminated on what had happened when she read the message from the mainland spy. During a possession, Legaba was part of her, and she was part of Legaba. She knew what the spider-god knew and felt what he felt. When Legaba rode her this time, he assured her the prophecy he had given to one of Jass Imbiah's predecessors soon after the end of the Storm Wars was about to be fulfilled.

When Retribution Time comes, the dead will fight beside the living, and the final victory will be ours ....

Why now? she had dared to ask Legaba, even as she had screamed his message to his worshippers over and over. *After so many years, why now*?

Instead of telling her, Legaba showed her. She saw the arrival of the Fidi ship in Khambawe's harbor, and she saw the pale people from far away, of whom the Uloans had retained fewer memories than had the mainlanders. The islanders paid less attention to the past than the blankskins; their main concern was the vengeance they foresaw in the future.

However, it was not the coming of the Fidi that caused Legaba's declaration that Retribution Time had finally come. It was the new deity the outlanders had brought to Abengoni. Unlike the enervated, largely absent Jagasti, this outland god, whose name was Almovaar, was potent ... dangerous.

Legaba showed Jass Imbiah an image of the new god's Seer: a pale, white-haired man surrounded by an aura of eldritch power that stretched to the sky. The man's eyes glowed like circles of fire, and hands appeared to reach out to grasp her before Legaba dispelled the illusion of his presence.

And Legaba told her the man's name: Kyroun.

Here is your true enemy, Legaba said. **If you do not destroy him, he will destroy you.**

Even as Legaba's call for Retribution Time thundered through her throat, straining her vocal cords beyond their limit, Jass Imbiah had experienced an emotion unlike any other the Spider God had ever shared with her when he rode her.

It was not fear. The notion that fear could touch one of the Jagasti was inconceivable to Jass Imbiah. What Legaba had imparted to her was ... apprehension. And if this new god and his Seer could cause such disquiet to Legaba, how could she, a frail mortal despite the power that she wielded, prevail?

But she knew she had no choice. Her god had declared that the moment for which generation after generation of Uloans had waited had finally come. Preparations for Retribution Time would be long and hard. Jass Imbiah would need all the strength she could muster, and all the *ashuma* Legaba could infuse into her. And she knew even that might not be enough for the task ahead of her.

"Legaba," she whispered hoarsely. "Help I."

And the flames of the candles tilted toward her, as though she were drawing strength even from the feeble energy of their glow.

PART TWO
RETRIBUTION TIME

CHAPTER ELEVEN

ADAPTATIONS

1

Shortly after dawn, Tiyana found Kyroun at Khambawe's City of the Dead. The immense cemetery extended well beyond the outskirts of the city of the living, sheltering the remains of a hundred generations of Matile. The Matile interred their deceased in oval-shaped crypts of stone. Simple piles of gravel covered the graves of commoners; those of emperors and the Jassi were surmounted by carefully carved miniature palaces that proclaimed their occupants' grandeur in the afterlife. The corpses of rich and poor alike were carefully mummified to enable their flesh to remain as close to whole as possible in death to what it had been in life.

Long ago, a small section of the cemetery had been set aside for visitors from the Fidi countries who had died in Khambawe back in the days when the two lands were still in direct contact. That was where the bodies from the dead of the *White Gull* were buried. Dardar Alemeyu had allowed the present-day Fidi to observe their own funerary customs, even though he and other Matile found those practices as incomprehensible now as their ancestors had centuries in the past.

Kyroun stood in front of a row of earthen mounds, each marked by a single slab of stone at its head. The mounds were strewn with flowers, and the names of the dead were inscribed on their markers. Beneath the mounds, the Fidi dead were interred in flimsy wooden boxes rather than the stone crypts that held the Matile. The markers on the older graves were weathered by the long passage of time; their inscriptions barely legible, the flowers that had been laid upon them long since vanished, their dried petals blown away by sea-winds.

The *White Gull* survivors had politely declined the Matiles' offer to build crypts for their dead, or to mummify their bodies. They could not understand their hosts' compulsion to preserve corpses and keep them forever in stone cells. And the Matile could not fathom the impermanence of the wooden coffins the Fidi carpenters had built.

"But the wood of the boxes will rot away, and the flesh of the bodies will be eaten by ground-worms, and, ultimately, absorbed by the soil," Jass Gebrem had said to Kyroun during a discussion in which the Seer had tried to explain the Fidi practice. "They will become as one with the earth."

"Exactly," the Kyroun had said.

Shaking his head in bewilderment at the Fidis' unfathomable disregard for the sanctity of the flesh of their forebears, the Leba had politely ended the conversation. And the foreigners were allowed to practice their peculiar customs without comment or interference, just as they had in the distant past.

When Tiyana reached Kyroun's side, she remained silent while he stared at the graves. Gebrem had told her of his conversation with the Seer, and she remembered it now as she stood next to him.

Kyroun had conducted funeral rites for his people months ago, consecrating the souls of Almovaads and non-believers alike to the afterlife promised by Almovaar. And every day since then, he had visited their graves in the City of the Dead. Only the Seer went there; never the Acolytes, the Adepts, or the other Almovaads. It was as though Kyroun was performing a penance only he could understand.

Sometimes Jass Gebrem joined him among the dead; sometimes Tiyana. Kyroun had not said a word to either of them during his daily vigil, although he talked willingly before and after his self-imposed ritual. But he had never discussed his sojourns in the burial place.

Not until now.

"So many lives lost," he said in a near whisper.

A breeze stirred the petals on the graves. Unlike the ones that had been strewn on the mounds of earlier burials centuries ago, these flowers neither wilted nor faded. They remained as fresh as they would have been had they been placed there the day before. But Tiyana knew that no else had put flowers on the Fidi graves since the burial ceremonies – Kyroun had forbidden his followers to do so.

More Fidi magic, Tiyana thought as she looked at the undying blooms. However, thinking about the sorcerous power the Seer commanded no longer stirred suspicion or uneasiness within her. The passage of time had diminished her distrust and suspicion of the newcomer. So had Kyroun's unfailing kindness and courtesy, to which she could not help responding. Eventually, Nama-kwah's warning during the First Calling ceremony had become little more than a faint echo in the back of her mind, easily ignored.

"So many deaths on my hands," he continued, not looking at Tiyana. "They put their faith in me. And I failed them."

Kyroun turned to Tiyana. The anguish in his gray eyes was almost unbearable to see. But Tiyana held his gaze. Her own eyes mirrored her empathy for his sorrow. She waited for him to say more, sensing that he wanted to speak openly to her about the suffering he had kept to himself for such a long time.

"And the others, whose graves are on the bottom of the sea ... I failed them as well," he said sadly. Then he looked away and bowed his head.

Tiyana took his hand in hers.

"The choice was theirs, Kyroun," she said to him. "They knew the risks. They knew there was no guarantee that your journey would succeed, or that they would live through it."

"But I would have succeeded in saving them, had I been strong enough," Kyroun protested, looking at her again.

"You were as strong as you needed to be," Tiyana said. "You were strong enough to do what no one else could have done."

They were conducting their conversation in the Matile language. The sorcery Kyroun had employed to provide translation when he first arrived was no longer necessary; by now, most of the Fidi had achieved a working mastery of their hosts' tongue, although their accents were unmistakable and sometimes difficult to understand. Kyroun, on the other hand, spoke the language as fluently as he would have had he been born in Khambawe.

Kyroun and Tiyana stood in silence for a time, still holding hands. Tiyana was clad in a plain white *chamma*, and silver and gold jewelry glinted at her wrists and throat. Her hair had grown to shoulder-length, and multi-colored beads dotted her many braids. Her demeanor was more serious, as if she had acquired several years of maturity in a matter of only a few months.

The season of First Calling was over, and the rains had departed after giving renewed life to the land. Abengoni's hot, sun-drenched, dry-season weather had been kind – almost rejuvenating – to Kyroun. The pallor was gone from his skin, and his carriage had become that of a younger, healthier man. But his eyes were still haunted by guilt and regret, of which he seldom spoke to the other Almovaads, and only now to Tiyana.

Tiyana squeezed his hand, as though her touch could banish the guilt that plagued him like an ailment for which he could find no cure.

She thought about all that had transpired since the Fidis' ship had arrived in the harbor. The newcomers had long since been permitted to leave their crippled ship. Even though Alemeyu had made them Gebrem's responsibility, he had also proclaimed the newcomers as Emperor's Guests, with free access to everything the Matile could provide for their comfort. And the Tokoloshe had taken a special interest in the Fidi who were called "Dwarven," the ones who so uncannily resembled themselves. The dwarves often visited the secluded Tokoloshe embassy, sometimes staying overnight.

The others, Believers and ship's crew alike, had been domiciled throughout Khambawe; many people willing to take the strangers into their homes, and having Fidi guests soon became a symbol of social standing. However, Pel Muldure, the captain of the *White Gull*, his first mate, Lyann, and most of the crew had elected to stay on the ship to oversee its repairs. The absence of Athir Rin onboard had been noted with relief.

The Emperor had given Kyroun a suite of rooms in the Gebbi Senafa. However, the Seer spent most of his time with Gebrem and Tiyana. His hours with the Leba were consumed by long discussions about sorcery, history, power, and gods. Only to Tiyana had he revealed any uncertainties or misgivings, and never before as much so as he had this day.

Only Tiyana knew the extent of Kyroun's disappointment when he learned that the house of his distant ancestor, Yekunu, had long ago been razed and replaced by a succession of other dwellings over the centuries. He had hoped to turn the site into a shrine to Almovaar.

Now, his guilt and shame over the deaths of his followers had become another secret they shared.

And secrets are all *we share*, she thought, even as a flash of annoyance about what others thought momentarily furrowed her forehead.

Tiyana had rarely stayed at the Beit Amiya since the Emperor's charge to her and her father of responsibility for the Seer. Still, she knew many of the other Vessels whispered behind her back about the growing bond between her and the leader of the Fidis, a man who appeared to be older than her father. She knew how deep some of them thought that bond had become.

And she ignored those rumors even as she performed only the minimum duties her service as a Vessel of Nama-kwah demanded. She did not seem to notice that a distance had developed between her and her friends, a gulf that was growing with the passing of each day.

She looked into Kyroun's eyes. With her free hand, she touched the skin of his face above his beard.

"You are not to blame, Kyroun," she said. "You were obeying the will of Almovaar, just as I obey the will of Nama-kwah."

Kyroun remained silent for a long moment. Then he took Tiyana's other hand, and they stood like that for a while, sharing a moment of mutual compassion.

"You really do understand, Tiyana," Kyroun said. "I am fortunate it was you who reached out to me just before I would have given up my struggle."

They smiled together. Then, hand-in-hand, they walked out of the City of the Dead, leaving the grave-flowers to wave in the wind.

2

Morning light streamed through the small porthole in the captain's cabin of the *White Gull*. In the narrow bed in the cabin that was his again now that Kyroun had moved to the palace, Pel Muldure and Lyann lay in each other's arms. Lyann's breathing came in the slow cadence of sleep. Muldure was wide awake. Already, he was planning the final stages of the repair job on the ship.

Kyroun had ordered the overhaul, as was his right since he owned the vessel. Had the Seer not done so, Muldure would have asked him to. He could not have borne to see a seacraft remain so badly damaged, even if it didn't belong to him.

The work had gone well thus far. With the help of Matile carpenters, his diminished crew had re-planked the hole the collision with the wharf had punched into the ship's hull. The broken mast had been replaced, and the Matile had provided new rope to replace snapped rigging. The Matile were also weaving new sails to replace the ones that had been ripped apart when Kyroun's sorcerous shield could no longer hold back the storm.

Muldure marveled yet again at the Matiles' generosity. In his time, he had sailed to more than a few places in which the inhabitants would have gleefully looted the crippled *White Gull* and sold its passengers and crew into slavery. At the very least, the "hosts" would have demanded goods, money, or unpaid labor in exchange for their hospitality. The newcomers' lives would have been in peril at almost every moment.

But not with the Seer aboard, he thought. *Not with the power he possesses ....*

He suppressed a shudder, then berated himself for the discomfort that even thinking about the Seer still aroused within him. He remembered their first meeting on the Fiadol waterfront, and the way Kyroun had almost compelled Muldure to join in a venture at which he would ordinarily have laughed loud and long. And he suppressed another shudder.

Lyann stirred, as if in response to Muldure's tension. Then she opened her eyes and sat up. As she raked a hand through her tangled yellow hair, the single sheet fell away from her tanned, sinewy body. Like Muldure, she was not wearing any clothing. Catlike, she stretched, back arching and breasts pushing forward.

Then she looked down at Muldure, saw that he was awake, and smiled. He smiled back at her.

"I've been thinking," he said.

Lyann widened her eyes in mock concern.

"Uh-oh; we're in trouble now," she said.

Muldure laughed and pulled her down to him, trapping her in his arms. They wrestled playfully for a few moments, then kissed deeply. After a while, Lyann pulled away and looked into his eyes. The expression on her face was serious now.

"What is it you're thinking?" she asked.

"The repairs are almost done," he said.

Lyann waited, knowing there was more on his mind.

"Kyroun's voyage was successful. He has found his so-called homeland. The Believers are happy here. And ... no one has tried to kill us."

"So?" she asked.

"So why does Kyroun want the ship repaired? What does he need it for, if the voyage has ended to his satisfaction?"

Lyann had no answer to those questions. She made the only response she could think of: a shrug of her shoulders and a roll of her eyes.

"I'll tell you something, Lyann," Muldure said then. "This ship ought to be ours."

Lyann slid away from him, drew her knees up to her chest and crossed her arms in front of her sheet-covered shins. Her expression showed her reaction to what Muldure had said: *Oh no. Not again.*

"Kyroun might not see it that way," she said in a level tone.

"He owes us," Muldure insisted. "He owes us for the lives of everyone who died on this ship – and the *Swordfish*."

Lyann looked at him. She was experiencing a familiar, sinking feeling.

She had known Muldure for more than a decade. At sea, in a fight, or in bed, she would rather have him at her side than anyone else she had ever known. But she was well aware that when Muldure was not involved in direct action that required all his resources, both physical and mental, he was prone to self-destructive lapses in judgment.

She remembered his foolhardy venture into privateering. When her attempts to talk him out of it proved unsuccessful, she had joined him in the enterprise and shared his disgrace when disaster struck, as she had known it would. And she had stayed with him through the bitter consequences, as well as the seemingly suicidal venture the madman known as the Seer of Almovaar had proposed.

Luck, superb seamanship, and Kyroun's sorcery had carried them through the Sea of Storms. The decision to transport the Almovaads had not been difficult. Landbound by decree, Muldure was dying by inches. It was far better for him to go out gloriously at sea with a deck under his feet. Lyann had been prepared to die with him then. But now ...

"Are you thinking what I think you're thinking?" she asked.

Muldure sat up, his bare shoulder brushing hers.

"Do you really want to stay here?" he asked, deflecting her question.

"Why not?" she replied. "The Ma-teel couldn't treat us any better. When was the last time you ever saw anyone being this accommodating to strangers?"

"True. But this city is dying around them. I can see it. I can feel it."

"Kyroun thinks he can bring the place back to life."

"Maybe he can. But I don't want to stay around to find out."

Lyann looked at him without speaking. She didn't have to say anything to convey her mood, which was worsening by the moment. Finally, Muldure sighed.

"All right, Lyann," he said. "I'm just thinking now. I'm not going to do anything stupid."

Lyann laughed.

"When have I heard *that* before?" she said.

Then she kissed him deeply, rose from the bed and padded naked to the privy that was closed off from the rest of the cabin. The light from the porthole picked out the long scar a sword-slash had etched across her back years ago.

Muldure had killed the man who inflicted that wound. Lyann had been part of his life ever since, first as a grateful friend, then as a lover.

Throwing the sheet aside, Muldure swung his legs over the side of the bed and stood up. There was work to be done. Muldure was still determined to learn the purpose of the repairs. However, a reckoning with Kyroun would have to come once that work was done.

3

Even in the glare of the noonday sun, the Tokoloshe embassy appeared only slightly less sinister than it did in night's darkness. The monoliths, the squat, cubical building and the barren grounds were all a uniform shade of gray, as though all other colors had been leached away from them long ago.

From the outside, it was difficult to imagine that anyone could – or would even want to – reside in the grim edifice, which was devoid of any sign of an entrance. It was as though a god or giant had sculpted a perfect cube of granite, put it down, and walked away, never returning to retrieve it.

Life itself seemed unwelcome in this forbidding place. Yet inside and underground, the Tokoloshes' domain teemed with activity.

Pale light suffused the interior of the embassy. The torches in the walls were not burning; the light was cast from incandescent balls that floated among the stalactites hanging from the roof. These spheres did not serve as receptacles for disembodied faces from the Tokoloshe homeland; illumination was their only purpose.

In the main hall, a feast was underway. The Tokoloshes' guests were the Dwarven people from the *White Gull*. Similar feasts had been held almost every day since the outlanders' ship had appeared out of the mist. For the Dwarven, it was as though they had already entered the paradise the Seer said awaited all Almovaads after they died. Some dwarves had joined the new religion; others had not. But all, Believers and non-Believers alike, took part in the revelries their hosts provided.

The main table was laden with plates heaped high with meat – mostly beef and *quagga*, but also wild game, including buffalo, zebra and elephant. The Tokoloshe had quickly learned that the dwarves shared their taste for well-cooked meat, as well as hearty appetites that belied their short stature. Along with the meat, the guests quaffed *talla* and *kef* from stone cups.

Tokoloshe women, who were never seen outside the embassy, kept the dwarves' plates and cups filled. Their squat bodies were scantily clad, and beads bedecked their long, frizzy hair. They did not appear to mind the way the visitors' hands wandered across their bodies while the food was being served. Indeed, the Tokoloshe men encouraged their guests to take such liberties.

A drumbeat boomed through the hall: slow, steady, unchanging, with none of the elaborate rhythms favored by humans. The slow, steady beat was familiar to the Fidi Dwarven. But never before had they seen a drum like the one the Tokoloshe musician played.

Hewn from the trunk of a massive tree, the instrument stood on four legs anchored by feet in Tokoloshe shape. At each end of the drum, a Tokoloshe face had been carved. A narrow slot ran down the top of the instrument. The drummer pounded out his hypnotic beat with sticks as thick as a bull's leg bone. In the dim light cast by the spheres, the legs and face of the drum sometimes appeared to move.

Rumundulu looked at the dwarf who sat in the place of honor next to him. Although they were still learning each other's languages, he had discovered much about the outlander, whose name was Hulm Stonefist. And he had found out even more about Hulm's people.

He learned that they preferred to dwell under the ground in caverns and tunnels, as did the Tokoloshe. He learned that while they were not immortal, the dwarves were much longer-lived than humans – as were the

Tokoloshe. He learned that the newcomers valued plain stone above gems and precious metals – as did the Tokoloshe.

But there were also differences ... differences that ran deeper than the shade of the two peoples' complexions.

All Tokoloshe were born with the potential to perform sorcery. Some possessed greater abilities than others, but the gift was present in all. It was an advantage that offset the numerical superiority of the humans during their long history together.

Among the Dwarven people of Cym Dinath, however, magical talent rarely appeared, and was seldom nurtured when it did. However, Rumundulu was inclined to believe the dwarves' capacities were latent rather than absent, needing only stimulation and tutelage to blossom.

The other difference lay in the dwarves' fertility. While not nearly as prolific as the fecund humans, the Dwarven birth rate greatly exceeded that of the Tokoloshe. And the Tokoloshe found that fact to be of great interest indeed.

A Tokoloshe woman poured *talla* into Hulm Stonefist's cup. Her breasts brushed against his shoulder as she bent to serve him. Hulm's eyes were drawn to the tuft of hair that grew in the cleft between them – a sight that was stimulating to Tokoloshes and Dwarven alike.

The woman smiled at Hulm as she walked away. And she exchanged a secret glance with Rumundulu – an acknowledgement of the promise she and the other women had made when the Tokoloshe became aware of the existence of others of their kind.

Rumundulu drank deeply. His *talla* did not contain the ingredient that had been added to what the dwarves were quaffing. The ingredient was by no means harmful; its purpose was merely to increase the concupiscence the Tokoloshes' guests were already experiencing.

"She likes you, my friend," Rumundulu said.

"I know," Hulm said, a broad grin splitting his face.

He took another swallow, and his eyes tracked the woman as she made her way across the room. Rumundulu's elbow nudged him with enough force to have knocked a human off the bench. Hulm merely grinned even wider as he rose and followed the woman as she walked through a door that led to another, darkened chamber.

Behind him, the Tokoloshe smiled knowingly.

4

Under the diffuse illumination of the Moon-Stars, Sehaye stuffed a message-tube down the gullet of yet another *gede*. He had sent many such messages to the Uloas since the day the Fidi ship had appeared out of the mist. He had written about the ease with which the newcomers had been accepted among the mainlanders, and about the influence their leader, the Seer Kyroun, appeared to wield with the Leba, if not the Emperor.

He had no way of knowing what effect his information was having at the court of Jass Imbiah. Sehaye had never received any communications from the islands, nor did he expect to – not until Retribution Time.

The Moon Star's light glinted on the sea as Sehaye leaned over the side of his boat and placed the *gede* beneath the surface of the water. As well, the light shone unmercifully on the smooth, unscarred skin of his forearm. He grimaced in disgust at that sight. In his mind, he could see the spider-scars that should have been there to denote his devotion to Legaba.

Legaba, him can see under you skin, Jass Imbiah had assured him years ago, when he had first been told that he was destined to be a spy among the blankskins, at the time when other children were receiving their first marks of Legaba. Jass Imbiah had also told Sehaye that when Retribution Time came, Legaba would raise his hidden spider-scars from the inside to the outside of his skin.

I and I hope that day soon come, Sehaye thought. Although he was always prudent in maintaining the Matile style of speech when he talked, his thoughts often came to him in his native dialect. The division between the speech patterns reflected the incipient division of his identity, even his soul itself – blankskin on the outside, Uloan within.

He looked away from his forearm and back down to where he had dropped the *gede*. He expected to see only the widening wake the construct left behind as it sped off on its long journey to the Uloas. But he saw no wake. The *gede* had not departed. It remained where he had placed it.

Puzzled and more than a little apprehensive, Sehaye reached out to nudge the *gede* into motion. He drew back his hand when the construct turned at stared up at him with its blank, stone-like eyes.

Then the *gede* opened its mouth and spoke two words that filled Sehaye with a combination of terror and joy. The voice that came from the *gede's* mouth belonged to Jass Imbiah.

Retribution Time, it said.

Then the *gede* sank out of sight, leaving Sehaye staring at the empty space where it had been. He didn't gaze for long. His spirit soared, even as he also felt a stab of fear at what was to come. He knew what he must do now that the words he had long awaited were spoken. Grasping his oars, he began to row back to shore, back to the mainland that was about to meet its doom at the hands of the Uloans and Legaba.

CHAPTER TWELVE

Ship's Rat Snared

1

"That's it. Give 'em a good toss," Athir Rin said to the Matile at his side. The Matile, a tall, lean young man dressed in threadbare clothes, threw a pair of cubes made from bone against the wall of the seedy *talla-beit*, or tavern, in which the Ship's Rat was plying his latest illicit trade. With a sharp click, the cubes hit the wall, then landed on the *talla-beit's* floor.

Athir bent over and counted the markings on the cubes, then invited the Matile to do the same.

"Seven," Athir said. "Looks like I win again."

He opened the leather pouch belted to his waist and held it out. With a sullen glower on his face, the Matile dropped several gold coins into the greedy, open mouth of the pouch. They clinked against the other coins that filled the bag a bit beyond its halfway point.

"Want to try one more time?" Athir asked.

"Forget you," the Matile said curtly.

With a slight curl of his lip, the Matile turned on his heel and stalked out of the *talla-beit*. Athir smiled in a way he hoped would appear to be friendly rather than triumphant.

"Anybody else feeling lucky?" he inquired.

None of the rest of the *talla-beit's* patrons said anything. However, Athir could sense the beginning of some hostility toward him. He knew it would soon be time for him to take his game elsewhere, for the sake of his own skin.

For Athir, life had been good since he said farewell to the *White*

Gull. As always, he thrived in the meanest streets. He had rapidly picked up enough of the Matile language to communicate and learn what he needed to know to prosper in his new surroundings, rather than merely survive them. During his wide wanderings – forced and voluntary alike – Athir had learned that regardless of the countless variations of culture or custom in the world, in large cities like Khambawe, there were always places where people like him gathered: places outside the reach, and sometimes even the interest, of the law. And he had developed an unerring instinct for finding such locales.

The *talla-beit* he was in now had become his favorite, even though it was in the Ukili district, close to the *tsotsi* territory that was known as the Maim. Athir had learned about the *tsotsi*s soon after he had jumped ship. However, he had not attempted to contact them, or join their ranks. From what he had heard about them they were fighters and killers as well as thieves and drug-sellers, and that wasn't his preferred style of operating. He would kill in self-defense, and he had no compunctions about doing so. But he preferred to keep his victims alive, and take from them without letting them know they were losing anything until it was too late. He was content to ply his trade on the peripheries of the *tsotsis'* domain, and leave the gangs to their endless cycle of street warfare, strong-arm robbery and *khat*-trafficking.

When he first began to frequent the *talla-beits* after he had picked up enough of the Matile language to make himself understood, Athir discovered that the customers' favorite gambling game involved moving pebbles around a board that had shallow holes scooped into the wood. He found the pastime boring, but he didn't allow the Matile to know that.

When he felt the time was right, which was when the *talla-beit* patrons no longer regarded him primarily as a pale-skinned outlander who had come on a mysterious ship out of the mist, but as just another slum-dweller who happened to look a little different, Athir introduced them to the thrills of dice-throwing. The new game quickly became popular, and Athir's assets, which he kept hidden in various caches in the Ukili, grew just as rapidly. Soon, the "Fidi with the bones" became an accepted, if not necessarily well-liked, figure in more than a few *talla-beits*.

Athir was prudent enough not to win all the time. His dice had been weighted by a master craftsman in Vakshma, Cym Dinath's City of Thieves, and he had spent many months mastering their use. With a subtle twist of his wrist, Athir could control the way they fell, and he could choose when he won or lost. The trick was to find the balance between winning enough to stay ahead and losing enough to keep the Matile interested in playing his game.

"Nobody else?" he said half-heartedly.

No one answered. And Athir didn't like the way some of the Matile were looking at him.

He got along with the Matile well enough, and even liked them to certain degree. They seemed more tolerant than many other people he had known, and the authorities didn't care very much about places like the Ukili – as far as Athir knew, they didn't even demand bribes to look the other way while criminal activities were occurring. Athir did, however, give a cut of his profits to the owners of the *talla-beits* he plied. And, of course, he was careful not to let any of them know how wealth he was really amassing.

Athir sighed – but only inwardly.

I should have let him win a little more, he thought ruefully of his last mark. But there was no point in regrets now. The time had come to make a graceful exit, then come back to this particular *talla-beit* later ... much later.

Before he could open his mouth to give his farewell speech, Athir felt a slight tug at his belt. He looked down, and saw that his pouch was gone. He looked toward the *talla-beit's* entrance. And he caught a glimpse of white-clad legs scissoring their way out the door.

2

"Mugguth's balls!" Athir cursed, unable to believe he could have been so inattentive, yet still be alive.

Not forgetting to snatch up his dice, the Ship's Rat sprinted out the *talla-beit's* doorway. Behind him, several of the patrons exchanged sly smirks and knowing glances. Others merely shrugged. Within moments, all of them had returned to their cups of *talla*.

Outside, the sun was close to setting and shadows spanned the narrow street in front of the *talla-beit*. Looking both ways, Athir quickly spotted the fleeing thief. As Athir charged after him, Matile men and women dodged from his path, then shook their heads at the foreigner's audacity –

or, more likely, ignorance. They knew who the Fidi was chasing, and they would never have done the same themselves, unless they no longer cared about living.

The thief cut around a corner. Athir slowed and pulled out the slim, keen-edged dagger that was the only weapon he needed. Then he peered around the corner. He saw a long alley with an end that was swallowed in shadows. Of the cut-purse, there was no sign.

Cautiously, Athir eased into the alley. He knew it was foolhardy to pursue a potential foe into unfamiliar territory. But the pouch contained his hard-earned winnings for the day. Of course, the coins it contained were not all that he had. He had other loot stashed elsewhere. Still, to have had the pouch taken from him so easily galled Athir's pride as a master of the thieves' trade.

He took another few steps forward, peering intently into the shadows, still seeing nothing. Then his instincts warned him – too late. He heard a soft rustle of clothing behind him. And the point of something sharp prodded into his back.

In front of him, the Matile thief glided noiselessly from a space between two buildings in the alley – a space Athir had not been able to detect in the semi-darkness. The thief came closer. Athir's purse dangled from one of the Matile's hand. In the other was a spiked, mace-like weapon unlike any Athir had seen before.

Behind him, the sharp point prodded Athir again, deeply enough to cut through his clothing and draw blood from his skin. Athir got the message. He opened his hand and let his dagger drop to the ground. The sound it made as it landed was the only thing he could hear in the alley, the entrance of which seemed to have suddenly receded a vast distance from the nearby street.

As his eyes became accustomed to the half-light of the alley, Athir recognized the thief. It was the young man whose money he had won in the *talla-beit*. Beneath the braids that hung over his brow, the Matile's eyes gleamed with a feral light. Gone was the resentment Athir had seen in them in the *talla-beit*. He realized now that had been only an act; what was in this youth's eyes now was something to be dreaded far more than mere anger over losing a few coins.

Athir was also beginning to suspect what this young man truly was, and he was becoming very afraid. When the thief spoke, he confirmed Athir's suspicions – and his fear, which was beginning to crawl in his stomach.

"You, Fidi," the Matile said. "Why you try to be *tsotsi*? Only *tsotsi* can be *tsotsi*. Heard?"

Other figures emerged from the shadows in the alley. They appeared as if by magic from spaces Athir would never have noticed even if the alley had been bathed in bright sunlight.

Say something – anything! Athir told himself.

"Uh, hey, I'm sorry, friend," Athir managed. "I didn't know this was your territory. Why don't you just keep the pouch? I'll take my business elsewhere, and I won't make this mistake again. Does that sound all right to you?"

The *tsotsi* tossed the pouch toward Athir. Reflexively, he reached out and caught it. Then he gave the *tsotsi* a quizzical look, even as the others gathered behind him. They were all young, but they were as hard-looking a lot as Athir had ever encountered.

"Don' want your gold, Fidi," the *tsotsi* said. "*You* be what we want."

"Me?" Athir asked, more afraid than ever.

Rather than reply, the *tsotsi* bent down and picked up Athir's dagger. He held it in one hand and compared it to the fearsome weapon in his other hand.

"This your teeth?" the *tsotsi* demanded, looking from the dagger to Athir and back again.

"I – I guess so," Athir said, trying to fathom the *tsotsi's* meaning.

The *tsotsi* laughed.

"That ain't hardly no teeth," he said.

Then he held up his *tirss*.

"*This* be teeth," he said proudly. "Heard?"

"Uh, yeah, heard," Athir said, reckoning that was what the *tsotsi* wanted him to say.

He waited a moment, then asked a question to which he didn't really want to know the answer.

"You going to kill me, *tsotsi*?"

"Don' know yet," the *tsotsi* said. "Jass Mofo decide. He the one want you. We gon' take you to him now."

The *tsotsi* stuck Athir's dagger in the belt that held the loop into which he then placed his *tirss*. Then he made a gesture.

Immediately, the sharp point was removed from Athir's back. At the same time, something was thrown over his head, cutting off his vision. Then the point poked him again, and he understood its message: get moving.

He began to walk.

I'm still alive, he thought, as he had on numerous similar occasions. But this time, he wondered if the Ship's Rat's luck had finally run out.

3

Blindfolded and stumbling, Athir allowed the *tsotsis* to poke and prod him through the squalid back streets of Khambawe. Although he could see nothing, the fetid smells that reached Athir's nose told him all he needed to know. His travels had taught him that offal smells the same everywhere, and these streets had to be choked with the stuff. He guessed that this was the infamous Maim. He had known he would have occasion to enter the *tsotsi* district sooner or later.

But not like this ...

His captors had remained silent, and discouraged him from trying to communicate with them. He attempted to remain optimistic. *They haven't killed me yet*, he reminded himself. And they hadn't played any cruel tricks on him, like walking him into walls or letting him trip over obstacles in the street.

Once, he heard a crunching of bones, followed by high-pitched, inhuman laughter. The *tsotsis* broke their silence at that sound. They made Athir stand still while they cursed and tossed objects at the source of the sound until the laughter stopped and rapidly receding footsteps signalled the departure of whoever – or *what*ever – it was. Athir thought he could detect the clicking of a beast's claws. And he was glad he couldn't see what it was that loped away.

Finally, Athir was hustled up a short flight of steps, then pushed through an entrance into a building. Immediately, the odors changed. Fragrant smoke and aromatic oils replaced the reek of decaying garbage. He could also hear music – a slow, hypnotic, rhythmic drumming.

The hands that gripped Athir's arms jerked him to an abrupt halt. He heard the shuffle of footsteps around him and a cacophony of hushed voices. The drumming suddenly stopped. He heard footsteps moving away from him, and others shuffling, as though to get out of the way of whoever was walking. For a long time, no one said anything. The unseen hands held him easily, but firmly. Finally, someone pulled the makeshift blindfold off his head.

Athir blinked. The light in the building was dim, but he could still make out the piles of loot scattered throughout the room, as well as elegantly made furniture pushed haphazardly against walls covered with intricately woven tapestries. *Tsotsis* swarmed around him, looking at him with idle curiosity rather than open hostility. Some of them were chewing *khat*, and were looking at him and through him at the same time. The *tsotsis* who were not transported by *khat* seemed to be fascinated by his sand-colored hair and his pale complexion, which seemed resistant to the browning rays of the Abengoni sun.

Athir was struck by their youthfulness, and the lithe, catlike grace of their bodies. But it was their eyes that made the deepest impression on him – those of the women as well as the men, and even the children. Athir Rin had gazed into the eyes of thieves, outlaws, murderers and other rogues in more than a score of far-flung countries in Cym Dinath and beyond. But never before had he seen such an absence of warmth, or any other kind of positive sentiment. The *tsotsis*' eyes reminded him of the cinders left by a burnt-out fire. They were the eyes of people who expected nothing – and gave less in return.

Athir forced himself to return the gazes of the *tsotsis*. Long-honed intuition told him these youths who were near, into, or just barely out of adolescence wouldn't hesitate to gut him like a fish if he showed any sign of the fear that continued to gnaw at his stomach and tickle his spine.

Then the crowd of *tsotsis* in front of him parted, and a lone, regal figure approached.

Their leader, Athir presumed.

This new *tsotsi* stood taller than average, which meant that he towered over Athir. Beads of gold and silver decorated the braids that hung from a strip of hair on an otherwise-shaved scalp. Thick chains of gold and silver hung across his bare, sepia-colored chest. A wispy mustache and chin-beard decorated his grim, dark face. His clothing and ornaments were those of a wealthy man, but he wore it as though its opulence meant nothing. He had the type of frame that could make rags look like royal robes.

Unlike the other *tsotsis*, this one's eyes glimmered with a spark of curiosity – and something else. He looked at Athir for a long time before speaking. Beads of sweat popped out across Athir's browline as he began to realize who this dangerous-looking *tsotsi* probably was. And Athir knew then that he was in even deeper trouble than he'd thought.

"What you be named, Fidi-man?" the *tsotsi* finally asked.

"I'm Athir Rin."

"I be Jass Mofo," the *tsotsi* said. "This be the Ashaki set. Baddest set in the Maim. Heard?"

"Heard," Athir replied.

He didn't say anything more. But his heart sank to his stomach as his surmise of the *tsotsi's* identity was confirmed. Amid the scant amount of information he had acquired about the *tsotsis* was the fact that Jass Mofo was considered the most ruthless and dangerous *tsotsi* in the entire Maim.

"What you doin' in Ukili?" Jass Mofo demanded. "What you doin' tryin' to be *tsotsi*?"

"Like I told the other guy, I'm new here," Athir said. "I didn't know the Ukili was part of your territory."

Annoyance flickered in Mofo's eyes. He wasn't accustomed to any indication of ignorance about his domain. Even the Emperor knew where Jass Mofo ruled. What was wrong with this outlander?

Jass Mofo gestured at the plunder scattered casually throughout the smoky chamber – a treasure hoard greater than the wealth of more than a few members of the Matile nobility.

"See that?" Mofo asked.

Athir nodded.

"That be mine," Mofo said. "All of it."

He gestured again, this time indicating the *tsotsis* who surrounded both of them, all of them looking with great deference at their leader, and disdain at the scrawny outlander.

"See they? They mine," he said.

Then he pointed to Athir.

"And you," Mofo said. "You mine. Heard?"

Athir knew better than to attempt to argue the point.

"Heard," he said.

He had nothing to add to that statement. He knew his life was hanging on the balance of the whims of this young lord of thieves. He tried not to wince as Jass Mofo studied him ... assessed him, as if he were a freshly stolen prize. It was a gaze Athir himself had often bestowed on his victims.

"No other set got a *tsotsi* like you, Fidi-man," Mofo said at last. "And this game you run – the one with the bones – no other set got that, either. I do believe you be good for this set."

"Heard," Athir said without prompting. "I'd be honored to be part of your enterprise. You can count on me, Jass Mofo."

Jass Mofo laughed.

"Not that easy to be in Ashaki set, Fidi-man. You got to step over. Heard?"

Athir gritted his teeth. He had a good idea what "stepping over" would mean.

"Heard," he said, hoping his voice reflected resignation rather than the fear that was devouring him inside.

4

Athir was sore. His body was bruised. He was bleeding. But he was alive. And he was now a *tsotsi* of the Ashaki set.

Although he normally preferred to work alone, Athir had occasionally found himself pressed into affiliation with criminal gangs, just as, from time to time, he found it expedient to offer his services to the crew of a departing ship. Unlike ships' crews, though, gangs required initiations. And wherever Athir had encountered gangs, their initiations were always the same: the prospective member was required to run through a brutal gauntlet, with the gang members striking blows with fist, feet and, sometimes, weapons.

The *tsotsis*' "stepping over" had been a gauntlet like any other. The only difference Athir could discern was in the incredible quickness of the *tsotsis*. Athir himself was far from slow, and in previous gauntlets he had run, he had been able to minimize the injuries he suffered by dodging and rolling with the torrents of blows that had rained down on him.

But he had not escaped many of the blows the *tsotsis* sent his way. Their hands moved like dark blurs, darting toward him with the swiftness of a viper's tongue. Only moments after he began to "step over," Athir knew he would need all the skills he had gleaned from a lifetime in back alleys simply to survive this initiation into the *tsotsi* ranks.

When the ordeal ended, no one congratulated Athir. He believed he did detect a brief glint of approval in the eyes of Jass Mofo. Mofo had not participated in the gauntlet. Like all rulers, he left matters like that to his underlings.

A young *tsotsi* woman had led him to the room in which he would recover from the effects of his "stepping over." Athir's aches were not so debilitating that he could not appreciate the subtle sway of her slender hips as she walked in front of him, or the lithe play of muscles beneath her dark-brown, mostly bare, skin. However, he wasn't yet aware of the connections and protocols of the *tsotsi* set; he didn't know who among them might be willing to kill him if he so much as touched even one of his guide's beaded braids.

Before she left him at the entrance of his room, the woman pressed a wad of *khat* into his hand.

"Chew this," she advised. "It make you feel better."

Then she departed without a backward glance.

Athir followed her counsel. The *khat* gave him a sharp jolt when he started chewing it; then it began to ease him out of his pain.

Khat wasn't nearly as potent as other narcotics he had sampled, such as Dream Lotus or Firedust. But it was sufficient. Just as the Ashaki *tsotsis* were sufficient ... for now. He didn't plan on remaining with them a moment longer than he had to ....

He was thinking of ways to escape when Jass Mofo came into the room.

When he saw Mofo, Athir started to rise. Mofo motioned him to stay where he was.

The *tsotsi* chief had shed most of his aristocratic trappings. He was clad only in black leather *senafil* studded with silver, along with several chains of silver and gold around his neck. And he still looked like a Jass.

"Fidi *tsotsi*," he said, smiling as though he liked the way those words sounded.

Athir remained silent.

"How you feelin'?" Mofo asked.

"Fine. Yourself?"

Mofo ignored that question. Instead, he asked one of his own that caused fear to crawl once again in Athir's stomach. The semi-stupor to which the *khat* had taken him vanished abruptly, and the pain from his injuries greeted him like an old friend.

"You thinkin' about runnin', Fidi *tsotsi*?"

"No," Athir said quickly. "Not at all, Jass Mofo. I would never do that. I'm proud to be a part of your fine organization."

Mofo snorted in disbelief.

"Best not be thinkin' about runnin'," he said. "Once you Ashaki, you always Ashaki. Till you die."

"Heard."

"Good."

Then Mofo knelt next to Athir. The Ship's Rat felt as though he were sitting next to a hungry leopard.

"Show me how you make the bones fall the way you want them to fall, Fidi *tsotsi*," Mofo said.

"Sure," Athir agreed, fishing his dice out of their hiding place in a fold of his garments.

"Here's how you throw a seven."

He flicked the dice against the room's bare stone wall. They bounced once, twice, then lay still on the floor. One face showed three markings, the other four.

"It's all in the way you move your wrist," Athir explained. "Very subtle."

Mofo nodded.

"Like killin'," he said.

Athir tried to swallow his fear as he continued Jass Mofo's first lesson in the art of throwing weighted dice. And all he could think about was running.

CHAPTER THIRTEEN

SOON COME

1

Jass Imbiah stood alone on Jayaya's beach, at the place where Sehaye's *gede* had arrived. No *ubia*-vine dared to come close to her; the altered *ashuma* that surrounded her like an unseen shield provided protection against *mwiti* and animal predators alike. As for human evil-doers, the mere sight of her – *chamma* billowing in the salty breeze, spider-scars clearly delineated by the light of the Moon Stars – was more than sufficient to ensure her well-being.

"Too narrow," Jass Imbiah said softly. "Me shoulders, them too narrow. Much too narrow for the task that is set for I."

The Moon Stars transformed the crimson sand of the beach into a black blanket nearly indistinguishable from the darkness of rolling sea. Jass Imbiah tried to find solace in the sound of the waves breaking against the shore. But calm of any kind eluded her, as it had since Legaba had ridden her on the day the message arrived from the mainland.

She shook her head slowly from side to side, as though that action could ease the responsibility she had to uphold: the undertaking of Retribution Time, the ultimate culmination of the Uloans' destiny, the final vengeance. Jass Imbiah knew what she and her people would be required to do now that Legaba had declared that Retribution Time was here. Her predecessors had also known. They had known; they had prepared; they had waited – but the call to Retribution Time was never heard.

Soon come, generation after generation of Uloans had told each other. *Retribution Time, it soon come.* And they never allowed themselves to doubt that one day, Legaba would lead them to their long-awaited reprisal against the blankskins and give the Uloans dominion over the mainland.

Jass Imbiah had never had even a moment of misgiving – until now. The source of her doubts was not in the truth of the words of prophecy that were uttered when the Storm Wars ended with so many of the Uloan Islands reduced to smoking lumps of rock barely breaking the surface of sea. And it wasn't a lack of faith in Legaba that drove her to seek solitude on the beach this night.

It was herself she doubted. So much of what was to come depended upon her, for she alone was the Vessel of Legaba. The Spider God's *ashuma* would ensure the success of Retribution Time – *if* she could contain and control it in her frail, aged body without breaking apart like a dry twig snapped underfoot.

Earlier that day, Jass Imbiah had met with an assembly of *huangi* from all the inhabited islands of the Uloas at her palace in Ompong. They had discussed their final preparations for Retribution Time down to the most minute details, and Jass Imbiah, the *huangi* of *huangis*, had imbued them all with confidence that they would triumph. But her confidence in herself was not as firm.

"Me shoulders too narrow," she said again.

Her faith in Legaba was as deep as the ocean. Her belief in herself as the god's Vessel was much shallower. As she stood on the shoreline, Jass Imbiah fought a battle within herself – a battle against her fears that she would fail not only Legaba, but her people as well.

My shoulders are more than wide enough, a familiar voice said inside her head.

"Legaba," Jass Imbiah said, with a sigh of relief in her tone.

She prepared herself to be ridden again. But Legaba did not intend to put her through the ordeal of possession this night.

Jass Imbiah heard a stirring in the sand. The sound was coming from the place where the ocean met the beach. She looked down, expecting to see a *gede*, although now that Retribution Time had come, there was no further purpose for the magical constructs.

She saw a shape coming toward her, barely visible in the black-crimson grains. But she could see clearly enough to realize that this was no *gede*. The shape was a round dome of weed, with legs radiating from its center like those of a spider. Jass Imbiah remained motionless as the weed-spider reached her. Jass Imbiah knew the weed from which the spider was formed did not come from Nama-kwah's realm of the sea, but from Legaba's, which was a much different place.

And she welcomed its arrival ...

The weed-spider's legs reached under her *chamma* and coiled around her body. The susurrating sound of their movements blended with the rumble of the waves as the weed-thing spread until it completely enveloped Jass Imbiah.

The web of weed did not constrict or smother her. She welcomed its touch as its substance was absorbed into that of her spider-scars, in the process imbuing her with *ashuma* – more potent than any she had ever experienced before; more than she had ever believed possible for her to bear. This was not like the times Legaba rode her, speaking and acting through her during the occasions when he possessed her. This time, Legaba was bestowing upon her a part of himself, directly from his Realm.

Jass Imbiah shivered in agony as the absorption continued – and, despite the pain, pleasure as well. But she neither moved nor cried out. When Legaba was finished, the web of weed was no longer visible. And the rest of the spider-shape in the sand disappeared.

Jass Imbiah's eyes shone like stars. She stretched her arms and legs, and the air around her crackled as if charged with lightning.

Now, your shoulders are wide enough, Legaba told her.

Then he was gone.

And Jass Imbiah was ready to do what she had to do, free from self-doubt and trepidation.

2

Throughout the Shattered Isles, activity teemed. From the largest islands – Jayaya, Makula, and Omanee – to mere flyspecks of rock that were home to only a few dozen inhabitants, the Uloans labored to prepare for their invasion of the mainland. This would be a far greater venture than the sporadic raids they had carried out over the centuries since the end of the Storm Wars. This was Retribution Time.

The skirl of steel ceremonial drums echoed throughout the islands, urging the Uloans to redouble their efforts. Spurred by the knowledge that the time that had long been soon to come had finally arrived, the islanders spared no effort to carry out Jass Imbiah's commands, for they knew that their ruler's words were also the words of their god.

In crystal-clear pools, the *huangi* held rites of purification. Dozens of Uloan warriors at a time immersed themselves in the water while the *huangi* uttered incantations that washed away all doubts and fears, leaving only the desire to fight and die for Legaba, and to annihilate the mainlanders. If they died in that cause, their spirits would become one with Legaba, and they would live forever in Legaba's Realm beyond the horizon of the world.

On altars atop the islands' highest hills, other *huangi* conducted sacrifices. As the populace of entire towns and villages looked on in awe, the *huangi* slaughtered pigs and goats and huge, flightless birds, the only domesticated animals that remained on the islands after the Storm Wars, and bathed in scarlet streams of blood as the beasts died. For in the worship of Legaba, blood was power, and power was blood. After the sacrifices ended, the malignant *ashuma* of the Spider God coursed like liquid fire through the *huangis*' veins.

In their forges, blacksmiths dipped the swords, spears and maces they made into vats filled with the sap of *mwiti*-plants from the Uloan forests. The viscous liquid clung to the points and edges of the weapons. Thus treated, the blades would leak poison into the wounds they inflicted, rendering them doubly lethal.

Carpenters repaired all the available warships and fitted new rams to their prows. New vessels were also constructed at a frantic pace. Even fishing boats were modified to hold as many warriors as possible. Not since the height of the Storm Wars had so many fighting ships been amassed for an assault on the mainland.

And in the most remote areas of the islands, the secret places in which the Uloans interred their dead, the bravest of the *huangi* performed the ultimate ritual of Retribution Time, one for which prophecy and many generations of ancestors had prepared them, the "soon come" time that had finally arrived.

The Uloans had long ago departed from the burial customs of the mainland. Their cities of the dead were not merely symbolic; they were real. Full-scale replicas of Uloan dwellings had been erected in the hidden valleys between the islands' rugged hills. And in those dwellings, the Uloan dead waited.

Powerful *ashuma* kept the *ubia*-vines and other intruders away from the charnel-cities. The *huangi* unwove the spells of protection before they entered, then restored them to prevent any interruption of what they intended to do. The cities of the dead were built on barren ground.

Nothing stirred; the coral dwellings were wrapped in cocoons of silence. The families of the deceased did not visit their relatives after their funeral rites were completed, for they knew that the dead would walk again at Retribution Time.

Inside the houses, clay effigies sat on stools, reclined on beds, leaned near windows. The effigies, called *jhumbis*, were not intended to represent likenesses of the corpses they encased. Thick layers of dull, gray clay covered the bodies from head to foot, creating lumpish caricatures of the human form. On the faces, cowrie shells took the place of eyes and sharp shards of clamshell substituted for teeth. There were no other features.

Jass Imbiah had dispatched a single *huangi* to each city of the dead. The *huangi* inspected the houses, ensuring that all the *jhumbi*s inside remained intact. They all were; not even the insects that feasted on carrion flesh would go near them.

Satisfied that the *jhumbi*s had not come to harm during their long time of quiescence, the *huangi* went outside to altars that had been built long ago in anticipation of this day. Stripping off their feathered garments, the *huangi* reclined on the flat surfaces of the altars. And they raised long, sharp daggers high over chests incised with scars in the shape of spiders.

From far away in Ompong, Jass Imbiah spoke to them simultaneously, whispering a single word the *huangi* heard in their minds – *now*.

Then, as one, the *huangi* plunged their daggers into their own chests, and dragged the blades down to their groins, opening their own bodies in devotion to Legaba and Retribution Time. They shrieked the name of their god as they died. And their life-blood poured out of grooves cut into the altars and soaked the soil underneath.

Inside the houses of the dead, the clay that covered the *jhumbi*s began to change as the *huangi*s' blood was absorbed in the ground. The hard shell softened and molded to the contours of the corpses inside, so that the *jhumbi*s' forms more closely approximated that of the human. Cowrie shells settled into hollowed eye-sockets; shell shards lined gaping mouths, creating sharp-toothed grimaces.

Then the *jhumbi*s stood up. And they shambled out of their dwellings, leaving patches of clay behind where they had sat or stood. With slow, measured steps, they trudged past the bodies of *huangi* sprawled on bloodstained altars. And they walked out of the cities of the dead to rejoin the living, and play their allotted role in Retribution Time.

3

Awiwi's tears dampened Bujiji's chest as they lay in the darkness of his house in Ompong. His fingers traced the spider-scars on her back as she lay quietly at his side. She wept because Bujiji was only one day away from sailing off with the armada that would bring Retribution Time to the mainland. Like all the other Uloan warriors, Bujiji had vowed before Legaba that he would return to the islands in triumph over the blankskins – or he would not return at all.

Awiwi's faith in the prophecy of Retribution Time, and in the ultimate ascendance of the islanders over the mainlanders, was complete and without question. But that faith had not prevented her tears from falling as she lay with her lover one last time before the war began, because she knew that the victory could not come without a price.

Bujiji had reassured again and again her that he would return to her arms. When the *huangi* had purified him in a pool in the forest near Ompong, it was as though Legaba's own power had passed through the pores of his skin and entered his body, infusing every muscle and nerve with the Spider God's *ashuma*. He felt immortal; invincible. The blankskins would fall before him like grass crushed underfoot and, unlike the *mwiti*-grass, his victims would not rise again. Victory was assured.

As well, Bujiji had long since overcome the consequences of his near-tardiness in retrieving Sehaye's message from the mainland, and had not blamed Awiwi for it. Jass Imbiah had not punished him for the marks of the *ubia*-vine's teeth on the message-tube, and he had even gained a measure of repute as the man who had brought the news that initiated Retribution Time. When the war against the Mainland was over, he could expect even greater renown to come his way.

But when he had explained that to Awiwi earlier this night, she had wept.

Bujiji understood the reason for Awiwi's tears, which flowed until she fell asleep. Her faith was not as strong as her fears. For that reason, he didn't tell her about some of the other things he had seen during the intense preparations for Retribution Time. He had seen the *jhumbis*, who were kept in places separate from those inhabited by their living kin. The *jhumbis* were ancestors; they were revered and they would play an important part in what was to come. Even so, the sight of them was terrifying. Bujiji could well imagine the effect the *jhumbis* would have on the blankskins.

As well, the *jhumbis* had a purpose beyond that of spreading fear on the mainland. Bujiji had seen the *huangi* train the *jhumbis* in rowing the Uloan warships. And he had seen the results of those efforts: the *jhumbis'* preternaturally enhanced strength had propelled the massive warcraft like giant arrows through the waters off the coast of Jayaya.

Bujiji was thinking about what such speed could do against the blankskins' warships when Awiwi spoke.

"Bujiji. Listen to I."

A heartbeat of silence passed before Bujiji responded.

"I and I thought you was asleep," he said.

"Bujiji. I and I having a child."

This time, the silence lasted longer. But during that time, Bujiji held Awiwi close to him in a clasp that was at once firm and tender.

"How long you know this?" he asked.

"Not long."

"Why you not tell I sooner?"

"You were readying yourself for Retribution Time," she said. "I and I not want to make problem for you."

Again, Bujiji fell silent. Then he gave Awiwi another, longer embrace.

"This I and I promise you, Awiwi," he said. "Our child will walk on the Mainland. And the blankskins – they will be slaves to he."

Bujiji's prophecy only partially reassured Awiwi. But she did not tell him what she thought. It was not the right time to do so. Instead, she nestled her head on his shoulder and clung to him as long as she could until the time came for him to go.

4

The Uloan armada stretched across the horizon as it sailed into the misty strait that separated the islands from the mainland. No farewell ceremonies marked its departure; Jass Imbiah had told the *huangi* there was neither time nor *ashuma* available for such rites. All the *ashuma* she and the *huangi* could muster would be needed for Retribution Time. The task of controlling the *jhumbis* would, by itself, consume more *ashuma* than the islanders had ever produced. And that task was only one of many they still faced.

On the island's crimson beaches, the women, children and elders watched as the many contingents of ships set sail to the place at which all the island's fleets would converge before heading for the mainland. There was no cheering or other show of celebration among the crowds gathered on the beaches. The Uloans' jubilation would be deferred until the future, when the ships would return in triumph.

No one doubted the inevitability of victory. The prophecy, spoken by a dying Vessel of Legaba in the grim days that followed the final devastation of the Storm Wars, had said that during Retribution Time, the dead would walk alongside the living on streets cobbled with the skull-domes of the Mainlanders. The clay-covered inhabitants of the cities of the dead would arise only once, and that one time would be the signal of doom for the Mainland. The only uncertainty was when that time would come. Now, after many years of hope and despair, the uncertainty was over, as was the waiting.

If the people on the beaches feared for the lives of their husbands, sons, and brothers, they did not acknowledge such misgivings. Some – perhaps many – would die as Retribution Time unfolded. Yet the final victory over the blankskins would be worth the price in lives, however high it might be.

Awiwi stood with the others on the beach of Jayaya. She watched the ships recede over the horizon, soon to be swallowed by the mist. Earlier, she had seen Bujiji march onto one of those ships, in company with scores of other warriors from her island. He had not attempted to catch a final glimpse of her. And if he had seen her, he would not have acknowledged her farewell wave. Like those of the other warriors, his eyes were focused straight ahead, in the direction of the mainland. It was as though the fighters' eyes could already see Khambawe through the curtain of mist that hung between the islands and the Mainland.

When the ships finally passed from sight, the crowds on the beach of Jayaya, and the other islands, dispersed; heading back to their homes and avoiding the *ubia*-vines and other hazards as they went. Now another, shorter time of waiting would begin.

Awiwi placed her hand on her belly. It was too soon to feel any movement from the new life that was growing inside her. But she knew it was there. The *mambi* – the medicine-woman who, among other things, helped to bring the life-spirits of children into the world – had told her it was so.

"Bujiji, him will return," Awiwi said to her child. "You will greet he when the ships come back from battle. And them soon come."

To reassure herself as well as her child, she repeated her words.

"Them soon come."

CHAPTER FOURTEEN

Attack

1

In the Audience Chamber of the Gebbi Senafa, Emperor Dardar Alemeyu sat in private council with the two most important people in the Matile Mala Empire, next to himself: Jass Gebrem and Jass Eshana. All three were seated around a low table. Its surface was carved with scenes similar to those on the tapestries that hung throughout the palace. Other than the inevitable palace guards, no one else was in the chamber. Dusk was falling, and the light from the windows painted the royal chamber in shades of gold and gray.

The topic of this council of royal kinsmen was the Fidi, the guests from afar who were still stirring curiosity in Khambawe months after their arrival. Jass Eshana was telling the others the latest news his network of informants had passed on to him about the foreigners.

"There is division among them," the Dejezmek said. "Those who are called the Believers mingle with our people more than the non-Believers do. The Believers ask many questions; they want to know as much about us as possible. And they seem happy to answer any questions our people have about them."

He paused. His listeners said nothing, waiting to hear more before they commented.

"Often, the Believers talk about their god, Almovaar," Eshana continued.

"What do they say about him?" Gebrem asked.

"That he offers much and demands little."

The Leba snorted, but said nothing more. But he knew what

the others were thinking: the Jagasti had neither offered nor demanded anything from the Matile for centuries. That thought had gnawed at him for years, even as he continued to practice a religion that was hollow at its core despite a few tantalizing shimmers on its surface from time to time.

"What about the non-Believers?" the Emperor asked.

"They seldom venture far from their ship," Eshana replied. "They are not unfriendly, but they mostly keep to themselves. Their captain, Muldure, seems to care about little other than finishing the repairs to the ship as soon as possible."

Gebrem and the Emperor exchanged a glance that was filled with unspoken questions: *Why was repairing the ship so important? Was Muldure planning to leave Khambawe? Was Kyroun?*

"I should mention another split in their ranks, Mesfin," Eshana said. "The Fidi who are called 'dwarves' are living at the Tokoloshe Embassy. And we have no informants there, so I have no idea what they are doing."

The Dejezmek left his other thoughts unspoken. He had never trusted the Tokoloshe. And if the Fidi dwarves were now in league with them ... He thrust that speculation aside and continued his report.

"Also, one of the Fidi – a non-Believer – has been spotted running with the *tsotsis* in the Maim."

"He'll have a short life then, won't he?" Alemeyu said, his mouth curving downward in disdain for the criminals who plagued the city.

Then the Emperor turned to Gebrem.

"And what of Kyroun, the 'Seer' of the Almovaads?" he asked. "Although I should, perhaps, be directing this question to Tiyana, not you."

Anger rose in the Leba, but he kept it under control. *Goading, goading, always goading, cousin*, he thought. *Will it ever end?*

"My daughter is very diligent in carrying out the task I assigned her, Mesfin," he murmured aloud. "She is learning as much about the Seer as she can. Concerning your question, it appears that Kyroun is so consumed by guilt over the deaths that befell many of his followers on their way here that he may be more dangerous to himself than to anyone else."

Alemeyu nodded, then opened his mouth to comment on what he had heard. Before he could say anything, Gebrem suddenly stiffened. His eyes widened and his nostrils flared like those of an impala sensing the presence of a lion.

"What is it?" the Emperor asked, leaning forward. Jass Eshana leaned forward as well, eyes narrowed in concern.

"*Ashuma*," Gebrem said. His voice had become raspy, as though someone was attempting to strangle him.

"Is it Kyroun?" Eshana demanded.

"No," Gebrem gasped. "Uloans!"

2

Jass Gebrem's warning nearly came too late. As dusk became darkness, Jass Eshana had only a limited amount of time to organize Khambawe's defenses before the attack the Leba's *ashuma* had detected came. The city was in a frenzy, its populace gathering weapons and barricading their homes. For Gebrem's *ashuma* had told him this was no coastal raid, as was usual from the Uloans. This was a full-scale assault against the city – the first in several generations.

A hastily assembled wall of warships and other vessels guarded the entrance to the harbor. The Fidis' ship, however, was still not sufficiently seaworthy to join the others. Eshana dispatched soldiers to stand beside Captain Muldure and his crew on the *White Gull*'s wharf to help defend the foreigners' ship. As for the Believers, they had joined Kyroun in the city to aid in preparations for the defense of the city.

Squadrons of other soldiers lining the docks formed Khambawe's second tier of protection. In the shadows of the Ishimbi statues, they stood in silent, armored ranks, shields raised, swords and spears poised to strike and thrust. Archers were stationed on rooftops and in windows of buildings in the wharf district. Their arrows would be the Matiles' first greeting to any Uloans who breached the barrier of ships in the harbor. Then the rest of the soldiers, aided by officers mounted on *quagga*s, would charge forward and drive the invaders off the docks.

That was how the last Uloan raid against the city had concluded. The first indication that circumstances would be different this time came with the wail of steel drums in the distance. Only a few Matile – fishermen driven close to the Uloan Islands by errant winds – had ever heard that sound. And they had described it as akin to the outcries of ghosts or demons.

Now, it was as though all the doomed souls in the Uloan Islands and the Matile Mala alike had united to howl a chorus of damnation and woe. On the ships and the docks, some of the soldiers covered their ears to keep out that sound, which had obviously been enhanced by *ashuma*. Their officers angrily ordered them to keep their hands on their weapons, even as they wished that they could cover their own tortured ears.

Eventually, the skirl of the steel drums faded – only to be replaced by voices raised in a repetitive chant. At first, the words were unintelligible, like the muttering of thunder in the distance. As the invaders drew closer, however, the two words they were saying over and over carried clearly through the mist, as though everyone in the Uloan islands was speaking in a single, demented voice:

"Retribution Time!"

Then, like gigantic beasts of prey, the vanguard of the Uloan war fleet burst through the harbor mist. The ships' sails were furled. Single banks of oars propelled the invaders' vessels at a speed that was both unnatural and alarming, leaving high tails of water in their wake. And they did not do what they had always done in the past.

Instead of dispersing to engage the Matile ships individually, the Uloan vessels focused their attack directly at the center of their enemies' line of defense. Before the astonished Matile could maneuver their ships out of the attackers' path, the rams on the Uloan prows punched hard into their hulls.

Planking cracked and caved at the devastating impact of the rams' points. The Matile ships lurched violently, hurling soldiers and sailors off their feet and into the harbor. Their cries were barely audible over the snapping of timbers and groaning of wood wrenched asunder as the Uloan rams probed deeper into the stricken ships' bowels.

The gap in the Matile defense line grew wider as the momentum of Uloan ships' uncanny speed forced the ships they had targeted to move aside. Savaging their victims the way a big cat shakes its hapless quarry, the Uloan warcraft reversed the motion of their oars, pulling away and leaving the Matile ships to founder and sink. The surviving Matile sailors swam frantically toward the docks. Weighed down by their armor, the ship-borne soldiers went down like stones.

Realizing what their foes were attempting to do, other Matile ships moved to close the gap. But they were too late. In a seemingly endless stream, Uloan vessels now hurtled toward the docks. The magnitude of the onslaught was even greater than Jass Gebrem had thought. Not since the Storm Wars had the islanders mounted such a massive assault on the mainland. Those Matile who had time to reflect wondered if the Uloans had finally become irrevocably insane, and intended to destroy not only the Mainlanders, but themselves as well.

Through a desperate effort, the defenders managed to close the gap before all the Uloan ships could break through. As the remaining Uloans came under attack, the outer part of the harbor became a maelstrom of clashing warships as the Matile vessels launched a vicious counterattack against the invaders. But they could only engage part of the invaders' fleet. The rest of the Uloan ships were ranging free, unimpeded by defenders.

Most of the ships that had taken advantage of the opening in the line of defense made for moorings at the docks – spots the Matile ships had vacated to join the defense line. However, three of the Uloan vessels veered away from the rest and headed directly toward the *White Gull* at a speed that was impossible for human rowers to have attained. It was as though the Fidis' ship was a specific target for the invaders.

The Uloan ships fanned out, then struck with devastating impact. One rammed the *White Gull* amidships; the others hit its bow and stern. The three loud, crunching impacts came nearly simultaneously. After the Uloan ships pulled free, the *White Gull* began to sink. Pel Muldure's frenzied curses were loud enough to be heard even above the din of the sea-battle and the Uloans' cries of "Retribution Time."

As soon as the other Uloan warcraft slid into the Matiles' moorings, they disgorged their cargoes of invaders, who marched stiffly across hastily dropped gangplanks and climbed onto the docks. Shields raised, weapons pointed outward, the Uloans began a slow, deliberate march toward their waiting foes.

The way the Uloans looked startled the Matile soldiers who faced them. The warriors seemed to be fully encased in gray, form-fitting armor of a sort no one had ever seen before. Masked helmets of the same color covered their heads.

Ordinarily, the islanders fought nearly naked, like the Thabas, with bright paint decorating the scars on their skin. The uniform, armored grayness of the invaders was disconcerting. And some of the Uloans were smaller than others, as though women and children had donned the gray armor along with the men. The movements of all were awkward, as though they had awakened from a long sleep. But they marched steadily forward, and in silence as well, for the cries of "Retribution Time" had suddenly ceased.

"Loose arrows!" the commander of the Matile archers cried from the roof of an overlooking building.

A thousand bowstrings twanged. A thousand arrows arced over the heads of the Matile soldiers toward the invaders. The Uloans made no attempt to escape or protect themselves as the arrows struck, nearly every one of them reaching its target. At the commander's order, two more volleys of death tore into the Uloans.

And not a single invader fell.

Most of the arrows had bounced from the gray patina that covered the Uloans' bodies. Others were embedded point-deep, as if they had become lodged in hardened mud. The Uloans made no effort to pull the arrows free. Undamaged, the invaders continued to march forward. As they came closer, the Matile realized their foes were either more – or less – than human. And with that awful understanding came the beginning of the kind of fear that steals courage and causes battles to be lost.

From his vantage point alongside the commander of the archers, Jass Eshana watched the advance of the invaders. More Uloan ships had broken through and tied up at the docks. Hordes of other Uloans disembarked without interference, since the Matiles' attention was focused on the first wave of attackers.

The newcomers did not have the peculiar crustation that covered and protected the others. The familiar daubs of bright paint adorned the scarification patterns on their bodies. Screaming maniacally and shaking their weapons, they fanned out behind their vanguard. As soon as they landed, the invaders again began their maddening chant: "Retribution Time!"

Eshana and the commander of the archers, whose name was Jass Kidan, looked at each other in dismay.

"Everyone on those damned islands who can fight must be out there," Jass Kidan said in a near-whisper. "And the ones in front ...."

"*Ashuma*," Jass Eshana said.

He turned an archer who was staring wide-eyed at the scene below.

"Go to Gebrem," the Dejezmek instructed. "Tell him his skills are needed now, and tell him why."

The archer nodded, slung his bow over his shoulder and headed for the nearest passage off the roof of the building. The sound of shouts and the clash of weapons rang in his ears as the Uloan and Matile forces met.

3

In the Beit Amiya, Tiyana knelt before the altar of Nama-kwah. The Mask of the goddess covered her face and an aquamarine *chamma* hung loosely around her. Her body was bent in an arc, muscles rigid as she invoked the *ashuma* of the deity she had served all her life.

An ancient statue that depicted Nama-kwah as a woman wearing a *chamma* made of fish scales loomed above her. The face of the idol duplicated the one on the silver mask. Its stone arms were spread wide, as though the goddess were embracing the sea, and the Matile people as a whole. In the past, that caress was as tangible as that of a lover.

Now ...

Mouthing incantations that were many centuries old, Tiyana entreated Nama-kwah to roil the waters of Khambawe's harbor; to raise foaming waves large enough to sink the Uloans' ships and break them into kindling; to spin whirlpools that would drag the invaders into the goddess's deep Realm; to send sharks and other sea-predators to savage the survivors.

In the distant past, when Tiyana's ancestors among the Amiyas had knelt in the same spot and spoken the same words to the stone effigy, Nama-kwah would have acted, and her *ashuma* would have infused Tiyana, and it would have given her the power to do more than merely dance on the waves. But now the Goddess was silent, just as she had been during First Calling, when the Fidi ship had arrived in the midst of her dance on the waves.

Then Tiyana remembered that Nama-kwah actually had spoken to her then, whispering a single word: *Danger*. At the time, she thought the goddess was warning her about the Fidi. Now, she realized that Nama-kwah had foretold the massive attack by the Uloans.

Nama-kwah's silence had returned in the Matile's time of need. Tiyana didn't feel even a tingle of *ashuma*. The Goddess had abandoned her idol; it was no more responsive than any ordinary piece of carved stone.

And she had abandoned her Vessel as well. Yet Tiyana continued to speak the ancient words. She could think of nothing else to do.

Similar scenes occurred at other altars as other masked Amiyas entreated the Jagasti to whom they had been pledged as children.

The Amiya of Ufashwe, God of the wind, asked for a tempest to overwhelm the Uloan ships. The Amiya of Sama-wai, Goddess of illness and decay, called for a plague to strike the Uloans down. The Amiya of Chaile, God of fortune good and ill, prayed for the Uloans' swords to break and their shields to turn brittle. The Amiya of Alamak, Goddess of the Stars, called for fiery stones to fall from the sky onto the heads of the invaders.

Like Tiyana's, the prayers to those and all the other Jagasti went unheeded. All except one – that of Keshu, Amiya of Halasha, God of iron and war. Keshu asked only that the soldiers of Matile fight courageously. That prayer was the only one that was answered, though not by Halasha.

Jass Gebrem stood apart from the others. *Abi* in hand, he attempted to consolidate whatever *ashuma* the Amiyas could gather; to coalesce it into a single surge of force that would destroy the Uloans. He was performing the incantation exactly as his forefathers had, centuries ago. But he might as well have been attempting to pour water from an empty jar. Nothing was happening. It was as though the Jagasti no longer existed.

The only *ashuma* Gebrem and the others could wield was whatever they could find within themselves. And he knew that would not be sufficient to defeat the Uloans ... not when their attack was so massive and overwhelming.

Earlier, for a single, awful moment, Gebrem felt the presence of his Uloan counterpart, Jass Imbiah, in his consciousness. Jass Imbiah was laughing at his attempts to resist her power ... and that derision in that laughter had pushed him to the brink of madness.

Even as he tried to gather his and the Amiyas' meager *ashuma*, the Leba fought off a wave of despair.

What can I do? he asked himself yet again. *What can I do?*

A sound near the entrance to the Beit Amiya broke Gebrem's concentration. He looked toward the source of the sound – and his eyes widened in surprise.

Kyroun stood in the doorway. Behind him were the Almovaad Adepts, most of whom he had come to know. All were dressed in robes of deep indigo, the color of a dark sky. As the Amiyas became aware of the presence of the Believers, the sound of their chants and incantations died down.

Anger rose in Gebrem. The Beit Amiya was forbidden to all, save the Vessels and their *shamashas*. He knew Kyroun and the Almovaads could not have been aware of the breach of sanctity they had just committed at the worst possible time. Now, they would learn.

But Kyroun spoke before Gebrem could begin his rebuke. And what he said quelled the Matile's outrage.

"Please allow us to help you."

Gebrem stared at him.

"You have nothing to lose," the Seer said. "And there is no price to pay for our assistance."

Gebrem kept staring.

4

Pel Muldure swung his sword at the nearest *jhumbi*. His blade bit deep into the gray shell that covered the *jhumbi's* body. A cloud of powder flew through the air as Muldure pulled his sword back. The *jhumbi* staggered a moment. Then it pressed forward, forcing Muldure to retreat another step.

The *jhumbi* swung its sword at Muldure, who easily evaded the slow arc of the blade. He struck again, chopping a chunk from the *jhumbi's* mask-like face. The *jhumbi* did not react. Drawing its sword back for another swing, the walking corpse moved forward. Muldure took another step backward.

He stole a glance at Lyann who was, as always, fighting at his side. She moved more than quickly enough to avoid the *jhumbis'* weapons and strike counter-blows of her own. But Muldure could see she was growing weary. They all were – the crew of the *White Gull* as well as the Matile soldiers who had fought alongside them since the beginning of the Uloans' invasion.

Step-by-step, the defenders had been driven from the docks, leaving their dead sprawled in pools of blood. The retreat was grudging ... but unavoidable.

Yet the *jhumbi*s were not invincible. Soon enough, the defenders had discovered that the creatures could be brought down by hewing through their knee joints and severing their legs. Even then, the *jhumbi*s used their arms to continue to crawl forward and strike and clutch at their foes' legs.

Still, a legless *jhumbi* was much less dangerous than an ambulatory one, and that result was the best the defenders could hope for. However, it took many blows to cut through a *jhumbi's* gray covering, and during the time involved in striking those blows the defenders were vulnerable to retaliation from other *jhumbi*s and the scarred, painted Uloans who shrieked and capered among them, darting in and out to inflict further carnage. Their blades were treated with a poison that delivered agony with the merest prick of the skin.

Already, some of the Uloans had skirted the Matile flanks and infiltrated the streets of Khambawe, killing anyone in their path and setting buildings ablaze. Smoke was beginning to blot the rapidly darkening sky. And even more Uloan ships were landing and disgorging more invaders to add to the horde.

Rage and frustration offset the fatigue that was creeping into Muldure's muscles. When the Uloans sank the nearly repaired *White Gull*, the captain had gone berserk. It took the combined efforts of Lyann and two other sailors to prevent him from charging single-handed into the enemy. When he became calmer, he led the defense of his crew and the Matile soldiers as effectively as a military commander could have done. But his thoughts were decidedly unmilitary.

So this is how Kyroun's great quest ends, Muldure thought bitterly as he swung his sword yet again. *In death for us all ....*

Then he stumbled over the body of a fallen Matile. The *jhumbi's* sword came down. Off-balance, Muldure raised his own weapon in time to deflect the blow. But the force of it drove him to the ground.

The *jhumbi* lifted its sword again. Lyann pulled Muldure to his feet before it could come down again. Together, they retreated yet further, as did the other defenders.

Suddenly, a chill breeze, colder than anything they had ever felt in the hot climate of Abengoni, brushed against the defenders. And the *jhumbi*s staggered to a halt, as though they had collided with an adamantine barrier. Then an unseen force hurled them backward. Many *jhumbi*s crashed to the ground; others spun in erratic circles. The Uloan warriors among them fell to the ground as if stunned by blows to the head.

Muldure exchanged a glance with Lyann.

"Kyroun," he said.

Lyann nodded in agreement.

"What the hell took him so long?" she wondered.

Only a moment later, Lyann and Muldure realized their assumption was erroneous.

With a booming war-cry, a combined force of Tokoloshe and dwarves charged from the mouth of a street leading to the docks. Muldure recognized his friend Hulm Stonehand in the forefront of the squat warriors.

Like a self-propelled battering ram, the Dwarven fighters crashed into the ranks of the disoriented *jhumbi*s. The warriors' diminutive stature proved an advantage: the *jhumbi*s' knees were in a direct line with the arc of the dwarves' and Tokoloshes' swords and axes.

Several *jhumbi*s fell as the Tokoloshe and dwarves hacked away at them. But the animate dead quickly recovered from the sorcerous ambush that preceded the charge, and they rained down blows that stunned even the most powerful of their new foes. Some of the dwarves and Tokoloshe began to fall, but they continued to stand their ground while the Matile and the Fidi regrouped behind them.

The invaders' momentum stalled. And the Matile commanders took full advantage of the change in circumstances. From his vantage point, Jass Eshana saw what had happened. And he knew what the city's defenders had to do next if they were to have a chance to win this battle.

"Attack!" Eshana shouted, eyes blazing beneath the lion's-mane crest on his helmet.

Forgetting their fatigue, the newly heartened defenders rushed toward their foes, living and dead alike. For the first time since the Uloan ships arrived, the Matile had hope of winning their battle for survival.

But that prospect proved short-lived ...

5

Dardar Alemeyu stood on the highest balcony of the Gebbi Senafa. From that point, he could gaze out over much of the panorama of Khambawe. During the daytime, the Jewel City stretched below him like a colorful carpet laid out for a deity. At night, the torches that lit Khambawe's streets and homes glittered like stars shining in a sky fallen to earth.

But this night, torches were not all that was aflame in Khambawe. On street after street, burning buildings blazed like sunbursts. Slowly, inexorably, those fires were creeping closer to the palace.

Alemeyu was clad in garments of war. Armor of leather and steel decorated with silver and gold sat loosely on his lean frame. Atop his head was a helmet covered almost completely with hair taken from the manes of lions. It was said to have been handed down from the great Dardar Issuri himself, as was the sword that hung in a gold-chased sheath at his side.

Many years had passed since an Emperor personally had led Matile troops into battle, however. On this night, the Sword of Issuri would remain in its sheath.

Tradition required Alemeyu, as Emperor, to don the martial raiment of an imperial commander. Reality dictated that he remain far from the scene of combat. For good or ill, the Dejezmek, Jass Eshana, would lead the remnants of an army that had once held sway over a continent in what Alemeyu sensed was the final battle against an ancient foe.

Alemeyu looked at Issa. The Empress was dressed for travel rather than war: loose cotton tunic and *senafil*; no *chamma* or jewelry, save for the inevitable hair ornaments that glistened in the light of the torches on the balcony.

Issa gazed at the fires, which still burned at a long distance from the palace. Faint sounds of fighting drifted to her ears, and Alemeyu's. Moment by moment, those sounds intensified.

"They are getting closer," Issa murmured.

"I know," said Alemeyu.

He said nothing about the even worse news Eshana's messengers had been delivering: the full-scale invasion of Uloans; the walking dead fighting at the islanders' side; the steady advance of enemy forces. The intervention of the Tokoloshe and the dwarves had slowed that progress only temporarily; the Uloans were swarming through the city like an invasion of vermin at a garbage heap.

"Mesfin."

The voice came from behind the royal pair. It was Bekele, the officer Eshana had assigned to see to their safety. Bekele was a strong-limbed young man who reminded Alemeyu of himself at a younger age, when he was still a prince and not yet obliged to sit on the Lion Throne.

Alemeyu and Issa turned to face the soldier.

"What is it?" the Emperor demanded.

"Jass Eshana has sent another message," Bekele said. "He thinks it best that you leave the Senafa now, and go to the Gebbi Zimballa – the Old Palace."

A sharp hiss marked the sudden intake of Issa's breath. Alemeyu said nothing.

"Soon you will not be safe here, Mesfin," Bekele continued. He said nothing more. The final decision belonged to the Emperor.

"We will go," Alemeyu said.

They followed Bekele from the balcony. Later, surrounded by the Emperor's Guard, and accompanied by Makah, the Emperor's cheetah, they departed from the Gebbi Senafa. Behind them, a long line of servants carried items that were the last legacy of a long dynasty. Now, they were going to the place where that dynasty had begun.

CHAPTER FIFTEEN

STREET CHAOS

1

Athir Rin was well-acquainted with fear. Indeed, dread was his best, and perhaps only, friend. Without its constant companionship, he would have been dead many times over. Fear kept him alert. And as long as the Ship's Rat stayed alert, he stayed alive.

Never before, however, had Athir's companion been as persistent as it was now, as he ran in the midst of the Ashaki set of *tsotsis* through the dark streets leading out of the Maim and into a city under siege.

Fear had first spoken to him earlier in the day. He had been giving Jass Mofo yet another lesson in the exacting art of throwing weighted dice.

Mofo had already made excellent progress in a short time. Athir himself had not mastered so much of the art so quickly, and he had been considered a fast learner by a mentor whose compliments were given only grudgingly. Unlike his own teacher, Athir always made certain the *tsotsi* chief knew how well he was doing at acquiring this new skill. And he suspected his teacher would not have been so quick to criticize a pupil like Mofo.

But patience was not a primary characteristic of the *tsotsis*. Life in the Maim was intense, frantic and deadly. *Tsotsis* lived for the moment, not the future. Athir had always considered himself an impulsive person. Compared to the *tsotsis*, though, he felt like a priest trapped amid infidels.

Jass Mofo had thrown the bone cubes against the wall of his "throne room" for what seemed the hundredth time that morning. He was attempting to throw a four. But when the dice stopped rolling, the dots showing on their upturned faces added up to five.

Jass Mofo made a sound that was halfway between a snarl and a curse. Athir's command of the Matile language wasn't sufficient to allow him to make out all the words that followed. He felt it was just as well that he didn't understand everything the *tsotsi* was saying. He was simply glad it wasn't directed toward him

This was the first time Mofo had missed after six scoring consecutive successful tosses. In eight throws out of ten, he could make the bones fall as he intended. But eight out of ten was not good enough, nor was nine out of ten. Mofo didn't need Athir to tell him that a crooked dice-roller's tosses had to be perfect every time. And getting to ten-for-ten from eight-for-ten was not a rapid process, not even for someone with Mofo's obvious natural talent.

That wasn't what Athir chose to tell him.

"You're really doing well, Jass Mofo," he reassured. "It'll be just a matter of time before you're better than I am at this."

Mofo stared at Athir. And that's when Athir's colleague, fear, settled into its home in the pit of his stomach. The climate in Khambawe was hot, but when Mofo gave him his bleak-eyed glare, Athir felt a chill stir inside like a stiff wind from the Northlands.

"Time be short in the Maim," Mofo said.

He kept his eyes fixed on Athir's. The Ship's Rat didn't dare to look away.

"Could be, time short for you too, Fidi-*tsotsi*," he added.

Athir remained calm on the surface. Inside, his companion was becoming clamorous. He knew the novelty of his presence among the Ashaki was wearing off, and it was unlikely Mofo would fully master the bones before becoming weary of the Ship's Rat. His mind raced in search of something to say that would divert Mofo from the anger that was becoming visible, building by the moment as he glared at the dice. Before Athir could say anything, though, an excited *tsotsi* burst into the room.

"Jass Mofo! Jass Mofo!" the *tsotsi* cried. "The Uloans come! They be killin', burnin' everywhere! Whole city be crazy!"

Mofo's mood changed immediately. He forgot about his frustration with the dice, and his growing impatience with the newest recruit to his set. He smiled, and to Athir that simple movement of Mofo's lips looked like the baring of a carnivore's teeth.

Other *tsotsis* who had overheard the news now gathered around Jass Mofo and Athir. They anticipated what their leader would say next, and they were eager to hear it.

"This be our time now," Mofo said, the feral grin still on his face. "This city – everything in it belong to us. And we gon' take it all! Heard?"

"Heard!" the Ashaki set shouted in a single voice.

Then they whooped and waved their spiked weapons. One *tsotsi* snatched up a nearby drum and began to pound out a battle-rhythm. The others, still shouting, broke into a spontaneous dance.

Jass Mofo glanced at Athir.

"You gon' do more than throw bones now, Fidi-*tsotsi*," Mofo said menacingly. "Heard?"

"Heard," Athir acknowledged.

His expression was as wan as the tone of his voice. And his internal companion was becoming relentless, its message impossible to ignore as he joined the *tsotsis* in their preparations for the looting spree of a lifetime.

Now, he was ranging with the *tsotsis* as they moved beyond the confines of the Maim. Never before had so many members of this set, or any other, ventured out of its territory at the same time. They preferred to do their work in the city by themselves, or with, at most, one or two companions, so they could blend more easily with the surroundings of their victims.

Now, however, the streets were either deserted or filled with fleeing, panic-stricken people to whom the sight of a full set of *tsotsis* on the prowl was as nothing compared to what they had already experienced from the Uloan invaders and their *jhumbis*.

Navigating the night shadows, the *tsotsis* were headed toward the wealthier part of Khambawe, where the Jasses and wealthy merchants kept their *aderashes*. Flames illuminated the night sky, and the *tsotsis* could hear outcries drifting up along with acrid smoke.

Athir had only a vague notion of who or what the "Uloans" might be. However, he sensed he was in great danger a he struggled to keep up with the fleet-footed *tsotsis*. The *tsotsis* were a gang, not an army. His inner companion was warning him that disaster loomed, despite their supreme confidence that they could do whatever they wanted now that the city was in upheaval. For emphasis, his companion clutched at his stomach with an icy hand.

Jass Mofo urged the set onward. hey needed to reach the loot-laden dwellings of the Jasses before the other *tsotsi* sets – or the Uloans – did. The Ashakis rounded a corner – and nearly collided with the vanguard of another gang of *tsotsis*. The hands of the newcomers bristled with weapons, and fire-filled light glittered madly in their narrowed eyes. Those eyes suddenly widened in recognition when they saw Jass Mofo and the others.

"Ashaki," one of the others cried, spitting out the name of Mofo's set as if it were a deadly curse.

"Hafar," Jass Mofo said, naming the set that was the Ashakis' most dangerous rivals in the Maim.

The Ashakis didn't fail to notice the bulging sacks that several of the Hafars were carrying. The rival set had obviously learned of the Uloans' invasion well before the Ashaki, and had managed to beat their enemies to the prize. The triumphant expressions on their faces conveyed their scorn for the Ashakis' tardiness. But that didn't disturb Jass Mofo.

"You done our work for us, Hafars," he said. "Now, we gon' take what's ours."

A moment later, Athir found himself in the midst of a screaming, blood-spilling melee as the *tsotsi* sets tore into each other.

2

Bujiji lifted his face and screamed into the night sky. So did the rest of his band of marauders. Theirs was a cry of madness and ecstasy, and it was answered by shrieks of terror from the beleaguered inhabitants of Khambawe.

The Uloan warrior carried a sword in one hand and a torch in the other. Firelight emphasized the scars the covered his scalp, and in the wavering illumination, the interplay of light and shadow lent an illusion of life to the image of Legaba carved on his chest. To the Matile who fled before him, he looked like the incarnation of a demon from the time when the serpent Adwe circled the world.

He lowered his face. And he spotted new prey: a Matile family, all terrified, no one armed. Like a pack of the wild dogs that roamed the plains of the Mainland, Bujiji and the others swept down on the Matile before they could flee. With shouts of "Retribution Time" roaring from their throats, the Uloans butchered all the members of the family, from the doddering patriarch to a girl-child ripped from her mother's arms and skewered on a sword.

Then Bujiji tossed his torch into the house from which the family had attempted to escape. Flames caught on a tapestry that hung from a wall. The fire spread quickly, as had all the others the Uloans had set throughout Khambawe.

At the beginning of the invasion Bujiji's band, numbering only about three dozen, had split from the main force while the battle at the docks was still raging. Doing so had been part of the battle plan Jass Imbiah had received from Legaba. While the main part of the Matile army was locked in struggle against the *jhumbis*, small groups of marauders would fan out to wreak havoc on the rest of Khambawe.

Bujiji glanced down at the corpses of the family he and the others had slain. Blood seeped from the tangled braids on their heads, and spattered their unscarred skin. Never before had he seen his people's hereditary foes at such close range.

As his eyes lingered on the infant, Bujiji was reminded of Awiwi and the yet-to-be-born child she carried. But that thought quickly vanished. Burning and killing dominated his mind. It was Retribution Time, and as much as he and others had done so far, there remained more to do. Much more, even though the poison the *huangi* had infused on their sword-blades was losing its potency, diluted by the blood that coated the weapons from point to hilt.

Now, Bujiji looked behind him. Bodies littered the street. Houses were ablaze, their brightly painted walls turning black. Even the trees burned like giant torches. He turned to look ahead. The street was deserted. He and the other marauders had slain the last of those who had been slow to flee, and he saw no one else to kill.

Still, a sound reached his ears – a sound that rose above the roar of the flames. It was shouting – and a clash of weapons. The other Uloans could hear it as well. They looked at Bujiji, waiting for his command.

"Follow I," Bujiji said.

The Uloans sprinted toward the sounds. Blood dripped from their weapons, leaving a crimson trail on the street. The shouting became louder as they drew closer to its source. So did the clangor of weapons and the cries of the wounded and dying.

Bujiji frowned in puzzlement. As far as he knew, no other Uloans had penetrated this part of Khambawe. And he had no idea whom any Uloans might be fighting – the Matile soldiers should still be trapped on the docks by the *jhumbis*, and most of the other city-dwellers his band had encountered had been weaponless.

Still, if other Uloans were involved in this fighting, they could combine forces, Bujiji thought. And they could inflict even more Retribution Time destruction. That thought brought a smile to Bujiji's face.

They turned a corner – and nearly ran into a maelstrom of swinging weapons.

Even in the firelit darkness, a quick glance was sufficient to show the Uloans that none of the combatants was a fellow Islander, even though the fighters did not resemble any other Matile they had seen – and slain – so far. Still, they were all blankskins – the enemy.

Bujiji shook his head in amazement. Matile were fighting other Matile even as their city was being overrun by invaders. The battle was so intense that the Matile, all of whom appeared to be youthful, were not even aware of the Uloans' presence.

Them blankskins crazy, he thought.

Combined, the Matile combatants outnumbered Bujiji's band. But those numbers meant nothing; the mainlanders were fighting each other. Bujiji exchanged a glance with his marauders. They reached a quick, silent agreement that the risk they were about to take was worthwhile if it meant more dead blankskins. Then they charged into the thick of the fighting and plunged their weapons into anyone who stood in front of them.

3

Jass Mofo swung his *tirss*. Its tips tore through the face of the Hafar *tsotsi* in front of him. Strips of skin and an eyeball flew through the air as the screaming Hafar went down, hands clutching his ruined face.

Mofo's eyes darted left and right. No one else dared to come near him. His Ashakis and the Hafars were battling in a mutual frenzy. The bags of booty the Hafars had been carrying lay unattended, for now, in the street.

The Ashaki leader could not determine which side was winning. There was no time to consider the circumstances; he could sense another Hafar attacking him from behind.

With the quickness of a cobra, Mofo ducked and whirled. The

hooked tips of the Hafar's *tirss* passed less than an inch from his face. Continuing his spin, Mofo struck at the Hafar's midsection. His weapon's spikes shredded lean abdominal muscles and left wounds like those of a leopard's claws.

Howling in pain, the Hafar doubled over. Mofo landed a contemptuous kick to his foe's head, and the Hafar fell to the ground, where he writhed in agony before Mofo dispatched him with another vicious strike, then kicked him again for good measure. He turned, expecting another attack. But no one else approached him.

Again, Mofo scanned the scene of battle. His gaze caught the Fidi, Athir, who looked as though he was attempting to sneak away from the fighting. The foreigner was holding his dagger as if he thought it could ward off a blow from a *tirss*. Mofo had tried to teach Athir the use of the *tirss*, but the Fidi proved to be a poor pupil.

Mofo opened his mouth to shout at Athir. Then he closed it at the sight of a group of strangers suddenly joining the battle, cutting down Hafar and Ashaki alike.

The newcomers had struck silently, without warning, doing a great deal of damage before their presence was known. Now they shouted as one: "Retribution Time!"

At first, Mofo thought the intruders were some previously unknown set of *tsotsis*. A closer look, even in the firelit darkness, revealed their shaven heads and the spider-shaped scars on their bodies, and the madness blazing in their eyes; a vehemence that easily matched the inchoate fury that drove the *tsotsis*.

Mofo had never before laid eyes on an Uloan. But who else could these interlopers be? They certainly weren't Fidi; their skins were dark, not light like Athir's.

The Uloans' initial rush had cut a bloody swath through the *tsotsis*. Then Ashaki and Hafar alike turned their attention to the islanders while at the same time continuing to slash away at each other. It didn't take long for Mofo to understand that neither *tsotsi* set could survive such a three-way conflict – not with the Uloans fighting only one foe, while the *tsotsis* battled two.

Mofo came to a quick conclusion. Then he fought his way toward Jass Nunu, the leader of the Hafars. When he found his counterpart, their eyes met across the storm of slaughter that roiled between them. Jass Nunu was a little older than Mofo, but in many ways not as cunning.

At least, not until this night, considering that the Hafars were the first to take advantage of the unforeseen pandemonium unleashed by the hordes of screaming, scarred invaders.

"Nunu!" Mofo cried. "Truce! Heard?"

As Mofo had anticipated, his rival shared his conclusions.

"Heard!" Jass Nunu shouted in reply.

"Ashaki! Truce!" Mofo bellowed in the general direction of the members of his set.

"Hafar! Truce!" Nunu echoed.

Until later, both *tsotsi* leaders thought.

The moment they heard their leaders' commands, the *tsotsis* stopped fighting among themselves and turned their full attention – and wrath – on the Uloans. Taken aback by the sudden shift in the flow of the battle, the islanders fell back in confusion, and all the surviving *tsotsis'* weapons tore savagely into their ranks, forcing them to retreat.

Then a voice rose from the ranks of the Uloans.

"Retribution time!" Bujiji bellowed.

Immediately the intruders echoed the cry, then surged forward again, weapons swinging and mouths distended.

4

As their combat raged on, neither the Uloans nor the *tsotsis* could gain an advantage. The *tsotsi'* nihilistic viciousness was more than matched by the Uloans' fanatical frenzy. Mangled bodies lay sprawled in the street; gore slid across stone, but battle-rage on all sides was unabated, and blood-lust was not yet slaked.

Hyenas from a pack that had followed the *tsotsis* out of the Maim were already dragging some of the corpses away. The fires the Uloans had started crept closer to closer to the scene of the battle. But the combatants didn't feel the heat from the approaching flames, and they paid no heed to the hyenas.

Jass Nunu had gone down. His head and body lay several feet from each other. For now, the surviving members of the Hafar set were content to obey Jass Mofo's commands. They would name a new Jass later – if any of them survived the invasion.

Gore covered Mofo's leather battle-gear. Weariness seeped into his muscles as he struck, backed away, then struck again. His *tirss* was growing heavy in his hand. His speed was diminishing, and that loss was bringing him closer to death.

Never before had he and the other *tsotsis* been forced to engage in such sustained battle. *Tsotsi* fights tended to be fierce but short, with the losing side fleeing down the nearest alley once its cause appeared hopeless. But the Uloans fought to the death; even the gravely wounded in their ranks continued to swing their weapons until loss of blood or limbs brought them down. Slowly, the tide was turning against the *tsotsis*.

Had only one set of *tsotsis* been involved in the fray, it would have long since cut its losses and escaped. But there were two. If one fled, the other would quickly spread word of its lack of courage throughout the Maim, and that would be the end of the reputation the set needed to ensure its survival in the streets. Thus, the *tsotsis* stood, fought – and died, even as they dealt death in return.

During a brief respite, Mofo spotted the Uloan who appeared to be leading the others. As he looked at the muscular Islander, he realized he had only one chance to win the battle and save his set. He took it.

"You! Scar-head!" he called. "You and me! We fight for all! Heard?"

The common tongue of the Matile and Uloans had diverged greatly during their long period of hostilities, and the *tsotsis* spoke a variation of the language that was unique to them. Still, Bujiji understood Mofo's meaning well enough. It was a challenge he could not resist.

"Die, blankskin!" the islander replied.

The rest of the fighting subsided as the leaders approached each other on the blood-spattered street like gladiators in an arena. Bujiji was the larger and stronger of the two; Mofo the quicker and more agile. Both warriors were battle-weary, but the killing lust flared unabated in their eyes. Bujiji carried a curved sword to oppose Mofo's *tirss*. Blood dripped copiously from each man's weapon.

Sword and *tirss* flicked out in a few exploratory passes. Then Bujiji swung his sword. Instead of parrying with his own weapon, Mofo leaped backward to avoid the sword's deadly arc. He didn't want to catch his *tirss* on the edge of the sword.

Not yet ....

Mofo feinted, then jabbed his *tirss* at Bujiji's face. Bujiji swung in return and struck off one of the *tirss's* spikes, which pinged against a wall on the side of the street. The Uloan laughed when he heard the sound. He anticipated hearing it again.

Bujiji pressed forward. Mofo retreated, staying out of the bigger man's range, jabbing with his *tirss* to keep his foe at a distance.

"Why you run, blankskin?" Bujiji taunted. "I and I catch you soon enough."

Mofo did not reply. He kept moving.

Suddenly, Bujiji leaped forward and slashed at the *tsotsi's* head in an effort to open the *tsotsi's* defenses. But it was Mofo who saw the chance for which he had been waiting as he reached out with his *tirss* to parry the blow. The spikes of his weapon caught the Uloan's sword in mid-swing. With a practiced twist of his arms, Mofo yanked the trapped sword out of Bujiji's hand. The blade clattered to the street. And Bujiji stood defenseless.

Mofo did not pause to savor his triumph. The moment the Uloan's sword fell away from the *tirss*, Mofo swung with all his remaining strength. The spikes of the *tirss* bit deep into the side of Bujiji's head. Their tips punctured the Uloan's skull and lacerated his brain. Bujiji died instantly, a stare of astonishment frozen on his face. He was dead before any outcry could escape his throat

Still holding the shaft of his *tirss*, Mofo refused to allow Bujiji to fall. He glared at the other Uloans and called out, mockingly, "Retribution time!"

Then he released his hold on his weapon. Bujiji's corpse crumpled to the street. And the rest of the *tsotsis*, Ashaki and Hafar alike, descended on the suddenly demoralized Uloans with redoubled fury, their bone-weariness forgotten.

When the slaughter ceased, all the Uloans were dead; none of them had fled even though their leader had fallen and the tide had quickly turned against them. Most of the *tsotsis* were dead as well. Of the handful who survived, some were Hafar, a few more Ashaki. The difference didn't seem to mean much of anything anymore. The Ashakis' triumph over the Hafars and Uloans was hollow; only continued existence mattered to the victors.

The fires were still approaching, the flames so close now that the hyenas had ceased their scavenging and slunk back into the shadows. By the flames' increasingly lurid light, Mofo searched again for the Fidi, Athir. But the Ship's Rat was nowhere in sight.

Neither were the bags of loot over which the Ashaki and Hafar had been fighting before the Uloans intervened.

5

In a place that was a safe distance from the fires, Athir emerged from the sewer in which he had hidden the *tsotsis*' booty. He took a deep breath of night air, and coughed as a whiff of smoke entered his lungs. The last of the sacks was safely concealed; he had no need to endure the dank, fetid floor of the sewer beneath his feet any longer. Even the smoke smelled better than the waste-tunnel.

While the combat between the *tsotsis* and Uloans raged, Athir had found it a simple matter to remove the booty while avoiding fighters on both sides. No one had noticed him, and he hadn't been forced to kill anyone while he stole the loot behind their backs.

Although Jass Mofo had forced him into becoming an Ashaki, Athir didn't much care which side won the fight. The entire city seemed to be locked in a mad death-struggle that would end in great destruction. But Athir had survived many battles – even long wars. He knew that sooner or later the fighting would end, and life would continue, and people like him would always be around to take advantage of the aftermath of destruction.

He scraped as much of the sewer-offal as he could from his skin and clothes. He would wash the rest of it away later. For now, he needed to find a place to wait out the tide of devastation that was rapidly engulfing Khambawe. Whoever won in the end, the Ship's Rat would be there to seek new advantages in the aftermath.

CHAPTER SIXTEEN

SPIDERWEBS

1

The Gebbi Senafa was enveloped in an illumination that had not been caused by the fires that were ravaging so many other parts of Khambawe. Light from inside the building blazed from its windows and transformed the jewels embedded in its front door into constellations of multicolored stars. Ranks of soldiers patrolled the walls. The troops were positioned in a way that suggested greater numbers than were actually present, for Jass Eshana had ordered his men to give the impression that the Palace was to be defended at all costs to ensure the safety of the Emperor.

But, as planned, the Emperor was already elsewhere.

The Uloans had, indeed, attacked the Gebbi Senafa. However, the force that attempted to scale the walls and break down the bejeweled gates was smaller than the defenders had expected. And loud as their cries of "Retribution Time" had echoed, and intense as the efforts of the *jhumbis* had been to batter their way through the doors had been, the islanders' attack had been less furious than an attempt to slay an Emperor would have warranted.

But the defenders had no time to ponder the nature of the Uloans' attack. They were far too occupied with shooting volleys of arrows into the ranks of their foes and extinguishing the fires the Uloans attempted to set. The defenders were satisfied that they were diverting their foes from the Emperor's true location. Never did it occur to the Matile that they, in turn, were being distracted from the Uloans' true intentions, which took some of the intruders away from the Gebbi Senafa.

Even as fire and slaughter threatened to engulf the whole of

Khambawe, a segment of the Uloan invasion force had, toward the beginning of the battle, detached itself from the main body of attackers and drifted from them like a shadow cast by some gigantic winged creature hovering high above the scene of carnage. At first, the glare of fires from the city's streets illuminated the invaders' way as they moved away from the city – and the Gebbi Senafa. That light faded as its all-devouring source grew more distant.

These Uloans were silent. No cries of "Retribution Time" resounded from their throats. There were no shouts of triumph, or hatred, or bloodlust. Only the shuffle of many moving feet could be heard above the crackle of flames and the cacophonic din of the battle raging behind them.

The group encountered only a few people along its route, along which they travelled purposefully, as if they were absolutely certain of where they were going, even though none of them had ever before been in Khambawe. The luckless few city-dwellers who caught sight of them were dispatched immediately. However, the Uloans involved in this offshoot of the invasion did not venture to seek out other Matile to slay. And the buildings they passed remained unscathed, for these Uloans carried no torches for purposes of either illumination or destruction. Yet despite the darkness of the smoke-shrouded sky, they travelled unerringly, slowed only by the ponderous pace of the *jhumbis* that accompanied them. It was as though some unseen guide were unerringly leading them to their goal.

Soon they left the burning city behind. The smoke in the sky dissipated, and the light of the Moon Stars and the lesser stars illuminated the route ahead of the invaders. They continued in a near-silence that was even more ominous than the loud war-cries of the comrades they left behind.

The houses they passed now were deserted. Once they learned of the Uloans' attack, the inhabitants of Khambawe's outskirts either rushed into the city to aid in its defense, or gathered their belongings and fled into the countryside. Most of those who stayed behind managed to avoid death by hiding in cellars, or groves of trees. The Uloans made no efforts to root them out. Only a few more were luckless enough to be seen and killed by the invaders.

After the Uloans passed, the survivors left their hiding-places and scattered, leaving no one to tell the tale of what they had witnessed. As it was, none of them knew the invaders' destination.

The Uloans moved on, heeding the directions given to them by their unseen guide, who spoke in the voice of Jass Imbiah to the feathered *huangi* who led them. It pushed them forward, tramping through a field of flowers toward an immense, ancient edifice that had stood since the days before the destinies of the Matile and Uloans had diverged.

At the end of the field, the Uloans came to a halt. The voice that guided the *huangi* spoke a final time, ensuring that the invaders knew what they had to do. Once the voice was satisfied, it again urged the Uloans onward.

And as they moved forward, the Uloans continued to keep their "Retribution Time" chant in abeyance. They would shout it to the skies later, after they finished what they had been told to do: an act that would bring Retribution Time closer to its ultimate fulfillment ....

2

The old Gebbi Zimballa Palace had been erected during the reign of Emperor Dardar Birhi, the monarch who had begun Khambawe's transition from a modest seaside fishing town to its eventual status as the Jewel City of the Matile Mala Empire. With the passage of centuries, its splendor had diminished, and the efforts of even the finest painters and stonemasons could not forestall its eventual decline. Long ago, the Emperors had moved their residence to the newer Gebbi Senafa, which was located closer to the city. Yet the people of Khambawe did not demolish the old building, out of respect for its importance to their history. They continued to maintain the edifice, although it was seldom visited by anyone other than scholars who made use of the library still located within its walls.

Now, in Khambawe's time of peril, the Gebbi Zimballa had found another purpose to serve: refuge.

Inside the old palace, the Emperor and Issa tried to make themselves comfortable in the chamber that had been hastily prepared for them. According to the history woven into faded tapestries and preserved in leather-bound tomes that few other than the most dedicated historians had reason to peruse, the chamber had once served as the throne room of Emperor Dardar Birhi. When he was a child, Alemeyu had been an avid reader of those ancient volumes, and he remembered now that the territory

Birhi had ruled was about the same size as his own diminished empire. The irony inherent in that similitude was not lost on Alemeyu.

Both the Emperor and Issa left their steaming cups of *kef* untouched on a golden tray. Food and drink were not their primary concerns now.

Still clad in the armor of Issuri, Alemeyu sat on a throne of granite worn smooth by many the generations of previous monarchs that had used it. The royal seat in the Gebbi Zimballa was far less imposing than the Lion Throne in its successor palace. The carvings on its back and sides were barely visible. They represented the triumphs of Khambawe's earliest rulers over their rivals in other cities. Many years had passed since the last time an Emperor had sat on this throne. On its arms, Alemeyu could see traces of dust his retainers had left behind in their rush to make the long-disused chamber ready for him.

The Emperor had not reprimanded them for their neglect. This night was no time for formalities or protocol. He had already decided that he would not abandon the seat of his distant ancestors if Khambawe fell this night. In Birhi's time, the Zimballa had been as much a fortress as it was a palace. And in this old fortress, the last of the Matile Mala Emperors would live ... or die.

There was only one throne in the Gebbi Zimballa. For that reason, Issa sat on the topmost of the seven steps that led to the dais on which the throne was mounted. On those steps were carvings that, like the ones on the chair itself, had been diminished by time to mere scratches in the stone. Issa paid scant heed to the record of history upon which she rested. She sat with her arms wrapped around her knees, which she had pulled close to her chest. Her eyes were drawn to the shadows cast by the torches that were the only illumination in the chamber.

The few furnishings left in the throne room were familiar enough, despite their great age. But the shadows they cast seemed somehow sinister, like hands with grasping fingers pressed against the wall.

Makah, the Emperor's cheetah, lay curled like a house cat at Issa's side. The cheetah's eyes stared unblinking at the entrance to the chamber. If the spotted cat saw the shadows, it paid no heed to them.

With a slight shudder, Issa looked away from the shadows. She and the Emperor were alone in the old throne room. A retinue of soldiers was posted outside the door, and throughout the rest of the old palace as well. They, as well as the Emperor and Issa, knew if they were forced to fight here, it was likely to be their last battle.

Issa looked up at Alemeyu. The firelight cast no shadows on his gold-chased armor. Instead, the muted illumination rendered to him a radiance that she would, at another, less-fraught time, have admired. However, that luminescence did not reach his eyes.

Alemeyu was staring beyond Issa, and beyond the shadowy walls of the throne chamber. He could have been looking into the future or, perhaps, the past. Or he might have been looking into himself.

Whatever the Emperor was seeing, it displeased him. Beneath the golden helmet that crowned his head, Alemeyu's brows were knotted in a frown.

"I wish we had more news," Issa said, for not other reason than to break a silence she was beginning to find oppressive.

Her voice caused Alemeyu's head to snap forward, then back, as though he had suddenly awakened from a deep slumber. His brow smoothed, and his mouth turned upward in a fleeting smile.

"Considering what we have heard so far, I'm surprised you would say that," he told her.

That comment brought a smile in return from Issa – also fleeting. At the beginning of the invasion, a succession of runners had come from the city. The descriptions of defeat and destruction they brought with them fell like stones in Issa's heart, as well as Alemeyu's. Then the messengers stopped arriving. And that, in itself, bore a meaning that was ominous.

It was Alemeyu's brief smile, along with the tension that accompanied their long wait, that then caused Issa to say words she never imagined would ever spill out of her mouth … words she had never wanted anyone – including herself – to hear, despite the truth in them.

"Alemeyu," she said. "I am sorry I could not give you – and the Empire – an heir."

The Emperor looked at her in silence for a moment that seemed to stretch into eternity. As she returned his gaze, Issa was reminded of the day they had wed – an elaborate ceremony attended by the Degen and Imba Jassi, with Jass Gebrem pronouncing the ritual words that bound them to each other until she or the Emperor died, or one of them put the other aside.

Alemeyu had put three previous wives aside because they had not been able to continue the line of Issuri. Issa's predecessors had been well compensated, but they lived in tacit, unofficial exile from the Degen Jassi. They no longer even resided in Khambawe. Their continued presence in the court and the city would have been an affront to the Emperor's current consort, and an embarrassment to him.

On the day they were wed, Issa had vowed that such a fate would never be hers. *I will bear him a child*, she told herself fiercely. *I will* ....

But as the years passed, no heir was born. And before the Fidi came, before the Uloans came, she had known that before long, the Emperor would put her, too, aside.

Then Alemeyu spoke.

"The fault for that is not yours, Issa," he said. "It is mine."

3

As the voice that guided them had instructed, the Uloans halted well out of the view of any watchers on the walls of the Gebbi Zimballa. Without torches, and clad for the most part only in their dark, spider-scarred skin or, in the case of the *jhumbis*, smooth clay, they were invisible to all but the keenest eye. And the sounds of their leaders' murmured conversations did not carry to the ears of the palace's defenders.

The invaders listened closely to their guide. Then they fell silent ... and waited. A few moments later, the dark mass of the Uloans wavered subtly, like a shimmer of heat on a plain at the height of the dry season. And then they moved forward, making no attempt to conceal themselves.

They marched quickly across the remaining stretch of ground, making no sound other than the soft crunch of their feet against the flowers. Anyone watching from the ramparts could have seen them. And many of the soldiers whose sole duty was to defend the Emperor and Issa were gazing directly at the invaders coming toward the old palace. Yet they saw nothing... heard nothing.

The walls of the palace were riddled with pits and cracks ... easy hand- and foot-holds for a determined climber. And the Uloan invaders were nothing if not determined. Like a swarm of spiders, they scaled the palace's exterior. They left the *jhumbis* behind. But the walking dead would soon have their own part to play.

Only when the Uloans made their way over the ramparts did the soldiers finally become aware of their presence, as the air shimmered again. A moment later, the dumbfounded Matile found themselves facing a nightmarish horde of spider-scarred, wild-eyed invaders. For a moment, they were startled into immobility. And their recovery came much too late.

The Uloans drove their swords deep into the bodies of their foes, punching their weapons' points through leather armor and piercing hearts and entrails. Screams of agony shattered the silence of the palace, which was suddenly no longer so far removed from the slaughter that was occurring in the city.

Once the initial shock of the Uloans' sudden onslaught – as though they had materialized from the night itself – passed, the Matile soldiers retaliated, hacking and slashing in a frenzy of hatred and fear. Light from the Moon Stars reflected from spatters of blood and glinted in the glaze of dead men's wide-open eyes.

For all its desperate heroism, the Matiles' resistance had no chance for success. The first surge of the Uloans' onslaught had decimated the ranks of the defenders. And their abrupt appearance, seemingly out of nowhere, had left the soldiers confused and disoriented, even as they fought grimly and hopelessly for their lives, as well as those of their rulers.

In the midst of the unequal battle, several of the invaders broke away and cut down the Matile who were guarding the gates to the palace. Some of the Uloans died before their grisly task was completed. But those who lived were sufficient in number to pull the gates open, allowing the *jhumbis* to lumber inside.

Only then did the Uloans raise their triumphal cry: "Retribution Time!"

And, as the islanders mercilessly drove the remaining defenders away from the walls, shadows followed them.

4

Issa blinked, unsure that she had heard Alemeyu correctly. She realized that she had. But she still couldn't believe that the Emperor would ever have made such an admission.

"Alemeyu, you don't have to ..."

The Emperor held up a hand to forestall her.

"There is nothing else to say," Alemeyu told her. "I have always known that I am the reason I have never sired a child with you, or any of the others."

Issa did not know how to respond to that admission. She looked at Alemeyu as though she had never seen him before. In his eyes, she could see the shadows of dead dreams and many years of self-recrimination.

"I know what others say about me beyond my presence," Alemeyu continued. "My ears are everywhere."

"I never spoke of the problem to anyone," Issa said, still looking directly into Alemeyu's eyes.

"But you knew the truth, just the same."

Issa dropped her gaze.

"Yes," she acknowledged. "I knew."

After a moment of silence, Alemeyu spoke again.

"I would have put you aside once the talk became more than mere whispers that only the walls could hear," he said.

Issa looked at him again, and a sharp retort sprang into her mind. Before she could give it voice, Alemeyu continued.

"It would have been for the good of the Empire," he said.

Issa's spark of anger faded as quickly as it had ignited, for she knew Alemeyu was only speaking the truth.

"For the good of the Empire," she repeated dully, dutifully.

The Emperor rose from his throne then. He reached down, clasped both of Issa's hands in his, and gently raised her to her feet. As he looked into her eyes, she could see that for a moment at least, that shadows that haunted him were gone.

"Issa," he said softly. "No matter what happens now, I will never put you aside."

Unshed tears stung the corners of Issa's eyes as she smiled and squeezed Alemeyu's hands. She opened her mouth to speak – but a sudden yowl from Makah stopped her.

The hair around the cheetah's neck and shoulders bristled like a ruff. The great cat was still staring at the open entrance to the throne room. The soldiers who stood on guard did not appear to notice whatever it was that had disturbed Makah. A moment later, the cheetah bolted from the throne room. And a moment after that, a sudden commotion of battle reached the ears of Alemeyu and Issa.

The Emperor let go of Issa's hands and called to the guards at the entrance.

"What is going on out there?" he demanded.

Amid the patter of rushing footsteps, one of the guards entered the chamber. He was trying, unsuccessfully, to compose his face into a mask that would hide his fear.

"The Uloans are here, Mesfin," he said.

Alemeyu and Issa looked at each other. The shadows had returned to his eyes, and hers as well. Then the Emperor drew the Sword of Issuri from its gilded scabbard.

"Stand behind me," he told Issa.

Then he turned to face the entrance, swordhilt gripped tightly in both hands, even as the guards moved into a defensive formation and the sounds of fighting drew nearer to their door.

CHAPTER SEVENTEEN

ALMOVAAR COMES

1

The Beit Amiya was dark and silent. No Vessels stood before the unheeding images of the Jagasti. Instead, in front of each statue, an Amiya's mask lay face-down – a clear, if unspoken, reproach.

The Matile Mara Empire had been forsaken by its deities at a time when its people needed them most. No longer would the Amiyas be Vessels for the *ashuma* that had been passed down to them by the Jagasti since the day Etiya sang. The Vessels were now empty, waiting to be filled with the spiritual essence of a new deity.

In a courtyard outside the abandoned Beit Amiya, the Vessels gathered around the Seer Kyroun and Jass Gebrem. With the Vessels were the Almovaad Acolytes and Adepts: the Believers who had followed their Seer across the vastness of Cym Dinath and through the Sea of Storms. Now the new home that had been promised for the end of their long, dangerous journey was going up in flames. They could see long tongues of fire licking at the sky beyond them; they could hear the bizarre war-cries of the invaders and the hopeless wails of their victims; they could hear the crackling of flames and the occasional roar of collapsing buildings.

Yet their faith in Almovaar remained unshaken. And they were prepared to pass that faith – and its concomitant power and blessings – on to the Matile.

The Almovaads and the Matile sat on the ground in a wide circle that surrounded Kyroun and Gebrem. The two spiritual leaders were also seated. Gebrem's *abi* lay in front of them on the sward of clipped grass that stretched away like a dark-green lagoon.

"Almovaar will aid us this night," Kyroun said.

His comments were addressed to the Matile, not the Believers, who already knew what their Seer was going to say and do.

"But you must help me to summon him," Kyroun continued. "And to do that you must vow, for now hereafter, to serve Almovaar alone, and no other god or goddess of any kind."

"Be it so," the Almovaads said in unison.

Kyroun turned deferentially to Gebrem.

"The choice is yours," the Seer said. "And there is not much time left to make your decision."

From her place in the circle, Tiyana looked at her father. She knew him well enough to see what the others could not: his anguish; his deep humiliation. Gebrem had wielded most of the scant *ashuma* that remained to the Matile, and done so with all his faith in the Jagasti and the Empire, and to the best of his not-inconsiderable ability. And now even that tantalizing remnant of the power of *ashuma* was gone, as if it had never existed, as if it had never enabled the Matile to rule half a continent and sail across the world, as if the Matile were no better than the Thabas who lurked in their hills to the south ....

Now Khambawe, the Jewel City, was about to be incinerated.

Tiyana caught Gebrem's eye. Her father returned her searching gaze for a long moment, communicating a great deal to her without any necessity for words. Then he looked away.

"Be it so," Gebrem said quietly, echoing the words of the Believers, to whom he had now committed himself and the Amiyas.

Tiyana winced inwardly. She knew how much it cost her father to say those words. And she knew how much it cost her and the other Amiyas, for Gebrem was speaking for all of them as well as himself. He had previously discussed the matter with the Vessels, and they had all agreed that the Fidis' god should be given the opportunity to save the Matile.

Kyroun gave Gebrem a slight bow of acknowledgement.

Then he said: "Now we begin."

2

The masks in the Beit Amiya did not remain in their places for long. Dark, furtive figures scuttled from the shadows that dominated the main chamber. Quick hands seized the Jagastis' masks and stuffed them unceremoniously into sacks.

Kalisha glanced at the other *shamashas* who, like her, were fronting for *tsotsi* sets. Once it became clear that the Beit Amiya had been abandoned, the clandestine *tsotsis* had met and decided to partition the plunder the Vessels had left behind as though it no longer had any value to them. It had value to the *tsotsis*, though. Kalisha's sack was loaded with fine chains of silver and gold, as well as jewels pried loose from their mountings.

And now, the mask of Nama-kwah was hers. It rested in the sack on top of the rest of her booty.

She looked up into the face of the goddess's idol, half-hidden in darkness. Then she glared at a bigger, older female *tsotsi* whose covetous stare indicated that she might consider breaking the pact the thieves had reached. Already, avarice was undermining that agreement, and the *tsotsis* were beginning to dispute the ultimate distribution of their loot.

With one hand, Kalisha clutched her sack to her chest. With the other, she reached into her waistcloth and pulled out her dagger. The other *tsotsi* decided she could be satisfied with the contents of her own sack after all. Kalisha was small, but she had long since established herself as a deadly foe who could not be intimidated; a person whose dagger was quick to strike and quick to draw blood.

After her would-be foe retreated, Kalisha looked left and right to determine whether there were any others who thought they could rob her of what she had rightfully filched. There were none. Still on her guard, Kalisha quickly made her way out of the building.

As she left the Beit Amiya for the last time, the young *tsotsi* smiled in anticipation of what Jass Mofo's reaction would be when she emptied her sack at his feet, especially when he saw the Mask of Nama-kwah. And this time, she would chew the *khat* he was certain to offer her.

3

Jass Eshana swung into the saddle of his *quagga*. Dozens of other Matile soldiers also mounted up, the *quaggas'* hooves stamping against the street as the animals snorted and neighed in anticipation. The Dejezmek hefted the lance he carried, and was reassured by its weight and balance. The long, heavy weapon he and the others would carry held his last, desperate hope to break the back of the Uloans' invasion.

Ordinarily, he would never have considered using cavalry in a street battle. The narrow confines of the city's streets worked against the effective use of mounted troops. But this conflict had been far beyond the ordinary since the moment the Uloans and their *jhumbis* had swarmed onto Khambawe's docks. The battle was going badly for the city's defenders. Defeat appeared imminent. Even so, a new, unexpected change in tactics could well turn the tide in the Matiles' favor.

Eshana had assembled his hastily gathered force in a wide square normally used as a produce market. Here, the *quaggas* would have ample room to maneuver while the Dejezmek worked out the final details of his battle plan. When the Uloans reached the market, a surprise would be waiting for them.

Saddles creaked and harnesses jingled as the last defenders of Khambawe awaited Eshana's order to attack. Firelight glinted from the steel tips of their lances and pooled in the wide eyes of their steeds. Hands reached out to soothe the eager *quaggas*.

The Matile heard the Uloans long before they came into sight. Their incessant chant – *Retribution time!* – punctuated a chorus of maniacal shrieks.

Then they appeared, bursting into the market-square like a swarm of locusts. Blood dripped from their weapons and trickled across the scar-patterns on their faces and bodies. Flames of frenzy blazed in their eyes as they bellowed their chant as if it were a challenge to the world.

Eshana knew the Uloans had reached a state of complete battle-madness, in which they would kill and keep killing until no more of their enemies stood before them – or until no more Uloans remained on their feet. The islanders' advance had to be broken – now.

"Forward!" the Dejezmek commanded.

He spurred his *quagga* toward the Uloans. His troops followed him. He lowered his lance and tensed his arm muscles to absorb the jarring shock that would come when the point of his weapon impaled flesh and bone.

At the sight of the mounted force that confronted them, the Uloans halted their advance. But the contorted expressions on their faces never changed; their screaming never stopped. Showing a discipline that contrasted with their maniacal appearance, the islanders parted ranks, opening a path for the *jhumbis* that had come behind them.

The *quagga* Eshana rode was battle-tested. It had faithfully carried him on punitive attacks against rebel Jasses who no longer respected their ties to the Empire. And he had ridden it on lion hunts, in which he and the *quagga* came within spear-length of the great cats before he plunged his lance into their tawny hides and took their manes as trophies.

But something about the *jhumbis* – perhaps a stench of the supernatural that was beyond the perception of humans, but not animals – panicked Eshana's *quagga* this time. Eyes rolling in fear, the beast stopped short and reared, pitching Eshana from his saddle.

The other *quaggas* reacted similarly. In the blink of an eye, a potentially devastating cavalry charge became a turmoil of screaming, stampeding *quaggas*, fallen riders and broken lances. As the few Matile who had not been thrown struggled to control their steeds, the Uloans, led by the *jhumbis*, rushed forward in a wave of imminent mayhem. And the "Retribution Time" chant filled the market square.

Of this, Eshana knew nothing. He lay where he had fallen: neck broken, dead eyes staring sightlessly at the smoke-streaked sky.

4

"Clasp hands," Kyroun instructed.

Everyone in the circle obeyed. Tiyana's right hand was enfolded in that of her friend, Keshu. With her left, she held the hand of a blue-robed Almovaad – Byallis, with whom she had become acquainted, if not friendly. She noted that Ruk, the giant Northlander, was seated on the other side of Keshu. Keshu was a big man himself, but he appeared small next to the Acolyte.

She also caught herself staring at Ulrithana, the Shadimish Adept. In general, Fidi were different on the surface from the Matile. But Tiyana sensed in Ulrithana an *otherness* that went deeper than dissimilarities in skin and hair color. She could not understand it more than that, and there was no time to explore the matter any further.

"Open your minds and hearts to Almovaar," Kyroun instructed. "Prepare yourselves to enter into the Oneness. Allow Almovaar's essence to become part of you."

In her mind, Tiyana bid a regretful farewell to Nama-kwah. At least, she now knew the Goddess's final warning had referred to the Uloans, not the Fidi, as she had once suspected. And she supposed she should be grateful for that much. Then Tiyana opened herself to Almovaar's Oneness.

She kept her eyes on Gebrem and Kyroun. The Seer led the Believers in a chant that had the rhythm of a song. Byallis had turned her head toward her, and now began to mouth the chant into Tiyana's ear. And she saw Ruk speaking into Keshu's ear as well.

The words, in the language of the Fidi, were meaningless to her. And she knew Gebrem didn't understand them, either. Yet as the chant grew louder, she saw her father's lips move. And she heard his voice join that of Kyroun, pronouncing the same words as if they were in his own language.

Although the sight and sound startled Tiyana, she did not have time to react to it any further. For now her own mouth had begun to move, and the words of the chant were drawn involuntarily from her throat.

Fingers of fear touched Tiyana's spine. She heard Keshu's deep voice beside her, speaking the alien syllables. When she tried to look at him, she found that she could not move her head. Again and again, she tried to perform the simple movement, and she could not do it.

Now the fear-fingers clutched hard. Tiyana tried to pull her hands out of the others' clasp. It was impossible. Her body no longer belonged to her; it no longer responded to the commands her brain gave it.

Still chanting involuntarily, she stared at the *abi*, which still lay in front of Kyroun and Gebrem. The rod was beginning to glow ... and change.

In the silvery light that surrounded the *abi*, the symbols of the Matile gods that had been engraved along its length ages ago shimmered, then faded until the metal rod became smooth and featureless as a shaft of starlight. A moment later, it rose into the air and hung in front of the Seer and the Leba. To the wide-eyed Tiyana, the *abi* – if it could still be called that – appeared to beckon to her father, as well as the Seer.

Kyroun ended the chant. All fell silent. Then he reached out and grasped the glowing rod. It appeared to merge with his hand.

The Seer looked at Gebrem.

"We must do this together, in the Oneness," he said.

Gebrem hesitated. The disappearance of the symbols from the *abi* marked a turning point. Instincts instilled by the practice of *ashuma* told him there would be no way he could go back to his old life once he touched the transformed instrument of power.

And just what was that life? he asked himself.

His city was burning around him. His people were dying. The world he had known was ending. Gebrem's hand crept toward the rod that had been passed down unaltered for countless generations. Now it had changed. And it was time for him to change as well.

His fingers curled around the rod.

And everyone assembled in the circle, Amiya and Believer alike, cried out in agony and wonder at the force that suddenly flowed like a surge of lava through their bodies and souls.

5

Deities do not die. Weak or strong, worshipped or abjured, they dwell in their infinite, timeless Realms beyond the world. Within that isolation, the petty concerns of the mortals' sphere can be as distant, or immediate, as the gods and goddesses desire them to be ....

In their Realms, the Jagasti dwelt in isolation. Long ago, they had forsaken direct involvement in the lives of their worshippers. They retained a tangential and superficial role over the centuries that had passed since the calamity of the Storm Wars. Now the people who venerate them were in peril. But the Jagasti could do nothing; they had spent too much of their endless time in their own Realms, and their potency in the mortals' world had diminished accordingly – and voluntarily. And so their Vessels had abandoned them and turned their worship to a new divine being.

Once they had walked among the Matile, and were part of their lives. Now they could only watch helplessly as a new conflict shook not only the world of mortals, but the Jagastis' Realms as well.

Only one deity continued to play a direct role in the world of mortal -- Legaba. The other gods had long since cast him from their company. They considered him a fool and left him to pursue his twisted dreams. Now that those dreams were becoming a terrible reality, they still did nothing ....

6

Legaba's Realm was a gray, gloomy place replete with leafless black trees. The branches of the trees intertwined like huge spiderwebs, and were bowed down as though in perpetual sorrow. Neither sun nor Moon Stars shone in Legaba's Realm. Still, a dim twilight illumination glistened in drops of water that clung like oily perspiration to the tree trunks. The trees did not grow out of soil, but out of water ... dark water covered with green slime and festooned with grass that was sharp as the blades of knives.

Legaba's Children – pythons, toads, crocodiles, water-rats and other creatures of the dank swamplands – crawled and slithered through the trees and splashed noisily in the foulness that surrounded their maker. More than anything else, though, the Realm teemed with spiders ... spiders of all shapes and sizes, from tiny creatures no bigger than a thumbnail to gigantic predators the size of lions.

In the midst of his endless swamp, Legaba loomed like a mountain. His immense, arachnid body was larger than an elephant's. Eight eyes burned like crimson coals in his formless face. But instead of the eight limbs of the spiders that surrounded him, Legaba had dozens, each one thicker than a python's coils. Those limbs waved constantly, as though stirred by an errant breeze. But there was no wind of any kind in Legaba's Realm ... only an oppressive humidity that weighed the air down like a gigantic blanket of wetness.

Legaba poured his twisted *ashuma* into the supplicant souls of his minions in the mortals' world through the medium of Jass Imbiah. He knew they were winning their battle. And when it was over, the ultimate victory would belong to him, not his followers, regardless of what he would lead them to believe.

He also knew his own battle had yet to begin. The one who aided the doomed worshippers of the other Jagasti was coming to him. He knew it. He could feel it. As if in anticipation of what Legaba had already sensed, his Children swam, scurried and dove away from him, even the spiders. For they knew the coming battle would be his alone, not theirs.

Suddenly, Legaba's limbs ceased their movement. His eyes flared like small suns. Then, with a loud, rending sound, the fabric of his Realm was ripped apart as though it were nothing but a sheet of flimsy cloth.

A white-gold opening split the dark sky. The aperture quickly extended down to the swampy soil. Trees toppled; stagnant water bubbled and hissed, fleeing creatures screamed as they were boiled alive.

Then, out of the substance of the light, Legaba's adversary took form. Manlike in shape, Almovaar stood as tall as a tree. Like a silhouette of light, his face and body showed no features.

A substance that resembled sand turned into motes of light that swirled around him. No words passed between the two deities as Almovaar confronted Legaba. None were necessary.

Almovaar stretched his arms, and the trees closest to him burst into golden flames, casting unwelcome illumination on the desolation that surrounded Legaba. In response, Legaba's numerous limbs stretched with frightening speed toward Almovaar. One by one, they wrapped around the intruder until he could no longer be seen, his light snuffed out as though it had never existed.

Then Legaba's tentacles contracted, squeezing inexorably, compressing the once-imposing manifestation of Almovaar into a sphere no bigger than a berry.

Legaba's multiple eyes flared in triumph. Then the sphere exploded, and bits of Legaba's flesh hurtled through the fetid air. Legaba's body shuddered, and his fragmented tentacles hung limp, powerless, even though they continued to move.

His form restored, Almovaar towered over Legaba. His effulgence blazed even brighter, and Legaba's vast bulk appeared to shrink under the merciless illumination.

Then a javelin of light appeared at the end of Almovaar's hand. At first, the weapon was part of the deity's substance. And then, suddenly, it wasn't. Like a bolt of lightning, it flashed toward – then into – Legaba.

Legaba's tentacles writhed wildly, smashing limbs from the nearest trees. His body bulged and contracted like a blacksmith's bellows. His eyes sizzled and sparked, then grew dim as Almovaar's spear of light consumed him from within.

Golden fissures appeared on Legaba's surface. They spread and connected until they formed a web that ensnared him in immobile agony. Legaba lay helpless, netted like some gigantic fish. Or like a spider snared in its own web. Of his Children, there was no sign.

Almovaar cast a final, disdainful glance at his vanquished foe. Then, in a blinding burst of incandescence, he vanished from Legaba's grim Realm, leaving only his net of golden fire behind to dispel the darkness.

Deities cannot die. Immortality is both their blessing and their curse. But they can be made to suffer – as can their worshippers. @

7

Like Legaba, Jass Imbiah sat at the center of a vast web. She confidently wove its strands from her place on one of the many ships that crowded the harbor of Khambawe. She monitored and controlled the movements of her fighters and *jhumbis*. Her *huangis*, some of whom remained with her on the ship while the others were positioned in other sea-craft and in the city, had easily held the negligible *ashuma* of their Matile foes in check.

For a fleeting moment, the more-potent magic of the Tokoloshe had caused Jass Imbiah some concern. But the Tokoloshes' numbers were too few, and the *ashuma* Legaba continually poured into Jass Imbiah was more than enough to offset the minor threat the Tokoloshes' magic posed.

Although the Uloan ship rocked gently, Jass Imbiah remained motionless, eyes staring straight ahead, face composed in a mask of concentration. In the depths of those dark eyes, however, the *huangi* gathered around her could detect an ember of triumph that was about to burst into an all-consuming incandescence.

Khambawe was burning. Its people were dying in droves. Jass Imbiah had tested the power of her Matile counterpart, Jass Gebrem, and found it sadly wanting. She had taunted him to demonstrate her contempt, then unleashed the full magical might Legaba had invested within her.

Now, as Legaba had promised Jass Imbiah's ancestors, Retribution Time had come. Soon, the mainland would belong to the Uloans ...

Jass Imbiah went rigid. The *huangi* tensed in anticipation. They believed Legaba was about to ride her a final time, imbuing her – and them – with the final measure of *ashuma* needed to ensure victory.

The *huangi* were wrong in their assumption. But Jass Imbiah could not tell them that, or anything else. She could not tell them Legaba was ... *gone*. One moment, he was as much a part of her as her bones and blood;

the next he had vanished like a ray of sunlight cut off by a cloud. And in an awful burst of insight, she realized that the cloud would never pass, and Legaba was gone from her forever.

She longed to cry out in protest and despair. But she couldn't. The moment Legaba left her, another presence filled her in his place. It was the adversary Legaba had revealed to her on the islands after the message from the mainland had arrived.

In her last instant of life, Jass Imbiah attempted to shout a warning to the *huangi*. But no sound escaped her throat. Instead, her mouth stretched across her face in a rictus that caused blood to drip from its corners. Her eyeballs bulged in their sockets. Her nostrils flared to an unnatural width.

Then, before the horrified gazes of the *huangi*, Jass Imbiah's body imploded, as though her skull and bones had suddenly turned to water. Like a burst bladder, her body collapsed within her robes. Her remnants stained the floor of the ship's cabin.

And the *huangi* stood alone ... powerless... helpless ....

CHAPTER EIGHTEEN
The End of the Uloans

1

Waves of sorcerous potency streamed through Jass Gebrem. Blue radiance enveloped his body. His transformed *abi* shone like the most brilliant of all the Moon Stars. In that blaze of light, he could barely make out the features of Kyroun, who remained at his side. The Amiyas and Believers who surrounded them were little more than blurry shadows that blended with the background.

Within the Oneness, Gebrem, Kyroun and the others had witnessed Almovaar's victory over Legaba in the Spider God's Realm. And they had seen the demise of Jass Imbiah, as well as the resulting panic among the suddenly powerless *huangi* and their followers. And they knew that although the battle had shifted in their direction, it had not yet been won. There was more that needed to be done if Khambawe was to be saved.

No longer did Gebrem feel helpless to do it. The greatest amount of *ashuma* he had ever managed to summon was as nothing compared to the magical strength that now flowed through every fiber of his body. His ancestors must have known power like this, he thought, when they held sway over half of Abengoni ....

This, he exulted, *is how it must feel to be a god!*

Kyroun came into focus, then. The Seer's face bore an expression of reproach, if not disappointment. And Gebrem immediately understood the reason for that reaction. Matile were dying in the streets, and here he was, reveling in personal power rather than concentrating on how he would use it to defeat the Uloans. A sudden shame flooded through him. Perhaps he did not deserve this gift from the new god ...

Then Kyroun spoke inside Gebrem's mind.

I had similar thoughts when I was first granted this power, my friend. There is no need for shame. There is only the need to do what has to be done.

I understand, Gebrem said.

The Leba reached out. His hand closed around the glowing shaft of his *abi*. At the moment, he had neither plan nor strategy to save Khambawe, only the raw capability. But the moment his fingers touched the *abi*, he was given the knowledge of what he should do.

And, with the help of the others in the Oneness, he did it.

2

In the burning, blood-soaked streets of Khambawe, no one noticed the coming of the blue mist ....

The Uloans, sensing victory within their grasp, pressed inexorably forward. They fought tirelessly, and the *jhumbis* gave them an advantage the Matile were unable to overcome. Many invaders fell, but the Matile were too hard-pressed to organize a co-ordinated strategy to repel the invaders.

Although they refused to surrender to the Uloans, the Matile were beginning to succumb to an inevitable fatigue and despair as the fighting wore on. Even so, some of the surviving city-dwellers had taken up fallen weapons and were fighting at the side of the soldiers. And they wreaked their share of vengeance against the marauders who burned their homes and killed their families.

Yet despite their most desperate and courageous efforts, the defenders were unable to forestall the destruction of the city and their lives. Now, their only solace was that they were prepared to sell their lives as dearly as possible.

The smoke that had enveloped Khambawe like a deadly, choking fog rendered the mysterious mist nearly invisible. Only the leaping flames of a thousand fires provided illumination through the swirling gray clouds that had become a barrier between Khambawe and the rest of the world. It was toward the flames that the mist drifted.

Floating in tiny tendrils, the mist appeared as insubstantial as morning dew – until it reached the fires that were devouring the buildings of Khambawe. The moment the substance of the mist touched a licking flame, a small hiss sounded – and the flame went out. This happened again and again, as though the fingers of a gathering of giants were reaching down to snuff out hundreds of candles.

One by one, the fires were extinguished. At first, the combatants did not notice what was happening because they were fully absorbed by their fight for survival. But as more and more flames disappeared, darkness gradually descended until Matiles and Uloans alike paused in their struggle and watched with haggard and apprehensive expressions on their faces as the last of the flames winked out.

With a pall of smoke obscuring the Moon-stars, a shroud of near-total darkness enfolded Khambawe. The fighting ceased altogether, for the combatants could no longer see their foes. Even the *jhumbis* stopped moving. The only sound that could be heard was the labored breathing of people who had pushed themselves beyond the limits of their endurance, but didn't realize they had done so until now.

Then a point of light appeared in the sky ... a speck that rapidly grew into an orb the size of the sun. The new night-sun was clearly visible even through the smoke. It was as though the hidden Moon Stars themselves had coalesced into a single sphere of radiance. From that sphere, a flood of silvery-blue luminescence poured down on Khambawe, its illumination picking out the smoldering ruins of buildings; the dead and wounded that littered the streets; the pools of blood awash in the gutters; the lines of fatigue that scored the faces of those left standing.

As the Matile and Uloans blinked in the unnatural illumination, the *jhumbis* stood immobile. The clay that covered their skin seemed to be attracting the light ... and absorbing it. Within moments, the *jhumbis* glowed like torches – yet they cast no heat. Even so, the *jhumbis* did not move. Their weapons remained in their hands, but they no longer swung in deadly arcs. The *jhumbis* looked like crude effigies of clay rather than fearsome creatures of nightmare. They stood forlornly, helplessly within nimbuses of pale luminescence.

Then cracks began to form on the *jhumbis*' coverings, spreading like spiderwebs. And the bits of shell that formed their eyes and teeth loosened and dropped to the ground, where they broke into tiny pieces. The cracks widened, and the gaps were filled with a pale, foul-smelling ichor that streamed down their bodies and pooled at their lumpish feet. And flakes and shards of clay from the *jhumbis*' body-coverings rained into the spreading puddles of ooze that mingled with the blood in the streets.

Then the *jhumbis* swayed, staggered, and finally collapsed, as though the eldritch forces that animated them had abruptly disappeared. Their weapons clattered to the stones that paved the streets, and where seemingly invincible enemies once stood, there now lay nothing but heaps of clay, bone, shell, and rapidly decomposing viscera.

An eye-watering stench rose from the remains of the *jhumbis*. But to the beleaguered Matile, that noisome odor was as welcome as a fresh sea-breeze. For with the demise of the *jhumbis*, the Uloans had just lost their most effective weapons and their most reliable shields. Now, they would be forced to continue the fight on the defenders' terms.

Even worse for the Uloans was the sudden disappearance of the goading influence of the *huangi* from the depths of their minds: a constant prodding and encouragement that kept fear and weariness at bay and pushed them to efforts well beyond the limits of human endurance. As long as that presence was there, the warriors were nearly as tireless as the *jhumbis*, if not nearly as impregnable. Even deep wounds had less effect on them than scratches; their courage blazed like an unquenchable fire. Even death did not daunt them, for they believed that in death, they would live forever in Legaba's Realm.

Now, their link to Jass Imbiah and, through her, to Legaba was gone. As their weapons dangled slackly in their hands, the Uloans stood confused and uncertain in the glare of the silver-blue sphere in the sky. Their maddening chorus of "Retribution Time" had fallen silent since the flames had vanished and the blue light appeared. And now, no Uloan was willing to resume the shouting of their battle cry.

At that moment, the defenders of Khambawe needed no command from their leaders to take advantage of the opportunity that fell into their hands. A murderous rage lifted their spirits and banished the fatigue from their limbs. Now it was they, not the Uloans, who were the tireless ones. Yelling in triumph and vengeance, they fell upon the dispirited Uloans like a pride of lions ravaging a flock of sheep.

3

Tiyana was lost in the Oneness of the Almovaar. No longer was she only herself. Along with Gebrem, Kyroun and the Amiyas and Almovaads, her individuality melded with the essence of the Almovaads' god. What one of them saw, they all saw. What one thought, they all thought. What one did, they all did. And what one knew, they all knew ...

Tiyana had known Keshu since they met as children consecrated to the House of Amiyas – she because of her bloodline; he because his affinity for *ashuma* had been recognized and encouraged. They had been friends from the beginning of their time in the service of the Matile deities. But only now, in the consciousness they shared with Almovaar, did she become aware of the love he had hidden from her all that time.

He concealed it because her father, the Leba, was of the highest royal blood; while Keshu's sire had been a sword-maker from a small village close to the Thabas' country. A union between them would be precluded by custom, if not law. So Keshu had remained silent and kept his longing deep within himself. But she hadn't ever known of it – until now.

Their difference in social standing had never mattered to Keshu and Tiyana before, because he had so carefully kept his true feelings to himself. And now ....

She couldn't think further about it now. She could not even turn her head to look at Keshu. The Oneness continued to hold her – and him – in an unbreakable grasp.

That always happens the first time, an unspoken voice assured her.

Again Tiyana tried, and failed, to turn her head. Still, she knew the speaker was Byallis, the Adept whose hand held hers.

You can learn how to shield your thoughts, Byallis continued. *I will teach you, after this is over.*

In an eyeblink's time, the woman allowed Tiyana to know in full who she was. Her complete name was Byallis ni Shalla, and her home was

Ul-Enish, a city located near Lumaron, Kyroun's home. Ul-Enish had been one of the first stops on the Seer's westward journey, and Byallis had readily chosen to join the Almovaads to escape the drudgery and abuse she endured as a servant to a mean-spirited lord who had been happy to see her go.

Kyroun had uncovered a talent for sorcery Byallis had never known she possessed. And she had risen to the highest rank of the Initiates.

So can you, Byallis assured her. And she gave Tiyana's hand a squeeze.

Before Tiyana could respond, a new vision entered into the Oneness. Almovaar was showing them how the battle was progressing. It was as though they were birds hovering over the blood-washed streets of Khambawe. The Matile in the Oneness winced at the sight of the burned buildings and the bodies in the streets. But they saw something else that lifted their hearts – but also fuelled their anger.

They saw the Uloans in full rout, pursued like hares by soldiers and any other Matile who could hold a weapon. Fear led urgency to the islanders' flight, and they were outdistancing their dogged pursuers. Once they reached the docks, boarded their vessels and sailed away, they would be free from further retaliation, for the Matile's ships had all been destroyed.

Driving the Uloans back to their islands would be victory enough for Jass Gebrem. Surely a defeat as devastating as the one the Matile were now inflicting would deter the Uloans from attacking the mainland again....

What if it doesn't, Kyroun whispered in Gebrem's mind in the Oneness. *What if they try again, ten, twenty, one hundred years from now?*

Gebrem did not reply. But he was thinking the same thing.

There is a way to ensure an end to this now and forever, Kyroun continued. *Your people have always known that an end is needed. And now, you can produce that end.*

And, for the second time since he had come to Khambawe, the Seer pulled his ancestor's small Ishimbi statue from the folds of his robe.

The moment Gebrem saw the replica, he remembered the legends of how his ancestors had utilized the Ishimbi during the Storm Wars. A skeptical part of him had doubted those old stories, for all that they were memorialized in books and woven in tapestries. Now, though, he believed them. And, gathering and focusing the *ashuma* that coursed through him, he began to do what Lebas of the past had done in the Matile's time of need.

4

In the witch-light that dispelled the darkness of night, Pel Muldure could see the enemy drawing farther away. He was not surprised that the scar-covered madmen were escaping. They knew the Ma-teel sought vengeance; there would be no mercy for any islander caught alive in the city their invasion had come close to obliterating.

Muldure, too, wanted revenge – for the deaths of his crew members and the loss of his ship. It infuriated him that he and the others had survived the Sea of Storms, only to face death and destruction at the hands of an enemy that wasn't even theirs.

Of course, with his surviving shipmates, he could build another ship. But that would take time. And once a new ship was seaworthy, where would he sail it? Back into the Sea of Storms?

That didn't matter so much now. What mattered most to him was catching and killing as many of the invaders as he could.

Not so brave now that your walking lumps of clay are gone, are you? he thought vindictively.

He cast a glance toward Lyann, who was running at his side. Her clothing had been cut to shreds, and gore spattered nearly every inch of her exposed skin. She had several open wounds, but no blood flowed from them. She should have been too exhausted to move. But she wasn't. And neither was he.

He knew such stamina was unnatural; that rage alone could not account for it. Clearly, it was a gift bestowed by the same sorcery that created the light; and like all such boons, its price would be tallied later. For now, though, he was satisfied that he still had a chance to kill a few more of the invaders before they were gone.

The Matile and the *White Gull* crew formed a ragged, intermingled line of pursuit. Military discipline had long since vanished; Matile officers ran alongside ordinary soldiers without issuing commands. Streams of civilians joined them, ranging in age from small boys and girls to elderly men and women. Some of them wielded weapons they had picked up from corpses; others made do with sticks, clubs and pieces of broken masonry. The hatred Muldure saw on their faces made him happy he wasn't an Uloan, and didn't look like one.

Far behind came the Tokoloshe and their paler-skinned Dwarven kin. Although their arms were stronger than those of almost any human, the legs of dwarvenkind were not nearly long enough to keep pace. They labored on, hoping that the final battle would not be over by the time they reached it.

No cries of triumph rose from the throats of the pursuers. And the Uloans' "Retribution Time" chorus had long since fallen silent. The only sound in the city was the pounding of feet against the stones of the streets and the harsh inhalation and exhalation of breath from pursued and pursuers alike.

Soon the docks came into view. The wharves were strewn with corpses from the earliest stage of the battle, before the invaders had broken through Khambawe's first line of defense. The Ishimbi statues appeared to glare down at the Uloan ships, which had already moved to a safe distance from the docks. From the decks of the sea-craft, crewmen tossed ropes that dropped down the hulls, then stretched like snakes on the surface of the water. The ropes would provide rescue for those among their fleeing comrades who managed to live long enough to reach them.

Leaping over the corpses, the surviving Uloans hurried toward their ships. Before diving into the water to make their escape, they turned to face the Matile one last time. When the first of their foes came within throwing distance, the Uloans hurled a lethal hail of weapons. Scores of spears, daggers, even swords hurtled toward the Matile. Those who were quick enough raise their shields in time survived. Those who had no shields, or could not lift them swiftly enough, died or were grievously wounded.

Then the Uloans began to dive into the water and swim toward the lifelines. The Matile who survived their foes' final fusillade charged forward, intent on putting whatever laggards they could find to the sword. Cries of frustration rose from their throats as they realized they were not going to reach the Uloans in time.

And no one heard the creak of stone coming to life ... not until the Ishimbi statues began to move ....

The sudden animation of the Ishimbi brought everyone to a halt.

For a long moment everyone, Matile and Uloan alike, stood frozen, eyes wide in fear and wonder as the Ishimbi walked toward the harbor. Legs that had no feet dented the docks; arms that had no hands moved as though they were reaching for the enemy. It was as though a stand of trees from the distant forest had come to life and were marching to the aid of Khambawe.

The bottom of an Ishimbi's leg crushed a luckless Matile who was too awestruck to step aside. As if the man's death were a signal, the city's defenders scrambled out of the walking statues' path.

Many Matiles cried out in exultation when they realized that an ancient legend had inexplicably come to life. It was said that in their last effort to help their people during the Storm Wars, the Jagasti had brought the Ishimbi to life and used them to spare Khambawe from destruction.

Now, the legend was repeating itself.

"The Jagasti have returned to us!" the Matile shouted. And they joyfully cried out the names of their normally aloof pantheon.

But the Fidi – Believers and non-Believers alike – whispered the name of another deity.

"*Almovaar* ...."

In sudden terror, the Uloans who were still on the docks leaped into the water. The splashes of their frenzied swimming echoed above the sounds of the Ishimbis' slow progress. When the gigantic statues reached the edge of the docks, they simply stepped into the air. Then they plunged straight down into the harbor.

The sound of their landing in the water echoed like a series of thunderclaps. Gouts of water geysered upward and landed like a torrent of salty rain on the faces of the Matile and the Fidi. Waves rolled out from the point of their landing, drowning many Uloans before smashing into their ships. The ships rocked wildly, but remained afloat.

Cautiously, the Matile made their way to the dockside. They saw the Uloan sea-craft retreating, even as the survivors swam frantically toward the lifelines. The ships moved more slowly than they had when they entered the harbor, for there were no *jhumbis* left to pull the oars with inhuman speed. Already, the swiftest-swimming Uloans were dodging oar-strokes and clambering up the sides of the hulls.

Then the featureless heads of the Ishimbi broke the surface of the water like those of gigantic fish. The statues rose higher, until their dripping, handless arms became visible. Then they moved forward. And the muffled thud of their leg-stumps against the harbor's bottom reached the ears of

Matile and Uloan alike. Their advance toward the ships was as inexorable as the approach of the rainy season, and even though they did not move swiftly, they pushed their way through the water faster than the Uloan oarsmen were able to row.

As though with one voice, the Uloans screamed out their hopeless fear. They begged Legaba and Jass Imbiah to save them. But those cries went unanswered as the Ishimbi reached their ships. Oars splintered like sticks against the Ishimbis' adamantine forms. Then the Ishimbis' arms struck their first blows against the hulls.

The ships shuddered as though in agony. Huge holes appeared where the Ishimbis' arms hit – above and below the water's surface. The Ishimbis struck again and again, turning the stout timbers of the ships into kindling. Scores of Uloans fell into the water like ants from a hill torn apart by the claws of a badger. Some sank; others struggled desperately to the surface of the water, where they stared in dread and resignation at the destruction that surrounded them in the city they believed they were destined to destroy.

Rapidly, the ships disintegrated, then sank. When the last vessel of the invading fleet went down to the bottom of the harbor, the Ishimbis stopped moving. It was as though they were ... waiting.

In silence, the defenders of Khambawe lined up at the edge of the docks and stared out at a scene of sheer desolation, starkly illuminated by the night-sun the power of Almovaar had placed in the sky.

Floating scraps of wood and sail-cloth were all that was left of the Uloans' ships. Human forms bobbed amid the flotsam – most of them dead, others alive. Some of the survivors swam aimlessly, pushing corpses and wreckage aside. Others simply floated and stared at the sky. And there were those who shouted defiance and waved their fists at their enemies.

The defenders, Matile and Fidi alike, looked at each other. They knew what the Ishimbi were waiting for; they knew what had to be done. Although their blood had only shortly before pulsed with the lust to kill, they loathed the thought of undertaking the final, gruesome task that lay before them.

Still, it had to be done ...

Soldiers stripped off their cumbersome armor. Everyone, military and others alike, put aside their heavier weapons, took up whatever knives and daggers they could find, and placed them between their teeth. Then they jumped into the water and swam toward the defeated, weaponless Uloans, who remained hopelessly defiant while they waited to be slain.

CHAPTER NINETEEN

Aftermath

1

The glare of the new day's sun painted a pitiless portrait of the devastation the Uloans' invasion had wrought on Khambawe. The night-sphere fashioned by the Almovaad Adepts and the Amiyas in their Oneness had long since disappeared. Even the mist that constantly drifted in from the sea had thinned, laying bare the extent of the worst damage that had been done to the Jewel City since the long-ago end of the Storm Wars.

In the harbor, wreckage from sunken and half-sunken ships pounded against the docks like the drums of a death-god. Bloated corpses blanketed the surface. The small amount of water that could be seen between the bodies and the ships was tinged with red. Already, sharks and other sea-scavengers were devouring the remains, of which most were Uloan. But more than a few Matile dead provided food for the scavengers as well, for the Uloans had fought until the last of them died. As the sea-creatures competed viciously for their repasts, the harbor roiled as though a storm stirred its waters.

The Ishimbi statues once again stood in their places at dockside. They were still wet, and the dampness caused the dark stone surface of the gigantic carvings to glisten in the sun. Tufts of seaweed from the harbor clung to the Ishimbi, mute testimony to the events of the night before, which before then would have been thought to be possible only in legends.

On the streets of Khambawe, the survivors of the melee wandered in weary aimlessness, or lay exhausted amid the bodies of the fallen. Lakes of blood congealed on the paving stones. Burnt skeletons of trees stood like mute sentinels guarding a realm of ghosts. Charred timbers poked from piles of rubble where buildings proud and humble alike once stood. Soot obscured the brightly painted facades of the houses that remained standing. Market stalls lay smashed and overturned, their goods a clutter of trampled garbage.

Although it was too soon for the piles of human corpses to begin to putrefy, the inert *jhumbis* had long since disintegrated into heaps of clay, bones, and liquescence, exuding a reek that competed with the smell of smoke that continued to hang in the air. In the meantime, like the sharks in the harbor, the packs of hyenas that haunted the fringes of Khambawe had emerged to feast at a banquet of carrion. The survivors were too exhausted to drive them – or the buzzing clouds of flies that hovered over the bodies – away.

However the hyenas, whether they were *irimu* or not, avoided the noisome remains of the *jhumbis*.

So did the flies.

This was the face of the Matile's victory, a success harder-won than any of the triumphs of the ancient days of conquest and glory. It was an achievement that would eventually be written into volumes of history and woven into new tapestries that would adorn the walls of the Senafa Palace, and be remembered in countless songs and stories. It was the final, definitive victory over the Matiles' worst enemies, who were their kin before the different paths they took forced them into a conflict that obviated those ancient blood-ties.

Yet for all that, an utter defeat could not have looked much worse than the triumph the Matile had managed to achieve.

2

Tiyana awakened slowly, painfully. Outside her eyelids, the sun glowed so insistently it was impossible for her to keep her eyes closed any longer. She remembered what she had seen in the Oneness before the insensibility of sheer exhaustion overcame her: victory ... *the Uloans routed ... the Ishimbi walking ... the final, horrific slaughter in the harbor ...*

She blinked, opened her eyes, sat up ... and bit back a scream as a lance of agony pierced through her. Every muscle in her body ached; every heartbeat was a pulse of pain. Even her bones cried out in protest against the price the application of the *ashuma* of Oneness had exacted. Tiyana closed her eyes again, and waited until the worst of the aches subsided.

Of the incredibly powerful *ashuma* she and the others had wielded the night before, nothing remained – not even a tingle. The Oneness was gone as well. Her mind seemed a weightless thing, drifting without direction inside her head.

She had allowed herself to think that the power Almovaar bestowed would be limitless, and without consequences, as legends averred the *ashuma* gifted by her own gods had been. Now, she sighed inwardly at the foolishness of such an assumption.

Of course there would be a price to pay, she thought. And she understood then that Nama-kwah and the other Jagasti had not exacted a price from the Amiyas when they worked their small magics because the deities had little left to offer in exchange for any demands they might make on the bodies and minds of their worshippers.

Tiyana decided to try opening her eyes again. Her vision wavered, then swam into focus. She saw the other Amiyas and Initiates sprawled on the grass, their circle broken. In the middle of the circle, Gebrem and Kyroun leaned on one another like a pair of drunkards. The *abi* rested between them. No longer glowing with *ashuma*, the instrument of power seemed nothing more than a simple metal rod now, bereft of the Jagasti-symbols that had distinguished its significance before the Amiyas had declared their loyalty to Almovaar.

Byallis lay next to Tiyana. The Fidi woman's eyelids opened slowly. Her eyes were brown, like Tiyana's. Her hair was brown as well. But her skin was almost translucently pale, even after the months she had spent under the Abengoni sun. Seeing the Adept more clearly now, Tiyana's gaze took in Byallis's round face, full features and the plump body beneath her sweat-soaked robe. Perspiration had also plastered Tiyana's own *chamma* to her skin.

Byallis smiled at Tiyana. Tiyana smiled back. She was about to speak. Then she felt movement at her other side.

Keshu had already risen to his feet. Tiyana gazed up at him. He was looking away from her as he stretched his body. She watched his muscles ripple like those of a young bull beneath his dark skin. And she felt the beginnings of a second awakening inside her, despite the exhaustion that enveloped her like a blanket.

Then Keshu turned his gaze to her. As their eyes met, Tiyana remembered what she had gleaned from his thoughts the night before. Keshu also remembered. And his eyes shifted away from hers in a combination of chagrin and embarrassment; reactions echoed in Tiyana despite the arousal in her loins.

Before Tiyana could decide whether or not to speak to Keshu, she heard other movement behind her. Painfully, she twisted her body around and saw the four Callers of Nama-kwah standing nearby. The Callers had not participated in the incantation of the night before; they were singers, not Vessels. Soot covered their faces and *chammas*, and the hems of their garments bore bloodstains – mute witnesses to their nightmarish struggles to survive the brutality of the Uloans' invasion.

Tiyana tried – and failed – to distinguish her friend Yemeya from her sisters, whose names were Jubiti, Tamala, and Zeudi. It was Yemeya who spoke to her; the others remained silent, as though grief had constricted their throats.

"Tiyana, there is something you should see in the Beit Amiya," she said.

"What is it?" Tiyana asked.

"You need to ... see."

Tiyana tried to rise but stumbled, her legs still weakened and her mind disoriented. Then a hand touched her shoulder. It was Keshu, reaching down to help her to her feet. A tentative smile touched his lips, then vanished. An unspoken question remained in his eyes. After a moment's hesitation, Tiyana placed her hand in his, and he raised her gently and effortlessly. Then he released her hand and pulled Byallis up as well. He did not look at either of the women once they were on their feet.

Some of the other Almovaads and Amiyas had also risen, but they were still disoriented. The Callers, however, were focusing their attention on Tiyana, Byallis and Keshu. They gave Byallis a curious gaze, wondering what she and the other Fidi were doing in the Amiyas' sacred compound. When Tiyana told them who the Fidi woman was, and what she and the other Almovaads had done to save the city, all four Callers bowed their heads and raised their palms as a sign of respect and gratitude.

"You may come with us, Byallis," Yemeya said.

"Thank you," the Adept said.

As the group crossed the grass on their way to the House, others – Amiya and Almovaad alike – gave them quizzical looks, but didn't follow.

And Kyroun and Gebrem remained inert on the ground, as though their efforts had used up all their vitality, leaving them as empty as drained *talla* cups.

When they entered the Beit Amiya, the Callers led them to the hall where the stone images of the Matile deities stood – or, as they soon saw, had once stood.

Tiyana let out a wordless cry at what she saw. Keshu bit back a curse. Byallis simply stared and shook her head in disbelief, appalled at the sight of sacrilege even though it had been perpetrated against deities that were not her own.

Sometime during the night, the statues of the Jagasti had fallen – or been deliberately toppled. They were now nothing more than scatterings of broken stone in front of their pedestals. Only the marks of long-dead sculptors' carving distinguished the pieces of the gods and goddesses from the rubble that littered the streets outside the Beit Amiya.

Keshu was the first to find his voice.

"This has to be the work of *tsotsis*," he growled.

"*Tsotsis*? Here?" Tiyana asked in disbelief.

Keshu walked to the pedestal that had held the image of Halasha, the Jagasti he served. He pushed some of the statue's pieces away from the front of the pedestal. His actions revealed that the mask Keshu had worn during his Calling ceremonies, and placed in that spot in a bitter act of renunciation the night before, was gone. He went over to Nama-kwah's pedestal and pushed its remaining rubble aside as well. Beneath the rocks, there was nothing. The silver mask that had once fit so well over Tiyana's face had vanished.

"Your father had always suspected there were *tsotsis* among us, posing as *shamashas*," Keshu said to Tiyana. "But we could never uncover them. They were too clever."

"But why would *tsotsis*, who respect neither laws nor gods, want to destroy images of the Jagasti?" Tiyana wondered, thinking of the nameless girl who had attended her after the First Calling during which the Fidis had arrived, and wondering if she had been one of the *tsotsi* infiltrators.

"What are the Jagasti to the likes of them?" Keshu retorted.

Before anyone could answer that question, another Amiya, who had come into the House behind them, spoke.

"The Leba and the Seer have awakened, and they want all of us to be gathered together," the Amiya, a woman who had been the Vessel of the river-goddess Ateti, announced. "They say something is wrong."

3

Despite the final killing in the harbor, there were still Uloans alive in Khambawe. They were the blankskin spies ... spies like Sehaye, whose message concerning the coming of the Fidi had been the catalyst that began Retribution Time.

For a long time, Sehaye had cursed the fate that had caused the *huangi* to choose him as a gatherer of the mainland's secrets. His childhood and adolescence had been a nightmare of taunts as his skin remained featureless while that of the others around him became living testimony to their adulation of Legaba.

The *huangi* had told him he would be facing more danger than any of his tormentors could imagine; and as an infiltrator, he would be performing an exemplary service for the Spider God. And Jass Imbiah herself had assured him that when Retribution Time came, he would receive his spider-scars in a ceremony of blood and honor.

Yet it was Sehaye's lack of skin-marks that had saved his life. Throughout the invasion, he had hovered in the shadows, furtively slaying Matile who could not distinguish him from themselves. More than once, he had been forced to flee his fellow islanders, because he had no time to make them realize he, too, was a Uloan.

Ultimate triumph over the mainlanders had been well within his people's grasp. But then the mist came. And the night-sun shone. And the *jhumbis* died a second time. And Legaba abandoned the Uloans. And the Ishimbi walked. And the fleeing invaders were gutted like fish in the harbor ....

Sehaye cried out and shook his head violently. He was wandering the ravaged streets, hoping to find other Uloan spies. He had not been acquainted with any of them in the past; the *huangi* had forbidden such contact so that the secret of their presence could be more easily maintained. For all Sehaye knew, he was the only Uloan left alive in Khambawe.

But he did not want to believe that …

A few Matile who had seen his outburst stopped and stared at Sehaye. But they said nothing to him; his behavior was far from unusual. The shouts and screams of those whose minds had been unhinged by the trauma of the invasion and its ensuing carnage echoed throughout Khambawe.

Sehaye did not trust himself to talk. He could no longer think, let alone speak, in the mainland language the *huangi* had forced him to learn. He had not been allowed to go to the mainland until he could mimic their speech flawlessly. If he opened his mouth now, however, he would give himself away to the mainlanders. And he knew what they would do to him, stunned and bewildered though they may be in the face of their costly triumph.

Why them not kill I? he asked himself for the hundredth time. He could not answer that question. He could only continue his aimless journey: stepping over corpses, dodging scavengers, wading through pools of blood, adding his crimson footprints to those left by his enemies.

One day, he was convinced, Legaba would speak to him and give him an answer. And this belief was the only thing that was keeping him alive.

4

Even in daylight, Kalisha moved furtively through the Maim. Her stealth was so habitual it seemed instinctive, as was the case with all *tsotsis*. To relax one's vigilance even for a moment in the Maim was to die. On this day, though, she need not have bothered with caution. The Maim's filthy byways were nearly deserted. Even the hyenas had moved on to richer harvests of decaying flesh in other parts of Khambawe.

There were *tsotsis* in the streets – members of sets other than the Ashakis. But neither they nor Kalisha attempted to intimidate or avoid each other. The Uloans' invasion and its outcome had left the *tsotsis* as disoriented as everyone else in Khambawe. And with the rest of the city in ruins, there was nothing left to loot, and thus no reason to assert old – or new – rivalries among the warring sets.

Earlier, Kalisha had wrapped a gold-striped *chamma* she had stolen from the Beit Amiya around her slight frame. Its ends trailed on the ground behind her as she walked. The *chamma* concealed a leather sack that contained the Mask of Nama-kwah. The sack was strapped firmly around her waist.

Ordinarily, she would have had to hide the *chamma*, too, or risk having it ripped from her body by other *tsotsis*. But on this day, most of the *tsotsis* she encountered were openly displaying the clothing, jewelry and weapons they had purloined while the rest of the city was fighting the Uloans. Some staggered and reeled, already drunk on stolen *talla*. Others were chewing *khat*, and losing themselves in the dream-like escape the leaves provided.

Some of them recognized her.

"Amiya-girl," they called, sometimes with a laugh.

Kalisha smiled and returned the greetings. Inside, she laughed at them in turn. In her mind, what she carried under her *chamma* was far more valuable than the insipid baubles the others so proudly displayed.

She could not wait to show the Mask of Nama-kwah to Jass Mofo. Her anticipation of his reaction pushed aside the nagging anxiety she felt as she realized that she had not yet seen another Ashaki *tsotsi* in the Maim.

Her sense of apprehension intensified when she reached the Ashakis' mansion – and found no one guarding the entrance. But she did notice large pools of congealing blood marking the places where the set's sentries usually stood. With that sight, her heart began to beat so loudly she was sure anyone near her would be able to hear its frantic pounding against her ribcage.

Kalisha almost ran away then. However, she could hear a murmur of voices coming from the mansion. Whose voices were they, though?

She quivered like an antelope caught between a leopard and a lion. But she didn't bolt. She felt a compulsion to know who was inside – Ashaki or foe. Was Jass Mofo still alive? Or was he as dead as the sentries whose blood thickened on the stones? It would only take one quick look to find out....

Kalisha edged her way to the entrance. She avoided the blood pools. Trusting the daylight shadows to hide her, she crept into the entrance. And her breath caught in a rasping wheeze in her throat at what her eyes showed her.

There were no enemies, *tsotsi* or otherwise, in the mansion – only Ashakis. But the numbers of the set were direly depleted. A row of mutilated bodies of Ashaki women and children lay in a row along one wall. Their wounds were horrendous; even the youngest children had not been spared.

Kalisha recognized Jass Mofo's woman, Kimbi, among the dead. Her throat had been slit from ear to ear, and her eyes stared sightlessly at the destruction that surrounded her. Her dazzling jewelry and elaborate clothing had been taken from her – along with her life.

Mofo, along with the other survivors, was in the great chamber, which was now nearly empty. The pile of plunder that was the Jass's throne was gone; only bits of worthless metal and scraps of shredded cloth remained. Kalisha knew then that Mofo had made one of the few miscalculations in his life.

For not all of the *tsotsis* had joined the massive looting spree in the city. Some of the sets had decided that pickings in the Maim would be easier, with so many fighters gone. And Mofo had not left enough defenders to guard his people and goods. And so, while the main body of the Ashaki had fought to the death against the Hafars and the Uloans, someone else had overwhelmed the sentries and looted the Ashakis' *aderash*.

To make matters worse, no new booty was in sight. Mofo and the others had returned empty-handed from their foray. Dried gore encrusted the spikes of their weapons, and blood from their own wounds stained their clothing red. Despite their youth, the *tsotsis'* faces bore marks of weariness that belonged on the faces of people who were much older than they.

The low murmur of conversation ceased when Kalisha entered the chamber. No one bothered to challenge her with the Ashaki signal as she made her way through the sad remnant of the set.

She approached Jass Mofo. Bleakness stared at her from the Ashaki leader's eyes. It was as though a fire had gone out inside him, leaving only cold ashes behind.

"What you got for me, Amiya-girl?" Mofo asked in a flat, perfunctory tone.

Kalisha unwrapped herself from her stolen *chamma* and let it fall to the floor. Then she reached into the pouch and pulled out the silver Mask of Nama-kwah. She held it out to Mofo as if it were an offering to a king.

"I take it right from the Goddess," she said. "No one see me; no one try to stop me."

Mofo's eyes remained lifeless as he gazed at the Mask. Without changing expression, he abruptly snatched it out of Kalisha's hands and hurled it away. The Mask sailed through the air and clanged against the far wall of the chamber. Then it fell, dented, to the floor.

Kalisha could not believe what Mofo had done. The Mask of Nama-kwah had more value than all the loot the Ashakis had previously accumulated that year, and would easily make up for what had been stolen by the *tsotsis* who had looted the mansion. It did not matter to her that other *tsotsis* had stolen the other Jagastis' Masks and most likely taken them back to their sets. To her mind, the Mask of Nama-kwah was the most beautiful – and valuable – of them all.

And Mofo had simply thrown it away, as if it didn't matter in the slightest.

She stared at him as though he had suddenly gone mad, as if she did not know him anymore.

"You go, Amiya-girl," Mofo said to her. "We all dead here. Everythin' be gone. Nothin' here for you now. Nothin' here for none of us. Heard?"

Kalisha did not reply. Tears filled her eyes, but she refused to allow them to fall. She gathered up her stolen *chamma*. And she went to the Mask, picked it up and enfolded it in the garment. Then she ran out of the mansion without looking back.

The blighted streets of the Maim beckoned her. She answered their call, for she had nowhere else to go.

5

Gebrem and Kyroun strode swiftly through the streets of the well-to-do section of Khambawe. Although the area had not suffered as much damage as those closer to the docks, the Uloans and the *tsotsis* had still exacted a toll of destruction. Soot smeared the painted walls of estates and pools of gore congealed in the gutters.

Despite their advanced years, the two holy men were practically running to their destination – the Gebbi Zimballa, the place of refuge to which the Emperor and Empress had been taken. When they had awakened from their weariness-induced torpor, Almovaar had issued a warning that was heard by both the Seer and the Leba: Alemeyu and Issa were in danger. But the deity had told them nothing more than that.

The Amiyas and Initiates followed. Survivors in the street gaped at the grim-faced procession of magic-users who had saved Khambawe. Some followed out of curiosity, then others, then more. Soldiers and civilians alike streamed behind the clerics as they made their way to the haven, which was located beyond the city.

Despite the fatigue from which they were just beginning to recover, Kyroun and Gebrem did not falter when they passed the last of the estates on Khambawe's perimeter. Silently, they proceeded through a swath of clipped grass, artfully arranged flowerbeds and groves of fruit trees. In the distance, they could see the Gebbi Zimballa. They noticed that the flowers were trampled, as though many feet had trod them into the ground.

And they saw something else coming rapidly toward them.

A yellow, black-spotted shape streaked past the crowd so swiftly that only a few realized that it was the Emperor's cheetah, Makah. The beast was running as though it were pursued by demons, and it paid no attention to the people in its path. And everyone saw the red trail the great cat's bloody paw-prints left on the grass. The spoor came from the Emperor's refuge.

Kyroun and Gebrem hesitated only a moment before breaking into a run. Uneasy murmurs rose from the throng that followed them.

Soon they reached the royal refuge. Its broken doors hung askew from their hinges. No guards came out to greet them. The only sound to be heard was the ominous buzzing of hordes of flies.

Inside, the Leba and the Seer and the others saw what they had steeled themselves to find. Mangled corpses lay in heaps throughout the courtyard of the refuge. Others hung from windows and sprawled on stairways. Among them were the noisome remains of many of the Uloans' *jhumbis*, as well as the spider-scarred bodies of the islanders themselves.

Gasps and choking sobs escaped the throats of some in the crowd. Those who could no longer weep simply stood and stared in disbelief. The Gebbi Zimballa was supposedly the safest spot in Khambawe; even during the worst days of the Storm Wars, it had never fallen. *How could so many Uloans have breached it*, many Matile asked themselves. It was a question none of them could answer.

Shaking his head in sadness, Gebrem moved forward, leading the others through the palace, searching through the jumbled corpses for familiar attire, a familiar face, dreading what he knew he would find. Then, in the ancient throne room, he saw a glimmer of the blood-spattered, ceremonial armor of the Emperor.

Dardar Alemeyu's face was a crimson mask that was almost

unrecognizable. Behind him lay the hacked body of the Empress Issa. Alemeyu clutched the Sword of Issuri in his stiffened hands. The blade was crimson to the hilt. Many Uloan bodies were scattered around him, along with those of the Matile soldiers who had guarded him to the death. The Emperor had died defending his wife and his people – a death that would raise him to heroic proportions in the future annals of the Matile.

So there was something beyond vainglorious arrogance in you after all, Cousin, Gebrem mused as he gazed down at his boyhood rival and adult nemesis. *There was courage ...*

He allowed himself a moment to mourn what might have been, had he and his relative begun their lives as friends rather than enemies.

"So ... Eshana will be Emperor," he murmured aloud.

Although Gebrem's tone was low, a soldier overheard him.

"No, Jass Gebrem," he said. "The Dejezmek is dead. I saw him go down during the charge in the Market Square."

All eyes then turned to Gebrem. For he was the one who stood next in line to Jass Eshana in succession to the throne. Now, Gebrem was the new Emperor of Matile Mara.

6

Great throngs crowded the beaches of all the Uloan Islands. The sea-breeze stirred the garments of the women, the children, the aged, and the infirm who had not been able to participate in the glory of Retribution Time.

They were awaiting the triumphant return of the Uloan armada. The *huangi*s had promised them that once Retribution Time was done, the ships would take the islanders to the mainland, where they would rule over their ancient enemies, who would be their slaves forever.

Every day, the people of the Islands came to the beaches and waited. They waited silently. But the moment the first sails were spotted, they would sing songs of triumph.

And every day, the horizon remained empty.

All the *huangi* had gone away with the armada. Jass Imbiah had needed them to help her focus the *ashuma* of Legaba. So the Uloans had no way of knowing the outcome of the invasion. Yet their faith in Imbiah and Legaba sustained their hopes as they waited, and day after day, the ships failed to return.

If doubt crept into the minds of the Uloans, none dared to give it voice. It was true that the end of Retribution Time was taking longer than any of them had anticipated. But it would soon come. Soon come ....

In the meantime, the *ubia*-vines grew bolder, slithering onto the beaches and wrapping themselves around the ankles of the unwary. The other *mwiti*-plants in the forests appeared to be gathering their forces, as if for battle. The safeguards the *huangi* had left behind were slowly losing their potency. If that protection finally disappeared ... the Islanders blocked that possibility from their minds. The ships would soon come. They had to. The final victory would be theirs. After all, Retribution Time had come.

In the meantime, the Uloans stood on their beaches like living sacrifices to the sea ... waiting ... waiting ... waiting ....

CHAPTER TWENTY
AMONG THE JAGASTI
1

Nama-kwah floated in the borderspace between Khambawe's harbor and the Ocean-beyond-the-ocean, the boundary between the world of Abengoni and the Realms of the Jagasti. Behind her, the Children of Nama-kwah swam in endless swirls that stretched far beyond any horizon that could ever have existed in the demesne of men and women. The luminous, multicolored fish and other sea creatures appeared to be performing a ritualized dance. They swam close to the unseen, yet clearly demarcated, barrier between the Realms of the Goddess and the world of humanity. Then they recoiled, as though in horror, and quickly swam away. And then, as if part of a performance, the Children of Nama-kwah repeated their sequence. It continued over and over, as though the Children had fallen under some spell of compulsion that could never end.

Light from a source that was not the sun glinted subtly from the jewel-like scales that descended from Nana-kwah's head and covered most of her sinuous body. Her elongated arms and legs moved gently in the water. The goddess did not need such movement to keep her afloat, but she enjoyed the sensation of the water that flowed smoothly over her scaled skin.

Considering what was happening on the other side of the divide, it would have been understandable if even a goddess like Nama-kwah followed her first impulse and swam far away, never to return. Like her Children, however, Nama-kwah could not stay away for very long. Like them, she kept returning, motivated by a morbid fascination with what she saw.

Corpses drifted through the murky water of Khambawe's harbor like leaves in a windstorm. Many had fallen to the ocean floor, where they lay in scatters and clumps – maimed, wide-eyed witnesses to the appalling carnage that had accompanied the defeat of the Uloans' invasion. The water was still tinged crimson with the blood that had been spilled copiously in the final slaughter. And the wreckage of dozens of sunken, shattered ships also littered the bottom of the harbor, turning it into a carpet of broken boards and masts.

Matile, Uloan … the identity of the wrecks and the corpses did not matter to the ocean currents that rocked them, lending a macabre semblance of life to the cadavers and animation to the smashed hulks of the ships. And it also didn't matter to the sharks and the lesser scavengers that were devouring the dead.

Deep indentations on the sea-bottom delineated the path the Ishimbi statues had taken during their destruction of the Uloan fleet. Even though she was a goddess, Nama-kwah had still been impressed by the sheer scope of the sorcery that had been summoned to cause the gigantic statues to walk into the harbor. She remembered a time when she herself would have helped to provide such power to the Amiyas. But that time was no more, and long gone.

On the other hand, the massive killing had impressed her much less. It had sickened her, but she had remained to witness it just the same, even though she was under no obligation to do so.

She could have stopped it. She and all the other deities the Matile had worshipped and served for so long, and for so little in return – together, they could have stopped the horror. But they had chosen not to do so. And now, as she watched the sea claim the spoils the humans' slaughter had given it, and her Children swam back and forth in a mindless dance of attraction and repulsion, Nama-kwah reflected on why the Matile had finally been abandoned in their time of need.

Abandoned by all – including herself.

But she had tried not to desert them completely. Yes, she had tried to forestall the tragedy that was to come. And her thoughts returned to the repeated attempts she had made to change the minds of her fellow Jagasti, even as she observed the result of her failure …

2

Nama-kwah had prepared carefully for her journey to the Realm of Ufashwe, the God of the Wind, who was Nama-kwah's closest friend among the Jagasti. Although the elements the two deities controlled were complementary in nature, the air in Ufashwe's Realm could prove dangerous to her if she entered it without taking the proper precautions.

Complementary ...

Nama-kwah's smooth brow had creased in a frown as she remembered how hollow a conception that had been during the time of the Storm Wars, when the *ashuma* that had been granted to the humans had escaped the control of even the Jagasti, and continued to rage unchecked to this day in the ocean off the coast of the Abengoni continent and the beaches of the Uloan Islands. In that part of the Beyond World, the Jagasti no longer held even a semblance of sway. The Beyond World's own elementals of sea and sky were at war, a war that could not come to an end because of the mindless nature of its protagonists.

And the rest of the Beyond World had, for the most part, been abandoned by the Jagasti – all except Legaba, the seeker of power, who had striven to ensnare the Realms of Jagasti and humans alike in his far-reaching webs, only to bring himself, the Realms, and the world of humanity close to ruin.

Like Legaba, Nama-kwah also paid more attention to the Beyond World than did most of the other Jagasti. But her reasons involved sentiment rather than a hunger for adulation. Her latest – and now last – Vessel, Tiyana, had intrigued her. The young woman reminded her of other Amiyas who had served her in times long past – Amiyas whose deeds had become legendary among the mortals. She had touched Tiyana more than she should have. And Tiyana had, in turn, touched Nama-kwah, for even among the short-lived people of the Beyond World, there were those whose qualities had earned the admiration of the Jagasti.

Nama-kwah remembered Etiya and her songs. And the shaman, Jaussa, and his curiosity. And Jass Issuri, the first Emperor, and his courage.

During the Dance on the Waves that had accompanied the First Calling ritual, Nama-kwah had attempted to warn Tiyana of the chain of events that was about to occur ... events the goddess was capable of foreseeing, but not forestalling. Giving that warning was all she could do.

Even so, Nama-kwah could not ignore the entreaties Tiyana had sent to her in the House of Amiyas at the time when all the Vessels had vainly beseeched Jagasti to save them from the Uloans ... from Legaba. Alone, Nama-kwah could do little. But with even some of the others at her side – together, this time – catastrophic destruction might not prove to be the inevitable result of their intervention.

And so she would go to Ufashwe.

At the margin between her Realm and the Wind God's, there was a blue space that was neither sea nor sky ... more than either, but less than both. There, Nama-kwah had metamorphosed. The scales on her skin merged into a single, smooth, opalescent covering that contained a second skin of water that would keep her body moist in Ufashwe's sky-beyond-the-sky.

Then she raised her arms, and gossamer growths like the specialized fins of a flying fish formed between her arms and her sides. She stretched experimentally, and was satisfied that her makeshift wings would endure the buffeting of the winds in Ufashwe's Realm.

Turning, she looked back at the multi-hued swarms of fish that thronged behind her. Where she would now go, none of them could follow and survive. With a gesture of farewell to her Children, Nama-kwah launched herself forward, out of her Realm and into Ufashwe's.

As she propelled herself through the blue border, Nama-kwah could feel the resistance of the water diminishing; at first gradually, then more and more rapidly until, finally, it was gone. The blue lightened, until it became not the color of a calm sea, but the shade of a sunny, dry-season sky. But there was no sun in this sky, even though it was bright rather than dark, and the air was warm, and white wisps of cloud dotted the blue like flowers in a field. Ufashwe's Realm was like a daytime that had neither sunrise nor sunset.

Beneath her, Nama-kwah saw no ground ... only more sky, and more clouds. Gentle winds swirled around her, lifting her translucent wings, keeping her aloft. The warmth of the wind caressed her, even through the protective covering she had created for herself.

One moment, Nama-kwah was flying alone through the infinite sky, well aware that her presence would soon be known to Ufashwe. Then, without warning, she was surrounded by birds that seemed to have materialized from the sky itself. Avians of all shapes, sizes and colors swooped and swirled around Nama-kwah, subtly guiding her toward Ufashwe. The songs and cries of the birds mingled into a chorus rather than a cacophony, and their music was pleasing to Nama-kwah's ears.

These variegated birds were Ufashwe's Children. Like the fish that were Nama-kwah's Children, the flock mirrored the birds that existed in Beyond World: eagles, flamingos, parrots, ibises, ox-peckers, guinea-fowl, marabous, honey-guides, hawks and songbirds. Ufashwe's sky-Realm lent beauty even to the vulture and other despised scavenger-birds.

Birds of other types flew amid the flock – creatures that would never be seen in the sky over Abengoni. Large in size and wingspan, with long, elegant beaks and crystalline, almost transparent feathers, these birds were of Ufashwe's own making; manifestations of his dreams. They looked at Nama-kwah with eyes that glinted with intelligence, and when they opened their beaks, they sang like no bird had ever sung in the World Beyond. They mingled freely with their fellow Children, neither receiving nor expecting any deference because of their differences.

In Ufashwe's Realm, the birds that were his Children enjoyed eternal flight. Never would they need to alight on the ground or cling to a tree-branch. The sky was theirs – forever.

More of Ufashwe's Children appeared, until they almost completely surrounded Nama-kwah. Although the birds conceded her the space necessary to spread her wings, she could no longer see the sky. She could see only an ever-changing mosaic of feathers, beaks and eyes. Other birds joined the song, and their music echoed in her ears as she flew.

She allowed Ufashwe's Children to carry her along with them, knowing that they would eventually take her to the Wind God. She listened to their songs, and thought about what she was going to say to her fellow deity when she saw him.

After a time, she could sense that the flight of the flock was slowing. Then, abruptly, they were gone – vanished, as though they had never existed. And Ufashwe hovered before her, suspended in the never-ending sky.

3

Like the birds of his own creation, Ufashwe was covered with feathers that were made of clear crystal. But the wings that spread from his back to encompass a wide swath of sky were pure cloud ... white, billowing, beautiful. His face, like Nama-kwah's, was similar those of the Matile. But, also like Nama-kwah's, Ufashwe's visage was a vision of perfection, without any of the blemishes and irregularities that characterized human faces.

Ufashwe's eyes shone like diamonds. Those eyes looked deep into Nama-kwah's, and probed even deeper into her being. He knew why Nama-kwah had come into his Realm. And he knew how he would answer her still-unspoken question. And he knew how she would respond.

Regret is certain to come, he thought.

Even so, he greeted her by reaching out with a hand that was bedecked with tiny, crystalline feathers. In turn, Nama-kwah extended her own hand, still sheathed in its protective covering, which was sufficiently translucent to show the jewel-like scales that covered her skin.

Their fingers touched, and a current of *ashuma* passed between them in an exchange of warm feelings.

A moment later, they withdrew from the contact. With a gesture of his pinions, Ufashwe beckoned Nama-kwah to join him in flight. Together, they winged through the endless sky of Ufashwe's Realm, floating over or arrowing through the clouds that formed a white landscape amid the bright blue background.

Soon, they were joined again by Ufashwe's Children. The flock kept pace with the two deities. This time, however, the birds' songs were stilled, out of respect for the silence Ufashwe and Nama-kwah maintained as they allowed the eternal wind to buoy them through the sky.

Finally, after a period of time that could not be measured by any reckoning humans employed, Nama-kwah spoke. Her words echoed not only in the sky, but also in his mind.

"Brother, the Children of the Beyond World need us," she said. "Will you help me to help them?"

"Sister, I cannot do as you ask," Ufashwe replied, his voice as soft as a rainy-season breeze.

"And, as you well know, *you* cannot do as you wish with the People of Beyond," he continued. "So it is better not to wish it at all."

Nama-kwah looked at him with eyes that were filled with the tears of the sea.

"But they need us, Brother," she insisted.

They addressed each other as Brother and Sister because all the Jagasti – even the despicable Legaba – were siblings, spawned at the same time in the same womb located in the fecund center of the Worlds-Beyond-the-Realms. The people of the Beyond World of Abengoni had emerged from an entirely different womb; they were not of their deities' creation. Still, the Jagasti had adopted them after they heard Etiya's song, and nurtured them until ….

"Remember what our 'help' has done to them in the past, Sister," Ufashwe said implacably.

Nama-kwah turned away from his unblinking gaze. Her memory of the calamitous Storm Wars was as fresh as though it had happened only recently rather than centuries in the past.

"Legaba will destroy them," Nama-kwah said.

"Legaba is, and has always been, a fool," Ufashwe returned. "And so are those who blindly worship him."

Nama-kwah did not have to give voice to her agreement with Ufashwe's opinion. For after the Storm Wars had come close to ending the world they had fostered, the Jagasti had agreed to keep their interventions to a minimum, and never again bestow power that could be misused.

All … except Legaba.

Legaba had become too similar to the people who paid him obeisance and reveled in his power. The Spider-God's adherents had desired domination over their fellow humans; Legaba craved similar ascendance over his fellow Jagasti. The pact the others had made had contained Legaba's ambitions, and reduced his capacity for mischief. But he could not be suppressed entirely.

In the end, an approximate equilibrium had prevailed for centuries. Legaba could trifle with the Uloans, influencing and manipulating them as he desired. But the scope of his sway would be confined to the Islanders alone. The rest of the Jagasti would refrain from interaction beyond a proscribed level with the Matile. Nama-kwah and a few others had come close to that limit on several occasions. Except for participation in Callings and other rituals, Ufashwe had confined himself to his own Realm, as did the majority of the other Jagasti.

Now, that equilibrium had been broken. Legaba was once again seeking supremacy in the Beyond World. And a new deity, who was not of the Jagasti, had come to the Matile.

Ufashwe gave no indication that he had contemplated the coming of the foreign god, whose name was Almovaar. But Nama-kwah had. So had the other deities, and the Wind God had as well after the Jagasti had communicated throughout their Realms and decided how they were going to respond to the advent of the new god and the reawakening of Legaba's senseless aspirations.

And they had decided to do ... nothing.

Legaba's latest design for dominance would be countered by the coming of the new god. The Jagasti had scrutinized Almovaar from afar since the time they discovered his presence in the Beyond World. His strength was formidable; he had been able to shield himself from their attempts to deeply probe him and his Realm. Still, they had learned enough about him to realize that he was more than capable of thwarting Legaba's schemes.

Thus, most of the Jagasti had chosen to end even their minimal involvement with the Beyond World. The Matile were free to embrace another god. The Jagasti, in turn, were free to create their own Children in their own Realms, and be satisfied with their complaisant behavior, which was so different from the obstreperousness and unpredictability of the mortals.

The Jagasti were not as one in their thinking. Even so, those who disagreed with the majority still agreed to comply with the majority's wishes. All – except Nama-kwah. The Sea Goddess found herself unwilling – or unable – to accept the ultimate abandonment of the Matile, even though she alone was powerless to forestall it.

She spoke of her misgivings to Ufashwe.

"I do not trust this new god," she said. "We should be the ones to contain Legaba, not him."

"Nevertheless, the Children of the Beyond World have chosen him," Ufashwe said.

"But only because we have given them no alternative," Nama-kwah responded. "They did not abandon us; we abandoned them."

Her sharp tone created an eddy of tension between them, and the Children of Ufashwe wavered in their flight alongside the two Jagasti. The heads of the birds cocked toward the deities, and sounds of distress emanated from their beaks. Ufashwe and Nama-kwah flew on in a silence that was finally broken by the Wind God. Before he spoke, he swept his cloud-wings in a gesture that took in half the sky.

"This is where we belong, Sister," he said. "Our Realms are of our own making. And so are our Children. Let the Beyond People have their new god. And let us have our peace."

"I fear for what will happen to them, Brother," Nama-kwah said.

"They are no longer our concern, Sister," said Ufashwe.

The finality of his tone precluded any further discussion. Nama-kwah knew she could never convince Ufashwe to join her in another intervention into the World Beyond. And if he, to whom she was closest, remained indifferent to her entreaties, so, too, would the others.

Deep within, she understood him. Had she not developed such a close bond with her Vessel, Tiyana, Nama-kwah might have shared Ufashwe's lack of concern. Like him, she would have been satisfied to relegate herself to her Realm, among her Children. She could not completely surrender her fondness for her soon-to-be former worshippers. But she could not help them, either.

She reached out her hand to Ufashwe to signal the end of their discussion. His hand touched hers, and again the *ashuma* flowed between them.

"Farewell, Brother," she said.

"Farewell, Sister."

Then Nama-kwah veered away from Ufashwe and flew back to her Realm. This time, the Children of Ufashwe did not accompany her.

4

And now, it was over. Legaba had been defeated by the new god. The Matile had forsaken the Jagasti, just as the Jagasti had abandoned them. The destruction had been immense, although not comparable to what had happened during the Storm Wars. That time had marked the first retreat of the Jagasti from involvement in the Beyond World. But that retreat had been only partial. A minimum of contact with the ephemeral lives of the people of that world had been maintained – just enough to offset the continuing ambitions of Legaba.

Now, Nama-kwah reflected as she hovered in the water of the borderland and watched the corpses and the wreckage continue to defile Khambawe's harbor, the withdrawal of the deities would be complete. Legaba was no longer a threat. He would remain dormant in his Realm for a long time, even as its passage was perceived by the Jagasti.

And now the Matile had Almovaar. His coming had disrupted the equilibrium that had kept Legaba in check. That was the danger of which she had attempted to warn Tiyana during First Calling.

And now, Tiyana was gone from Nama-kwah. The vessel had abandoned the Mask of the Sea Goddess, and Nama-kwah had no had other means to contact her Vessel. And the Beyond World was lost to Nama-kwah as well.

But what was that world, compared to her Realm, and those of the other Jagasti? Her Realm belonged to her; she could shape and reshape it as she pleased, unlike the Beyond World, which shaped itself.

Still, she felt a lingering attachment to the Beyond World and its impermanent, intractable people. And she knew something else. Her Mask had fallen into other hands ... the hands of one who was not an Amiya, and had not been trained in the ways of communing with the Jagasti. It was only a tentative link, and not a very strong one. But it was the only connection Nama-kwah had left. She would maintain it, because she did not trust this new god, Almovaar.

Almovaar had made no attempt to communicate with the Jagasti, and his Realm was impenetrable to any incursions from them. Nama-kwah wondered what he was hiding in his Realm. But of all the Jagasti, only she had expressed any curiosity about the newcomer. The others, like Ufashwe, were content to leave the Beyond World to its own fate.

So, too, would Nama-kwah. Still, she would keep her connection with the holder of her Mask. That was all she had left of the Beyond World.

Turning away from the aftermath of the carnage, Nama-kwah swam through the border waters and back into the clean, clear blue of her Realm. Her Children trailed behind her in a long, luminous line. And behind them, the scavengers of the sea continued their grisly work of devouring the dead.

PART THREE
CITY OF BELIEVERS

CHAPTER TWENTY-ONE

Rebirth

1

Like a heavy, moist curtain, the last shower of the rainy season descended on Khambawe. The earlier torrents of the season had washed away the blood of the fallen, as well as the malodorous ichor that had been all that remained of the Uloans' *jhumbis*. The streets of the Jewel City glistened in the dim sunlight filtered through the ranks of clouds that hung low in the sky.

The corpses and wreckage from the terrible day and night of the battle against the Uloans had long since been removed from the city's harbor. The hordes of sharks that had feasted on the dead had returned, well sated, to the open sea, as had the scavengers of the sea-bottom. Only the few Matile ships left unscathed from the combat remained on the water's surface, bobbing placidly at their berths. Other, newer, sea-craft were in various stages of construction.

The Ishimbi stood in their age-old location as though they had never walked; never helped to seal the demise of the Uloan invaders by destroying their ships. Rain had stripped away the mud and gore that had covered the statues' stone skin, but the seaweed from the harbor remained. Garlands of flowers laid daily by grateful Matile still festooned the Ishimbis' feet.

Evidence of the rebuilding process abounded in the streets of Khambawe. Burned buildings, of which there were many, had been either demolished or reconstructed. New houses rose in the vacant gaps along the streets. Charred trees had been removed; the ones that remained were now flourishing in emerald splendor, and new ones sprouted in place of those that were burned. The market squares again flourished, with wares of all types on display over which good-natured haggling continued past sundown.

However, there were still abundant reminders of the time of death and destruction. The City of the Dead had almost doubled in size, with a new section set aside for the peculiar graves of those who had come from Beyond the Storm. No one in Khambawe had been left untouched by death in some way, with family and friends newly buried in the City of the Dead. Even so, the time for mourning was over. Few now visited the metropolis of tombs. There was too much that needed to be done. The extent of the destruction the Uloans had caused was so great that another cycle of wet and dry seasons would have to pass before the Jewel City would be whole again.

Before the coming of the *White Gull* and the Almovaads, the expanse of Khambawe beyond the City of the Dead had been alive only in appearance. Beneath the surface of the city's life, the advance of decline and decay seemed irreversible; the end of the Matiles' civilization a mere matter of time. But now, the foreshadowing of doom that had loomed like a death-shroud over the city was gone. Now, the people of Khambawe and other cities were celebrating hope.

From the earliest of their days, the Matile had held a Coming-of-the-Sun ceremony to mark the end of the rainy season, just as First Calling heralded its beginning. The Coming-of-the-Sun was conducted on land rather than the sea, with the Amiyas for the Jagasti of the sun and sky leading the celebration of the season's change.

But now, for the first time in hundreds of years, there would be no Coming-of-the-Sun rite. The people of Khambawe had renounced their old, powerless deities. The Beit Amiya was now the Temple of Almovaar, and the Amiyas had become Adepts in the magic of the new religion the Fidis had brought with them. And nearly all the Matile had, in effect, become Almovaads – Believers. The few who had not converted kept their skepticism to themselves. And no one advocated any restoration of the Jagasti.

Another event had been planned to take the place of the Coming-of-the-Sun. When the rainy season came to an end, Jass Gebrem would be formally crowned Emperor of Matile Mara – the first Leba ever to ascend to the Lion Throne.

The coronation would confirm in ritual what had long since been reality. Gebrem had, in fact, ruled the Empire since the day the remains of

Dardar Alemeyu and Issa were interred in the royal section of the City of the Dead. Among some people in Khambawe, however, an undercurrent of intrigue flowed as they speculated on who the true Emperor was: Gebrem – or the Seer Kyroun, whose growing influence in the Matile court was obvious to all observers.

Until the sun broke through the clouds, the streets of Khambawe would remain empty, as custom dictated. Within their homes, the Matile adorned themselves with their finest clothing and jewelry in anticipation of Gebrem's enthronement.

Regardless of how some viewed the current state of their kingdom's politics, nearly everyone eagerly anticipated the coming ceremony. The event symbolized not only a transition of rulers, but also a change in the destiny of the Matile people.

2

Long before the end of the day, the sun finally vanquished the clouds, and the last rain ended. Khambawe glistened as though it were a newly built city rather than one that counted its age in thousands of years. For all its antiquity, however, Khambawe had changed. And so had the people who now happily thronged its streets.

The Matile were answering the summons of music that wafted in gentle, but insistent, waves throughout the city. Drums mimicked the heartbeat of a newly invigorated populace. Horns and flutes heralded the advent of new possibilities; fresh dreams; revived purpose. Stringed instruments – some of which were Matile, others brought by the Fidi – enticed people's feet to dance.

The music was sourceless, pervasive; no part of the city was beyond its reach, yet no one could see who played it. It was yet another sign that a new magic had come to Khambawe ... a magic that had proved much more effective than the *ashuma* of the old days.

By the thousands, the Matile streamed through the streets toward the palace of the Emperor. From the humblest to the highest, they were clad in their finest *chammas* and other garments. There was no separation by social status: nobles of the Degen Jassi mingled freely with merchants, artisans, even beggars. All had suffered grievously during the Uloans' invasion; no family was unaffected by its consequences. Everyone, rich and poor, had fought against the invaders with equal ferocity and desperation. And everyone who survived had paid a price for the victory.

The influence of the Fidi in Khambawe was clear. More than a few of the Matile had dyed their hair in shades of yellow and red in honor of the newcomers, even though the hair of many of the Fidi was dark. The beads and metal ornaments that decorated their braids blended well with the exotic hair coloring. And many Matile wore solid-blue *chammas* that marked their status as Initiates among the Almovaads. Every day, more Matile in Khambawe were joining the new religion whose god had saved them from destruction.

The more traditional people from the outlying provinces had not yet taken up the hair-coloring trend or the blue *chammas*, although some had become Almovaads after they heard about how the city – and the Empire – had been saved. As always, their simpler garments and hairstyles contrasted with the ostentatious finery of their urban kin. On this day, though, the Matile's regional rivalries had been put aside. The country-dwellers knew full well that if Khambawe had fallen, the Uloans would have attacked them next. If not the Uloans, then the Thabas, who would have been emboldened once they heard that the heart of the shrunken Empire had been shattered.

The Fidi walked with easy familiarity amid the crush of Matile. Whether or not they were Believers, the Matile were grateful for the role the people from Beyond the Storm had played in saving their city from the Uloans. And they expressed that gratitude with all the hospitality they could muster.

The Fidi had changed as well during their time among the Matile. Most of them had adopted elements of Matile dress and hairstyles. Their *chammas* bore blue-green stripes that symbolized the sea from which the people of Cym Dinath had come, and their hair ornaments clicked in rhythm with their footsteps, just as they did with the Matile. The Abengoni sun had darkened the skin of all but the fairest of the outlanders, so much so that in some cases it was difficult to distinguish their color from that of some of the Matile who surrounded them.

Smiles and pats on the back greeted the people from Beyond the Storm as they walked in the procession to the Palace. Since the end of the battle against the Uloans, the Fidi had wanted for nothing, even as they provided more than their share of assistance in the rebuilding of Khambawe.

Only the Tokoloshe and the Fidi dwarves remained apart from the rest of the crowd. Yet even they mingled with each other as though there were no differences between them. The streets echoed with the booming sound of their laughter at each others' jests.

As the crowds drew closer to the Emperor's palace, singing began – a harmonious blend of male and female voices, which, like the instrumental music, had no discernable source. Although the words of the songs celebrated the glories of past centuries, this time they signified more than mere nostalgia for the irretrievable past. This time, they heralded a promise for the future.

The destination of the crowds wending through Khambawe's streets was the Gebbi Senafa. Its jewel-encrusted doors stood wide open, with the customary contingent of guards absent on this day. The audience chamber of the Palace was large enough to accommodate hundreds of people. Still, even that capacity was too small to hold everyone who wanted to witness the coronation of Jass Gebrem. And in the past, that wouldn't have mattered.

Far fewer Matile had had even the slightest desire to attend the enthronement of Dardar Alemeyu, whose aged father had died in his sleep. Alemeyu's ascension to the throne had not been a momentous occasion, and only the elite of Khambawe had appeared at the event. The rest of the populace was neither wanted nor needed at the ceremony, and few of them regretted their exclusion. Alemeyu was not a popular man before or after he became Emperor.

As tradition dictated, only the higher-born and renowned had been permitted entry into the audience chamber to see the crown pass to Alemeyu's head. Others had to be content with second-hand accounts or street rumors. And the doors of the Gebbi Senafa remained closed.

This time, though, the palace doors were open – not to allow the entrance of the public; but, instead, an exit for the royal entourage who would be part of Gebrem's enthronement. The coronation would take place not inside the palace, but outside. Khambawe had buzzed like a beehive with chatter about the change in tradition. Never before had such a thing occurred. Then again, never before had a foreigner's hands been the ones to place the crown on the new Emperor's head, as would happen on this day....

After lengthy deliberations over precedent and protocol, the Degen

Jassi had decided that everyone throughout the Matile lands who desired to witness the crowning of Jass Gebrem should have the opportunity to do so. To that end, an enormous pavilion had been raised on the grounds in front of the palace. Hundreds of weavers had worked day and night, with the help of the Almovaads' new magic, to create what amounted to a tapestry large enough to envelop an entire building.

The tapestry was decorated with scenes from the triumph over the Uloans, with the people rendered in the ancient round-faced, large-eyed Matile motif. The cloth, light beige in color, was translucent enough to allow the sunlight to shine through, illuminating the woven scenes and suffusing its interior in an amber glow. Slowly, the pavilion filled with celebrants. On this day, soldiers in glittering accoutrements served as ushers rather than guards.

For all its size, the crowd was relatively subdued. The people gazed somberly at the cloth walls of the pavilion. Surrounded by scenes of the battle that were animated by the motion of the breeze, it was as though the survivors were reliving that night – but bloodlessly, at a distance, with the horror and anguish abridged in black thread against pale cloth.

But there were other sights to see as well.

In the large space left by the gaping palace doors, a platform had been erected. It was hewn from the finest timber; the colors of the rare woods blending like those in a painting. Its polished surface was bare, save for the Lion Throne of the Emperor, which sat within a three-sided canopy that depicted the succession of emperors dating back to Jass Issuri himself. After Jass Gebrem was crowned, his likeness would be woven into the canopy, which was brought out of its storage place in the Palace only during coronations.

Although the platform towered high above the crowd, there were no steps ascending to its surface. Many in the crowd wondered how the heavy throne had been placed there, and how Jass Gebrem and the others who would be involved in the coronation intended to mount the platform in the absence of steps. But no one asked those questions aloud amid the hum of conversation that complemented the sourceless singing and drumming.

Then, abruptly, the music stopped. As though on cue, so did the crowd's chatter. It was as though the entire population of Khambawe were holding its breath. And all attention focused on the platform.

3

"Are you nervous?"

Tiyana turned and looked at person who had asked the question. It was Byallis, the brown-haired Adept who had helped her to maintain her equilibrium during the manifestation of Oneness that had allowed the Amiyas and Almovaads to combine to defeat the Uloans' magic.

"Yes," Tiyana admitted.

She was sitting on a carved, hardwood bench in front of a mirror in the House of Almovaar, formerly the Beit Amiya. Her hair, which had grown to a length below her shoulders, was being re-braided by a Matile Acolyte.

In previous times, a *shamasha* would have performed such a task. When, in the aftermath of the battle against the Uloans, it had been discovered that many, if not most, of the *shamashas* were fronting for the *tsotsis*, the position of *shamasha* was abolished, and those who had not already left the Beit Amiya were dismissed. Now Acolytes – new recruits from all parts of the Empire who were in the beginning stages of their apprenticeship in Almovaad sorcery – performed menial duties in the House as part of their training to become Initiates.

"So am I," Byallis said.

They both smiled.

The friendship between them had grown since the night the Uloans had invaded. Because of Tiyana's changed status, her other friendships – even with Yemeya – had suffered. Tiyana was the only child of the new Emperor. Therefore, she now stood next in line to the Lion Throne.

Women had ruled the Matile Mara Empire in the past, but only when the previous monarch produced no male heirs. One Empress, Shumet, was almost as legendary as Jass Issuri. Under her command, Matile armies had pushed the Empire's borders far to the south, deep into Thaba territory. Shumet had also recaptured Gondaba, a city that had attempted to break free from the Empire just as the Uloan Islands had later done.

As a child, Tiyana had learned the history of Shumet. But she never imagined she would one day emulate that legendary ruler.

As Empress-in-waiting, Tiyana found that a distance had developed between her and those she had known since their shared childhood. Before, she had been only one of many in her generation of the Jassi, the Matile nobility. Now, as the future sovereign, the lives of everyone in Matile would one day be in her hands.

She knew the questions that the others were asking themselves now. How much would Tiyana remember about the past? What grudges did she hold? What slights and insults were hidden in her heart, never forgotten? And what favors did she give or receive that would one day demand reciprocation?

But none of those concerns mattered to Byallis. As an outsider and an Adept of the Almovaads, the intrigues of Matile royalty were irrelevant to her. Thus, Byallis was free to become Tiyana's confidante, the ear into which she poured her hopes and misgivings about the new direction upon which she and her people had embarked. Byallis listened ... and sometimes, she advised.

Byallis was swathed in a blue *chamma* that left one of her plump shoulders bare. Her hair was braided Matile-style, with blue beads woven through its length. The sun had finally darkened her skin, although it was still much lighter than Tiyana's.

Her face bore the serenity typical of the most unwavering Believers. Unlike Tiyana, Byallis harbored no qualms about the future. Whatever happened would be Almovaar's will, and whatever that will might be, she would accept it without question.

The acolyte, a Matile girl not much older than Kalisha – whom Tiyana had long-since forgotten – finally finished her work. Tiyana's hair was now a fall of silver, amber and gold beads, framing her dark face. Her *chamma* was the color of a cloudless blue sky, and it hung in immaculate folds from her slender frame.

After inspecting herself in the mirror one last time, Tiyana turned to the acolyte.

"You have done well," she said. "Thank you."

She would never have said anything so complimentary to a *shamasha*. The girl smiled shyly in acknowledgement, then departed.

Tiyana looked at Byallis for a moment. The coronation ceremony was new to the Fidi woman, and the preparations had been at once elaborate and meticulous. But Byallis showed no signs of apprehension, regardless of what she had said about being nervous.

One day, I might have such serenity, Tiyana mused in her mind.

"No one among the Matile has ever tried what we are about to do," she said aloud to Byallis.

"No one among us has, either," Byallis returned.

Byallis smiled as she spoke. The smile became a giggle, then a laugh. Despite her nervousness, Tiyana soon joined her.

Then, within the part of their minds that all Adepts shared, a Summoning to the Oneness came. And the women's laughter stopped.

"It's time," Byallis said.

Tiyana nodded and rose from the bench. Arm-in-arm with Byallis, she went to the place in which all those who were participating in the coronation ceremony were to gather.

4

The silence inside the pavilion had stretched from moments to many minutes. Anticipation – but not yet impatience – hung like a low cloud over the vast assemblage of people who awaited the coronation.

Along with the other surviving members of the *White Gull's* crew, Captain Pel Muldure stood in a place of honor at the forefront of the crowd, along with the Matile who had fought valiantly against the Uloans. Lyann was, as always, at his side.

Muldure was resplendent in full Matile regalia: embroidered tunic and trousers, and a white *chamma* with sea-green stripes. A leather band studded with silver held his hair in place. If he was still brooding over the destruction of his ship and further loss of crew members, neither his eyes nor his demeanor showed it.

Lyann had eschewed Matile clothing, saying it was uncomfortably confining. She was clad in a shirt and breeches made to her specifications by Matile seamstresses. Her only concession to the culture of her new locale was a single strand of multicolored beads woven into a lock of her unbraided hair.

Her well of patience wasn't as deep as that of the others.

"When is this thing going to get started?" she grumbled.

"When they're ready," Muldure said.

"Or when the Seer decides to pull the strings," Lyann snorted.

"Don't say that!" a voice admonished sharply.

Both Muldure and Lyann turned to the source of the comment. It was Herrin Junn, formerly one of the rowdiest and most profane seafarers Muldure had ever come across. Now, Junn's burly body was wrapped in the blue robes of a Believer. The forces that had vanquished the Uloans had also shaken Junn's lifelong cynicism and, like several other *White Gull* crew members, he had pledged himself to the Almovaads.

Lyann found Junn's new piety amusing. For Muldure, however, it was insufferable.

"The Seer does not rule this place," Junn said. "He merely advises."

"Of course," said Muldure. "And the *White Gull's* sitting at anchor out in the harbor, waiting to take us home."

Junn's eyes narrowed and his lips compressed into a thin line of disapproval.

"Do not mock the Seer!" he hissed.

Lyann's sharp elbow to the ribs suppressed the sardonic retort that came to Muldure's mind. He expressed his annoyance with a scowl instead.

Suddenly, the air above the platform shimmered like a pulse of heat on a sun-scorched savanna. And a bang loud as a thunderclap caused everyone in the pavilion to close their eyes and cover their ears. Many cried out in surprise and, in more than a few cases, fear. Some even fell to the ground. When the echo subsided and the people opened their eyes again, the platform was no longer empty.

Mouths agape in wonder, the crowd gazed at the glory of the people of power among the Matile and the Almovaads. This was a feat of sorcery that easily matched, or surpassed, anything the *ashuma* of the storied past could have accomplished.

Gebrem was the center of the assemblage. He had materialized in front of the throne that was about to become his. Gebrem's demeanor was solemn, a reflection of his mood. Never in his life had he imagined that he would succeed his cousin, Dardar Alemeyu. Now, he knew the reality of the responsibilities that rested on an Emperor's shoulders. For all the lifelong abrasiveness of their relationship, he wished Alemeyu were still alive.

The royal *chamma* that had enveloped Alemeyu was now wrapped around Gebrem's own gaunt frame. His head, with its mass of graying braids, remained bare. The Crown of Issuri would weigh upon it soon enough.

For the moment, the Crown rested atop a waist-high pillar of crystal in front of Kyroun, who stood at Gebrem's side. The Seer's unbraided white hair stirred in the gentle breeze that billowed the sides of the pavilion like a ship's sails. Draped over Kyroun's Fidi robes was a *chamma* dyed a blue so dark it was almost black. It was as though the Seer was cloaked in a segment of starless night sky.

The Kyroun held the transformed *abi*, symbol of the status of Leba. The shining rod remained smooth, bereft of the symbols of vanished Matile gods. The Degen Jassi had earlier agreed that Kyroun would become Leba in Gebrem's stead. A few traditionalists had objected, arguing that no one who was not of Matile blood had ever before been Leba. When Gebrem pointed out that Kyroun was indeed of Matile blood, however distant, because of his ancestor, Yekunu, the critics had fallen silent. Besides, this Leba would be the servitor and interlocutor for one god rather than many. That, too, was a break from tradition.

Tiyana was at Gebrem's other side. Already, her bearing was that of an Empress. Gone was the insecure Vessel of Nama-kwah who had feared for the future and longed for the past. Now, Tiyana almost never thought about Nama-kwah; nor did she miss the fleeting contacts she had experienced with the goddess when she was an Amiya. Her new relationship with Almovaar was constant, a reassuring anchor at the center of her being. Her magical strength was no longer ephemeral; it flowed through her as naturally as her blood.

The rest of the Degen Jassi shared the platform with the Leba and the imperial pair of father and daughter. The ranks of the ruling class had been thinned after the slaughter the Uloans had inflicted. Many of those who would have shared the splendor of Gebrem's coronation this day were buried in the City of the Dead.

In contrast, the Imba Jassi were almost fully represented. Only a few of them had been in Khambawe when the Uloans had invaded, and they now outnumbered their city-dwelling counterparts. What this change would mean in the future was yet to be decided.

Although the raiment of the rulers of the outlying lands could not match that of the Degen Jassi, the bearing of the rustic lords was just as dignified. Still, they, too, harbored apprehensions. Under the loose rule of earlier Emperors, the Imba Jassi had enjoyed tacit independence. With a new ruler whose power was strengthened by that of the Almovaads, how long would this level of autonomy last?

That question would be answered at another time. For the glory of this day reflected as much on the Imba Jassi as it was on the people of the city.

A lone drummer occupied a corner of the platform. He was clad in the garb of the primeval Matile, harkening back to the time before the first Leba harnessed the power of *ashuma*. The skin of a lion cloaked the drummer's lean frame, and ornaments made from lions' teeth and claws adorned his arms, legs, and hair.

His drum, called the Negarit, was ancient, made before the time of Jass Issuri and handed down through countless generations. It was huge; the drummer could not have circled it with both his arms. A patina of age coated its dark wood, obscuring hints of figures and symbols carved by the hands of long-dead tribal craftsmen. Only during coronations was the Negarit removed from its place of honor in the Palace, and only the descendants of the first drummer were allowed to play it.

But when the drummer, whose name was Wolde as was that of all his ancestors, struck the Negarit's surface with the ebony sticks in his hands, the sound was clear and resonant, as though the drum had been carved that very morning.

As Wolde's arcanely amplified beat echoed throughout the pavilion and far beyond, Kyroun began to recite the long list of Emperors and Empresses of Matile Mala, names only now known to him.

"Issuri," he began. "Tebede. Mangasha. Tsegaye. Hailam. Bekele...."

These were names most Matile knew as well as their own. Names of pride, names of power. Names of those who had lifted the Matile Mara Empire to its greatest glory; names of those whose folly had led to its downfall. And, finally, the name of the one who would be entrusted to renew the Empire's greatness:

"Dardar Asfaw Gebrem."

The Seer and the crowd fell silent. Gebrem raised his arms, and a soft glow suffused the Crown and Sword of Issuri. Then both royal objects rose from the pedestal and floated toward Gebrem. Gently, the Crown settled onto Gebrem's head. And the Sword drifted into his waiting hands.

Gebrem raised the Sword high above his head and held it steady. The glow from both the Crown and Sword enveloped him, transforming him into an incandescent icon and suffusing everyone else with him on the platform. As he stood before his people, the new Emperor overshadowed even Kyroun. It was as though Gebrem personified the Matile's imminent return to the greatness of the past in the aftermath of their near-obliteration.

A spontaneous cheer rose from the crowd: a cacophony of chants and ululations that originated back in the time when the Matile herded cattle and fought clan wars and dreamed of something more, something beyond the confines of their fields and pastures. Caught up in their hosts' fervor, the Fidi joined the celebration, adding victory songs from their own lands to the tapestry of triumph.

As waves of approbation continued to wash over him, the Emperor Gebrem locked eyes with Kyroun. The Degen and Imba Jassi had met several times, well in advance of the coronation, to discuss what should be done during its immediate aftermath. Alternatives had been discussed. Plans had been made. Tasks had been assigned.

"Now, my friend, our work truly begins," Gebrem said.

Kyroun nodded.

5

One person in the crowd was not the same as all the others, even though he looked like the rest of the people, and shouted and sang in celebration as loudly as anyone else. But he was different – unique.

As far as he knew, Sehaye, the islander spy, was the only Uloan left alive in Khambawe. He had not crossed paths with any others. There was no longer any danger of discovery; he had long since overcome the madness that had claimed him after Retribution Time had turned into a calamity, although some of it remained, touching his consciousness like strings of spider-silk. In the immediate aftermath of the battle, his disoriented behavior had not been noticed, for it was not unusual. Eventually, his mind calmed, and he did what he needed to do in order to stay alive.

He often thought a similar madness had afflicted the other spies in the city, whose identities in any case remained unknown to him. He did not want to know who they were, or whether or not they still lived. He only knew there had to be a purpose in his own survival. And that purpose would become clear when Legaba decided it was time for him to become aware of it.

In the meantime, Sehaye focused his attention fully on the royal platform: on the pretender who wore the crown that rightfully belonged to Jass Imbiah; on the foreign interloper who had wrongfully assumed the role of Leba. He sensed those two were somehow involved in his own destiny. But he did not yet know how, nor could he even guess what lay ahead.

He knew the answer would come. Legaba would give it to him. And when he received it, he would be ready to act.

CHAPTER TWENTY-TWO
Complications

1

The Emperor Gebrem meditated alone in Dardar Agaw's chamber, where Alemeyu had spent so much of his time. Gone were the elaborate panoply and accouterments that had accompanied his coronation. His crown and royal vestments were close at hand, but now was not the time to wear them. He was clad in simple garb: plain white tunic over *senafil*, like most Matile of lesser rank. The long braids of his hair were unadorned. When he presented himself to his new god, he did so as an ordinary man, even though he had become much more – a man who possessed the ultimate in both secular and sorcerous power; a combination that had never before been seen on the Lion Throne. Even the great Issuri had been only a warrior, and not a sorcerer as well.

Gebrem sat cross-legged on the bare, stone floor, his hands folded in his lap. His eyes were closed, and his lips set in a straight, unsmiling line within his beard. Gebrem still looked like a man who was approaching old age, his hair rapidly becoming more gray than black. Inside, though, every fragment of his being radiated a vitality he had never known even when he was a youth – the power of Almovaad magic, a power far greater than anything he had ever experienced when he utilized *ashuma*. At times, Gebrem felt as though he could do anything he cared to do simply by waving his hand. But he also knew better than to fall into the foolish trap of acting as though that belief were true.

Now, his body was in the chamber of the long-dead Emperor Asfaw. But his soul was in the Realm of Almovaar ....

Gebrem stood in the midst of a desert unlike any that existed in

Abengoni. Golden sand stretched as far as his eyes could see, merging in the distance with a saffron sky in which no sun was visible. Yet there was light everywhere, emanating from the sky and glowing from every grain of sand.

Dunes rose like the multi-humped back of some gigantic beast slumbering just beneath the surface. Rills of sand rolled like water down the dunes' slopes, whispering in a language Gebrem could not understand. There was no indication of life's presence in this sere landscape ... none of the hardy plants and animals that clung to existence in the vast expanses of the Khumba Khourou wasteland, which lay far to the south of Matile Mala.

Yet even though there was no life, there were ... shadows. They were human in shape, but Gebrem saw no one who might have cast them no matter where he looked. After a moment's thought, Gebrem realized that these shadows must be Almovaar's Children ...

Heat burned into the soles of Gebrem's bare feet. A dry, searing wind whipped the braids of his hair into a frenzied tangle and billowed the tunic and trousers away from his lean frame. But the Emperor ignored both the heat and the wind. For he had been to this place before in the months that followed the defeat of the Uloans, though always with Kyroun at his side.

However, the Realm had always been empty the other times he had been there. Never before had he seen these shadows. They stretched in elongated silhouettes on the sand, not menacing Gebrem in any way, but also not reassuring him with their presence. They neither moved not made any sound.

Now, for the first time, he was in Almovaar's abode on his own, without the Seer present to guide him. After much reflection, Gebrem had decided that if he were to be the true ruler of Matile Mala, it was necessary for him to encounter his new god without the benefit of Kyroun's well-meaning intercession.

And he had questions to ask Almovaar ... more than he had first imagined, now that he had seen the shadows.

He waited. The shadows waited with him. Before long, an eddy of sand appeared in front of him, a tiny whirlwind no higher than his knees. Slowly, the spiral increased in size until it towered high above him, loftier than the stelae that rose throughout Khambawe, higher than the tallest tree in all the forests of Abengoni. The mighty pillar of sand whirled in front of Gebrem, blasting his face with heat, scoring his skin with granules of grit that stung him mercilessly. Within that pillar, Gebrem could detect the vague, shifting outline of a human form that disconcertingly resembled that of the shadows on the sand.

And still, Gebrem waited, along with the shadows. In his Realm, the god -- Jagasti or not -- was always the first to speak. When he did, Almovaar's voice was wind and sand, sibilant as a breeze, yet hard as a stone cliff-face.

You are here alone, *Almovaar said.* **Where is the Seer?**

"Kyroun is not the Emperor of the Matile Mala," Gebrem replied. "I am. There are things I must learn that only you can tell me. And those things are of greatest concern to the Emperor, not to the Seer."

A gust of wind nearly blew Gebrem from his feet. Sand stung his face and other exposed areas of his skin, and he shut his eyelids tight, lest he be blinded by the flying particles. Still, he stood firm, refusing to acknowledge the sudden fear that was threatening to overwhelm him. And he wondered how long it would be before the relentless wind forced him to flee Almovaar's Realm.

Abruptly, the wind subsided into a breeze that gently plucked the grains of sand from Gebrem's skin and clothing. When he opened his eyes again, Gebrem saw that the shadows were gone.

You have cut the cord that bound you to Kyroun, *Almovaar said.* **And you have woven your own cord that binds you to me. That is to the good. I have waited for this moment to come. And now it has. Ask of me what you will, Dardar Asfaw Gebrem.**

"You have saved the Matile Mala from destruction," Gebrem said. "And because of you, we will soon be as great as we were before; perhaps even greater. Everything of which I have long hoped and dreamed will now come true."

He paused, gathering courage to utter his next words.

"But why did you choose us? Why not some other people, elsewhere in the Fidi Lands? Why did you bring Gebrem back to the land of his far-distant ancestors? What is it here that you want, or need?"

A lengthy silence followed. Gebrem waited. He knew time did not pass in the same way for a deity as it did for a mortal. He often wondered whether time even existed for eternal beings like Almovaar and the Jagasti ...

You needed me, *Almovaar finally said.* **You still need me. For those who are such as I, it is better to be needed than forgotten and forsaken. That is something your Jagasti will learn soon enough.**

Gebrem nodded. The answer was less than he wanted, but still more than he had expected from the deity.

"I have another question," Gebrem said.

Almovaar waited.

"There is a price for everything," Gebrem continued. "Before our Jagasti became powerless, we paid a price for the *ashuma* they gave us. And for what you have given him, Kyroun has paid. I can see it in his eyes, even though he does not speak of it."

He paused, secretly dreading what he knew he had to ask next, and also knowing that he would never rest if he did not ask it.

"What, then, is the price we Matile must pay in return for what you have given to us?"

Gebrem steeled himself for another blast of searing, sand-filled wind from the god. It never came. Instead, the shadows reappeared, surrounding him until they blotted out the golden glow of the sand of Almovaar's Realm.

Then Almovaar told him what the price would be. And when Gebrem fully comprehended what it was, he devoutly wished for the sand and the wind instead of what he heard.

2

In the heart of the Tokoloshe embassy, a woman was the center of all attention, even though most of the Tokoloshe and their Dwarven kin were elsewhere. The woman was on her back, on a bed. Her stomach was distended, and her breath came in short, choking gasps. She was in labor. And she was the first Tokoloshe woman to be in that state for a long time, even by that long-lived people's reckoning.

Several other Tokoloshe women surrounded the one who was about to give birth. They were far from certain about what they needed to do; they could only rely on memories of ancient folklore, as well as their intuitive understanding of the birthing process, and the magic all Tokoloshe carried at their core. Yet for all their capabilities in a score of arcane arts, birthing was far more difficult for the Tokoloshe than it was for either humans or Zimwe. Tokoloshe pregnancies lasted longer, and their babies were larger in proportion to their mothers' bodies, and thus much more difficult to deliver.

The woman in labor, whose name was Izindikwa, struggled to fend off the pain that lanced through her in unrelenting cycles. The others around her chanted birthing-spells that were, at best, only half-remembered.

Izindikwa tried to concentrate on the ball of light that hovered over her, spilling pale illumination onto her heaving abdomen.

But her concentration slipped away from her. And she uttered a low moan that quickly rose to a long, lingering cry of pain. The sound echoed throughout the embassy, and the women surrounding Izindikwa cringed as it continued despite their best efforts to soothe her. The oldest woman, whose name was Chiminuka, grimaced as though she was herself experiencing Izindikwa's agony.

Izindikwa's cries also affected the men, who were gathered in the great hall that had been the scene of joyous feasting, drinking and other merriment not long before. When Izindikwa's pregnancy had been confirmed months earlier, the celebration of the happy occasion had lasted more than a week. And when the women had indicated she was due to deliver, more festivities had followed. But now, with the birthing imminent, the Tokoloshes' gaiety was gone. They feared for Izindikwa's life – and that of her child.

"Is she going to die?" Hulm Stonehand asked.

He was sitting in a stone chair. On his lap, his hands were knotted into tight, rock-like fists. Sweat covered his broad brow and trickled into his thick beard. Like most fathers at birthing-time, he felt as though he were useless ... powerless. As harrowing and distressing as the combat against the Uloan invaders had been, to Hulm's mind this waiting was far, far worse, primarily because waiting was all he could do.

Hulm looked into the eyes of his friend, Rumundulu. Rumundulu could not answer him. Neither could any of the other dwarves and Tokoloshe gathered in the huge underground chamber. They sat at unadorned tables and stared at empty plates and mugs, or at their equally empty hands.

Izindikwa had been the only Tokoloshe woman to conceive after the copulatory tempest that had followed the dwarves' arrival from Beyond the Storm. Hulm was the acknowledged father of the child-to-be, and had received many accolades from the Tokoloshe. In that one child of hope, the future of the Tokoloshe people would be assured ... if the child survived.

Another scream from Izindikwa tore into the chamber. Hulm rose from his seat. Rumundulu laid a restraining hand on his arm. Hulm shook it off violently and took a step away from the table.

"Let me go!" Hulm bellowed. "I have to help her!"

Rumundulu reached out again to hold Hulm back.

"Help her how?" the Tokoloshe asked. "What can you do?"

Hulm looked as though he were about to strike Rumundulu. Other Tokoloshe and dwarves around them tensed in anticipation of a need to intervene in case Hulm followed through on that impulse.

Then the blaze in Hulm's eyes dimmed. His breath escaped in a sorrowful sigh, and he slumped back into his seat. Relieved, the others also relaxed – until Izindikwa's next outcry assaulted their ears.

Hulm's hands knotted into massive lumps of bone and muscle. Rumundulu laid his own hand on Hulm's shoulders.

"We can only wait, my friend," he said as softly as his rumbling voice would allow. "We can only wait."

Hulm remained silent. Still, his huge fists slowly relaxed.

In the birthing chamber, Izindikwa continued to battle the pain. Struggling to implement knowledge that had been learned but never before put into practice, the Tokoloshe women laid their hands on Izindikwa's abdomen. They could feel the movement of the infant inside her. Before, the movement had started, then stopped again. This time, it continued in a rapidly increasing rhythm.

"*Now*," said Chiminuka.

The Tokoloshe women unleashed a stream of benign, undifferentiated force from the centre of magic within each of them. There was no specific chant or spell involved; no spectacular flashes of eldritch energy; no rambling chants or incantations. It was the simple manifestation of the women's desire to end Izindikwa's suffering and ease the long-awaited passage of the new Tokoloshe into the world.

Izindikwa moaned. Then she convulsed. And then the head of her child began to appear. Chiminuka's hands helped the infant along as the muscles of Izindikwa's body slowly pushed it out of her womb. Each push was accompanied by another outcry. When the child fully emerged at last, Izindikwa fell limp and silent.

The child was a boy. He had the fair complexion and straight hair of his father, and the broad features of a Tokoloshe. The infant drew his first breath, then began to wail. His crying echoed through the embassy building like a summons to celebrate. And the men in the other chamber did exactly that, bellowing and laughing with joy and deal the now-grinning Hulm buffets that would have disabled all but the sturdiest of humans, blows that Hulm happily returned.

But when Chiminuka came into the room only moments later, the tumult died down. The expression on the Tokoloshe woman's face was far from celebratory. The infant's cries continued; otherwise, silence suffused the chamber.

"What is wrong, Chiminuka?" Rumundulu asked.

"The child lives," Chiminuka replied. "But Izindikwa is dead."

Hulm could only shake his head in disbelief as the others looked at him with expressions ranging from sorrow to anger. What was on their faces was only an echo of the maelstrom of emotions that suddenly roiled inside him.

And the newest Tokoloshe continued to wail, as though he were acknowledging the price Izindikwa had paid to allow him to be born.

3

Keshu was inside Tiyana – inside her body, inside her mind, inside her soul, inside her heart. The soft sounds of their love-making echoed in the semi-darkness of Tiyana's bedchamber in the Beit Amiya. Through the new *ashuma* of Almovaar, their passion had become manifest, embodied in a warm, amber glow that emanated from their enjoined bodies. Within the subtle luminescence, the beads of sweat on their skin sparkled like bright dots of gold.

Their union was more than merely physical; it was spiritual and magical as well. Just as the minds of all the Almovaads had merged to release the sorcerous power that had defeated the Uloans, so, also, could two individuals link at the deepest possible level of intimacy, to reach a Oneness with each other that could be shared by no one else.

That was where Tiyana and Keshu were now. Even as their bodies moved together beneath the single, cotton sheet on Tiyana's bed, their souls joined into a single entity, as though together they had become a whole beyond what either of them could be as individuals. It was that convergence, as well as Keshu's climactic thrusts, that pushed cries of ecstasy from Tiyana's open mouth.

In the time before the traditional world of the Matile was torn asunder, any sharing of love between Tiyana and Keshu would have been unthinkable, because of the difference in their stations, even though they were both Amiyas and as such, theoretically equals. But that theory would never have been allowed to progress to practice.

Once Tiyana's days as Nama-kwah's Vessel were over, she would have been given in marriage to one of the Degen Jassi, and she would have had children and lived the rest of her life as a wife of a member of the Emperor's Court. Her place in the line of succession to the Lion Throne meant little to her then; she had stood far behind Dardar Alemeyu's hoped-to-be-born heir and Jass Eshana, not to mention her own father.

Despite Tiyana's indifference to her status, if she and Keshu had become lovers prior to the coming of the Fidi and the Uloans, they would have had to do so in utmost secrecy. And if that secret had ever been discovered, Keshu would have been put to a painful death, and Tiyana would have been stripped of her rank and exiled into the lands of the Imba Jassi. Such was Matile custom, passed down without question over scores of generations.

But now, the age-old social hierarchy of the Matile no longer mattered. Its meticulously layered strictures of social strata lay in as much ruin as any of the heaps of charred rubble in Khambawe that the Matile had cleared to make way for new structures to arise. Among the Almovaads, all Adepts were of equal status. And both Tiyana and Keshu had quickly become Adepts, easily transferring their skills at harnessing the weakened *ashuma* of the Jagasti to the disciplines required to control the powerful sorcery Almovaar placed at their disposal.

And so they were free … free to fulfill their love in ways that would have been beyond their understanding in the time before the arrival of the Almovaads. Free to acknowledge what had become known to both of them only during the first time they had entered the Oneness.

Finally, their passion subsided. The golden glow ebbed even as the perspiration on their bodies dried. For a long time they lay quietly, still wrapped in each other's arms, skin touching skin, soul touching soul.

Keshu was the one who broke the long, sweet silence.

"How long will it be before you must do what the Emperor has requested of you?"

His voice was low, almost a whisper. He had asked his question as though he were reluctant to hear the answer. As it was, Tiyana's reply did not come until several long moments had passed.

"Soon," she said. "Too soon."

She pressed her face into the space between his neck and shoulder, as if she were about to weep. But she didn't. And in the deepest part of their

Oneness, of the connection the Almovaads' magic had given them, Keshu knew Tiyana would never shed any tears over the duty the Emperor and Seer had given her. They both knew the task they had chosen for her was a test ... a measure of Tiyana's capability to take her father's place on the throne when the time came for her to do so, as it must regardless of how intensely she hoped Gebrem would live forever.

"I wish I could go with you," Keshu said.

"I do, too," said Tiyana. "But there is so much that needs to be done. And so few of us to do it."

Keshu was silent. But he understood what she was saying. Not all of the former Vessels had been able to adapt fully to the transition from *ashuma* to the new sorcery the Almovaads practiced. Some of them clung unconsciously to previous times and old ways that had defined their identities. So for those who had done so successfully, the burden of helping to restore the Empire was heavier – but not too onerous to be welcomed and embraced, even when it forced lovers like Tiyana and Keshu to be apart for a time.

"Even though I want to go with you, I have my duty as well," Keshu said. "Still, even when we're far apart, I'll be with you. Our Oneness will last forever, Tiyana."

"I know," Tiyana whispered.

She embraced him fiercely, as though she were making certain her skin would remember the touch of his, no matter how long the responsibilities they had been charged to fulfill might separate them. Keshu returned her ardor. And soon, the glow of their passion again illuminated Tiyana's bedchamber, and soft sounds echoed from its walls.

4

Kyroun had been given his own complex of chambers in the Gebbi Senafa, which befitted his status among the Matile and his close relationship with the Emperor. In previous times, the Emperor and the Leba had been estranged because of the antagonism between Gebrem and Alemeyu, and Gebrem had resided in the House of Amiyas rather than the Palace. The Seer's presence in the Palace symbolized the alliance between the two men.

Now, though, Kyroun knew that partnership was about to be put to the test. And he could not foresee whether or not it would survive that trial, which Kyroun knew would come sooner rather than later.

Like Gebrem, Kyroun was clad in a plain garment and seated in a meditative posture on the floor in front of his bed. He could have joined Gebrem in the golden desert that was Almovaar's Realm, if only to observe what passed between the Emperor and his god. But he chose not to do so. There was no point; he already knew what Almovaar would say to Gebrem. However, he did not know how the new Emperor would react.

He would soon find out, though. And he was waiting for that moment. So he was not surprised when Kyroun entered the chamber, unannounced and without ceremony.

Gebrem looked as though he were still in Almovaar's bleak fastness. The hot wind had left the braids of his hair askew, even though only his spirit had been away, not his body. His eyes were red, as though tiny granules of sand still stung them. And when he spoke, his voice sounded like the rasp of a sliding dune, similar to the voice of Almovaar.

"You knew," he accused. "You always knew, Kyroun. Yet you didn't tell me. *Why?*"

Gebrem's eyes blazed. Kyroun could sense the gathering of the Emperor's nascent power. It was a power that might well have matched his own, for all that it was still new to Gebrem. The Leba had assimilated Almovaad magic far more quickly than any of the Amiyas; it was as though he were born to wield it. The Seer knew that his future, as well as that of Gebrem and the newly reborn Matile Mara Empire, depended on how he replied to Gebrem's anguished question.

He answered it with a series of questions of his own.

"If I had told you, would you have accepted Almovaar? And if you had not accepted Almovaar, would you – and the Matile Mala – be where you are today? Would you, or your daughter, or anyone else here still be alive? Would this city still be standing?"

Gebrem's eyes didn't waver from their intense lock with Kyroun's. But the flames of wrath in the Matile's gaze slowly diminished to embers. And the scowl on his features relaxed, becoming an expression of deep melancholy – and, perhaps, regret. Finally, Gebrem turned and departed from Kyroun's bedchamber without saying another word.

He never replied to the Seer's question. He didn't have to. For both men knew what his answer would have been.

CHAPTER TWENTY-THREE
Shadows After Dark
1

The tsotsis *must go*, the Emperor, as well as the Degen and Imba Jassi had agreed. More than a menace, the gangs of thieves were traitors as well. The people of Khambawe retained bitter memories of the way the tsotsis had looted their homes and robbed them in the streets even as the Uloans were rampaging through the city. The gangs had proven to be as destructive in their own way as the invaders.

In times past, Khambawe's authorities were helpless to stem the tide of lawlessness rampant in the Maim and beyond. No longer were they ineffectual. No longer would they allow the tsotsis to rule the streets after the sun went down.

No longer ...

Kece froze in fear when he looked back and saw a second shadow beginning to appear on the wall behind him.

Don't trust shadows after dark ....

That was the new watchword among the *tsotsis*. Life in the Maim had become more arduous than ever since the new Emperor had decreed his intention to reclaim the area and finally eradicate the infestation of outlaws from the city. The *tsotsi* sets, already decimated by the fighting against the Uloans and each other, were now hunted relentlessly by squadrons of soldiers and vigilantes. Those who were not killed on the spot were captured and taken away, never to be seen again. And rumors concerning where they had gone multiplied among the remnants of the gangs.

But soldiers could be evaded and, given the opportunity, killed. Not the shadows, though. Not the shadows.

Don't trust shadows after dark ....

Not long after the coronation of the new Emperor, the shadows began to appear without warning, etched on the walls and floors of the Maim. A *tsotsi* would suddenly sprout a second shadow behind him, and that *tsotsi* would die, no matter what he or anyone else tried to do to prevent it, or how far and fast the target attempted to flee. The *tsotsis* soon began to call the second shadows "Muvuli," which meant "Bringers of Death."

Now, it was Kece's turn to be stalked by a Muvuli.

Kece looked up at the night-sun, and cursed bitterly. Where there was light, there were shadows. And there was always light in the Maim. It was the same light that had shone over the entire city on the night the scar-heads from the islands had invaded. Now, the Maim was the only place over which the magical orb shone: muted in the daytime, brightly at night.

This witch-light was the Blue Robes' doing. Kece hated the Blue Robes more than anything else – other than the new Emperor, whom he and most other *tsotsis* considered to be little more than the foreigners' *shamasha*, doing their bidding and mimicking their ways.

Kece's second shadow stood only a short distance from the first. It duplicated the posture of its counterpart. When Kece instinctively reached for the hilt of his *tirss*, both shadows did the same. Then, when he realized his weapon would not help him, he drew his hand away from it. So did one shadow – but not the other. The Muvuli completed the motion that Kece and the first had stopped. Its movements were now independent of those of the *tsotsi*.

Eyes widening in horror, Kece watched as the second shadow raised its *tirss* high over its head. Then the Muvuli swung downward.

With a choked cry, Kece flinched away. The Muvuli's blow barely missed striking the other shadow on the wall.

Even though he knew flight was futile, Kece turned and ran, trying to outdistance both of his shadows. As his feet echoed hollowly through the deserted street, Kece cursed Jass Mofo for sending him and everyone else in the Ashaki set out in the streets to search for two people who could not be found.

The Muvuli struck again. This time, the blow landed, the spikes of the *tirss* sinking deep into the back of Kece's true shadow. Kece cried out as pain ripped through his own back and blood spurted from fresh wounds, even though it was only his shadow that had been struck. He staggered, struggling to stay on his feet, fighting to hold on to his life.

Another shadow-blow sent the *tsotsi* reeling to the ground. His blood rilled onto the street's paving stones. He continued to crawl forward even as the Muvuli struck again and again, hitting Kece's shadow and ravaging his flesh with each blow. Kece cursed, moaned, and finally screamed in agony as the rain of death-blows tore at him.

Finally – mercifully – Kece's life came to an end, and he lay still. The Muvuli stood alone on the surface of a house wall, and shook shadow-drops of blood from its *tirss*. Then it faded out of existence, its work done.

2

Jass Mofo and the rest of what was left of the Ashaki found Kece's corpse the next day. The *tsotsi* lay in a pool of congealed blood. His body remained undisturbed; that was how the others knew Kece had been slain by one of the Blue Robes' shadows. Ordinarily, the Maim's contingent of hyenas and wild dogs would have long since devoured the fresh carrion. But the scavengers never touched the remains of those whom the Muvuli had slain.

Mofo gazed dispassionately at the butchered corpse. The other *tsotsis* – fewer than a dozen of them – in turn gazed at their Jass with half-averted eyes and deliberately blank expressions on their faces.

No longer did Mofo exemplify outlaw royalty. The braids of his hair were matted and bereft of the silver and gold ornaments that had once weighed them down. His regal *chamma* was gone; he wore only soiled, torn black leather *senafil*. His hand was clenched tightly around the hilt of his *tirss*. If anything, the cold, affectless void mirrored in his eyes had grown deeper and darker since the night the *tsotsis*' reign in the streets had ended.

The *tsotsis*' power over the Maim and the other, poorer, parts of Khambawe had become only a memory now. The outlaws' former prey no longer feared them. The Emperor's soldiers ruled the city by day, and the Muvuli owned the night. One by one, the *tsotsis* were disappearing, either through death or capitulation to the new realities of the city.

But Jass Mofo refused to surrender. Two obsessions drove him onward, even as other *tsotsis* gave up their miscreant ways and attempted to become part of the new Khambawe – or if not that, escape it.

"He be careless," Mofo muttered as he looked down at Kece. "Should've watched he-self."

Ordinarily, silence would have greeted Mofo's statement. This time, though, one voice dared to allow itself to be heard.

"If you not send him out here, he not be dead."

Whispers of indrawn breath accompanied Mofo's motion as he turned to face the speaker, who was Jumu, the only Ashaki who still had the courage not to cringe before the leader of the set. Jumu had not been openly rebellious, but he had come close to reaching that line before. Now, he crossed it.

"What you say, Jumu?" Mofo asked softly.

"You got bad ears, or what?" Jumu said coolly.

Jumu didn't drop his gaze when Mofo looked at him.

Jumu tightened his grip on his *tirss*, and his face took on an expression of daring and determination. He had thought about this confrontation for a long time, and had convinced himself that Mofo had lost his edge, that the Ashaki Jass was no longer to be feared, that he was ready to be taken.

Jumu thought he was ready to challenge Mofo, to pit his prowess with the *tirss* against that of his leader.

He wasn't.

Mofo had grown leaner than he was before. But he wasn't any slower. And he had always been the quickest *tsotsi* in the Maim.

Before Jumu could say or do anything more, Mofo's *tirss* reached out to him – and bit. The impact of the weapon's sharp spikes sheared away half of Jumu's face. Then Mofo struck again, laying Jumu's chest open to the bone and exposing his still-beating heart.

Eyes wide and round, Jumu crumpled to the ground, dead before he had a chance even to cry out. His fresh blood mingled with the pool of congealed gore that surrounded Kece.

Mofo turned to the rest of the set and stared at them all, each in turn. None of them met his cold gaze.

Then he said the words the Ashaki had come to dread; the words they had been hearing every day since their loot had been stolen by the Fidi, Athir, who had beaten them at their own game.

"Find the Fidi-*tsotsi*," Mofo said. "Make him give back what he take from us. Kill him – slow. Then bring me his seed-sack. Heard?"

"Heard," the *tsotsis* replied in a ragged chorus.

"Find Amiya-girl," Mofo continued. "Bring her back, alive. She be my luck. Never should've let her go. Heard?"

"Heard."

Mofo nodded. Then he waved his hand in curt dismissal. And the set scattered, for soon the soldiers their henchmen would be patrolling the streets they had once ceded to the *tsotsis* and the hyenas. Though none would say it aloud, more than a few of the set wished that one of Muvuli would come and claim their Jass, so they could finally be free of him.

3

To find Athir Rin, the *tsotsis* would have had to make their way into the Gebbi Senafa. Then they would have needed to evade human guards and magical wards. And if they somehow managed to succeed in slaying the Fidi but failed to avoid capture, they would have received a punishment even worse than what the Muvuli that stalked the Maim could mete out.

The reason the erstwhile Ship's Rat was safe was that he had become an honored guest of the Emperor Gebrem. And even as the Ashaki set scoured every reeking alley and bolthole in the Maim, Athir was ensconced in his own chambers in the Palace, enjoying sumptuous food and the finest *talla* and *kef*, attended by a pair of young female servants who supplied him with more than just food and drink.

Athir took another sip of his *talla* and savored the tangy taste. It was much better than the rotgut he had forced down his throat in the *talla-beits* of the districts close to the Maim, or other dubious concoctions he had drunk in less-reputable corners of the world.

He grinned. And he had ample reason to be smug.

During the immediate aftermath of the Uloan invasion, Athir had taken the biggest risk of his life – and he won, even more than he thought he had when he made off with the *tsotsis'* plunder while they were fighting for their lives against the Uloans. The hoard of loot he had filched from the *tsotsis* had immense value. But for all practical purposes – and Athir acknowledged no purposes other than the practical – it was worthless and useless to him.

He knew that once the survivors of the carnage discovered that the *tsotsis* had been plundering them even as they were fighting for their lives and their kingdom, the ensuing eruption of indignation would be frightening in its intensity. Anyone who attempted to profit from goods stolen by the *tsotsis* would have been torn limb-from-limb by mobs of Matile, who now hated the *tsotsis* even more than they did the Uloans – and there weren't any more Uloans around for the Matile to kill.

Therefore, Athir needed to think of some other way to gain advantage from the loot he had taken from fellow thieves, which in his mind evened the score for the purse they had stolen from him in the Ukili *shebeen*. It did not matter to him that the loot was far greater in value than the contents of his purse.

Well did he remember the abuse he had suffered at the hands of Mofo and the Ashaki set during his "stepping over." He remembered the fear that had been his constant companion during the time he ran with the *tsotsis*, and the ill-concealed disdain and contempt in which he knew Jass Mofo held him. And those bitter memories made his decision an easy one, once he had worked out all the details in his mind. And the revenge that followed his carrying out of that decision tasted all the sweeter, like the finest Fiadolian wine.

It had been a simple matter for him to seek out a Matile army officer and spin a tale of being captured by the *tsotsis* during the fighting against the Uloans, and being forced to accompany them during their depredations. He had ultimately escaped their clutches, he said half-truthfully, but not before learning where the set that had captured him had cached its loot. Athir then offered to show the officer where the cache was located. And he asked for nothing in return.

Muldure and other members of the *White Gull's* crew would have seen through the Ship's Rat's story as if it were made of glass, for they knew him well. And even the Matile officer, whose name was Keteme, harbored some suspicions about Athir, as he would about anyone even slightly associated with the *tsotsis*. But in the debilitating immediate aftermath of the invasion, before the rebuilding had begun, even a glimmer of good news was better than none at all.

So Keteme allowed Athir to lead him and some other soldiers to the spot in the sewers in which he had cached the Ashakis' spoils. That course of action was Athir's toss of the dice.

Under normal circumstances, Athir would never have placed himself in such a vulnerable position. It would have been a simple matter for Keteme and his troops to slit his throat and keep the loot for themselves once it was in their hands.

But circumstances in Khambawe were far from normal, and Athir knew it. Most of the city lay in ruins, and outrage at the opportunistic depredations of the *tsotsis* had risen to a fever pitch. Few people were thinking clearly while bodies still lay in the streets and buildings lay in smoking ruins. Athir's calculations of his odds proved correct: this time, the soldiers' sense of duty superseded their all-too-human greed.

The Ashakis' hoard was collected, and the stolen goods were returned to the owners who had survived the invasion. Keteme, his men, and Athir divided what was left.

When the Emperor learned of Athir's role in the recovery of the *tsotsis*' plunder, he had, in gratitude, given Athir a room in the royal palace. Suddenly, the Ship's Rat had become a man of wealth and influence in the rebuilding city, much to the bemusement and disgust of his former shipmates, who were certain Athir had stolen the booty himself, then passed the blame on to the *tsotsis* when he found he couldn't sell it.

None of them had said anything to the Matile, though. The Ship's Rat simply wasn't worth the trouble, even though he now possessed much more material goods than any of those who had scorned him.

Wrapped in luxurious Matile garments, Athir leaned against the ornate cushions that supported his back and fingered the thin tail of hair that hung from the back of his head. He thought about Mofo and the other *tsotsis*, and how they were currently on the run, stalked by soldiers, shadows, and even ordinary citizens bent on vengeance.

And he laughed out loud.

"I love it," he said. "I just love it!"

He was speaking in his native tongue, which his servants did not understand. They laughed with him, anyway. For they knew this Fidi could be generous, given the proper enticements.

And, as Athir looked on in approval, they began to provide them.

4

Neither the Ashaki nor the Muvuli would ever be able to find Kalisha... not as long as she remained in the darkness of the Underground, an extensive labyrinth of tunnels and sewers of ancient vintage that lay beneath the streets of Khambawe. Kalisha was safe in the Underground. But she was also alone.

She sat still as a stone, the wet surface of a tunnel wall clinging to her back. At first, she had loathed the sensation of dampness constantly seeping into her skin. Now, she welcomed it, because it reminded her that she was still alive; that the gloom that surrounded her was not the endless dark of death.

Her fingers trailed idly across the Mask of Nama-kwah. By now, she knew every contour of the effigy by touch alone. Its shape was as familiar as that of her own face and body, emaciated though she had become during the long time she had spent in hiding. She sustained herself on fungal matter she foraged from the walls and whatever scuttling creatures she could capture on the ground. Water was plentiful, if not particularly palatable.

Her fingers paused at the dent in the Mask, the single blemish caused when Mofo had hurled it against a wall. Kalisha had smoothed it as much as possible, but despite her efforts, the imperfection remained. She hated Mofo for the way he had defaced her prize when he discarded it – and her. Her ambition to be his consort one day was now as dead as the *tsotsis'* rule of the streets.

And the Mask had saved her life.

Kalisha remembered the night a Muvuli had come for her. She had seen other *tsotsis* attacked, yet she had, child-like, refused to believe the same thing could ever happen to her – until it did.

Fear had clutched at her heart when she saw a second shadow materialize behind her. It had pulled a dagger from the silhouetted simulacrum of cloth at its waist, even as Kalisha's own weapon – and her natural shadow's – remained in its hiding place. She had stood frozen in fear as the Muvuli's blade rose, then began to fall ....

Then the light of the Blue Robes' night-sun glinted from the silver surface of the Mask. And a luminous shaft of illumination pointed the way to an open sewer – the way to the Underground.

Kalisha had not hesitated. She dove toward the opening even as the second Muvuli's dagger barely missed her own shadow's back. The dark mouth of the sewer swallowed her whole, and the Blue Robes' shadow could not pursue her into it. She was safe.

At first, she had loathed the noisome stench of the Underground. And she missed the sun's light and warmth. And she longed for the sound of other people's voices, and the sight and touch of them. Eventually, however, those yearnings passed. She came to realize that the Muvuli would never find her as long as she remained below. And neither could other *tsotsis* bent on stealing the Mask from her.

Before going into the Underground, Kalisha had not failed to notice the covetous glances some of the surviving *tsotsis* of the Maim had cast at the bundle that was always clutched in her arms. It had to contain something of value ... something worth stealing. Small as Kalisha was, however, there was a glint in her eyes that warned would-be thieves to beware. It was like looking into the eyes of a cobra.

Kalisha was not alone in the Underground. The Mask served as both her companion and her friend. The only time she spoke aloud was when she spoke to the Mask.

She remembered how Tiyana had donned the Mask during ceremonies at the Beit Amiya. She had seen Tiyana become one with the goddess. In her fronting persona, she had been all but invisible to Tiyana and the others she served, so they seldom, if ever, shooed her away. She had watched and listened; observing much, but understanding little.

More than once, Kalisha had wondered what it would be like to place the Mask's face over hers. How snugly would it fit her? Would she, too, become one with Nama-kwah, as Tiyana had?

Now, the Mask was hers. She could put it on any time she wanted, and her curiosity would be satisfied. And, on several occasions, she had begun to do so. But each time, something stopped her hands before they could place the Mask over her head. It was as though another, unseen hand placed itself gently, but firmly, over hers, exerting just enough pressure to restrain her without hurting her.

Eventually, Kalisha realized that the Mask would let her know when it wanted her to put it on. Until that time came, she would remain Underground, out of the reach of *tsotsis* and Muvuli alike. She would remain in the darkness as long as she had to. The Mask would tell her when she should put it on, and leave the Underground, and see the sun and the Moon Stars again.

She ran her fingers across the face of Nama-kwah. And she sang a wordless song in a voice corroded from lack of use.

CHAPTER TWENTY-FOUR
ULOAN FEARS
1

Legaba's Realm lay silent and inert. Its sky was like the inside of a leaden bowl: gray, flat and featureless. Its sourceless light had grown so dim that the landscape it illuminated was almost invisible, shrouded in a shadowy pall like the overhanging smoke from some massive, cataclysmic conflagration, or a fog that encompassed the entire world.

The trees that dotted the endless swamp drooped like gigantic, wilted flowers. Their branches hung even lower than they had before; some of them snapping off and falling, then floating aimlessly in fetid water. A colorless scum rimed the swamp's surface. Occasionally, bubbles would rise in the water, as though something underneath was struggling to breathe. Those bubbles were the only indication of life in all the dreary the dreary vistas of Legaba's Realm. His Children ... the crocodiles, the serpents, the hordes of spiders ... had all vanished after Almovaar's departure. The Spider God was alone.

Legaba himself had remained motionless beneath the shattered remnants of the trees that had once surrounded him like a palisade. Now, only jagged stumps remained. The fragments of their trunks and limbs had long since drifted away or sunk to the bottom of the swamp.

The Spider God had greatly diminished in size. Before, his bulk would have dwarfed even that of an elephant in the Beyond World. However, his losing battle against Almovaar had reduced his substance to an irregularly-shaped sphere about the size of a buffalo.

Legaba's innumerable tentacles were gone. The eight crimson stars that were his eyes no longer shone, leaving him as monochromatic as a piece of shale. Almovaar's lattice of golden fire, which had ensnared Legaba and rendered him helpless, had disappeared soon after its work was done. Still, the foreign deity's power left its traces behind in the form of lines scored deep into the crust of Legaba's surface. The effect was ironically similar to that of the web-like scars that his worshippers had etched into their skin.

Despite the ruin of his domain, Legaba was far from dead. But he was as dormant as a deity can become. He cared nothing for the decay that surrounded him; he was hardly even aware of it. His consciousness had become dim as an ember. There was no fuel left to sustain it. The most powerful among his worshippers, Jass Imbiah and the huangi, had all perished. The survivors scattered on the islands were too weak to engage his attention, and even if they were strong enough, he could not have answered their callings. And he had no more will to allow his Children to live. Now, all Legaba could do was dream.

He dreamed of what could have been ... what should have been ...what would certainly have been, had it not been for the intervention of that accursed alien deity, Almovaar ...

He dreamed of the triumph of Retribution Time: his worshippers overrunning the mainland, conquering, burning, killing all who resisted and enslaving the survivors, tearing down the monuments to the other Jagasti ...

He dreamed of walking the world again, while the other gods continued to cringe fecklessly in their Realms ...

He dreamed of the day when he would be the god of all the people of the Abengoni continent, his image scarred into everyone's skin ...

One of Legaba's eyes flared into life as those images filled his consciousness. The charred surface of his body rippled, as though something was stirring underneath, and he was on the verge of awakening. Then the scarlet blaze winked out again. And the defeated deity continued to dream.

2

The Uloan Islands writhed beneath a carpet of moving plant life. With the demise of Jass Imbiah and the *huangi*, and the defeat of Legaba by Almovaar, the *ashuma* that had kept the *mwiti*-plants at bay had subsided, then disappeared. Unfettered, the plants had soon begun to expand their movements.

Ubia-vines crawled out of the forests like a legion of grotesque serpents, overwhelming outlying villages and farms, attacking anything that moved or stood still. Grasses turned into lethal webs that enmeshed the unwary. Single blades grew higher than a man's head, and they wove ominous patterns in the air, and they danced with a disquieting frenzy in the absence of wind. Fruits throbbed like beating hearts, with poisonous ichor beading like perspiration on their skin and dripping onto the *ubia*-infested ground.

The petals of flowers large and small opened and closed like hordes of groping hands. Clouds of noxious fumes wafted from blooms that unexpectedly shifted their colors and shapes. The roots of trees erupted like tentacles from the ground, whipping spasmodically in the air and ensnaring even the largest animals foolish enough to blunder into their reach.

When the first few Uloans were swarmed by *ubia*-vines or smothered in deadly snares of grass, the others were too concerned about the return of the Retribution Time fleet to take much notice of the *mwiti*. But as the toll of death mounted and the infestation intensified, the Uloans retreated, abandoning their homes and moving closer to the beaches ... closer to the sea.

Slowly, but inexorably, the *mwiti* were forcing the Uloans out of all their settlements. Large cities – even Ompong, on Jayaya – were being overrun and deserted. Even the cities of the dead, from which the *jhumbis* had marched to join the invasion of the mainland, were not immune to the incursion. Vines crept across the walls of the empty house-tombs, and trees sprouted inside them. Their rapidly growing branches split the structures apart from within.

With no means to protect themselves, the surviving Uloans could do nothing other than retreat, giving ground grudgingly, but inevitably. It was as though all the *mwiti*-plants had developed a conscious purpose: to expunge human life from its midst. And there was a reason for that purpose... a reason the Uloans had long ago allowed themselves to forget.

The islands' beaches were the Uloans' final refuge. Beyond the edge of the sand, the islands' interiors had become seething masses of mobile, lethal vegetation. By day, the plants of the *mwiti* blotted out the horizon like a writhing green wall; at night, they slithered and crept closer to their prey. Soon, even the beaches would not be a haven for the Islanders. They would either have to find a way to defeat the *mwiti*, or die on the blood-red sand ... or in the sea itself.

And still, the Uloans waited for the ships to return.

3

A tiny, gurgling wail pulled Awiwi from her troubled sleep and rescued her from a terrifying dream. In it, the Retribution Time fleet had made its long-awaited return to the Islands. Along with all the other surviving women, children, and elders of Jayaya, she waited on the beach. As always, the Uloans scanned the empty horizon, hoping that this time, the sight of sails would reward their never-ending vigil.

In Awiwi's dream, the sails appeared, one after the other, until they covered the sea like fronds torn from palm trees during a storm. There were far more ships returning than had set off to wreak havoc on the mainlanders. But in her dream, that anomaly didn't register.

The ships drew closer. The cheers of the Uloans on the beach drowned out the rumble of the waves that lapped the shoreline. But when the ships came close enough for their occupants to become clearly visible, the triumphant shouts of the Uloans fell silent, as though a single hand had clutched and squeezed all their throats at once.

The shapes that lined the decks of the Uloan ships were not alive. The occupants of the ships were *jhumbis*, one and all. Not a single living Islander could be seen on the ships; only clay-coated figures with broken sea-shells as substitutes for eyes and teeth.

Like all the other women on the beach, Awiwi cried out in horror and protest at what she saw on the ships. She didn't try to look for Bujiji. She could not tell the *jhumbis* apart, nor did she want to. If Bujiji had now become a *jhumbi*, that meant he was dead and gone from her forever, even if he could still walk and do the bidding of the *huangi*.

Awiwi's own outcry awoke her, as it always did when nightmares like this plagued her sleep. But this time, there was another cry as well.

Instinctively, she reached for the infant at her side. Her hand touched him ... and then she could feel him being pulled from her grasp. His cries were muffled, as though something was covering his mouth – or constricting his throat.

In the dim Moon Star light that filtered through the flimsy thatch of her lean-to, she saw her baby son moving slowly toward the structure's entrance. He wasn't crawling. He was being dragged by an *ubia*-vine as thick as her wrist. The plant had wrapped part of itself around the infant's throat, and was choking him even as it inched its way into the darkness outside the lean-to.

With a wordless cry of rage, Awiwi reached for the coral dagger she kept at her side. Then she seized the part of the vine that was not wrapped around her son, and began to hack at its green flesh. Even as the *ubia*-vine writhed and buckled, the baby's cries weakened. Awiwi's slashes became wilder, missing as often as they landed. Some came close to cutting her baby. Yet enough of them eventually landed to rip the sorcerous life out of the *ubia*. When the vine finally lay still, Awiwi frantically tore its loops from her baby's body, not noticing that the infant lay silent.

Awiwi lifted him and laid her ear on his small chest. And she heard the tiny flutter of his heartbeat. He was unconscious, but alive.

As she held her baby to her breast, Awiwi sobbed quietly, tears falling from her face to the infant's brow. She had not yet given her child a name. None of the infants born in the Uloas since Retribution Time had been named. The father and a *huangi* had to be present for a proper naming ceremony to occur. But all the fathers and all the *huangi* had departed for the war on the mainland. Without their presence, the new children had to remain nameless.

As time passed, the *ubia*-vines had become bolder. If the *huangi* did not arrive soon, the human inhabitants of the islands were in danger of being overwhelmed by the animate vegetation.

"Legaba ... help I," Awiwi whispered into the darkness

She made that plea out of lifelong habit, even though she knew her words would be answered only with silence. Legaba was ... gone.

Awiwi refused to countenance the possibility that the Spider God had vanished forever. To think that would be to lose all hope. And the loss of all hope would be the final step into the abyss of oblivion.

But still ... Legaba was gone, leaving no trace of a presence that had existed since the time the Uloans began to worship him. And so were Jass Imbiah, and the *huangi*, and all the fighting-age men, and even the walking dead. Each day that they did not come back was another day closer to the end of the Uloans who remained on the islands. And they would remain, despite the *mwiti*. They could build boats, but there was no safe destination to which they could sail; certainly not to the Mainland, nor to the Sea of Storms.

The *ubia*-vine's attack had occurred swiftly, although to Awiwi its coils had touched her infant's skin for a loathsome eternity. Her outcry had awakened women in neighboring lean-tos, and some of them now came to her, and held her, and whispered soothing words into her ears. They knew all too well that on the next night, one of their children could be the target of the *ubias'* hunger.

They tried hard not to lose hope. But the struggle was growing too difficult, and before long, their will to live would be gone.

4

For many generations, the Uloans had lied to themselves about part of their past, until they had finally forgotten it ...

When the first explorers from the Matile mainland had reached the islands centuries ago, they had found human inhabitants as well as the animals and the *mwiti*. The population was small and scattered, and the people had a name – the Kipalende. A small-statured, peaceful race whose origins predated those of the Matile and Thaba, and even the Tokoloshe and the Kwa'manga of the Khumba Khourou thirstland, the Kipalende lived in harmony with the *mwiti*.

The Kipalende had no need to build dwellings; the trees shaped themselves into shelters for them. They had no need to hunt or cultivate food; the fruits of the *mwiti*-plants provided all the sustenance they required. In return, the Kipalende nurtured the *mwiti* and spread their seeds and pollen, and protected them from the depredations of hungry creatures such as the *munkimun*. The Kipalende knew neither want nor warfare, and they were unaware that there were other people in the world; people who could neither understand nor respect the way of life that had sustained them for thousands of years.

In an overweening arrogance born of their recent acquisition of the power of *ashuma*, the explorers, and the settlers who arrived on their heels, saw the Kipalende as nothing more than tree-dwellers only a step above the *munkimun* – an obstacle that had to be swept away or trampled beneath the feet of the Matile. The early settlers decided that they needed to remove the Kipalende. And that was what they did. In less than a generation, the Kipalende were gone – exterminated. In ensuing years, the Uloans expunged from their memories the fact that predecessors had existed on the islands, and so did the mainlanders.

But the Kipalende were not truly gone.

The *mwiti* possessed a shared sentience, but it was not like that of humans or animals. The source of their awareness was not restricted to specific organs such as eyes or ears. Changes in sunlight, variations in vibrations in the air or ground, shifts in the direction of the breeze that carried chemical signals… these shaped the consciousness of the *ubia*-vines and the rest of the *mwiti*.

And because the *mwiti* had extended their consciousness to join with that of the Kipalende, the plant life had shared the torment their human symbiotes had suffered at the hands of the invaders. And the *mwiti* had absorbed the spirits of the Kipalende, and kept that part of the doomed people alive long after the dust of their bodies became an element of the islands' soil. Now, the Kipalende were part of the *mwiti*, from the *ubia*-vines to the tallest of the trees.

No longer were the Kipalende timid. Their spirits had become vindictive, and they bent the inchoate consciousness of the *mwiti* to their influence, and to their goal: vengeance against the descendants of those whom had destroyed them. The powerful sorcery of the Uloans was all that prevented the *mwiti* from overrunning the islands in the aftermath of the Storm Wars. That had been the Kipalendes' best chance to fulfill their desire for reprisal, and their spirits slipped into dormancy when that opportunity was thwarted.

And now, that protective sorcery was gone. The unseen barriers that had thwarted the Kipalendes' revenge were gone. Freedom had come. And so had an unanticipated kind of Retribution Time for the Uloans who remained on the islands, with the reawakening of the Kipalendes' spirits.

The *mwiti* were now capable of a full range of movement. *Ubia*-vines slid more swiftly than serpents along the ground. Grass blades whipped, curled and wove together, into vast, moving webworks, as though the air had become a gigantic loom. Even the thickest of tree-branches had become as limber as the tentacles of a squid or octopus. Flowers grasped and clawed like an eagle's talons. Roots clutched the soil and propelled huge trees forward.

Immediately after the magic that had kept them at bay vanished, the *mwitis'* consciousness had momentarily overwhelmed that of the Kipalende. The plants had revelled in their liberty, and underwent a period of anarchic growth and movement, during which they posed scant threat to the now-vulnerable Uloans.

In the midst of the chaos, however, a glimmer of greater purpose kindled in the consciousness of a single, aged papaya tree in a forest on Jayaya Island. The papaya was hardly an imposing tree; others were far larger and bore brighter blossoms and more plentiful fruit. But the consciousness of the Kipalende loomed larger in this papaya than in any of the other *mwiti*, for it was the refuge of the greatest among them, a shaman who was the principal link between his people and the plant life. As the others dueled with branches and leaves and roots, the lone papaya remained motionless, easily fending off the intrusions of its more aggressive neighbors.

The Kipalende part of the papaya's consciousness reached out to the other *mwiti*, and it sent a message that soon worked its way into that of all the animate vegetation of the islands.

Destroy them, not us, the Kipalende shaman in the papaya urged. *The time for vengeance has come.*

Swiftly, the rest of the Kipalende spirits regained control over the *mwiti*. Swifter still came a new message from the spirit of their shaman.

Now it ends.

5

Awiwi cried out in fear and disgust as she kicked at an *ubia* that was trying to wrap itself around her ankle. The vine fell away. Then it snaked toward her again. Others followed.

Holding her baby tightly in her arms, Awiwi backed away. She had been retreating since the dawn of this terrible day. So had all the rest of those who had taken refuge on the Jayaya beach.

When the first light seeped into the morning sky, an army of *ubias* had swarmed out of the forest. The Uloans who were still asleep at the time died agonizing deaths, covered with *ubias* that leeched the blood out of their veins. Those who, like Awiwi, were fortunate enough to be awake had fought desperately to free themselves from their assailants. They fled their lean-tos and made for the beach, closer to the final embrace of the sea.

Behind them, their flimsy shelters were quickly overrun by swarms of *ubias*. People who had not been alert or swift enough to elude the attackers had become little more than struggling lumps barely visible beneath a writhing carpet of vines.

"Fire! Catch they on fire!" one of the elders shouted as he cut and tore *ubias* from his legs.

He rushed toward a cooking fire that still burned several yards away, and thrust a piece of wood from it into the mass of *ubias* that was still in front of him. With a sizzling sound, the vines shriveled and blackened in the flame. Wielding the brand like a flaming sword, the elder burned a wide swath through the *ubias*.

Others followed the elder's example. Risking their lives to reach other fires, they lit the wreckage of their shelters, pieces of driftwood, patches of dry grass – anything that was combustible. Soon, a rampart of fire blazed between the Uloans and their attackers. The hiss and pop of burning *ubias* punctuated the crackle of the flames.

But the respite proved only temporary.

As the Uloans stared in renewed horror, the sheer mass of the *ubias* began to snuff out the flames. Unlike even the most obtuse form of beast, the animate plants of the Uloas bore no instinctive fear of fire, for all their vulnerability to that element. And they also had no fear of death. For them, the loss of hundreds, even thousands, of their numbers had no consequence. All that mattered to the Kipalende part of them was the fulfillment of their deadly purpose.

Slowly, the flames died, leaving a mass of charred *ubias* in their wake. And a new wave of vines passed over the remnants of the others. Again, the Uloans retreated before the onrushing horde of *ubias*. And a new enemy emerged as tendrils from rapidly growing *mwiti* roots erupted from the ground and coiled around the Uloans' ankles and up their legs.

Overcome by a sense of futility, some of the Uloans simply ceased their struggles and allowed the plants to pull them down. Others continued to fight for their lives, even as the water of the ocean lapped at their heels.

"Legaba! Legaba! Save we!" many of them shouted, even though they knew their god no longer heard them.

Others uttered screams of rage and despair. And still others bore their fate in bitter silence. The end of their existence was in sight ... but so, on the horizon of the sea, was something else.

Awiwi was the first to spot what was drawing closer to them.

"Ships!" she shouted, her voice soaring above the din. "Ships! Them come back to save we!"

The other Uloans turned and looked to the sea. At the sight of the line of ships in the distance, they let out a long shout of relief and joy. But the cries of elation died in their throats when they realized the ships were not Uloan after all.

CHAPTER TWENTY-FIVE

Tiyana's Task

1

Pel Muldure was glad to have a deck rocking beneath his feet again – even if it was the unfamiliar planks of a Matile vessel, sailing in the equally unfamiliar waters between the Abengoni mainland and the Uloan Islands. His *White Gull* had been damaged beyond any hope of repair during the battle against the Uloans. So had most of the Matiles' ships. Much of the time between then and now had been spent repairing the ships that were salvageable and building others from scratch. The scuttled remains of the *White Gull* rested on the cluttered bottom of Khambawe's harbor, along with many of Muldure's regrets.

Muldure and some of his crew members who were knowledgeable about the ship-building craft had offered suggestions to their Matile counterparts as they worked. Some of the Fidis' suggestions were accepted; others politely disregarded. The vessel Muldure now helmed, the *Amdwa*, combined Matile and Fiadolian design concepts. Newly built, it was the flagship of the Matiles' refurbished war fleet. As such, the *Amdwa* was destined to carry the revitalized Empire's war-commanders, and even Emperors, into future battles.

This time, however, the ship carried neither Gebrem nor Kyroun, only Tiyana and a group of other Almovaad Initiates, as well as soldiers. The rest of the sea-craft in the flotilla also held complements of Adepts and Acolytes who were proficient in the use of the magic provided by Almovaar. For the entire voyage, both the seasoned and novice Almovaads had engaged in intense preparations for what they intended to do once they arrived at the islands. Strangely, the ships carried only a minimum number of fighting-men.

Now, across the water that separated the ships from Jayaya, Muldure could see tiny figures, barely discernable as human at that distance, engaged in a desperate – and apparently futile – struggle against foes he could not make out. Many of the people were already in the water, as though something was striving to push them into the sea's embrace. But he couldn't make out the enemies they were fighting. He could only see that the islanders were being driven ever-deeper into the water.

Muldure shook his head in bewilderment as he considered what he was seeing on the island, as well as what had occurred in Khambawe in the days before the flotilla had set out.

"Hardly any soldiers," he muttered. "No weapons to speak of. And a foe that is already beaten. What the hell kind of 'invasion' is this, anyway?"

At his side, Lyann shrugged.

"How do you know it's supposed to be an 'invasion' in the first place?" she asked.

Now it was Muldure's turn to shrug. The rulers of Khambawe had not informed him of the details of the mission to the Uloans' homeland. Along with the captains of the Matile ships, he had been told only that the Emperor and the Seer had decided the time had come to put an ultimate end to the conflict between the mainlanders and the islanders.

But no one outside the inner circle of Almovaad Adepts knew what that end would be, nor how it was expected to be accomplished ...

Behind the captain and the first mate, the crew – half of which was Fiadolian and the rest Matile – toiled at tasks such as furling the *Amdwa's* sails and securing its anchor. Shouts and curses in two languages accompanied the work.

Muldure chuckled as he listened to the chorus of complaints.

Sailors will be sailors wherever they are, he mused.

Tiyana and her fellow Adepts were still in the ship's main cabin, just as Kyroun had been when the *White Gull* entered Khambawe's harbor. With the Matile woman, however, Muldure experienced none of the uneasiness the Seer had always inspired. Despite the new power Tiyana had acquired, to Muldure's mind she was still the vulnerable young woman who had first come aboard the *White Gull* to give aid to strangers in need.

A stiff sea-breeze stirred the single strand of beads in Lyann's hair as she followed Muldure's gaze toward the island. Jayaya differed little from the thousands of other islands she had seen during her travels in the seas off

Cym Dinath. But she had never before seen vegetation that swayed *against* the wind ...

"Whatever Tiyana plans on doing, she'd better do it now," Muldure said. "It looks like those people are going to drown before we get to them."

Lyann nodded agreement.

A moment later, the cabin door opened. From it, Tiyana, Byallis, and a half-dozen other Initiates emerged and strode across the deck. On the way, Tiyana's eyes met Muldure's, but only briefly. After that brief contact, she looked straight ahead as she led the Initiates to the ship's rail. Then, as one, the Almovaads levitated from the deck and floated over the side of the *Amdwa*.

2

The last time Tiyana had stepped onto the surface of the sea, she had worn the Mask of Nama-kwah, and had striven futilely to establish contact with the goddess for whom she had been a Vessel. She had been painfully conscious then of the weakness of her *ashuma*. And even before the day the Fidi arrived, First Calling had been little more than an empty ritual, although she would never have admitted, or even acknowledged, that truth back then.

And now ...

Now she stood, rather than danced, on the waves. She wore no Mask; there was no need for her to impersonate a goddess who was no longer worshipped by her or her people. Instead of the elaborate webwork of diamonds and silver that accompanied First Calling, she wore only a plain blue *chamma* that whipped in the breeze. Her braids, decorated with sky-blue beads, descended below her shoulders and flew in the wind. She stood slightly above the waves, and could feel their delicate touch against the soles of her feet.

Tiyana's face was as serene as the Mask of Nama-kwah had been. She was secure in the power Almovaar had bestowed upon her. And she felt certain in the justness of its use, and in the responsibility her father and Kyroun had given to her and the other Adepts.

She focused on the island before her. It was still a fair distance away, but with the far-vision Almovaad sorcery bestowed, she could see the beleaguered Uloans still fighting hopelessly to survive, even as the relentless *mwiti* forced the people off the beach.

Byallis stood at Tiyana's right side, standing on the waves with practiced ease. At her left was a Matile man named Geremu, who was once an Amiya, and now an Adept second only to Tiyana in accomplishment. Tiyana nodded to them. They nodded back. They, too, had seen what was occurring on the island, and along with the other Adepts, they had, in the Oneness, agreed on what they had to do.

Arms spread wide, Tiyana began the task of gathering the magic she and the others needed to accomplish their goal. The others duplicated her stance. No longer was it they necessary for them to clasp hands to wield their collective energy; the link their minds shared in the Oneness was more than sufficient to draw upon Almovaar's resources, which they now did.

Without warning, blue lightning blazed from Tiyana's hands. Its crackling could be heard over the waves. The coruscation of eldritch force leaped from Tiyana to Geremu and Byallis, who added their own power, as did all the other Adepts, each in his or her turn, until jagged lines of energy surrounded them like a palisade fashioned from glowing serpents.

Then Tiyana thrust her hands forward, as though she were pushing against a wall. So did the others. And a myriad of lightning-like lines of force arrowed toward the island.

3

Awiwi's resistance had almost ceased. Sea-water swirled above her waist. Her body, and that of her child, was covered with *ubias*. The mouths of the vines burrowed into her skin. Rows of teeth pierced her flesh. Her blood began to flow into the *ubias'* tubular bodies, which expanded as they gorged greedily on her life-fluid.

Neither Awiwi nor anyone else on the beach cared any longer about the ships that had appeared on the horizon. Who the intruders were; whether they meant help or harm; none of that mattered because it was impossible for them to reach the Uloans in time to make any difference for good or ill.

Then the Almovaads' magic struck.

Awiwi staggered and fell into the water. So did the others around her. Choking and spitting salt water from their mouths, the Uloans struggled desperately to regain their footing before the tide had a chance to sweep them away. And their eyes widened in shock when they saw what was now happening to the *ubias* that still clung to their bodies.

Lines of blue, crackling fire enmeshed the vines. The humans felt only a slight tingling from the force-lines. But the energy's effect on the *ubias* was immediate and dramatic. The vines writhed as though they were on fire. Like a grotesque rain, they dropped from the Uloans' bodies and fell into the sea, where they continued to twitch and convulse until they finally subsided and floated motionless. Incoming waves washed them onto the beach, where they lay like limp strands of seaweed.

On the red sands, the *mwiti*-roots that had sprouted from the ground were also caught in the force that swept the island. They remained frozen in place like a forest of ribs. From the tentacular roots, the lines of force expanded, enmeshing the entire island in a netting of brilliant blue light. The outcome of the Almovaads' sorcery on the *mwiti* was immediate.

The grasses stopped waving, their life force suddenly snatched away. Fruits that pulsed like multicolored hearts either ceased their motion entirely, or exploded in bursts of pulp. Flowers that had clenched like hands fell apart in showers of petals that lay in heaps around their stems.

Vines that had engulfed entire towns shriveled and dropped away from walls and doors under the relentless assault of the Almovaads' sorcery. The branches and roots of great trees ended their growth and movement, and stood still again. Even in the villages of the dead, the desecrating plant-life was cleansed by the blue webwork, leaving the empty funeral-houses uncovered and undisturbed.

In the depths of the Jayaya forest, the lone papaya tree struggled stubbornly against its fate. Its trunk, branches, and leaves were ensnared in a lattice of glowing blue lines. The gigantic *mwiti* trees that surrounded the papaya had all fallen motionless. For all their size and grandeur, they had proven easy prey for the magic of the Almovaads. The Kipalende part of their consciousness had subsided in the shock of the surprise attack.

But the Kipalende spirit that had found shelter in the humble papaya was more resilient than the others. Even as its companions passively surrendered their recent gifts of sentience and movement, the papaya continued is resistance. Its limbs whipped as though it were in the midst of a typhoon. Its leaves scattered; its fruits plummeted to the ground.

Yet for all the cruel damage it was undergoing, the spirit in the papaya refused to submit to the force that was destroying its host. The Kipalende's vision of vengeance was too pervasive to be extinguished. Even as chips of its bark were torn from its trunk, the papaya continued its attempt to rally *ubias* and other *mwiti* that no longer responded to its calls.

Finally, the papaya's trunk split as though it had been struck by lightning. Its two halves teetered, then crashed to the ground. It lay in a tomb of its own leaves and branches. The Kipalende spirit was the last part of it to die.

On the rest of the Uloan islands, the undoing of the *mwiti* rampage continued as the Almovaads' strands of sorcery extended themselves far beyond Jayaya. By the time the assault was done, the animate plant life of the islands had either perished, or been transformed into ordinary vegetation. And the spirits of the Kipalende finally vanished from the islands: their dream of vengeance ended, their reason for continuing to exist defunct.

Eventually, the lines of blue fire that encircled the islands dimmed, then vanished, their work completed.

And on the beach of Jayaya, the surviving Uloans stared first at the reefs of dead *ubia*-vines that blanketed the sand, and the lifeless roots that jutted skyward like monuments to a fallen monarch. The Uloans' own dead lay there as well. Only a pitiful few survived.

Then the islanders turned to face the blue-robed newcomers who were now levitating toward them, their feet lightly skimming the waves.

4

As the Adepts approached the beach, the Uloans retreated out of the water and onto the *ubia*-strewn sand. Shock, fear, bewilderment and exhaustion glazed their eyes and deadened the expressions on their faces. Circular wounds from the *ubias'* mouths covered their bodies. Blood trickled over the raised tissue of their spider-scars. The islanders slumped in stances of extreme weariness.

The Uloans backtracked farther as the mainlanders' feet finally touched the sand. None of them had ever seen a blankskin. Captives had never been taken in the raids the Uloans mounted, and more than a generation had passed since the last time the Mainland Matile had made an offensive against the islands. Legends and hearsay told the Uloans what their ancient enemies looked like, but legends and hearsay did not match what they saw now.

The blankskins the Uloans thought they knew had never floated across the sea like birds. They had never swathed themselves in plain blue robes. And even in their most vivid imaginings, the Uloans had never pictured Mainlanders with pale skin, or hair in colors other than black, like that of many of the small group of intruders who now confronted them. Memories of the Fidi had faded more rapidly on the islands than it had on the mainland; to the survivors of the *mwiti* assault, these new people were even more disconcerting than those they assumed to be blank-skinned Mainlanders.

Who them be? the Uloans wondered as the blankskins looked at them. *Why them come? Why them save we?*

For their part the Adepts, Matile and Fidi alike, looked at the Uloans and asked themselves how it was that people such as these could have been such formidable foes to the Matile for such a long time. They saw only young and old women, old men, and children ranging from suckling infants to near-adolescents. Their spider-scarred bodies were gaunt, showing the effects of dwindling food supplies. Wounds from the *ubias* puckered their skin like open, bleeding mouths.

The silence stretched. Then an old man stepped forward. Despite the ragged clothing that barely covered his blood-spattered skin, and the trauma he had just endured, he was still carried himself with a measure of dignity. His name was Jawai. Although he had never possessed the magical talent necessary to become a *huangi*, he had always been a man to be respected. It was Jawai who had attempted to use fire to forestall the *ubias*, and it was Jawai who now took the initiative to find out what these powerful newcomers wanted.

Tiyana stood a few paces in front of the other Adepts. Jawai believed that she was the one who would have the answers to his questions. He tried to read her intentions in her dark eyes and the calm expression on her strange, unscarred face. He could not. It was like looking at a mask.

"From Matile-land, you?" he finally asked.

"Yes," Tiyana replied.

"Our warriors ... our *huangi* ... Jass Imbiah ... where them gone to? Why them not come back?"

"All of them are dead."

Tiyana said nothing more. She anticipated a chorus of wails and curses, and, perhaps, a physical attack, against which she was well-prepared to defend herself. But none came. She had only confirmed for the Uloans what they already knew, even though they had assembled at the beach every day to wait for ships that would never return. They had known that truth, but they had not been able to accept its reality. Now, at last, they were forced to do so.

"They would not stop killing," Tiyana said, feeling they needed an explanation. "They died bravely. But they died for no reason – for a mistaken cause. There is no 'Retribution Time.' There never was."

Jawai closed his eyes as though he had just been struck. When he opened them again, he looked at the piles of dead *ubias* and the immobilized roots. Then he looked again at Tiyana.

"Why you do this for we?" he asked, indicating the evidence of what the Believers' magic had accomplished. "Why you not kill we?"

"Because the war between us is over," Tiyana replied. "Because there is no more need for killing."

Jawai stared at her as though she had spoken the gibberish of the mad. So did the other Uloans. For half a millennium, the war against the Mainland had been the focal point of the Uloans' existence. Without that sacred warfare; without the promise of Retribution Time's triumph and the fulfillment of the destiny Legaba had promised them, they had nothing.

And they *were* nothing ...

"Legaba, him lie to I and I," Jawai muttered bitterly. "Where him be now? Where him be?"

"Legaba is gone," Tiyana said. "All the Jagasti are gone. A new god has come to take their place. His name is Almovaar."

"Almovaar ... him help you take Retribution Time from we?"

"Yes. And he has helped you, too. He was the source of the *ashuma* that we used to destroy the plants-that-move before they pushed you into the sea. Now, these islands belong to you alone."

Jawai shook his head as though he could not, or did not want to, comprehend what he was hearing.

"You can rebuild," Tiyana pressed. "You can teach your children love, not hate. You can live in peace with us. The hatred between your people and mine can end. All this can be. The choice is yours."

"Who *them* be?" Jawai asked abruptly, gesturing toward the Fidi who stood nearby. The Fidi were mingled with the Matile, but Tiyana knew the Uloan was referring to the outlanders.

"They are the Fidi, the people from Beyond the Storm," Tiyana replied. "They brought Almovaar to us. Now, we bring him to you."

Another silence followed as the Mainlanders waited and watched the islanders absorb the reality that their old way of life was gone forever, and it was their ancient enemies who were offering them a new way.

Some of the Uloans kept their eyes downcast. Others gazed openly at the blue-robed strangers, especially the Fidi, as though they could read their people's fate in faces that were innocent of scarification.

Then, with an expression of regret and resignation on his face, Jawai bowed his head sank to his knees in front of Tiyana. One-by-one, the other Uloans followed his example.

"You have beaten we," Jawai said softly. "Nothing left of we but the old and the young. No more *huangi*. No more Legaba. No more of we. I and I yours now."

The Almovaads looked at each other in consternation. Such an abject act of submission on the part of the islanders had never been their ultimate goal. They had no desire to enslave the remaining Uloans. But now they could see that without their obsession with Retribution Time, the islanders were like children whose parents had died. Even with the menace of the animate plants gone, the Uloans had still lost their will to live.

An infant's cry broke the silence. And that cry told Tiyana what she must do.

5

Awiwi tried to hush her baby son, but the pain from the wounds the *ubias* had inflicted was too much for him to bear. Then Awiwi sensed someone coming toward her. She looked up, and saw the woman who led the mainlanders standing over her.

When Tiyana reached down, Awiwi shrank away, her arms protectively cradling her infant. But when Tiyana's hand touched the boy, his cries ceased. Turning her back on Tiyana, Awiwi raised her baby's head so that she could see his face. He looked up at her, wide-eyed. Then he gurgled and smiled. When she looked closer, she saw that his wounds were no longer bleeding.

Awiwi felt Tiyana's hands on her arms. Gently, the Matile woman lifted the Uloan from her knees. Awiwi turned to face the mainlander, opening her mouth to shout at her. Then she felt a faint tingle from Tiyana's hands. Awiwi tried to pull away, but Tiyana held her firmly. Awiwi looked down at her arms ... and saw that the spider-scars were slowly disappearing from her skin. It was as though all the traces of Legaba upon her were being erased by the power of this new god, this Almovaar.

"No," Awiwi whispered in protest as the last of the scarification faded, transforming her into a hated blankskin. But her protest was half-hearted, and was finished almost before it had begun.

Inside, Awiwi had changed even as her skin transmuted. It was as though she had shed a reeking, ragged garment that she had worn for far too long. Legaba was gone from her. She was a new person. It was as though she, and not her infant, had only recently emerged from the womb.

Tiyana smiled at the island woman. Awiwi smiled back. Around them, other Adepts were following Tiyana's lead, lifting the Uloans from their knees and expunging the spider-scars from their bodies. Jawai was the last to accept the eradication of Legaba from his life. And he was the only one who still appeared to regret the changes the mainlanders had wrought.

It was a beginning.

The Uloans did not know the price they would ultimately have to pay for falling into the embrace of Almovaar.

Tiyana did not know it, either. Nor did the rest of the Adepts who were duplicating what Tiyana had done, not only on Jayaya but also the rest of the Uloan Islands.

Nobody knew, other than Kyroun and Gebrem.

And Almovaar ...

CHAPTER TWENTY-SIX

Dissent

1

For all the progress that had been made in the restoration of Khambawe, the task was far from complete. Many of the interior sections of the Jewel City still lay in ruins, waiting to be reconstructed. The Emperor had decreed that the entire city was to be rebuilt by the beginning of the next rainy season – what was once known as First Calling. Although much work remained to be done, the people of Khambawe were confident that they could fulfill the Emperor's edict, even if it did seem unreasonable to some.

But there were those in the city who bore scant regard for either the new Emperor or his many pronouncements. As well, they harbored deep-seated suspicions of the Fidi outlanders and the new god they had brought to Khambawe. They did not speak publicly about their misgivings, for their opinions were shared by only a small number of their fellow Matile; and in any event it was not considered wise to speak ill of the Emperor Gebrem or the Almovaads. To do so was not prohibited, but such opinions were more often than not shouted into silence by those who believed that they owed their lives to the foreigners. For that reason, the dissidents did not espouse their views in public, and they held their meetings in places where few others were inclined to go.

This night, several people approached a house that remained the most nearly intact on a street of ruins. They came singly, and they spaced their arrivals at irregular intervals. Light from the Moon Stars created a pale nimbus that softened the jagged outlines of the broken buildings. In the distance, the night-sun that hovered over the Maim was clearly visible.

Because of that silvery beacon in the sky, the people who approached the house were able to gather at night without any need to fear becoming victims of the *tsotsis*.

However, the dissenters felt no gratitude for that tangible gift from the new god. The night-sun and the rumors of sinister shadows that were killing off the *tsotsis* only exacerbated their misgivings. Their discontent was not based on loyalty to the Jagasti, who had abandoned – and been abandoned by – the Matile. Yet the doubters could not bring themselves to embrace the worship of the new god, whose adherents seemed to have profited rather than suffered in the wake of the near-disaster that had befallen the Empire.

The dissenters continued to converge on the half-fallen house until more than a dozen had made their way inside. The interior of the house remained dark until the last of the group had arrived. At the lighting of a single candle, their clandestine meeting commenced.

2

"How much longer will it be before we act?" a voice hissed out of the candle-lit gloom.

The speaker was a man named Adisu. He was a leather-worker whose goods and premises had been destroyed beyond repair by the rampaging Uloans. He had not been able to recover his losses nor resume his business, and the seeds of bitterness within him had now reached full fruition. And, like some others, Adisu blamed his misfortunes not on the invading Uloans, but on the Fidi and their new god. In his mind, he associated the islanders' massive attack with the coming of the foreigners, as if the Fidi had somehow been the cause of the Uloans' actions. Now, the invaders were long since defeated and destroyed. But the Fidi were still in Khambawe. And Adisu wanted them to be gone from the city.

"How long will we continue to allow these outsiders to rule us, change us, turn us into whatever it is they want us to be?" Adisu continued.

The light from the candle cast a wavering illumination on Adisu's dark face as he awaited a reply to his questions. When none was immediately forthcoming, he forged ahead impatiently, his voice low in tone, but infused with fierce urgency and repressed anger.

"There is no time better than now to make a move," he insisted. "Half of the sorcerers have gone off to the Uloan Islands, to do who knows what? They say they want to put an end to the scarred devils' threat, once and for all. But for all we know, they could be bringing the rest of them back here to finish what they started."

He allowed that ominous – and absurd – speculation to hang in the air before he pressed on.

"Whatever they've got planned, the point is, now we can do something about them, because they are at less than half of their full strength."

After a short silence, another voice spoke out of the near-darkness of the meeting place.

"And what would you have us do, Adisu? Even at half-strength, the Believers are much more powerful than we can ever hope to be."

All eyes turned toward the new speaker, whose name was Jass Kebessa. Kebessa was a minor member of the Degen Jassi whose status had been even further diminished with the coming of the Fidi and the defeat of the Uloans. His influence in the Emperor's court was scant because of his steadfast refusal to embrace the new religion of the Almovaads.

More than once, he had told anyone who would listen that he would rather believe in no god or goddess at all than a god of foreigners, regardless of how beneficial this Almovaar appeared to be. That stance caused his standing in the court to become negligible at best. However, by virtue of his rank, Jass Kebessa was the leader of the small cadre of dissidents.

"Would you have us incite an uprising?" Kebessa asked. "That would be a difficult task, indeed. Most of our people are in love with these newcomers. There is nothing they would not do for them … and nothing they would not do to anyone who caused harm to them. So … what would you have us do?"

"Something! Anything!" Adisu shouted, no longer caring whether anyone passing outside the meeting place could hear him.

"The longer we wait, the fewer our chances," the leather worker went on, his voice somewhat calmer. "Already, people are disappearing into thin air without any explanation."

"But those people are only *tsotsis*," another speaker interjected. "Most of us are happy to see those vermin disappear. Aren't you?"

The new speaker was Tamair, a middle-aged woman who had lost her husband and children when the Uloans had attacked, and had nearly lost her own life as well before the night-sun first shone and the tide of battle turned. What she had seen and experienced on that deadly night could never be effaced from her soul. The Almovaads wanted her to forget her past, and embrace their future. But Tamair preferred to remember. And she was suspicious of those who advised her to forget her old life and begin anew. She would never forget. Never ...

"What happens when the Maim is empty of *tsotsis*?" Adisu retorted. "Who will disappear next? Does this new god have a hunger that can never be satisfied, no matter how many people are taken?"

"We don't know," Jass Kebessa said. "We know only that the Emperor Gebrem is under the spell of this Kyroun, and when Gebrem opens his mouth to speak, it is the Fidi's words that come out. Kyroun is even made himself the Leba! And how much longer will it be before a Fidi, and not a Matile, sits on the Lion Throne?"

That speculation caused the others to fall into silence for a long moment, before Adisu spoke in reiteration of his opinion.

"We must act, then."

"But how?" Kebessa asked again.

"To kill a serpent, you must cut off its head."

These words came not from Adisu, but from a new speaker, one who had previously made few contributions to the dissidents' discussions even though he attended all the gatherings.

The speaker's name was Sehaye.

3

A slight smile curved Sehaye's lips as he wended his way through the rubble-strewn interior streets of Khambawe. The dissidents' meeting had ended, and his ideas had received much attention, even from the cautious Jass Kebessa. Almost without thinking, Sehaye avoided the broken stones and other debris that littered his path as he savored the outcome of the gathering. In another part of his mind, he wondered if he would soon help to remove the wreckage past which he was now stepping, rubble he had, in his way, helped to create.

In the time before Sehaye's countrymen had launched Retribution Time, the street he travelled had been free from detritus. But it had not been free of *tsotsis*, who had awaited in the shadows, poised to pounce on the unlucky and unwary who came within their reach. Now, the *tsotsis* were penned in the Maim, and were steadily disappearing. The only danger the street now posed for Sehaye was the chance of stumbling over some unnoticed obstacle.

Sehaye's smile broadened as he left the interior of the city behind and approached the dwelling he had appropriated in the aftermath of Retribution Time's failure. It was a modest house that had escaped the brunt of the destruction on the night of the invasion. Its previous owners had been killed, and no one else had come forth to claim it. Close to the area in which the dissidents met, although they never gathered in the same place twice in a row, as well as the other still-damaged areas in which he made his living, the location was ideal for Sehaye's purposes.

And he had finally found a purpose after a period of aimlessness, and at times madness, that had lasted until the time immediately following Jass Gebrem's coronation as Emperor. It was a gap he barely remembered, and he knew he was fortunate to have lived through it.

Even before the coronation, he could no longer maintain his previous identity as a fisherman. His boat had long since been lost. And after he had looked at the harbor the day after Retribution Time ended, and he had seen the spider-scarred corpses of his countrymen covering the surface of the water so thickly that he could have walked across them, he could no longer bear the sight of the sea.

Despite his wiry frame, Sehaye's back was strong. Soon enough, he was able to stave off starvation by helping to clear the rubble left from Retribution Time, and participating in the rebuilding of the city he had dedicated his life to bringing down. The irony of his position did not escape him, and there were times when he teetered on the brink of an abyss of despair.

Then, one day, a voice that came from within pulled him away from that brink. He was certain that the voice belonged to Legaba. Sometimes, though, he thought it might belong to a different source, one that he did not care to contemplate very long or very deeply ...

Why I make questions? he asked himself.

Voice helping I, he assured himself in the Uloan dialect he spoke only in the deepest recesses of his mind.

I and I listen and learn, he promised himself.

Sehaye became known as a silent but capable worker who did what he was told without asking any questions. Following the advice of his new inner companion, he watched and listened as he worked. At first, he was searching, as always, for fellow spies from the Islands who might have survived Retribution Time. But even if any such people existed, he had no way of recognizing them. Jass Imbiah had forbidden any contact among her mainland spies; if they became acquainted, they could inadvertently give each other away. After a while, though, he gave up that search. If he were to be the only Uloan left in Khambawe, so be it.

Where Jass Imbiah gone? he often asked himself bitterly. *Why she leave we?* That the ruler of all the Islands was dead, he had no doubt, even though he had not personally witnessed her demise. And he also knew he had no way of ever returning to his homeland. Even if he did, he would likely be killed as a damned blankskin before he could open his mouth to convince his fellow Uloans that he was one of them despite his lack of spider-scars.

Sehaye had listened more closely as he heaved rocks and repositioned beams. And he began to hear mutterings of discontent; the voices of those who did not accept the huge changes that had occurred in Khambawe and spread throughout the Matile Mala Empire, even though the catalysts of those changes, the Almovaads, had saved the dissenters' lives as well as those of the Believers.

And those were the voices the new speaker inside Sehaye's head wanted him to hear ...

Sehaye continued to listen as he worked. Then he began to speak ... softly, unobtrusively, using the words that the voice inside him suggested. At first, the dissidents were surprised that their taciturn co-worker possessed the ability to utter more than two words at a time. However, the more they listened to him, the more respect they developed for what he said.

Soon enough, the dissidents invited Sehaye to one of their gatherings. Although he remained relatively quiet, when he did speak, his words were well-received. He quickly became accepted among the dissidents' thin ranks. They entrusted him with their secrets because they were confident his mouth would stay as closed outside their meetings as it usually did during them.

At times, Sehaye wondered why the voice inside him harbored

any interest at all in the dissidents. During their gatherings, they did little other than complain incessantly about the dominance of the newcomers; the changes the new religion had wrought; and the possible perils of the Almovaar magic, which was in many ways even more powerful than the *ashuma* the Amiyas had wielded in the legendary past. They also grumbled about Kyroun's near-equality of power with that of Gebrem.

They even criticized the new fashions that were sweeping the younger people: the hair-dyeing to emulate the Fidis; the adoption of Fidi clothing, the intrusion of some of the foreigners' words into the Matiles' speech. Sehaye had rapidly grown weary of such useless talk, but the voice inside had persuaded him to continue to attend the dissidents' gatherings.

Recently, though, the dissidents' discussions had become more urgent. Rumors were spreading of a new war to come, to be launched by the Matile against the Thabas who were encroaching on the southern frontier.

Considering the near-annihilation the Matile had almost experienced when the Uloans invaded, the dissidents believed they were not alone in their trepidations about going into battle again so soon. The city was still recovering from the devastation the islanders had wrought. And there was even now another action being taken against the Uloans, on their home islands. Ships had departed the harbor, but no one knew what their ultimate intent would be once they reached their destination. The new authorities had remained silent about their purpose.

Sehaye had said nothing when the discussion touched on the islands. He needed to exert all the power of his will to prevent himself from attacking the Matile when they spoke of their satisfaction with the debacle his people had suffered. However, he did take satisfaction in the knowledge that the after-effects of Retribution Time would continue for a long time to come as the Matile rebuilt their city ... and his own schemes came closer to fruition.

Patience, Sehaye, the voice counselled. *Patience ...*

And so Sehaye continued to cultivate his ties with the dissidents, who continued to be satisfied with talk, not action.

Then, on this very night, the voice planted its final seed of suggestion in Sehaye's mind. The islander's eyes widened when the whispered words first welled within him. He wondered if madness had once again claimed him, as it had in the days that immediately followed the demise of Retribution Time. However, the more he listened, the more he realized that the voice was speaking the truth, and if he could persuade the others to accept the voice's proposal, Retribution Time would be, in a small but not insignificant way, fulfilled after all.

That thought caused Sehaye's smile to broaden as he reached his dwelling and went inside.

4

On another dark street of Khambawe, Jass Kebessa and Tamair walked side-by-side. Before the Uloans' invasion, Kebessa would never have associated so closely with someone of Tamair's lower social status. Now, he actively sought her companionship, even though most of his own family had managed to survive the terrible night of slaughter.

Even under the changed circumstances of the Renewal, as the Emperor Gebrem's reign was beginning to style itself, Kebessa continued to hide his true feelings from himself, convincing himself that he regarded Tamair only as a friend from whom he sought counsel.

"Do you think Sehaye is mad?" he asked as they walked along a street that was relatively free from rubble.

The street was closer to the main part of the city, which had by now been almost completely rebuilt. Other people were abroad this night, and the Moon Stars' light outlined their faces as they passed. If anyone recognized either Tamair or Kebessa, they gave no indication.

"Mad?" Tamair repeated. "Well, his idea certainly is."

After a short pause, she continued.

"In fact, I've never heard of anything more insane in my life – even in these times of lunacy."

Kebessa chuckled.

"That's why it just might work," he said.

This time, it was Tamair's turn to laugh.

"I never thought I'd hear something like that from him," she said. "He was always so sensible before."

"In a way, he's being sensible now."

That comment caused Tamair to stop walking and give Kebessa a quizzical glance.

"How's that?" she asked.

Kebessa stopped as well, and he returned her gaze directly, without pretense of ulterior motive.

"His scheme brings no direct risk to us," he said. "If it fails, no one will ever know that we were involved."

"That's only if Sehaye doesn't talk."

"I have a feeling he won't."

"Are you willing to gamble our lives on a 'feeling?'" Tamair demanded. "Hah! That's the way is has always been with you Jassi."

As Kebessa looked at her, a distance became evident in his eyes; a reminder of times past, and the way he would have regarded a woman like Tamair back then. Tamair could sense that distance as well.

"What we do will be for all of us to decide," Kebessa said stiffly.

Little else was said as they began to walk again. When they reached one of the principal streets of Khambawe, on which the light from night-torches overwhelmed the Moon-Stars' glow, they silently went their separate ways.

CHAPTER TWENTY-SEVEN
The Tokoloshes' Decision

1

Rumundulu struggled to conceal his shock at the words he had just heard. The words had been spoken by Mungulutu or, more precisely, Mungulutu's simulacrum, contained in his sphere of pale phosphorescence suspended high above the floor of the Tokoloshe Embassy. Light from Mungulutu's orb bathed Rumundulu's broad, dark face in an ashen glow, turning his features into a stark, expressionless mask.

He was alone in the innermost cranny of the Embassy: a cavern hewn deep in the bedrock below the surface of the ground. Only the foremost of the Tokoloshe who were delegated to dwell among humans were permitted to enter the chamber, which had been shaped by magical means into the form of an inverted bowl. Its walls were smooth; its floor as flat as any street in Khambawe. The chamber had neither furnishings nor decorations, nor anything else that would indicate it had ever been intended for habitation.

For several moments now, Rumundulu had remained silent in an attempt to comprehend the consequences of what Mungulutu had just told him. He concluded that his wisdom was too limited to encompass the enormity of Mungulutu's message; its significance loomed larger than anything he or any other Tokoloshe had ever encountered or contemplated. It was as though some huge hand had suddenly swept hundreds of years of history and custom aside, and left in its place only a yawning, incomprehensible chasm.

Rumundulu could only shake his massive head in disbelief as he pondered the unthinkable. He had been in a conference with Bulamalayo, his figurehead among the humans, when he felt the insistent, *pulling* sensation that told him he was being summoned by Mungulutu. Bulamalayo had immediately understood what was happening, and simply nodded as Rumundulu walked away with a rigid gait, as though invisible strings controlled his limbs.

Gaze fixed on a horizon visible only to himself, Rumundulu had not returned any of the many greetings his fellow Tokoloshe and the Fidi dwarves had given him. The Tokoloshe had seen such a detached gaze in his eyes before. Well did they know the reason it was there, and they were quick to step aside and allow him room to pass. However, some of the newcomers perceived Rumundulu's behavior as brusque until the Tokoloshe took them aside and explained the nature of the summoning their leader obeyed. The dwarves understood then, although their eyes continued to follow his passage.

Level by level, Rumundulu had navigated a dank, twisting trail of stone that burrowed through the depths beneath the Embassy. When he reached the bowl-shaped chamber, Mungulutu's simulacrum had awaited him like a single Moon-Star shining in the darkness.

Respectfully, Rumundulu had waited. Then Mungulutu spoke. And Rumundulu could only stare in stunned silence after the Stone King finished. Now, Mungulutu was waiting for Rumundulu to respond.

Rumundulu could have asked how Mungulutu and the other Lords of Belowground had reached their drastic and momentous decision. He could have asked what they expected to accomplish with their directive. He could have asked what the future was now expected to bring to their kind.

Instead, he could only utter a single word: a question he knew all the others would ask when he told them what they must do.

"Why?"

"We see shadows," Mungulutu replied.

2

Hulm Stonehand could only bear to gaze at his son a few moments at a time before anger and grief forced him to look away. Those feelings were not, however, shared by the Tokoloshe, who could not bestow enough attention on the infant who personified the future of their people.

The child had been named "Humutungu," which in the Tokoloshe language meant "hope." Hulm heard a slight echo of his own name in that of his progeny. But that realization evoked little within him other than sorrow. His grief over the death of Izindikwa, the mother of Humutungu, had not abated. Instead, the sadness had grown stronger and more pervasive with each passing day, until it had become as much a part of him as his flesh and bones.

Thus, he looked away as yet another Tokoloshe woman took a turn at nursing his son. The magic that had failed to enable Tokoloshe women to conceive in the past had, ironically, proved successful enough in filling those women's breasts with nourishment. For this, Hulm could summon only a vague sense of gratitude.

Of paternal pride, he could summon nothing.

In Hulm's abdicated place as father, dozens of Tokoloshe were willing to stand. Indeed, all the Tokoloshe males in the Embassy treated Humutungu as though he were their own son.

Now, as always, Humutungu was surrounded by a throng of admiring Tokoloshe, all of whom wanted to see and touch their miracle child. Hulm stood aside, not caring to get closer, but not yet willing to depart.

The woman who nursed Humutungu looked at Hulm, and smiled. Her smile remained even as Hulm shifted his gaze elsewhere.

Among the Tokoloshe, Hulm was regarded with a respect that bordered on reverence. They deferred to him almost as much as they did to their leaders, Rumundulu and Bulamalayo. And they made allowances for his aloofness, for they, too mourned Izindikwa. For them, however, her name would live forever in renown, for she had given birth to the future of the Tokoloshe even as she sacrificed her life.

None of the other Fidi dwarves stood with Hulm. Like the Tokoloshe, they respected his right to grieve in privacy. As well, most of them had established liaisons with Tokoloshe women, hoping to duplicate Hulm's accomplishment. As yet, none of them had done so. However, optimism remained fervent, among Fidi and Tokoloshe alike.

Hulm's gaze returned to Humutungu and the woman who was feeding the child. The infant was swaddled in a cloth the color of granite, embroidered with decorations that looked like flecks of mica. From the little he could see of the child's face, Hulm acknowledged the similarity of Humutungu's features to his own. But that likeness did not fill him with joy.

Instead, there was only a hollowness inside him. Not even his belief in Almovaar could fill that void. Although the dwarves had fully embraced the Seer Kyroun's teachings, and had faith in Kyroun's ability to bring them through the Sea of Storms, Almovaar had receded from their attention during the time they spent among the Tokoloshe. The Dwarven had not adopted the religion of their hosts, which involved the propitiation of gods and spirits that dwelt in the core of the world. But they were no longer so ardent in their devotion to Almovaad doctrine. As well, the Seer paid them scant attention in the midst of his involvement in the concerns of the Matile. For all that, though, they continued to give Kyroun their allegiance.

Once again, Hulm turned away from his child and the Tokoloshe who surrounded him – and saw Rumundulu and Bulamalayo standing in front of him.

"My friend, we must speak together," Rumundulu said.

The troubled look in the Tokoloshes' eyes told Hulm that this would not be an ordinary conversation.

3

The Emperor Gebrem and the Seer Kyroun were in the Gebbi Senafa – and in the Oneness. The co-rulers of the Matile Mara Empire sat facing each other in Agaw's Chamber. Kyroun's presence there was unprecedented; never before had anyone other than an Emperor been permitted to enter the royal sanctuary. Then again, never before had a foreigner held a position as high as Leba.

Both men wore plain, dark-blue *chammas*; the emblems of their status would have been out of place in the austere environs of Agaw's Chamber. Their eyes were closed, and the expression each man's face bore was both somber and serene.

Within the Oneness, the Emperor and the Leba were not in the Palace, or even in Khambawe. They were standing on the crimson sand of Jayaya's beach. Tiyana stood with them.

A warm, soothing breeze blew in from the sea. In the Oneness, the three Adepts could experience the touch of the wind – but they felt as though the wind was passing through their bodies rather than around them.

As if she were weaving a story-tapestry in the air, Tiyana showed her father and the Seer what she and the other Almovaads had accomplished on the islands. Even though the three of them were standing on the beach, in the Oneness they could be anywhere ... or everywhere, as in more than one place at the same time. An unwary Initiate could become hopelessly lost in the Oneness, fluttering frantically from dimension to dimension in search of his or her body before it succumbed to thirst and starvation.

They watched as the surviving Uloans rebuilt the homes that had been destroyed during the rampage of the *mwiti*-plants. Dead *ubia*-vines and stiffened *mwiti*-roots had long since been cleared away or used as fuel for cooking-fires. The foliage that remained on the islands grew lush and luxuriant, and moved only when it was stirred by the wind. The taint of

Legaba's *ashuma* had long since disappeared, along with the vengeful spirits of the Kipalende.

If the people of Jayaya and the other Uloan islands had possessed the ability to foresee what Retribution Time would bring them, they would have slain Jass Imbiah and all her *huangi*. As a result of what Jass Imbiah had unleashed, the islands' population had been more than decimated. The only men left were those who had been too old to join the invasion force; the rest of the survivors were women and children. Their cities and towns lay in ruins that were only now being reconstructed, and food and water were in scarce supply.

Still, the survivors were free from Legaba. No more spider-scars marred their skin. They were allowing their hair to grow, and their hopes as well. Most importantly, they were able to envision a future beyond the shattered dream of Retribution Time – a future with Almovaar, their new savior-god.

On all the inhabited islands, the Almovaads walked among the Uloans, teaching them new ways of living and believing. The islanders had long since become accustomed to the presence of those whom they had previously derided as accursed blankskins, and even the Fidi, whose aspect had at first been disconcerting. Now, some of the Uloans had donned the blue robes of the Believers.

Gebrem looked with pride at what Tiyana had achieved, much of which had been under her own initiative. Neither he nor Kyroun had suggested the removal of the Uloans' spider-scars. And they had not been aware of the presence of the Kipalendes' spirits in the *mwiti*-plants. The decisions Tiyana had made then had been hers alone; Gebrem and Kyroun had done nothing more than observe her progress from the vantage point of the Oneness.

Now she stood before them in that same Oneness, in and out of Jayaya at the same time, the red sand of the beach seeming to stretch into infinity while images of ghostlike Uloans hard at work reshaping their lives surrounded them. Tiyana was clad in a plain blue *chamma*, but she looked more like a goddess now than she had when she wore the Mask of Namakwah and danced on the waves during First Calling not so long in the past.

Sunlight glistened on her smooth ebony skin and flashed in brilliant daylight constellations from the gold and silver beads woven into the long braids of her hair. Confidence – but not arrogance – shone in her dark eyes as she smiled at her two mentors.

"Daughter, you have done well," Gebrem said.

"I agree," said Kyroun.

"Thank you, Father," Tiyana said.

Her words and her smile were meant as much for Kyroun as for Gebrem, for in the ways of Oneness and the Almovaads, he was her other father. Because of him, she was a new person. The Seer answered her with a smile of his own, which was echoed by the Emperor.

"But there is so much more to do," Tiyana added.

"Yes, there is," Kyroun said. "But the Uloans must do it for themselves. You cannot stay with them forever."

"It is time for you to return to Khambawe," Gebrem said. "There is much to be done among our own people as well."

Tiyana's smile faded as she realized that the some of the plans she had made for the further regeneration of the Uloans would now have to proceed without her. Then she sighed, and nodded.

"You are right," she said. "We will prepare the ships and leave within a few days."

"We will be glad to have you back," Gebrem said.

Again, Tiyana nodded.

With that, the Emperor and the Leba detached their consciousness from the Oneness. Tiyana and the scarlet beach of Jayaya faded like mist, and within an instant the two men's minds were back in Agaw's Chamber, their spirits now rejoined to their bodies.

As soon as they opened their eyes, the two men knew someone was awaiting them on the other side of the door – someone who had been there for a long time, and would remain until Gebrem and Kyroun emerged from the chamber, no matter how long that took.

The Emperor and the Leba rose to their feet. With a single gesture of his hand, Gebrem opened the chamber's door without touching it. Standing on the other side was the soldier who was in charge of the Palace guards this night, a man named Asenafe. Asenafe had fought with great distinction during the Uloan invasion, and Gebrem had rewarded him with a high position in the Gebbi Senafa.

For all his courage in battle, though, Asenafe appeared uneasy under the gaze of the Emperor and the Leba, who waited for him to speak.

"Your pardon, Mesfin, but the Tokoloshe, Bulamalayo, is in the Audience Chamber," the soldier said. "He says he needs to speak with you. There are others with him."

Kyroun and Gebrem exchanged a glance.

"What others?" Gebrem asked.

"Another Tokoloshe ... and one of the Fidi who look like the Tokoloshe."

After another exchange of looks with Kyroun, Gebrem said:

"Tell them we will see them."

"As you command, Mesfin," Asenafe said.

The soldier saluted, turned on his heel, and departed.

"This could be trouble, Gebrem," Kyroun said.

The Emperor nodded.

4

Instead of the Audience Chamber, the meeting between the Tokoloshe representatives and the rulers of the Matile Mara Empire occurred in the chamber in which the Emperor usually met with the Degen Jassi. It was in this room that the fate of Kyroun and the other Fidi had been decided. Now, the Seer helped to determine the destiny of the Empire.

As they listened to what the Tokoloshe envoys were telling them, both Kyroun and Gebrem soon realized that for all the immense power their wielded – sorcerous and otherwise – there were still eventualities that were beyond even their considerable ability to control. And that realization disturbed them more than they would have wanted to admit.

Already, they had been surprised when Bulamalayo revealed that Rumundulu was the real head of the Tokoloshe Embassy. Misdirection, however, was far from uncommon in the practice of diplomacy among Matile and Tokoloshe alike. But what Rumundulu and Hulm Stonehand, who represented the Dwarven, said next truly stunned both the Emperor and the Leba.

"We are closing the Tokoloshe Embassy," Rumundulu said without preamble. "The closing is effective at once. All Tokoloshe will depart from Khambawe and the lands of the Matile as soon as possible."

"And we will be going with the Tokoloshe," Hulm said. He looked at Kyroun, not the Emperor, as he spoke.

Silence followed as the two rulers reacted to the news. Gebrem was the first to break it.

"Our alliance ...." he began.

"Is intact," Bulamalayo said, speaking for the first time since revealing who Rumundulu was. His voice grated like gravel trod underfoot as he continued.

"However, we are needed in our homeland at this time."

Gebrem labored to maintain a calm exterior even as he attempted to absorb the considerable impact of Rumundulu's words. The connection between the Matile and the Tokoloshe stretched back many centuries, its inception coming long before the time of the Storm Wars. Together, the two races had prevailed over adversaries ranging from the ogrish Zimwe to the shape-shifting *irimu*, and they had kept the barbaric Thaba hordes first at bay, then in thrall.

For all that time, the Tokoloshe had maintained a presence in Khambawe, even during the Storm Wars and their aftermath. And the Matile owed the Tokoloshe a further debt of gratitude for their part in the victory over the Uloans, for without their aid, the city might have been overrun before the sorcery of the Almovaads could come into play. The prospect of such a sudden departure disconcerted Gebrem. Kyroun, being less knowledgeable about Matile history, was less concerned. But he could sense the obvious importance of this development to Gebrem.

As if he were reading the Emperor's thoughts, Rumundulu said:

"You do not need us anymore, Mesfin. Your new sorcery is more than sufficient to protect your people. And you don't need much protection at that, for your greatest enemy has been defeated beyond any hope of recovery. You may even be strong enough to prevent us from leaving Khambawe. – although I suspect neither you nor I would care to put that supposition to the test. As Bulamalayo said, we are needed in our homeland, and we intend to go there."

Gebrem understood that that no threat was implied in the Tokoloshe's words ... Rumundulu was only stating the facts of the matter at hand. A clash between the mystic forces the Tokoloshe and the Matile commanded would undo much of the rebuilding that had been accomplished since the defeat of the Uloans, and leave the Empire vulnerable to the growing threat posed by the Thabas to the south.

One question repeated itself like a drumbeat in the Emperor's mind: Why? Why was the entire populace of the Embassy "needed" in the Tokoloshes' mysterious homeland? Rumundulu's statement was vague, and told Gebrem little of what he truly wanted to know. Gebrem realized, though, that he was not likely to learn more if he pressed the Tokoloshe for answers.

But Kyroun did not hesitate to ask a question of his own, which he directed to Hulm.

"Why do you wish to accompany the Tokoloshe?"

Hulm had earlier prepared a detailed, precise discourse explaining his people's decision. Now, as he looked into the Seer's eyes, he remembered the first encounter between the Dwarven and the Almovaads ....

5

For millennia, the Dwarven of Cym Dinath had lived secretively, much more so than the Tokoloshe of Abengoni. Although they traded sporadically with humankind and sometimes ventured into the humans' world, for the most part they preferred to dwell in the territories they had carved out deep Belowground. They found humans to be too greedy and quarrelsome, their nature too dangerous and unpredictable, for extensive contact or alliances like the one between the Tokoloshe and the Matile to be made.

But Belowground was not without perils of its own. The Dwarven environment was far from static; the Belowground breathed and moved as though it was a living creature rather than an inert mass of stone and earth. One such movement – a titanic shift in the plates of rock deep Belowground – destroyed the territory in which Hulm's people had dwelt for millennia. Only a few had survived, none of them women or children. Those who still lived had no alternative other than to venture Aboveground.

There, they wandered in aimless sorrow, eking out a subsistence living as they attempted to find their way back Belowground. But they were no longer welcome in their old environs. For their fellow Dwarven considered them to be blighted by the disaster they had suffered. And they believed the wanderers carried the curse of that calamity with them. Thus, every time Hulm's people ventured Belowground, they were met with sharp imprecations and sharper axe-blades.

They were a weary, disconsolate group when Kyroun and the

Almovaads met them during their long journey west to Fiadol. When the Seer learned what had befallen them, he gave them more than sympathy. He offered them hope for a new life in a land far away from the disaster and subsequent rejection they had suffered. They needed only to become Believers in Almovaar.

And that is what they did.

During the most harrowing parts of the subsequent journey, the Dwarven had remained steadfast in their faith in Almovaar, and in the Seer's vision. They had even trusted to their new god when the Almovaad ships took to the sea, an element the Dwarven instinctively disliked, as did the Tokoloshe.

And now ....

"Seer, you told us that every Almovaad would find a home on the other side of the Sea of Storms," Hulm said, giving voice to what he truly felt rather than reciting the words he had rehearsed.

"Your people – the humans – have found a home among the Matile," Hulm continued. "But the lands of your people could never be a true home for the Dwarven. It is not like that with the Tokoloshe. They are us; we are them. The Tokoloshe do not believe we are tainted by what happened to us in our lost home. They welcome us. And we accept that welcome."

Hulm paused for a moment, still holding Kyroun's gaze.

"Seer, Almovaar has fulfilled his promise to give us a new home," he said. "And we will take Almovaar with us to the land of the Tokoloshe."

"We worship many gods and spirits," Bulamalayo interjected. "Your god saved us as well as you. We are grateful to him. He will be accepted among us."

"We followed you because you said we were needed here," Hulm said. "Now, we Dwarven are needed in the land of our friends. Like you, we cannot ignore that need."

Hulm and the two Tokoloshe were not aware that that Gebrem and Kyroun had slipped momentarily into the Oneness. From the standpoint of an outside observer, the two rulers appeared to be listening intently to what the others were saying. And, to an extent, they were doing exactly that. But only to an extent.

Is this what Almovaar wants? Gebrem asked in the Oneness.

He hasn't raised any objection, Kyroun replied.

We do not need another war ... yet, said Gebrem.

Then you will not have one.

The last voice was Almovaar's.

At once, the two rulers departed the Oneness. For a time that stretched over an uncomfortable period, they regarded their visitors, who fought to conceal their growing anxiety as the silence deepened. Finally, the Emperor spoke, directing his words to the two Tokoloshe.

"Your ancestors came freely among us long ago," he said. "And you may leave freely now. Go in peace."

Apprehension changed immediately to relief for the three visitors. And they concealed that emotion just as diligently as they made their farewells to the two rulers and exited the chamber.

6

Preparations for the Tokoloshes' departure from their Embassy had been uncommonly swift, but also orderly. The Tokoloshe gathered food, water and other provisions, all of which they would carry themselves, as they possessed no beasts of burden capable of travelling Belowground. The packs were huge, but they hefted them easily, for only the strongest of humans could come close to matching the physical might of the average Tokoloshe or Dwarven.

The mood was somber; even though many of the Tokoloshe had lived their entire lives in the Embassy and had yearned to visit their ancestral land. Despite that desire, they were still leaving the only home they had ever known.

Even though they had removed virtually all the Embassy's accouterments as well, the Tokoloshe still felt the need to set potent sorcerous wards to forestall the attention of looters, as well as those who were merely curious about the forbidding, cube-shaped structure that had sat untouched and unvisited in their midst for such a long time. As it was, the Tokoloshe did not know whether or not their kind would ever return to live among the Matile.

Special care was taken with the two-headed drum, which held high sacred significance among the Tokoloshe. Although one of them could easily have handled its weight, it was carried reverently on an ornate litter by two Tokoloshe men.

When all the preparations were done, the inhabitants of the Embassy gathered in a long, double-file line that snaked through the corridor that would lead ever-deeper Belowground. The Fidi Dwarven did not separate themselves from the Tokoloshe, as they might have done when they first arrived in Khambawe. Most of them were beside the Tokoloshe women with whom they had mated. Only Hulm Stonehand stood alone, apart from Dwarven and Tokoloshe alike.

One-by-one, the light-spheres that illuminated the Embassy were extinguished. But the pitch-blackness that descended when the last sphere went dark lasted only a moment.

Standing at the front of the column, Rumundulu whispered a syllable of power, and the large globe at the tip of the staff he carried blazed into incandescence, showing the Tokoloshe the way forward.

Rumundulu led his people further down, past the dome-shaped chamber in which Mungulutu had commanded him to close the Embassy and return to the homeland. They descended yet further, through tunnels humans would have found insufferably claustrophobic. For the Tokoloshe and Dwarven, however, the close confines felt like an embrace from the spirits that dwelt Belowground.

Soon they reached what appeared to be an impenetrable wall of rock. However, the light from Rumundulu's globe revealed a thin crack that split the stone from top to bottom.

Rumundulu opened his mouth to voice the syllable that would cause the crack to widen. Before he could speak, Humutungu began to wail. Despite the attempts of the Tokoloshe women to quiet him, the infant's cries continued unabated.

Rumundulu sensed an omen in Humutungu's outcries. He spoke quietly to Bulamalayo, who was at his side. Bulamalayo nodded, then went to the woman who held Humutungu, spoke to her in turn, and took the infant from her arms. Then he carried the still-crying Humutungu to Hulm.

"Take him," Bulamalayo said. There was a note of command in the Tokoloshe's rumbling voice.

Hulm only stared straight ahead, refusing to look at the squirming, wailing infant. Anguish was graven on his broad features.

"Take him, Hulm," Bulamalayo repeated. "He is yours. And he is ours. You do not have to love him. But you must accept him."

Slowly, hesitantly, Hulm extended his arms. Bulamalayo gently placed Humutungu in his father's grasp.

    Hulm forced himself to look at the infant. Humutungu's mouth was open wide as he cried. And so were his eyes ... Izindikwa's eyes. Hulm realized then that part of Izindikwa lived on in the child he was holding. And, at that moment, Humutungu's cries ceased.

    Then Rumundulu spoke a set of syllables that sounded harsh even by the standards of the Tokoloshe tongue. When he finished, a grinding, groaning noise accompanied the slow widening of the crack in the rock. Soon, the crack became a gap wide enough to allow passage. Rumundulu squeezed through, and the others followed. When the last of the group was on the other side of the gap, it closed again, and a shroud of darkness descended on the part of Belowground the Tokoloshe had occupied beneath Khambawe – a darkness in which shadows could not survive.

CHAPTER TWENTY-EIGHT
A Deal With The Tsotsis
1

Athir was lazing in his Gebbi Senafa suite when he heard the scuff of footsteps approaching his door. He half-rose from the long lounge-seat in his sitting-room and rearranged the satiny, colorfully patterned throw-cloth beneath him. Earlier he had informed a passing servant that he wanted more *talla*. From what he had gleaned of the workings of Gebbi Senafa protocol, he knew that the servant to whom he had spoken would, in turn, relay his request to the people who were in charge of dispensing food and drink in the palace. Then the servant assigned to his suite would bring him what he desired.

Ordinarily, such a sound of footsteps would have elicited an instant response from the Ship's Rat. His survival had always depended upon the quickness of his reactions to what his sharply honed senses told him. But the soft life in the Gebbi Senafa had dulled the knife's edge of tension that had always been inside him. And his best friend, fear, had fallen quiescent of late.

Athir's hand toyed idly with the thin tail of hair that dangled down the nape of his neck. Never before had he spent so much time in one place, or within the walls that did not belong to a prison. But then the palace was, in its own way, as confining as any place of incarceration had ever been.

Although he was fairly certain the *tsotsis* no longer posed a threat to his life, penned as they were in the Maim, he still wasn't willing to venture into the streets. He knew the *tsotsis* had penetrated much of Khambawe before their downfall, and there was still a remote chance that a determined few from Jass Mofo's set could capture him if he left the protection of the

Gebbi Senafa. Inside the palace, he remained safe, secure ... and bored.

Not that he didn't enjoy his new life of indolence and luxury. Who wouldn't? Still, with increasing frequency, his fingers itched to cradle the ivory cubes he continued to keep in their pouch at his belt. He missed the thrill of the hunt for victims for his petty larceny, as well as the inevitable flight from the marks' angry vengeance. The conflict between the dreamlike life he was living and his recollections of his former days was becoming a tempest inside him, and he could not drink enough *talla* to put that turmoil to rest.

A diffident knock on his door interrupted Athir's reverie. He rose from the couch, walked to the door and lifted its latch. Few people who dwelt in the palace bothered to secure their doors. But Athir's old habits were hard to discard, even if it seemed they were no longer needed.

The grin that was on his face when he swung the door open faded when he saw who was standing on the other side. He had been expecting one of the serving-women with whom he had become familiar in more ways than one. Instead, the servant who carried a fresh pitcher of *talla* and a cup already filled to the brim was a new man who had only recently been assigned to attend Athir's needs when the women were not available.

The Ship's Rat made no attempt to conceal his disappointment.

"Oh. It's you," he muttered. "Come on in."

He stepped aside and the servant entered, balancing the tray on the palm of one hand. After placing the tray on a low table in front of Athir's couch, the servant moved toward the open door. Without looking at him, Athir went back to his couch and sat down again.

He didn't particularly care to look at the new servant, who was a wiry, nondescript man with few, if any, distinguishing characteristics. Still, there was something about this servant that reminded Athir of himself. And he had no desire to confront his own aspect in the dark mirror of some Matile's face.

Athir heard the servant walk away, and he heard his door close. He looked up ... and saw that the servant had not left the room. Instead, the man was coming toward him – fast.

Immediately, Athir's torpid survival instincts awakened. But the arousal came too late. Moving as quickly as Athir ever had, the servant reached the Ship's Rat's side. Before Athir could say or do anything, he felt an arm snake around his shoulders. Then the sharp edge of a blade pressed against his throat, but not hard enough to puncture his skin.

Despite the caress of steel against his neck, Athir still managed to give voice to his greatest fear.

"Are you a *tsotsi*?" he asked.

He didn't recognize the servant from his time in Jass Mofo's set. But then, other than Mofo himself, the *tsotsis* had more or less looked the same to him.

Before he replied, the servant uttered a chuckle that was devoid of humor.

"I am far from being a *tsotsi*," he said.

"What do you want from me?" Athir asked.

"I brought you *talla*, as you requested. Now, all I want you to do is drink it."

Athir swallowed hard. Then he sighed in resignation. He had no weapon within reach. And the servant's grip was like iron; Athir could not hope to break free.

"Pick up the cup, put it to your mouth, and drink," the servant instructed. "And if you try to throw the *talla* in my face, I'll cut your throat."

Athir did as he was told. As he expected, he grew weak as soon as the *talla* reached his stomach, and a curtain of darkness quickly descended over his eyes. Before he lost consciousness, the Ship's Rat cursed himself for allowing the easy life to turn him into the prey, rather than the predator he had always been. As Athir slumped forward, Sehaye caught the Fidi before he could fall to the floor.

2

No one had questioned Sehaye very closely when he applied for work as a servant in the Gebbi Senafa. Because of the terrible toll Retribution Time had exacted on the populace of Khambawe, toilers of all kinds were in short supply. Anyone who was willing to perform menial tasks for low pay was more than welcome. The servants were no longer called *shamashas*, but the work they did remained the same.

In the same way, the Uloan's offer to help with the disposal of the palace's garbage had also been appreciated. The chief of the servants found Sehaye to be a hard worker, albeit taciturn to a fault. He spoke only when spoken to, and even then, he used as few words as possible, as though talk were a treasure he was hoarding.

The servant supervisor had far more pressing concerns than questioning the motives of a man who had volunteered to do one of the most hated chores in the palace. He thanked Sehaye for his diligence and put him in charge of hauling the two-wheeled cart that carried the palace's refuse.

So it was that Sehaye now pulled his cart through the halls of the Gebbi Senafa. Two long poles extended from hinges on the cart's side; Sehaye was positioned between them as though he were a *quagga* in harness. The cart was filled to the brim with food scraps, pieces of cloth, and various other discarded items. There was something else in the cart as well ... an inert, slumbering body. Its weight required Sehaye to exert more effort than usual as he pulled the cart.

Thank Legaba he doesn't snore, Sehaye thought as he struggled not to show his increased effort. He did not want anyone he passed in the halls to notice anything unusual – and they didn't. Indeed, they hardly noticed Sehaye at all. The closer he came to the palace's doors, the more he realized he'd had no reason to worry. The palace guards, the royal retainers, and even the other servants paid him not more heed than they would have to a piece of furniture.

Finally, Sehaye reached the gates, which had been kept open well into the night since the coronation of Emperor Gebrem. Before, they had been shut at sundown and guarded grimly until dawn. More people visited the palace now, for Gebrem was proving to be a much more accessible ruler than Alemeyu had been. And he was also more benevolent ... most supplicants came away from his audiences with more largess than they had asked for.

Sehaye trundled his cart toward the two palace guards who manned the gates. Ordinarily, the guards would simply wave him through, though not without a jest or two aimed his way to help alleviate the dullness of their duties. He never responded to the gibes ... which was likely the reason they decided to do more than merely joke with him this night.

"Hold it," one of the guards barked, lowering his spear to forestall Sehaye's passage.

"What's the problem?" Sehaye asked.

The Uloan was striving to conceal his nervousness. Both guards had stern expressions on their faces as they moved closer.

"New rules," said the guard who had stopped Sehaye. "Items of value have been disappearing from the palace. We've been ordered to inspect everybody and everything that goes out."

Sehaye wished he could will away the beads of sweat that were beginning to form on his brow. As it was, he could barely restrain himself from bolting as the soldiers reached toward the trash at the top of his cart. Then their hands stopped in mid-motion. And both guards burst out laughing.

"He really thought we were going to put our hands in that damned garbage," one of the guards guffawed.

"As if there was anything worth stealing from this stinking cart," the other one said, nearly choking on his own wit.

Sehaye waited as the guards continued to enjoy their prank. He even joined their laughter ... better to display mirth, however false, than to show even a hint of his desire to kill both the bastards on the spot. Their idiotic joke had brought him far too close to panic. Sweat still dripped down his face, but the guards were too absorbed by their rare bit of amusement to notice.

"Can I go now, with my 'stolen treasure'?" Sehaye asked when the guards' laughter finally subsided.

"Go ahead, go ahead," the more talkative of the two said. "Next time, though, you'll have to split your loot with us."

That set off another round of laughter, which echoed in Sehaye's ears as he pulled the heavy cart away from the Gebbi Senafa.

3

Before the invasion of the Uloans, the Maim had been the most dangerous part of Khambawe. During the time that had passed since the defeat of the Islanders, that distinction still held true – but for a much different reason.

In the past the Maim had, for all its squalor and decrepitude, teemed with life and a knife's-edge form of verve. Rival *tsotsi* sets had roamed the streets: preening, profiling, socializing, fighting. Brave or foolish people from the outer city would venture into the Maim on missions of illicit business – or unconventional pleasure. Even wildlife of a sort thrived in the blighted district. Hyenas and feral dogs fought over human carrion in fetid alleys, while hordes of rats lay in wait to devour whatever scraps the larger scavengers left behind.

And if some of the hyenas were really shape-shifting *irimu*, few in the Maim considered that to be a matter of importance. For back then, the *tsotsis* themselves had been *irimu* of a sort – deadly predators in human guise.

In the daytime, only a few vestiges of the Maim's previous vitality remained. *Tsotsis* could still be seen in the streets, but their movements were guarded and furtive. The bravado they had exhibited before was gone. Almost no one from the outer city came into the Maim anymore. The *khat* trade had ground to a halt, as had the other vices the denizens of the Maim offered to the rest of Khambawe.

And at night ... at night, the light of the Moon Stars and the blazing night-sun conjured by the Almovaads illuminated streets that were nearly entirely devoid of life. Even the scavengers avoided the bright glare that sought out the prey of the Muvuli. The light was harsh, accusatory ... as though it embodied the wrath and contempt the rest of Khambawe held for the *tsotsis'* depredations during the time in which the city was fighting for its survival.

Even though many of the Matile whose homes had been looted by the *tsotsis* while the Uloans were burning the city harbored bitterness in their hearts, no one visited the Maim to wreak vengeance on their own account. Although the Almovaads had assured the honest people of Khambawe that the Shadows posed no danger to them, only to the *tsotsis*, they were disinclined to put that pledge to the test. Besides, the Almovaads had convinced the people that the Muvuli were more than adequate surrogates for ensuring the destruction of the *tsotsis*. The shadows were picking the *tsotsis* off like lice from a scalp, one at a time ...

Had the voice in his mind not assured him of his safety, Sehaye would never have gone to the Maim even during the day, let alone at night. Yet he trusted that voice as implicitly as the Matile trusted the Almovaads. And the voice told him neither the shadows nor the *tsotsis* would harm him.

This was not Sehaye's first venture into the Maim. He had come once before, and had seen what no one other than the *tsotsis* themselves had witnessed.

From whispered conversations he had engaged in with people who lived on the fringes of the Maim, Sehaye had learned that one set of *tsotsis* continued to roam the district's streets at night, despite the constant danger of an encounter with the Muvuli. The members of that set were searching for something more valuable to them than loot – or their lives. The informants had told Sehaye the name of the set, and of its much-feared Jass.

Armed with that knowledge, and with the reassurances of the voice within him that he would not be harmed by the Muvuli, Sehaye had ventured into the Maim. Before Retribution Time, he'd had no reason to go there. The time he had spent in Khambawe had been devoted to selling the fish he caught and seeking information to pass on to Jass Imbiah. Otherwise, he had avoided the blankskins, primarily because the sight of them reminded him of his own want of spider-scars.

Even so, his lack of familiarity with the convoluted streets of the Maim had not mattered. The voice inside him, the voice that had become his friend, but also his insistent taskmaster, guided him unerringly. He had seen no shadow other than his own, and the dogs, hyenas and rats had avoided him as though he were part of the silver glare that turned night into a disconcerting semblance of day.

Hidden in an alley that contained his shadow and no others, Sehaye had waited until he heard rapid, scuttering footsteps coming down the street. Then the footsteps paused. A moment later, a *tsotsi* appeared in the opening of the alley. Fear was written plainly on the youth's face as he peered into the darkness of the alley. The *tsotsi* carried a *tirss* in his hand. He held the weapon in front of him as though it could somehow detect danger he could not see.

The *tsotsi* could not see Sehaye ... but Sehaye could see the second shadow that suddenly appeared on the street behind the *tsotsi*. He saw the Muvuli raise its *tirss* and plunge it into the back of the *tsotsi's* shadow. He heard the *tsotsi* cry out in fear and agony at the impact he felt on his own flesh, even though it was only his shadow that was being attacked. And he stared wide-eyed as both shadows gradually disappeared even as the *tsotsi* bled to death practically at his feet.

Striving to suppress his fear and giving himself over completely to the guidance of the voice within him, Sehaye had stepped over the body of the *tsotsi* as he emerged from the mouth of the alley. He cast a glance at the street-stones, then at the wall on the opposite side of the street, and breathed a sigh of relief at the sight of only one shadow – his own.

Now, he was back in the Maim ... at a different location this time, and for a different reason. The voice had told him the purpose of the previous visit had been to prepare him for what he would see when a shadow struck. Then, the life of a luckless *tsotsi* had meant nothing to either Sehaye or the voice. On this night, however, a *tsotsi's* life would mean everything ...

Sehaye waited in the darkness of another alley. The Almovaads' night-sun shone pitilessly, creating shadows that were unavoidable. And before long, another *tsotsi* crept into view, keeping to the darkness as much as he could, but unable to prevent his shadow from following him.

His efforts to avoid the inevitable were unsuccessful. As the *tsotsi* drew closer to the alley in which Sehaye was hiding, a second shadow appeared behind him ... a shadow with a *tirss* in its hand ... a *tirss* it was raising for a slash into the substance of the other shadow that shared the space on the wall.

This time, Sehaye was more than merely an observer. This time, he acted. Even as the Muvuli's weapon began to descend, Sehaye sprinted from the alley, seized the *tsotsi*, and dragged him back into the safety of the darkness. In the moment before he reached the alley, Sehaye was touched by an icy coldness unlike anything ever experienced by any Matile or Uloan, or anyone else in Abengoni. He shuddered even as the cursing *tsotsi* struggled to get away from him.

When an unseen point of the *tsotsi's tirss* pricked his skin, Sehaye uttered curses of his own. Then he twisted the *tsotsi's* arm behind his back and turned him so that he could see outside the alley.

"Look!" Sehaye commanded, forcing the *tsotsi's* head in the direction of the street.

The *tsotsi* obeyed ... and saw a shadow where no one stood to cast it. *Tirss* still raised, the Muvuli looked left and right, looking for its prey. The apparition was still searching as it faded from sight.

While he watched the Muvuli disappear, the *tsotsi's* body went slack in Sehaye's arms. Now, his lean muscles tensed. Sehaye tightened his grasp.

"Who you is?" the *tsotsi* hissed. "What you want?"

Sehaye knew better than to expect gratitude, or even courtesy, from a *tsotsi*. Instead of replying directly, the Uloan asked a question of his own.

"Are you Ashaki?"

The *tsotsi* started, then stared hard at what little he could see of Sehaye in the alley's gloom.

"Why you ask that?" the *tsotsi* demanded.

"I have something Jass Mofo wants."

"What that be?"

Sehaye leaned forward and whispered a name in the *tsotsi's* ear. This time, the *tsotsi* grinned.

"Mofo want that, for true. You coming with me. Heard?"

"Heard," Sehaye said.

4

The Muvuli did not unnerve Sehaye nearly as much as did Jass Mofo. And he had to struggle twice as hard to contain his fear as he had in the alley in the Maim, when a mere brush from the shadow's weapon had thrust a cold blade into his soul. The eyes of the Ashaki set's leader were even colder than the Muvuli's touch. Yet there was something else in those dark, empty chasms ... something that burned fiercely, yet emitted no warmth ... something that was as distant from sanity as the Moon Stars were from the world.

Sehaye was in the dilapidated *aderash* that was still the headquarters of the Ashaki set. A few candles provided illumination; these days, any other light after sunset was the *tsotsis'* worst enemy. The *tsotsis* who surrounded their Jass seemed more wraithlike than real: their bodies were thin to the point of emaciation, and their eyes, showing the influence of the copious amounts of *khat* they chewed, flickered like the candles that lit the huge, nearly empty hall from which they and Mofo had once ruled the night.

Now, the night ruled them.

The *tsotsi* who had led Sehaye to the *aderash* had left him in the custody of several others while he went to inform Jass Mofo of his arrival. Sehaye knew the repetition of the name he had whispered would bring Mofo to him immediately. He was not wrong. He waited only a short time before the *tsotsi* reappeared, with Mofo at his side. During the interval, the other *tsotsis* had eyed him as though he were fresh meat, and they were starving. Sehaye ignored their attention. He knew he was safe among them.

Or so the voice told him ...

But when Sehaye first laid eyes on Mofo, that assurance fled: voice or no voice. Jass Mofo reminded him of the sharks that had tried to tear the catches from his nets during his time as a fisherman. The *tsotsi's* previous finery was long since gone. The braids of his hair had become as tangled as a bramble bush, and his skin stretched tautly across the bones of his lean frame. Mofo looked as though he were cornered, and therefore even more dangerous than usual. The *tsotsi* eyed the Uloan for a long time before he spoke.

"You save Kutu from the shadow," Mofo said, nodding toward the *tsotsi* at his side. "You give Kutu a name. That name bring you here alive. You want to stay alive, you say what you want here. Heard?"

"This is not about what *I* want, Jass Mofo," Sehaye said. "It's about what *you* want. Word is, you want two things. I have one of them. The name tells you which one it is."

"The Fidi-*tsotsi*," Mofo said.

His eyes narrowed.

"Where he be?"

"In a safe place."

"How I know you got him?"

"Maybe this will convince you."

Slowly, Sehaye reached beneath the folds of his *chamma* and produced a long, thin tail of sandy-colored hair. As he held it in front of Mofo's eyes, Athir's hair-tail swayed like a pendulum.

With a sound akin to a snarl, Mofo snatched the hair-tail from Sehaye's hand. With his other hand, he pulled his *tirss* from its loop at his waist and thrust the weapon in front of the other man's face. Its points were close to Sehaye's eyes.

"Give the rest of him to me," Mofo said in a low voice.

"I want something in return," Sehaye said.

The points of Mofo's *tirss* moved closer to Sehaye's eyes. Sehaye did not move or blink. He knew his life depended on not giving in to the terror that was clawing him inside.

"I want; I take," Mofo said. "I take easy, I take hard. But I take. Heard?"

Sehaye knew exactly what the *tsotsi* meant.

"You can torture me if you want to, Jass Mofo," the Uloan said. "You can make me scream for my gods and my mother. But I will not tell you where you can find Athir unless you do what I ask. If you do it, not only will you have what you want; you will also be free from the Muvuli, and no longer be hated by the people of this city. Heard?"

No one had ever before spoken to Jass Mofo with such impunity. The remaining Ashaki waited for their Jass to savage Sehaye with his *tirss*.

Instead, Mofo lowered his weapon. He stared at Sehaye with an expression akin to interest. It was as though he was looking at something he had never seen before. In Sehaye's eyes, he recognized an implacability that might well have matched his own.

"What you want, then?" he asked.

Sehaye told him. And when he finished, Mofo did not kill him.

5

Athir opened his eyes to darkness. He blinked several times, but what he saw was always the same: a darkness so profound that he could not see his hand in front of his face. Or, more accurately, had he been able to move his hand into his field of vision, it would have remained indistinguishable from the darkness. But he could not move his hands, or his feet. His limbs had been bound so securely that he wondered how blood managed to make its way to his extremities.

However, Athir was not gagged. He could call for help if he so desired. He didn't. His abductor had obviously hidden him in a place where no one was likely to hear his cries, and had therefore not bothered to ensure his silence.

Although Athir could see nothing, the darkness did not affect his sense of smell. A foul odor permeated the place in which he was imprisoned. A strong smell of garbage surrounded him, and he struggled to prevent himself from retching. And there was another, underlying scent as well ... one with which Athir was familiar, having encountered it in other places in the course of his travels.

It was the dank, musty, acrid smell of a sewer. On more than one occasion, such places had provided an appropriate place of refuge for the Ship's Rat. And another sewer in this city had held the loot that bought him his now-departed time of luxury. But now, the underground was a prison. Or, perhaps, a tomb.

The latter was not likely, though. If the palace servant who had abducted him had wanted him dead, by now he would be. However, he had a feeling that he would not live much longer if he remained bound and helpless in the sewer. He had essayed a few abductions himself, and he knew the value of the victim was either loot or life. He knew of no one who would be willing to pay anything to keep him alive. So his skin had to be the prize in this game. And he knew exactly who it was that wanted that skin more than anything else.

The *tsotsis* ...

Rivulets of sweat began to trickle down Athir's face as he contemplated his chances for survival. Out of necessity, he had become adept at wriggling his way out of ropes, and sometimes even chains. He could not discern the nature of his present bonds. However, the job had been done in expert fashion. His arms were bound straight at his sides, giving his fingers nothing upon which to gain purchase. He tried the eel-like wriggle that had always worked for him in the past. He could move ... but only a little. And he knew if he continued such gyrations, he would eventually free himself. His bonds were so tight, though, that he knew a great deal of time would have to pass before that happened.

And he did not know how much time he had. He suspected it was far less than he needed ...

Then he heard faint, splashing sounds. And he knew he had no time left at all. For the sounds were coming closer to him. And he could see an object that was casting a silvery light in the pitch-darkness of the sewer.

As the object drew nearer, Athir could see that it was a mask, carved in the likeness of a woman too beautiful to be human, even though it was marred by a small dent. At first, the mask seemed to be floating disembodied in midair. Then, as his eyes became accustomed to the sudden light, Athir could see that the mask surmounted the emaciated, nearly naked body of a young girl.

"Who are you?" he croaked. "What are you doing down here?"

The wearer of the mask did not reply. As she came closer, Athir let out a low cry of fear and frustration. Not only was the girl wearing a glowing mask; she was carrying a small, lethal-looking dagger. And the dagger was moving toward him.

CHAPTER TWENTY-NINE

ESHETU'S STORY

1

Eshetu did not look like a man who belonged in, or anywhere near, the Gebbi Senafa. Indeed, he did not even look as though he belonged in any other part of the Jewel City, not even the disreputable Maim. He was a *kabbar* – a peasant farmer from the Matile hinterland, the lands of the Imba Jassi, where *teff*, the grain that was the main ingredient in *injerra*, was grown. His hands bore the calluses that betokened a life of hard farm work, and he wore the rural *harai* rather than the city-dweller's *chamma*. Both his *harai* and his waist-cloth were torn and threadbare. His unbraided hair grew in a huge, uneven mass, and many days had passed since the last time he had trimmed his bushy beard.

A badly healed scar traversed Eshetu's face from his left brow to his right cheek. By some miracle, the slash that had made the wound had not taken his eye as well. However, the scar was not Eshetu's most arresting feature. It was his eyes that indicated he was no longer a typical rural-dweller; that he had witnessed horrors that rivaled the worst depredations the Uloans had inflicted in Khambawe.

Ordinarily, a *kabbar* would never have had any reason to make the long journey to Khambawe. The people who lived in the outlying parts of the Matile Mala Empire seldom ventured farther than the next town or village. On rare occasions, they would go to a festival or ceremony in the nearest large town, or to the few cities in the region. Khambawe was only a name to them, a name signifying a place as distant and unattainable as the Realms of the Jagasti.

Yet here he was, being escorted by a soldier past a long line of people waiting to be ushered through the gates of the Gebbi Senafa. Inside, the petitioners would present their grievances or requests for favors to the Palace functionaries who looked after such matters. Petitions of greater importance would be passed along to the Emperor. Only on rare occasions would a petitioner be permitted to bypass the functionaries and be presented directly to the Emperor. Thus, the people in the line stared at Eshetu as he walked past them.

Eshetu had to remind himself that the Emperor was now Gebrem, formerly the Leba, and that Alemeyu was dead. Until he had travelled closer to the city, Eshetu had not even known that the Uloans had invaded the mainland. Not enough time had passed for the news to travel that far.

But he carried other tidings … vital information of which he was very certain no one else in the city was aware, other than the few to whom he had already spoken, albeit obliquely.

When he first entered the city, Eshetu had been overwhelmed by its size; its splendor; the sheer numbers of people crowding its stone-paved streets; the unimaginable wealth that ordinary people displayed as mere ornamentation in their hair and on their bodies. He also saw the remnants of the havoc the Uloans had wrought, as well as the city-dwellers' determination to rebuild. And, mingling with the throngs that filled Khambawe's streets, he saw the Fidi.

The Fidi …

At first, Eshetu had wanted to blurt his tale to the first person he encountered when he finally arrived in Khambawe. Caution prevailed, though, and he had taken the time to learn what had happened in the city since the time he had departed from his home village, which no longer existed.

In exchange for his help in the many back-breaking tasks that remained in the rebuilding process, Eshetu received food, *talla*, and information. The *kabbar* learned of the arrival of the Fidi ship, and the fact that a second Fidi sea-craft had sunk before it could reach Khambawe. He learned how the intervention of the Fidis' powerful god, Almovaar, had saved the city from destruction at the hands of the spider-scarred Uloans. And he learned of the Emperor Alemeyu's death, along with that of the Empress Issa, and the ascension of Jass Gebrem to the Lion Throne, and the elevation of the Fidi Seer, Kyroun, to the position of Leba, and the Matiles' eager embrace of the newcomers' religion.

Eshetu observed intently, and absorbed all the details he could glean about the numerous changes that had occurred in Khambawe since the invasion was repelled. At times, he was tempted to simply return to the frontier and find another farm to till. His news seemed of minor import compared to the aftermath of the battle against the Uloans and the transition from the veneration of the Jagasti to the worship of the new god, Almovaar.

But when he thought of how pervasive the influence of the Fidi had become in the capital of the Empire, and when he thought about what he had seen, which had prompted him to decide to undertake his long journey, Eshetu's resolve returned. Finally, he had told his tale to a soldier whose house he had helped to rebuild. The soldier had relayed Eshetu's story to an officer, who in turn had passed him along to another officer of higher rank.

Finally, the story had reached the ears of the Emperor – and, presumably, the Leba. A soldier from the Palace Guard had come to Eshetu with a summoning to tell his tale directly to the Emperor. Despite Eshetu's nondescript appearance, and humble *kabbar* status, the soldier had treated him with respect, and the crowds in the streets – even the *quagga*-drawn *gharris* – moved aside to make way for him and his stern-faced escort.

And now, he was about to pass through the portal that led into the Gebbi Senafa. In all the long years his people had dwelled near the border of the Thaba country, none of them had ever had an audience with, or even seen, an Emperor. And now, there was no one left back home to know that Eshetu had been the one to do so.

2

Gebrem looked at Kyroun. Then he looked away, not because he could not meet the Seer's calm gaze, but because he could no longer trust his judgment about the man who had saved the Matile Mala Empire and brought new hope for the future of its people. A small, unseen cloud of suspicion hung between then now ... a tiny, but persistent, shadow of doubt.

Only once before had such misgivings seeped into Gebrem's mind. That time had been in the beginning, when he first saw the Seer teetering with steely determination in front of the mast of the *White Gull* after the

Fidis' vessel had crashed into the docks of Khambawe's harbor.

The tale that the *kabbar* was telling throughout the city had, at first, startled Gebrem. As the implications of the story became clear, a sense of unease had crept into him, like a persistent ache or a chronic illness.

He did, however, have the satisfaction of knowing that Kyroun shared his sense of unease. As it was, relations between the two men had become somewhat strained since the departure of the Tokoloshe, though they had not disagreed over the decision to allow the Tokoloshe and the Fidi Dwarven to depart without hindrance. However, they had shared a dismay over the fact that for all the power and position they now possessed, there was nothing they could have done do to forestall the Tokoloshes' resolve.

That was the first setback the Emperor and Leba had experienced since the defeat of the Uloans.

And now, this ...

"We will learn the truth," Kyroun said mildly.

This time, the Emperor held Kyroun's gaze. If the Seer was troubled, nothing of it showed in his gray eyes.

"I hope so," Gebrem said.

A discreet knock sounded at the door of the small chamber Gebrem and Kyroun had chosen for their meeting with Eshetu. The chamber was unadorned, furnished only with chairs and a low table. Servants had left cups of *kef* on the table. Intricate designs were incised in the wood of the table and chairs.

Both the Emperor and the Seer wore plain blue *chammas* over their *senafil*. They had eschewed the other accouterments of their status. Kyroun had suggested doing so to put the *kabbar* at ease, and Gebrem had agreed.

"Enter," the Emperor said.

The door swung open, and the guardsman ushered a blinking, disoriented Eshetu into the presence of the two most powerful men in the Matile Mara Empire. The soldier, who would remain in the room, closed the door behind him. No one expected any trouble from the *kabbar*, but caution still prevailed, and the soldier's hand did not stray far from the hilt of his sword.

Recalling stories told over several generations about the proper behavior in the presence of the Emperor, the *kabbar* dropped to his knees. Then he prostrated himself on the plain stone floor.

"Get up, man, get up," Gebrem said impatiently. "It is not necessary for you to do that. No one has done that for years."

Abashed and astonished, Eshetu rose awkwardly to his feet. He almost fell, but caught himself in time.

"My apologies, Mesfin," he stammered.

"No apologies are necessary," the Emperor said. "Sit. Relax. Drink your *kef*. And tell us this news you bring from afar."

The *kabbar* sat, reached gingerly for the cup of *kef* in front of him, and took a swallow of the dark brew.

"I am told your name is Eshetu," the Emperor said. "And you come from …?

"Imbesh," Eshetu replied, putting the cup back on the table. "It is a village in Kembana."

Gebrem nodded.

"Jass Shebeshi's country," he said. "Your Jass did not attend First Calling. Before the Uloans invaded, Alemeyu spoke of correcting Shebeshi's defiance. But now, if we understand the news you bring correctly, that may no longer be a concern. He is facing other, more pressing, concerns."

"Yes," Eshetu agreed, showing spirit for the first time since he came into the presence of the Emperor and the Leba. "Shebeshi is a fool. And we will all pay for the idiocy of pushing the Thabas too far. My family is no more. Imbesh is no more. And if the Thabas attack again, Jass Shebeshi will be no more."

After a short silence, the Emperor spoke again.

"You have all our sympathy," he said. "And your family will be avenged."

Eshetu bowed his head in acknowledgement of the Emperor's promise. It was the Leba who spoke next.

"The tragedy that struck your people is not the only news you bring to us," he said.

"No," Eshetu said, shifting his gaze to Kyroun.

"You have seen people who look like me," Kyroun said.

Eshetu nodded.

Kyroun reached out and took one of Eshetu's hands in his own. Gebrem took the other. Eshetu's first impulse was to pull his hands away. Who was he, a mere *kabbar*, to be actually touching an Emperor and a Leba? But the grip of the other two men was too strong; he could not pull away.

"Tell us your story, Eshetu," Kyroun said. "As you speak, we will join you in your memories. And we will know the truth."

The Seer's last words were directed as much to Gebrem as they were to Eshetu. The Emperor inclined his head in acknowledgment of Kyroun's thrust.

Eshetu never knew whether he had begun to speak of his own volition, or if the sorcery wielded by the Emperor and the Leba pulled the words from his mind and his mouth. But speak he did, and at great length, until long after the time the sun sank in the sky and the Moon-Stars rose, while Kyroun and Gebrem shared his experiences in the Oneness ...

3

Eshetu lay beneath a mound of corpses. Their weight pressed heavily upon him, and he could barely draw breath. His only hope that he would be able to continue breathing at all was that the pile above him would prove deep enough to absorb the thrusts of the Thabas' *assegais*, the broad-bladed stabbing-spears that were the chief weapons of the warriors of the south.

The bodies were not enough of a barrier to drown out the sounds of Imbesh's demise. Eshetu could hear the crackle of the flames that were devouring the *tukuls*, the round, conical-roofed dwellings typical of the *kabbars* of the Matile countryside. He could hear the screams of women who would soon be taken south, never again to see their homeland. He could hear children crying. He could hear the anguished shouts of Matile men who, like him, were trying – and failing – to protect their families and their land. There were simply too many of the crimson-painted Thaba warriors. Always, too many.

And he could hear the hated war-cry of the Thabas, the sound all *kabbars* who lived on the borderland feared: "*Sigidi! Sigidi! Sigidi!*"

After a time that seemed to have no end, the cries from the Thabas and the Matile alike ceased. And no longer did he hear the loathsome sound of *assegais* ripping open the bellies of the dead and exposing their entrails, as though the Thabas were killing their enemies twice. Yet they did the same to the bodies of their own dead, a practice the Matile had never understood. There was much about the Thabas that the Matile did not comprehend, nor did they care to try.

Eshetu did not begin to burrow his way out of the mound of corpses until his air had nearly run out. As he pushed through a tangle of arms and legs, he thanked the Jagasti that the Thabas had not pulled all the bodies above him aside during their ritual of disembowelment. At the same time, he cursed the remote Matile deities for allowing Imbesh to be destroyed.

When he finally extricated himself from the bodies that had shielded him, Eshetu looked at what was left of Imbesh, and tears began to mingle with the blood that covered his face. Some of that blood was his own, spilled from the *assegai*-slash that had felled him as he fought. The rest of it had seeped down from the bodies that had fallen on top of him.

Although dusk was darkening the sky, flames from the burning *tukuls* and *teff*-fields would burn well into the night. Light from the fires picked out corpses strewn like chaff throughout Imbesh. Men of fighting age, the elderly of both sexes … all lying with their bellies opened by Thaba *assegais*. Several mounds of earth indicated the Thaba corpses that lay in the village as well, for the southern warriors left their dead behind, buried where they fell, taking only their ox-hide shields back to their home villages as tokens of their courage.

Imbesh's women of child-bearing age were gone, and the children themselves, along with the cattle of the village. Shetu knew the fate that awaited any Matile woman who fell into the hands of the Thabas. He thought of his sister, Sallamawit, and of Desta, the woman he intended to wed. And when he thought of them, and of his brothers, his father and mother and all the others who were either dead or carried off, he dropped to his knees next to the pile of corpses that had saved him. And he howled out his anguish, not caring if any Thaba stragglers heard him.

He never knew how long he remained that way: on his knees, screaming wordlessly until his raw throat could no longer produce any sounds. Finally, he collapsed in exhaustion as the *tukuls* and the fields continued to burn, and the corpses of his family and friends bled, and their blood soaked the land Jass Shebeshi had hoped to reclaim for the Matile.

When Eshetu awoke, the only sound he heard was the buzzing of the clouds of flies that had already settled over the bodies of his fellow villagers. He heard the sounds of other, larger scavengers on their way to the carrion-feast. When he opened his eyes, he saw that he was surrounded by smoking ruins and stiffening corpses.

Laboriously, he rose to his feet. He wondered why he was still alive, when the rest of the people of Imbesh were either dead or stolen. And he could not find an answer that satisfied him.

Without conscious thought, Eshetu searched for a weapon. Many were scattered among the ashes that were all that was left of the *tukuls*. Swords, daggers broken shields ... all used in the ultimately unsuccessful attempt to defend Imbesh from the Thaba hordes. Eshetu picked up a fallen sword and inspected it in the morning light. Its blade was blooded, but undamaged. Eshetu sliced it through the air, and drew grim pleasure from the sound it made.

It was then Eshetu decided what he would do. He would find out which way the Thabas had gone after their destruction of Imbesh. If the warriors had forged further north to ravage more of the villages of Kembana, he would try to get ahead of the invaders and give whatever warning he could. And if they were headed south, back to their homeland in the rolling hill country, he would follow them.

And when he caught up with them ...

He did not know what course he would take then.

Before departing from Imbesh, Eshetu had one more duty to perform. He did it poorly, and might as well not have done it at all.

The Matile of the countryside interred their dead in a fashion similar to that of the city-dwellers. Instead of small stone houses, however, the *kabbars* made *tukul*-shaped monuments from hardened clay. The prospect of properly burying the dozens of corpses scattered throughout Imbesh sickened Eshetu. He knew he could never do it before the scavengers ate most of them.

Instead, he placed a single handful of Imbesh's bloodsoaked soil on each of the bodies – people he knew well, or to whom he was related, now reduced to fodder for the flies and vultures and hyenas that would soon come. He hoped his people would forgive him when he saw them again... when he joined them in death. And he knew when that day came, he would have to answer to Metelit, the Jagasti who was the Goddess of the Afterworld.

After he dropped the last bit of dirt through a cloud of flies, Eshetu departed from Imbesh without looking back. The drone of the flies droned in his ears long after he had left the charred remains of his village behind.

Not much time passed before it became obvious to Eshetu that the Thabas had not pushed farther into Kembana territory. Imbesh had been their only target. The destruction of Imbesh was the lesson the Thabas intended to teach Jass Shebeshi. But Jass Shebeshi would need many more such lessons before he would acknowledge the foolishness and futility of his ambitions, Eshetu mused bitterly.

With no sign of the Thabas to the north, Eshetu turned and headed southward, toward the Thabas' own country. Although he retraced his steps part of the way, he bypassed the remains of Imbesh. He had no desire to again see what he had left behind there.

The Thabas' trail was easy enough to follow. They had no reason to attempt to conceal the marks of their passage. Long in the past were the days when Matile armies penetrated unimpeded deep into the Thaba hills to capture slaves for the mines and the fields. The Thabas had never forgotten those days. And they would not allow the Matile to forget them, either.

Their new chief-of-chiefs, Tshakane, seemed determined to turn the fractious Thaba tribes into a single *assegai*, aimed directly at the Matile. Jass Shebeshi had hoped to blunt the thrust of Tshakane's spear and to make a thrust of his own. Now, that hope was buried beneath the ashes of Imbesh.

As he continued his journey, Eshetu would sometimes see a discarded scrap of clothing or a lost ornament from one of the Imbesh women and children. The forlorn items reminded him that he, alone, could never rescue his people. But he could, in however limited a way, avenge them. If he could find a Thaba warrior alone, he could kill him. And then another ... and another ... as many as he could until his own life was taken. It was a bleak – and likely short – future. But the opportunity for revenge gave him a grim satisfaction.

Soon enough, the ground began to rise in gentle ripples, upward and upward until undulant waves of verdant, tree-clad, flower-spangled, river-threaded hills stretched before him – the Thaba country. And, in the distance, he could see the slow-moving mass that was the raiders and their captives. As the days passed, he cautiously drew nearer to them. But he could not carry out his plan for vengeance. The horde of Thaba warriors were as disciplined as any Matile army had ever been, and he could find no stragglers to kill.

With no other strategy in mind, Eshetu continued to shadow the Thabas. He survived by foraging; the land was as abundant as it was beautiful, and so he had no need to risk discovery by stealing supplies from the Thabas.

He made no attempts to discern Desta or Sallamawit among the indistinct mass of captives. He knew that to see them while knowing all-too-well that he could do nothing to rescue them would have pushed him beyond the edge of madness.

Days passed, each one no different from the next. The Thabas pushed southward, their pace matching that of the cattle they had taken from Imbesh. Eshetu watched and waited. Then the day came when a smaller group of Thaba warriors joined the ones who had destroyed Eshetu's village.

And that was when Eshetu saw the strangers.

4

"There were four of them," Eshetu said as Gebrem and Kyroun listened intently while reliving the *kabbar's* experiences through the medium of the Oneness.

"They all had pale skins, like yours," he continued, looking at Kyroun as he spoke.

"Three were men; one was a woman. One of the men was tall and brawny, like the Thabas. His hair was the color of fire. Another was shorter, with brown hair. He carried a drum unlike any other I have seen. The third man was small, with thick black hair and a black beard. His body was covered in blue robes – again, like yours. And the woman …"

Eshetu paused and shook his head as though he still could not give credence to what he had seen.

"She was taller than any of the men, and her skin was paler. Her hair was like strands of spider-silk. And her ears were … larger than usual, and their tips were like the points of daggers."

Again, Eshetu paused. He looked at both the Emperor and the Leba, as if he were gauging whether or not they believed him.

"Were these strangers captives?" the Emperor asked.

"I don't think they were," Eshetu replied. "They were carrying weapons. But the Thabas were still watching them closely. And it looked to me as though they didn't understand the Thabas' language – not that I understand it myself. Still, the strangers spoke differently, and the Thabas had to use gestures to make themselves understood."

Eshetu's fingers flexed involuntarily in the grasp of the Leba and Emperor, as though he were imitating the Thabas' gestures. Both men released their holds on the *kabbar's* hands. For reasons he could not have explained, Eshetu felt relieved that the contact had ended. However, he had still not finished his story.

"I had never seen such people before. But I remembered that I had heard of pale traders who had come from a land far across the sea – the Fidi – in the songs and stories of the old days. But even in the songs, there had never been any mention of people like the woman.

"I knew then what I had to do. The Jagasti had not allowed me to live only to throw my life away. They had spared me to be the one to see that the Fidi were among the Thabas, and to come here to tell that to the Emperor Alemeyu.

"And so I came to Khambawe, leaving women and children of my village in the hands of the Thabas. And when I came, I learned that the Fidi are also among the Matile; that Alemeyu is dead; and the Jagasti are no more."

Eshetu's story was done. He bowed his head and awaited the judgment of the two unimaginably powerful men who sat across from him.

"Look at me, Eshetu," the Emperor said.

The *kabbar* obeyed.

"You are a courageous man," Gebrem said. "The Empire needs more – many more – like you."

Eshetu bowed his head again in an expression of humility, then raised it as the Emperor continued.

"Before you told us your story, I promised you that Imbesh would be avenged. I reiterate that promise ... and I also promise that you will play a part in that vengeance. While we make our plans, you will remain here in the Palace as my guest."

Kyroun spoke then.

"You have my thanks as well. I am pleased to learn that some of my followers have survived the sinking of their ship, even though they are now held by the enemies of the Matile. They, like the survivors from Imbesh, must be rescued."

The Emperor nodded to the soldier, who had changed neither his stance nor his expression during Eshetu's recounting.

"Tewolo will take you to your quarters, Eshetu. We will talk again soon."

When Eshetu stood, his knees could barely support him. With only a few words, the Emperor had transformed him from landless *kabbar* to a man of position, a man of honor, a man of power. So much had happened to him that was beyond belief ... now, he said the only thing he could say:

"Thank you, Mesfin ... Leba. My life is yours. I will serve you well."

After Tewolo ushered the *kabbar* out of the small chamber, Gebrem turned to Kyroun.

"Do you know the people he saw among the Thabas?" he asked.

"I know all my followers," the Seer replied. "But I was not aware that any of them had survived the sinking of the *Swordfish*. Almovaar must have spared them for a reason ... a reason he has not seen fit to impart to us."

"Who are they?" Gebrem asked. In the Oneness, he had seen them as clearly as Kyroun had, but their identities remained a mystery to him.

"The red-haired one is Niall," the Seer said. "A quiet man and a good fighter, a loyal defender of Almovaar. The drummer is his friend, Diamid. The blue-robed one is Ferroun, who ranks high among the Believers, even though he does not possess the aptitude in sorcery necessary to become an Adept, or even an Acolyte. He was responsible for the organizational work that kept us functioning as we journeyed from Lumaron to Fiadol."

"And the woman?"

A long moment passed before Kyroun went on. As he spoke again, his tone was less assured.

"Her name is Aeliel. She is of the Elven – a secretive people who live apart from all others in Cym Dinath. Only rarely do the Elven dwell among us ... and to this day, I do not know why Aeliel joined the Almovaads. In the Oneness, she always shields her thoughts. Even I am unable to penetrate them."

"And now, they are among the Thabas," Gebrem said. "Our worst enemies, now that the Uloans are no longer a threat to us."

"It would seem that these Thabas are a more immediate threat than we had originally supposed," Kyroun said. "Even as we rebuild, they prepare to push across the frontier as a united force under their new chieftain, this Tshakane. We must strike them sooner than we thought."

"To save your shipwreck survivors?" Gebrem asked.

"To save the Empire," said Kyroun.

5

Later, in the Beit Almovaar – which had once been the Beit Amiya – Kyroun met with some of the Adepts who had not joined Tiyana on the voyage to the Uloan Islands. They were all Fidi; none of the Matile Adepts were present. When he told the others what he and Gebrem had learned from Eshetu, their eyes widened and their mouths gaped in astonishment.

"How could anyone have survived such a shipwreck?" Eimos asked. "The fury of the storms would have reduced the *Swordfish* to kindling without your protection."

"And why *those* four?" asked Ulrithana. "Why Ferroun?"

Kyroun suppressed a smile. The Shadimish Adept's dislike of the administrator had continued even after what she had thought to be his elimination from her life.

"More to the point, what are we going to do about it?"

The speaker was Hara, a plain-faced, yellow-haired woman from Fiadol. She had been one of the last converts the Almovaads had acquired before sailing away from the seaport. Although Hara had never so much as dabbled in sorcery in her previous life, about which she said little, she had become an Adept almost as quickly as Byallis. She seldom spoke. But when she did, even Kyroun often listened.

"I could not determine whether or not they were captives," the Seer said. "Either way, they will be in danger once the Emperor begins his campaign against the Thabas. They will have to trust in Almovaar for their protection until we arrive in Thaba territory. Once we are there, we can decide on how we will bring them back among us."

"Perhaps they weren't the only ones who survived the shipwreck," Eimos mused. "There could be others."

"Perhaps," Kyroun agreed. "If there are, Almovaar has not told me. But then, he did not tell me of the survival of those four. And I do not know why. Almovaar does not tell me everything."

"It is possible he did not want you to be disturbed in your task here," Ulrithana murmured.

Hara and Eimos exchanged a wry glance. They knew Ferroun was the "disturbance" to which the Shadimish woman was referring.

"Possibly," Kyroun agreed. "In the meantime, this news will not remain a secret for long. Nor should it. Soon, it will spread throughout Khambawe, and beyond. Many questions will be asked, by Believers and non-Believers alike. For now, our best – and only – answer is: 'Almovaar will show us the way.'"

The others nodded their agreement.

"For now, we will continue our preparations for the homecoming of Tiyana and the others, who have succeeded beyond our highest expectations."

"She bears watching, that Tiyana," said Hara, narrowing her eyes. "She grows very strong, very swiftly."

Kyroun turned to her.

"Almovaar will decide how strong she grows," he said reprovingly. "And how swiftly."

With that, the Adepts – with the exception of Ulrithana – departed the part of the House of Believers in which they had held their meeting. As soon as the others were gone, the Shadimish woman took the Seer's hand, and he led her to the private quarters that had previously belonged to Gebrem.

CHAPTER THIRTY
Tiyana's Homecoming

1

A strong sea-wind whipped through Tiyana's braids as she stood near the prow of the *Amdwa*. Her silver hair-ornaments clashed to create a discordant melody. Her blue *chamma* alternately billowed and clung to her body, depending on the vagaries of the breeze. Salt-tinged spray moistened her face and arms as she focused her gaze on the east, the way home. Khambawe as not yet visible across the sun-dappled waves, but Tiyana knew the Matile fleet would arrive home in a matter of hours.

To the north, she could see the vast, gray band of mist that marked the beginning of the Sea of Storms. As she looked at it, Tiyana remembered First Calling. And she remembered what the mist had brought to the Matile people that day.

She remembered Nama-kwah as well, and the final warning the Goddess had given her before ending the tenuous contact between them.

Danger ...

Tiyana laughed: a bittersweet sound carried away by the wind. At First Calling, she had believed the Goddess was warning her about the coming of the Fidi. Now she was certain that the warning had been about the Uloans. Had the Fidi and Almovaar not been present, the insane islanders would have demolished Khambawe.

She wondered if Nama-kwah was still watching her from somewhere in her Realm. And she decided that possibility no longer mattered to her. None of the Jagasti mattered anymore.

What mattered most to Tiyana now was her return home. Home to her father, whose pride in her accomplishments in the Uloan Islands meant more to her than all the other words of praise that showered upon her on the *Amdwa* and in the Oneness. Home to Keshu, with whom she shared a private togetherness even when they were far apart, as they were now. Home to the celebration the Believers were planning, the type of festivities usually reserved for a Dejezmek returning victorious from battle.

Someone was approaching her from behind. Tiyana knew this, even though the wind and the tinkle of the ornaments in her hair muffled the sound. And, without needing to turn around, she knew who was coming.

The magical power – she no longer thought of it as *ashuma* – that her delvings into Almovaad sorcery had awakened with in her had become as much a part of her as her blood and bones. Her awareness of her surroundings extended beyond her senses. She saw her, heard more … *knew* more.

Thus, when she did turn, she was not surprised to see Lyann, second-in-command to Captain Pel Muldure, coming toward her.

Lyann stopped at a respectful distance from Tiyana and inclined her head in greeting. Tiyana returned the gesture. She did not know the Fidi woman well, but she appreciated the fierce fighting Lyann and the other crew members of the lost *White Gull* had done in the battle to save Khambawe.

Lyann had allowed her yellow hair to grow, but not much. Now she had two strings of beads braided into her locks, one on each side of her sun-darkened face. But she continued to wear Fiadol seaman's garb of shirt and breeches, sewn to her specifications by Matile garment-makers. In Khambawe, some of the younger Matile affected similar garb.

"The sailing is smooth," Tiyana said.

Lyann nodded acknowledgement of the compliment.

"But you know," the Fidi woman said, "in all my years at sea, I have never been on a voyage as strange as this one."

Lyann's Matile was heavily accented, but Tiyana understood her.

"Not even the one through the Sea of Storms?" she asked.

"That was dangerous," Lyann allowed. "But this time, the purpose was not to risk lives …or to take them. It was to save lives … the lives of your enemies."

Tiyana smiled.

"Yes. That is different. But that is what Almovaar teaches us … to be merciful to all, even enemies who are no longer a threat."

She regarded the Fidi woman for a moment.

"Why are you not a Believer?" she asked abruptly.

Lyann looked away. Then she returned Tiyana's steady gaze.

"We have our own ways, Muldure and I," she said. "The sea is our mother, our father … and our god. For all that Almovaar can do, we still trust to the sea."

Tiyana nodded.

"The nature of the voyage is not what you wish to speak to me about, is it?" she asked.

"No, it's not," Lyann replied. "It's about Muldure."

Tiyana waited for her to continue.

"He doesn't like to stay in one place for a long time. Neither do I. And neither does the crew … at least the ones who haven't become Believers, and are content to stay here. The problem is, we don't have a ship anymore."

"You wish to return to your own land?" Tiyana asked.

"We can't do that," Lyann replied.

She gestured toward the roiling gray band that marked the boundary of the Sea of Storms.

"We would need the Seer's power to get us through that again. And he is not going back."

"What would you like to do, then?" Tiyana asked. "And how could I help you?"

"We have heard tales of how your ancestors explored the rest of this continent, as well as others, in days gone by," Lyann said. "But that was long in the past. Your people have been gone from the rest of your land for so long, it is as though your world is new again. If you Matile would want to go once again to these other places, Muldure and I would like to be the ones to sail there for you."

Tiyana nodded thoughtfully.

"That is a worthy idea," she said. "Only the Emperor could make the final decision on it, though. I will try to persuade him for you."

Lyann nodded.

"Thank you," she said.

"Muldure doesn't know you intended to speak to me, does he?" Tiyana asked with a knowing narrowing of her eyes.

"No," Lyann acknowledged. "This isn't his idea. But he'll agree to it."

The two women shared a wry smile that said much about their experiences with men. Then they watched the clear horizon to the east as the *Amdwa* brought them closer to Khambawe.

2

When the fleet sailed into Khambawe's harbor, a large throng awaited the ships' arrival in the shadows cast by the Ishimbi statues. Garlands of flowers festooned the gigantic statues, as they had during the coronation of the Emperor Gebrem. The dry seaweed that that remained from the Ishimbis' march into the harbor to destroy the Uloan warships remained encrusted to the statues. Although the plants' color had faded from green to brown, they had not flaked away with the passage of time. The clumps of weed were revered as reminders of Almovaar's deliverance of the city.

The harbor had long since been cleared of the bodies and wreckage left behind from the Uloans' invasion. Once again, the air smelled fresh and clean, and sea-birds swooped above the surface of the water.

Dignitaries comprised the bulk of the crowd that greeted the ships. The rest of Khambawe's populace was arrayed along the street that would be the route the Degen Jassi and the Almovaads would follow from the docks to the Gebbi Senafa. A string of *gharris* drawn by ornately caparisoned *quaggas* waited at the edge of the dock area to carry the procession along its course.

The Emperor and the Leba, each resplendent in the panoply of his position, stood at the forefront of the throng. If any suspicion or animosity lingered between them over the revelations of Eshetu, they kept it well-concealed. Once the celebration of Tiyana's return was over, the Degen Jassi would meet, and the implications of the *kabbar's* tale would be discussed in full.

Tiyana was the first to embark from the *Amdwa*, alighting with the grace of a bird onto the wharf. The rest of the Adepts followed, from the *Amdwa* and all the other ships in the fleet. In defiance of the usual silent decorum that accompanied such events, cheers rose from the dignitaries as the Adepts made their way toward them.

When she reached Gebrem, Tiyana tossed propriety aside and threw her arms around her father who, after a moment's hesitation, returned her embrace, much to the delight of the others in the crowd.

"You have done so well, my daughter," the Emperor whispered in her ear. "Yet there will be so much more for us to do."

Tiyana smiled and nodded her agreement. Then she went to Kyroun and embraced him in turn. He smiled at her, but said nothing. Tiyana thought she could see a hint of disquiet in his gray eyes. She decided she would talk with him later to find out if anything was troubling him.

Then she reached Keshu, who looked resplendent in the Fidi-style blue robes of an Adept. She knew what lay beneath those robes, and she intended to spend some time alone with him after the celebration of the fleet's return was over. They would have much to say to each other ... and they had a future to decide.

For now, they shared a long embrace.

"I have missed you," Tiyana murmured as she pressed her face against Keshu's robe and absorbed the touch and smell of him.

"Never again will we be apart," he promised.

He held her tighter, as though his embrace could meld her so close to him that even a command from the Emperor or the Leba would have no effect on his resolve to make Tiyana his wife. He knew Gebrem's eyes were upon him, weighing him on a balance between the shadow of the Empire's past and the splendor of its future. Keshu was confident that the new ways would supersede the old, and Tiyana's lofty status as the future Empress would not stand between them.

Other greetings were exchanged. Then, the entire aggregation of notables made its way to the *gharris* that were waiting to carry them to the Gebbi Senafa. Tiyana and Keshu climbed into the same *gharri*. The Emperor and Kyroun rode separately.

Musicians playing *melekhet* horns and drummers beating out a rhythm on *kebarus* signaled the beginning of Tiyana's procession of triumph. Amid the rumble of *gharri* wheels and the braying of the *quaggas*, the ranks of Khambawe's ruling class began their journey along a street strewn with blossoms and lined with cheering people.

3

Adisu the leather-worker and Tamair mingled their praise-chants with those of the rest of the crowd as the *gharris* passed and the music played. Other members of the dissident group were scattered throughout the throng on both sides of the street. All of them strove to conceal their knife-edged anticipation, as well as the apprehension that drew sweat from their palms. There was no part for them to play in what they expected to happen at any moment. Only afterward would they act, and they would do so with no blame attached to them at all ... if Sehaye's scheme worked. And if that strange, taciturn man was not as insane as he appeared to be ...

The *gharri* carrying the foreign Leba, Kyroun, passed by the two dissidents. The white-bearded man stared straight ahead, barely acknowledging the praise the Matile were giving him – adulation that, in the minds of the dissidents, he did not deserve.

"Look at him," Adisu muttered beneath his breath. "He cares nothing for us at all. He ..."

Tamair gave him a sharp jab with her elbow even as she sang a verse from a praise-song that was almost as old as Khambawe itself. Adisu understood the message she imparted, painful though it was. He joined the chorus of reverence for the Emperor Gebrem as his *gharri* passed. In contrast to Kyroun, the Emperor smiled broadly and raised his hand from time to time, as though the gesture was a benison to the crowd. With a slight nod to Tamair, Adisu struggled mightily to prevent his true feelings from surfacing again.

Neither bothered to look for Jass Kebessa. The leader of the dissidents would be far to the rear of the procession, as befitting his lowly status among the Degen Jassi. He would be safe from what was to come.

Now the *gharri* that conveyed Tiyana and Keshu was passing. For the briefest of moments, Adisu's anger receded as he looked at her.

Gebrem's daughter possessed the beauty and courage of a goddess. And Keshu had risen high from the ranks of the common classes, people like Adisu himself.

The respite lasted only for a moment before Adisu once again hardened his heart at the realization that even these two had fallen irrevocably under the insidious control of the foreigners.

Mounted soldiers accompanied the procession as it wound its way through the city. They, too, were resplendent in their polished armor and lion-mane decorations. Their weapons remained sheathed, for no one was expecting any trouble ... no one other than the dissidents.

Sehaye, where are they? Adisu demanded silently. *Where?*

A moment later, his unvoiced question was answered.

They struck with the quickness of cobras. The crowd had concealed them well; they had mimicked those who surrounded them with chameleon-like ease. The soldiers had no time to react; neither did the Adepts, for all their skill and power and preternatural awareness. So completely had the attackers hidden themselves that Adisu was oblivious to the fact that one of them had been standing at his other side all this time. He didn't know until the *chamma*-clad figure hurled itself at a passing *gharri*, rushing beneath the rearing hooves of the soldier-escort's startled *quagga*.

The music faltered, then stopped completely, to be supplanted by shouts, screams, the neighing of *quaggas* and the crash of overturned *gharris*. Sunlight glinted from the weapons the assailants wielded. *Tirss* ... the chosen weapon of the *tsotsis* ...

Even as the press of the panicking crowd pulled him one way, then the other, ultimately separating him from Tamair, Adisu exulted inside.

He did it! That crazy man Sehaye did it! No one will blame us for what has happened! They will blame the tsotsis! *The cursed* tsotsis *have freed us from the foreigners!*

Even as Adisu celebrated, his foot caught on a raised stone in the street, and he went down. The fear-maddened crowd around him did not notice as he flailed about in a desperate attempt to get back to his feet. But the feet of others pounded him like a hailstorm and kept him down. Some of the people in the crowd were running toward the procession to try to aid the Jassi and the Almovaads. Others were simply running away.

Collisions abounded. Others besides Adisu fell and were trampled. Some managed to rise and escape further injury; others were not so fortunate. Adisu was not among the fortunate ones. Even as he died beneath the pounding feet of the people he had plotted to save from the foreigners, he heard the cry of the *tsotsis* rising above the clamor of the crowd:

"*This be for your shadows!*"

4

"Tiyana! Beware!" Keshu shouted.

The spikes of a *tirss* swooped toward Tiyana like the talons of some gigantic bird of prey. Shock at the suddenness and savagery of the attack had left her immobile. The arm that swung the *tirss* was lean and sinewy; the face of the wielder was twisted in a snarl of hatred.

Before the *tirss* could complete its deadly arc and tear into Tiyana's flesh, a dark shape interposed itself between her and the weapon. An ugly, rending noise accompanied the bite of the *tsotsi's* "teeth" through cloth and flesh. Tiyana fell backward as two people stumbled against her. One of them was already dying; the other was screaming incoherent imprecations.

The *gharri* rocked wildly as the fear-maddened *quagga* that was pulling it reared and kicked its hooves indiscriminately at the mass of people swarming around it. A *tirss* raked across the beast's belly, spilling its blood and intestines even as it collapsed in its traces.

As she tumbled out of the *gharri*, Tiyana's head hit the stones of the street, and small replicas of the Moon Stars whirled in the sudden darkness in front of her eyes. Pain lanced through her skull. The weight of Keshu's body pressed down on her, and she could feel the movement of the assassin's struggle to pull his *tirss* free from the flesh in which it was embedded. She could hear the screams, the curses, the clangor of weapons, the pounding of feet and hooves. And she could feel Keshu's body sliding away as the *tsotsi* pulled it away to get to her.

Keshu is dead! she thought as she fought to retain consciousness. *Keshu is dead! He died to save me! Keshu is dead!*

The tiny Moon Stars faded. The blackness before her eyes broke into small, moving dots. Through them, Tiyana could see the *tsotsi* looming above her. He had pulled his *tirss* free from Keshu's body. Keshu's blood dripped from the tips of the tines onto Tiyana's face and arms. The *tsotsi* raised the weapon to deliver another flesh-rending strike.

Rage ripped through Tiyana like a wet-season storm. A cry of fury and desolation erupted from her throat. The sound of the cry turned into power – a spiral of radiance like that of the night-sun that shone on the Maim after the day-sun went down. Blue light, similar to the healing illumination that had, only days ago, cleansed the Uloans' bodies and spirits.

What Tiyana unleashed now had nothing of healing in it. The blue spiral wrapped itself around the *tsotsi* like a python made of light, pinning his arms to his sides. The *tirss* fell to the ground with a clatter scarcely audible above the tumult that engulfed the interrupted procession.

With hatred on her face that matched the *tsotsi*'s expression when he attacked, Tiyana concentrated her power. And the serpent of light constricted, slicing through the *tsotsi*'s flesh as though it were of no greater substance than the air that surrounded it. The *tsotsi* had time only to utter a truncated shriek of agony before the spiral sectioned his body into pieces.

As Tiyana struggled to her feet, she refused to look down at the spot where Keshu lay. She did not want to see him as a corpse. And she had no time to mourn him ... the awareness in which she had earlier taken such great pride, the awareness that had failed her and all the other Adepts when they needed it most, was now warning her that another *tsotsi* was approaching her from behind. Without turning around, she sent a whip of magical energy looping around the assailant's neck. The loop squeezed the sides of his throat together until he could no longer breathe.

Other flashes of blue amid the chaos signalled that Tiyana was not the only Adept to have survived the *tsotsis'* attack. With the moment of surprise gone, the tide was turning against the assassins. Instead of fleeing in panic, some of the people in the crowd were now turning on the attackers, in some cases tearing them to pieces as effectively as Tiyana's sorcery had done.

A deadly calm settled over Tiyana as she sought out the glint of a *tirss* and sent a blaze of vengeance that tore through the weapon's bearer. Loathing spilled from her soul as she searched for more *tsotsis* to slay. The *gharri* in which she and Keshu had been riding was still upright, but its *quagga* lay inert in a welter of blood. Using the *gharri* as cover, Tiyana picked off as many *tsotsis* as she could see.

With the momentum now against them, the surviving *tsotsis* fled. Some of the people in the crowd pursued them. Others stood in blank-eyed shock. Still others tended their wounds, and those of their fallen companions.

Tiyana sank to her knees beside the body of Keshu. He stared sightlessly, his face set in a grimace that bespoke courage and determination. The front of his robe was shredded and his spilled blood turned its blue color into a muddy red.

Tiyana took one of his hands in hers, and wished that the power of Almovaar could enable her to will him back to life. She knew that was not possible, and that knowledge brought tears to her eyes ... tears that flowed in twin streams down her cheeks.

"Keshu," she whispered as the echoes of the crowd's pursuit of the *tsotsis* faded. "You saved my life, but part of me has died with you."

"Tiyana."

She looked up to see who it was that interrupted the beginning of her grieving. It was a soldier. Blood spattered his armor. His dark face bore a grim expression.

"Please come with me, Tiyana," the soldier said. "The Emperor ..."

His voice trailed off.

Wordlessly, Tiyana released Keshu's hand, rose, and followed the soldier through the thin crowd of people who remained behind. They skirted overturned *gharris*, as well as bodies surrounded by knots of mourners, some of whom acknowledged her as she went by.

Although her tears had stopped falling, the wetness in her eyes blurred her vision. She had a premonition of what the soldier was taking her to see, and she did not want to see it; not now, not ever.

But she knew she must.

The *tsotsis* had concentrated their attack on the *gharris* that carried the most powerful people in the Empire. The Emperor and Leba had been the principal targets. So was Tiyana. And many others among the Degen Jassi and the Adepts had fallen victim to the assailants' killing frenzy.

The *gharris* of both Gebrem and Kyroun had been overturned. Tiyana saw Kyroun standing, head bowed, blood drying on his blue robe. Others stood in the same posture, and they stepped aside as the soldier led Tiyana through them.

And when she reached the Emperor's *gharri*, she saw her father lying on the street. His legs and arms had been straightened, and someone had respectfully closed his eyes. But no one could close the wound a *tsotsi's* weapon had torn across his throat, a ragged, gaping gash that had taken his life and left him covered in blood.

"I am sorry, Tiyana," Kyroun said. "I tried my best to save him. Would that I had died in his place."

Tiyana paid him no heed as, for the second time that day, she sank to her knees beside the body of a man she loved. Her grief was even greater now; her devastation overwhelming. A deep sadness replaced the rage that had fuelled the ferocity of her retaliation against the *tsotsis*. And even as a weeping Tiyana wrapped her arms around her father's bloodstained corpse, all the others around her – even Kyroun – knelt in the presence of their new Empress.

CHAPTER THIRTY-ONE
CONSEQUENCES
1

The light from a single torch guided Sehaye and Jass Mofo through the stifling darkness of the Underground. Their feet splashed through noisome mire, and the fetid air inside Khambawe's sewers seemed to lodge in the two men's lungs. Sehaye was carrying the torch, which was beginning to burn low. Jass Mofo walked behind him. The tines of the Mofo's *tirss* pressed lightly against Sehaye's back as they made their way through the muck. Sehaye did not like the touch of the weapon. But he did not complain. He was still alive. And above him, the *tsotsis* were carrying out their end of the bargain he had struck with Jass Mofo.

The voice that had guided him for so long had fallen silent after he and Mofo had sealed their pact. Sehaye longed for it to return. Without its constant advice and encouragement, he was becoming uncertain about the chances for success of the scheme it had suggested when it first began to speak inside him. He was no longer even sure that the voice belonged to Legaba.

But who else could it be? he wondered. *Who else would talk so to I?*

The *tirss* jabbed a bit deeper into Sehaye's back.

"How much farther we got to go?" Jass Mofo demanded.

"Soon come," Sehaye replied, unconsciously reverting to the Uloan way of speaking.

"Better be 'soon,'" Mofo said. "This light go out before we get to the Fidi *tsotsi*, you gon' be dead. Heard?"

Sehaye did not respond to Mofo's threat. He knew that when he led Mofo to the place where he had hidden Athir, the *tsotsi* chief would kill them both. Sehaye had trusted the voice to tell him the best way to avoid that fate. But now his guide was gone, and he would have to trust to his own wit and courage to survive. And he was far from certain that would be enough.

Jass Mofo eased the pressure from the *tirss*. Sehaye pushed onward. The light of the torch was weakening, but Sehaye knew they were coming very close to their destination now.

He could not forswear a grudging admiration for the *tsotsi* leader. Once Jass Mofo had accepted the scheme Sehaye had proposed, he not only commanded his own set to participate; he had also enlisted members of other remnant sets as well, including blood enemies of the Ashaki. The *tsotsis* knew that some – many – of them would die in the effort to cut off the head of the serpent that was slowly destroying them. But the Muvuli were killing them anyway. Attacking their oppressors appealed to them far more than passively waiting to be slain by shadows after dark. And to gain the gratitude rather than the hatred of the people outside the Maim ... that would be a lesser, but still worthwhile, reward.

For his part, Sehaye had arranged with the other dissenters to spirit the *tsotsis* out of the Maim. He himself led the *tsotsis* through the Underground, into which they had never before ventured because the Maim had always been more than sufficient as a home and sanctuary. Jass Mofo had berated himself for not having thought to make better use of the Underground. But then, if Sehaye's plan proved successful, they would not need its shelter in the future.

Sehaye wondered how the battle above was going. He and Jass Mofo were too far Underground know. Neither clangor nor cries could reach their ears.

Mofo had insisted on accompanying Sehaye alone. He knew the *tsotsis* would carry out his commands even in his absence, for they feared him more than they feared death. But then, as Sehaye had learned during the short time he had been among them, a *tsotsi* who feared death did not live long.

Despite the silence of the voice, Sehaye was certain that Retribution Time had finally been fulfilled in a way. Khambawe had not been destroyed, as Jass Imbiah and all the others before her had promised. But at least the Uloans would have gained a measure of vengeance for the blankskins' slaughter of the invaders. Sehaye hoped that Legaba had told the *huangi* back home what he had done.

If not, he would inform them himself. He had long ago decided that if he lived through this journey Underground, he would steal a boat and return to the Islands. The need for spying among the blankskins was over. He wanted to find a *huangi* who would bestow upon him the spider-scars he had missed all his life. No longer would he live as a Matile ...

The torch flame guttered lower.

"You time runnin' out," Jass Mofo said.

"Just follow I and quiet you-self," Sehaye retorted.

If Mofo noticed the change in Sehaye's way of speaking, he did not say anything about it. And Sehaye did not care whether or not he had. They were very close now to where the Fidi was hidden, and Sehaye was preparing himself for Mofo's reaction when he saw the prize that awaited him.

Then they reached the alcove, which was so dark that the weakening light of the torch failed to show what was inside.

"Him here," Sehaye said, holding the torch forward so that Mofo could see the trussed-up Athir.

The *tsotsi* pushed past Sehaye. The wordless sound that issued from Mofo's throat would have been frightening if it had been uttered by some predatory animal, let alone a human. He snatched the torch from Sehaye's hand and thrust its tip into the alcove.

Then Mofo's snarl of triumph turned into a shout of rage. He whirled and glared at Sehaye.

"What game you playin' on me?" the *tsotsi* demanded, his voice deadly in its calmness.

"What you mean?" Sehaye asked.

"Look!"

Sehaye peered over the *tsotsi's* shoulder. His eyes widened in shock when he saw that the hiding place contained nothing other than the ropes that had bound the Fidi. The strands lay in severed pieces.

"Help I, Legaba!" Sehaye shouted as he whirled away from Mofo and attempted to flee.

Then the Uloan had no more time to say or think anything else. The last thing Sehaye saw in life was the points of Jass Mofo's *tirss* flashing toward his face. And the last thing he knew was that the voice that had guided him to his doom could not have belonged to Legaba.

2

In another part of the Underground, far from far from his erstwhile place of captivity, Athir huddled in darkness broken only by the shining of the mask his rescuer wore. He was holding a wriggling creature he could not identify. The mask-wearing girl had placed it in his hands.

"Eat it," she said, her voice partially muffled by the mask.

Athir's stomach heaved even though he was starving, not having eaten since the last time his captor had visited him and fed him just enough to keep alive. In the dim, silver glow of the mask, he could not determine what he was holding. A rat? A lizard? Some unknown slime-dweller unique to this benighted place?

"Go ahead," the girl insisted when she noticed his hesitation. "Nothin' else down here to eat."

Fighting down a surge of nausea, Athir reached for what he hoped was the creature's neck. A quick twist of his hands snapped its spine, and the wriggling ceased. Then Athir lowered his head and bit into the creature's flesh. He swallowed hard and quickly, to make sure the chunks of raw, bitter-tasting flesh made it all the way to his stomach and stayed there. The girl's masked face watched him imperturbably.

When he had eaten as much of the creature as he could manage, Athir tossed its remains aside. They landed with a splash somewhere beyond his range of vision. Then the Ship's Rat took a long, close look at his rescuer.

"Who are you?" he asked. "Why did you set me free?"

"You know me, Fidi-*tsotsi*," she replied. "From the Ashaki. My name Kalisha. They call me 'Amiya-girl.'"

Athir remembered her as she was without the mask ... a somber girl who would appear from time to time with loot from the former Beit Amiya. His heart sank as he realized that she was a favorite of Jass Mofo.

So this isn't a rescue after all, he thought. *It's a cruel trick, just what I should have expected from Mofo...*

Athir tensed his muscles in anticipation of instant action. Kalisha was armed; he was not. But he was a full-grown man, and she was only a girl. Surely he could overpower her, then take the mask and use it to light his way while he searched for a way out of the Underground ... and then out of the city. The dagger wasn't even in the girl's hand now. And his own hands were quick.

As if she had been listening to his thoughts, Kalisha suddenly bared her dagger with a speed of hand that matched Athir's at his best.

"You stayin' with me," she said.

Athir relaxed. *Better to keep her talking, then find a way to distract her*, he thought.

"Why don't you take off that mask," he suggested. "It must get hard for you to breathe with it on all the time."

"Mask don' want to come off," Kalisha said.

"How's that?"

"I carry Mask for long time, it don' want me to put it on. Then one day, Mask tell me to put it on. Then it tell me where you be, and tell me to come get you. Now, I wait for Mask to tell me what to do with you."

"I ... see," Athir said noncommittally.

Inside, he shuddered.

This girl is crazy, he thought. And the mad were the most dangerous to deal with of all, because there was no way for even the shrewdest operator to anticipate what they might do next, or why. That was the reason Athir had never stolen from anyone he suspected of insanity.

"Do you think the mask might want you to take me out of these sewers?" Athir asked hopefully.

"No," Kalisha replied. "Too dangerous up there. Muvuli ..."

"So you're not going to take me to Jass Mofo?"

Kalisha shook her head. The mask moved with her, as if it had become part of her body.

"Mask want you. Forget Mofo."

Athir stifled a sigh of relief. Kalisha might be mad, and she was carrying a weapon. But at least he was better off with her than he would have been had he remained trussed in the alcove like a sacrificial offering. And he had shadows of his own to avoid above the Underground. If his enemies could pluck him out of the Gebbi Senafa, it might well be better for him to remain here, hopefully well beyond their reach. And, even though she was clearly deranged, at least Kalisha did not appear to want him dead. Not yet, anyway.

Sooner or later, though, the Ship's Rat would be free – Mask or no Mask.

"Come," Kalisha declared. "It better not to stay in one place too long."

"Truer words were never spoken," Athir muttered as he followed the glow of the Mask into the darkness.

3

Sadness suffused the Empress Tiyana as she sat in the Throne Room of the Gebbi Senafa. She did not sit on the Lion Throne; she would not have the right to do so until her formal coronation ceremony. She did not look forward to that event ... or to any other. Or even to living another day with the onerous weight of the sorrow that pressed down on her like a leaden shroud.

Instead, she sat at the bottom of the steps that led to the dais upon which the Lion Throne rested. The ancient, ornate seat loomed high above her. Its shadow penetrated beneath her skin and darkened her soul.

She imagined that Gebrem was still sitting on the Empire's throne. But in her mind, the image of her father became as it had been the last time she saw him, lying dead beside his overturned *gharri*. And she thought of the Lion Throne as a Blood Throne ...

Tiyana shook that image from her mind as she tried to concentrate on the Degen Jassi who were coming one-by-one to affirm their fealty to her. It was a ritual that dated back to the time before the Matile built cities of stone. Was it only yesterday that Tiyana stood by Gebrem's side while the Degen Jassi paid similar tribute to him after the death of Alemeyu?

That recollection brought a new wave of grief, which Tiyana struggled to suppress. The time for more tears was later. But not now. Not here.

Tiyana did not want to be Empress. Not this way. She would have preferred to be a *shamasha* if being so would have allowed her father and Keshu to live. But that was not to be. The Empire was in her hands now ...

hands that she kept clasped tightly together, so that the Degen Jassi would not see how badly they were trembling.

Her father ...dead.

The man she wanted to become her husband ... dead.

Others close to her had survived the attack. Kyroun ... her Fidi friend, Byallis ... her Matile friend, Yemeya. But the part of her that should have been grateful that they were still alive lay dormant, as though it had died along with Keshu and Gebrem. When she had more time to grieve alone, she would appreciate the good fortune of those who – including herself – had survived. Now, though, she could not.

The voices of those who were offering their allegiance to her seemed to be coming from a great distance, at the end of a long, hollow shaft of emptiness. She could barely hear them well enough to nod her acceptance at the appropriate times. Tiyana wished she could be somewhere – anywhere – else. But she knew tradition compelled her to be where she was now. It was her duty to be there.

She was the Empress ...

Then, for a reason she could not have explained, her attention suddenly focused on Jass Kebessa, a minor member of the Degen Jassi to whom she had previously paid scant, if any, heed. Yet now, as he knelt on one knee before her, bowed his head, and began to recite the ritual words, Tiyana heard him clearly. The internal distance that had muffled the words of others had disappeared.

"Mesfin, my life is yours," Jass Kebessa intoned, as had all the others who preceded him; as would those who were behind him.

"I pledge you my fidelity," Jass Kebessa continued. "I will serve you and the Empire well."

Still on one knee, he raised his head and looked at her.

Why are his eyes shifting, Tiyana wondered. *What is the meaning of the drops of sweat standing out on his brow?*

Jass Kebessa waited for her to give the nod that would send him on his way. It was taking longer for him to receive the time-honored signal than it had for others. Stinging perspiration crept into his eyes.

A slight touch from Kyroun prodded Tiyana into giving the awaited nod. Jass Kebessa rose, bowed, and made way for the next member of the Degen Jassi to give the Empress her pledge.

And, once again, grief put a distance between Tiyana and the words that would be repeated endlessly that day.

4

Much later, Tiyana lay awake in her bed at the Beit Almovaar. Despite the entreaties of the more tradition-minded members of the Degen Jassi, she had refused to sleep at the palace this night. She could not bear the thought of spending the night in her father's bedchamber. As it was, sleeping in the bed she had shared with Keshu carried its own complement of sorrows. But here, at least, she could wrap the sheets she had hoped to share with him forever tightly around her body, and she could still feel him and smell him as she slept the sleep of one who was completely drained, both physically and emotionally.

The burdens of her new position had not eased after the pledges of fealty were finished. After the Degen Jassi had departed, Kyroun had taken her aside and told her all of what had transpired in Khambawe during the time she had spent in the Uloan Islands. He told her about the continuing progress of the rebuilding, and the re-establishment of the links that had once held the Empire's territories together. He told her about the unexpected departure of the Tokoloshe.

And he told her the tale brought to him and her father by the *kabbar* Eshetu, who had seen survivors of the second Fidi ship among the Thabas, far to the south. He had discussed the implications of the latest Thaba incursions under their formidable chieftain, Tshakane, who appeared well on his way to becoming an emperor in his own right among the cattle-herding tribes of the highlands. And he told her how he and Gebrem and planned to act upon this convergence of events.

As well, he suggested ways in which she could quell the disquiet rampant in Khambawe in the wake of the *tsotsis'* treacherous attack, and how she could reassure the Matile that their Empire would retain its newfound stability and momentum even in the face of the assassination of Gebrem. And he had discussed how vengeance could be exacted against the perpetrators of the killings. The shadows, as it seemed, had not been sufficient.

Tiyana had only half-listened to him. She understood the gravity of his words well enough. But she could only vaguely attach what he said to herself, or to the future. As well, part of her harbored an unfair resentment toward him because he was alive and her father was not. And another part was mortified that she could wish death on the man who had saved the Empire.

Sensing the extent of the conflict within Tiyana, if not its exact nature, Kyroun brought the one-sided conversation to an end.

"We are all weary," he had told her. "Better that we get whatever rest we can. But heed this, Tiyana – the responsibility that has passed to you is yours until the day you die. It is what defines you now. I know you wish that did not have to be so. Yet so it is, and you cannot change it. Do you understand?"

"I understand," Tiyana said in a voice devoid of feeling, as though someone other than herself had spoken the words.

Kyroun had departed from her then, and Tiyana had returned to the Beit Amiya. Now she finally breathed in the slow rhythm of deep sleep, the white cotton sheet bunched and tangled around her body, which was curled into itself like that of a frightened child.

She was in her familiar bedchamber ... yet, at the same time, she was somewhere else ...

5

Tiyana stood in the midst of a landscape of sand. Plains and mountainous dunes stretched farther than her eyes could see, the horizon touching a sky the color of saffron. A gentle breeze blew grains of sand against her skin. But the sand did not sting her. Instead, the touch of the grains was like a thousand tiny caresses.

The sheet from her bed was draped around her like a *chamma*. Its ends stirred in the breeze and tickled her legs. Her many braids blew around her face, at times obscuring her vision.

Although she had never been in this place before, Tiyana knew it was the Realm of Almovaar. Kyroun had described it to her, and so had her father. At those times she had envied their access to the deity, and wondered if Almovaar would ever deem her worthy of entry to his Realm. Now that she was here, she wished only that Gebrem could be with her, and that she could be with Keshu.

She turned in a slow circle, searching for both men, for could their spirits not be alive in Almovaar's Realm, as the Believers were taught when they joined the religion? But she did not see either man.

She did not see Kyroun, either. She was alone, except for the sand, and the wind, and her sorrow.

Then the wind began to pluck at her sheet, pulling it away from her body. Tiyana struggled to clasp it closer to her, but the wind was insistent, like many hands pulling in all directions. When the wind began to buffet her and the sand suddenly started to sting, she released her hold on the sheet. The wind took it from her, and blew it away like a white, flapping bird that soon became lost in the yellow sky.

Now Tiyana stood naked in the sand, self-conscious even though there was no one present to see her. No one, other than Almovaar. And she could not see Almovaar.

She dared to call to him.

"Almovaar," she said, suddenly angry. "Show yourself!"

Again, the breeze blew around her. Again, grains of sand struck her. This time, instead of falling away, the grains adhered to her, dotting her ebony skin with numerous flecks of yellow hue. When she attempted to brush the sand away, it continued to cling to her skin and hair. She looked like the embodiment of a midnight sky speckled with golden stars.

Then, abruptly, a pillar of whirling sand formed before her, a column that grew until it towered higher than the stelae that pierced the sky in Khambawe. Gebrem and Kyroun had described their own experiences with this pillar. She knew she was now in the presence of Almovaar.

Her anger fled, and she sank to her knees before the pillar, and looked up at the mass of swirling sand. She knew she should wait for the god to speak. But she could not. There were questions to which she needed answers.

"Why did you allow my father to die?" she asked, in a voice not unlike that of a small child. "Why did you allow Keshu to die?"

I did not allow them to die, Almovaar replied.

"But you could have prevented their deaths."

No. That is beyond my level of dominion.

Tiyana fell silent, not understanding how saving the lives of the men she loved could be beyond the "dominion" of a deity who had rescued an entire people. But she had other questions to ask.

"Why have you brought me here?"

To show you what you need to see.

Tiyana opened her mouth to ask another question ... then she closed it when she saw a shadow that was not her own grow out of the sand like a tall, dark weed. Another shadow sprouted beside it. Then another. And another. More of them sprouted, until the golden sand turned black with their numbers. They were sticklike and immobile. Tiyana feared them.

"These must be the Muvuli that are taking the lives of the *tsotsis*," she whispered almost inaudibly.

They are my Children, Almovaar said. **They need sustenance. They obtain that sustenance from the people of the Beyond World. And my Children sustain me.**

Surrounded by the shadows, Tiyana remained silent, even as an ominous realization was beginning to take shape in her mind.

It is not only the *tsotsis* that fulfilled the needs of my Children, Almovaar said.

Before Tiyana's widening eyes, a portion of the pillar that was Almovaar became transparent. And pictures began to form in the space ... pictures of the Uloan Islands ... pictures of the people Tiyana and the other Adepts had healed, and freed from their age-old hatred of the Mainland and their dependence on the evils of Legaba. Pictures of these same people, huddled in fear, fleeing from the Muvuli in their midst, shadows that came for them after dark ...

"I did *that*?" Tiyana cried. "If I had known ..."

You would not have done it. And when my Children finished with the *tsotsis*, they would have sought their sustenance elsewhere.

"Among the other people of Khambawe," Tiyana said, a quaver in her voice reflecting the horror growing rapidly within her.

But there was no need for them to turn their hunger in that direction, Almovaar said. **The sorcery you unleashed among the Uloans brought the Muvuli to them.**

"And when they are finished with the Islanders ..." Tiyana said.

Almovaar was silent long enough to allow Tiyana to provide her own answer to the question she was about to ask. When he was satisfied that she knew the answer, he went on.

That is why you must make war against the Thabas. My Children will need more sustenance.

Almovaar's words whirled through Tiyana's head like debris uprooted in a windstorm. She could not speak. She could hardly think. Without conscious volition, her hand was raking across her brow in an attempt to dislodge the particles of sand embedded in her skin. Her efforts were not successful.

Power comes at a price, Tiyana, Almovaar said. **Kyroun was willing to pay the price. So was your father, once he knew what it was. So, too, were many others before them. But the choice was always theirs, not mine. The Muvuli are the price you pay for the restoration of the Matile's greatness. Are you willing to pay that price, Empress Tiyana?**

Tiyana did not reply.

You do not have to answer now. But you must answer soon.

Before the echoes of Almovaar's voice died, the pillar of sand vanished. So did the Shadows. Once again, Tiyana was alone in Almovaar's Realm. She remained on her knees, with her head bowed.

Now she knew why Almovaar had been shunned before he had appeared to Kyroun in the Fidis' faraway land. Now she knew why the Seer was being so insistent upon beginning a campaign against the Thabas. Now she knew why the *tsotsis* had killed her father and Keshu, and tried to kill her as well.

And now she knew her father had hidden this terrible secret from her.

Would he have told me the truth about the shadows, had he lived? she wondered.

Tiyana closed her eyes and waited for more tears to flow. When none came, she opened her eyes again ... and found that she was no longer in Almovaar's Realm. She was back in her bedchamber, the Moon Stars' pale light streaming through the window. Looking down, she saw that the sheet that had blown away in Almovaar's Realm had returned to enfold her. But when she sat up in her bed and let the sheet fall away, her eyes widened when she saw the light of the Moon Stars reflecting from the grains of sand that covered her skin from head to toe.

Even as she reached convulsively to brush the sand of Almovaar's Realm away from her, the grains suddenly dropped in a whispery cascade. Tiyana shook the sheet, and the sand fell to the floor.

Then Tiyana sank back onto her bed. She knew sleep would elude her now. She still had her sorrow. But she had no more tears to shed. And she had no answer to Almovaar's question.

EPILOGUE

Nama-kwah swam in swirling spirals in the waters of her Realm, leaving a silvery trail in her wake. She was in the part of her Realm that was closest to the Beyond World, but she did not look past the barrier that separated the two. Her Children followed, their movements mirroring her agitation. They were capable of sharing her mood, if not her thoughts.

The goddess could not confide her worries with her Children, for they were incapable of understanding her in that way. Nor could she speak of them with the other Jagasti. They would understand her far too well; and in such understanding, they would condemn her as Legaba had been condemned so long ago, as the people of the World Beyond conceived of time.

Had she done right with her latest intervention ... an act that forbidden by an accord among the Jagasti? Was she, in truth, no better than Legaba, or this new god, Almovaar, who now held sway in the land once favored by her and the others? And had the Jagasti been wrong to distance themselves from the Matile?

Nama-kwah had no answers to those questions. She knew only that she could not fully sever her connection with the Beyond World, as had the other Jagasti. She could not be content to spend her eternal life in her Realm, with occasional sojourns in the Realms of the other Jagasti. The Beyond World was ever-changing in ways that were outside her power, unlike her Realm, where she controlled all and could change its entirety at a moment's whim.

She had done something small in the World Beyond ... something slight enough to fall beneath the notice of the other Jagasti, if they even deigned to direct their attention beyond the boundaries of their Realms.

Nama-kwah had found a new Vessel.

Never before had a Jagasti bonded with as unlikely a Vessel as the one into whose hands her Mask had fallen. This Vessel was not a trained Amiya, but a thief-girl who possessed no understanding of the significance of the object she had stolen. For a time, Nama-kwah would not even allow the girl, Kalisha, to don the Mask, for she was not certain the thief could comprehend what the wearing of the Mask would mean, and what it would require from her.

As time passed, though, Nama-kwah sensed a quality in this Kalisha ... something much different from that of her previous Vessel, Tiyana, who had been born to be an Amiya and whose life had been set in that direction since her childhood. Yet in her own way, Kalisha, too, had been born to be an Amiya. But neither Nama-kwah nor Kalisha had been aware that she was so before disaster had struck the Matile, and the thief-girl had stolen the Mask.

When she was satisfied concerning Kalisha's capabilities, Nama-kwah had induced the girl to don the Mask and become her Vessel. And she had directed her new Vessel to find and free the Fidi-thief, for he, too, would play a part in the events that were unfolding in the Beyond World.

Two thieves ... one destiny.

Nama-kwah continued to swim in circles. She had done what she could; now, once again, the World Beyond would continue in its own way, separate from the workings of the Jagastis' Realms.

When the others discovered what she had done, they might well ostracize Nama-kwah in the same way they had isolated Legaba. And she well remembered that her own voice had been among those that had been raised against the Spider God. She had been convinced of the rightness of her cause then, and she was just as convinced now ... perhaps even more so.

Abruptly, Nama-kwah swam in a straight line toward the center of her Realm, far away from the border with the Beyond World. For now, she had done what she could. What was to come would be in the hands of her new Vessel ... and her previous one.

APPENDIX

CHARACTERS

Of the Matile:

Dardar Alemeyu, the Emperor of Matile Mala.

Issa, wife of Dardar Alemeyu and Empress of Matile Mala.

Makah, Emperor Alemeyu's pet cheetah.

Jass Gebrem, the Leba, or High Priest, of the Matile Mala Empire.

Membiri, deceased wife of Gebrem.

Tiyana, the Amiya, or Vessel, of the Jagasti Sea Goddess Nama-kwah; daughter of Jass Gebrem and Membiri.

Keshu, the Amiya of Halasha, the Jagasti God of iron and war.

Yemeya, one of the double-twin sisters who sing during the First Calling ceremony, and friend to Tiyana.

Jubiti, Tamala, and **Zeudi,** Yemeya's double-twin sisters.

Jass Eshana, the Dejezmek, or supreme commander, of the Matile military.

Jass Kidan, commander of the Matile archers.

Jass Kebessa, a minor member of the Degen Jassi.

Jass Hirute, a rural Imba Jassi noblewoman.

Jass Kassa, a member of the Imba Jassi, deceased husband of Jass Hirute.

Jass Tsege, a member of the Imba Jassi.

Jass Fetiwi, a member of the Imba Jassi.

Jass Shebeshi, member of the Imba Jassi and ill-fated ruler of a Matile hinterland
territory called Imbesh.

Bekele, an officer in the Matile army.

Keteme, an officer in the Matile army.

Tewolo, a soldier.

Asenafe, a place guard.

Adisu, a leather-worker.

Tamair, a widow.

Eshetu, a peasant farmer from the hinterland.

Sallamawit, the sister of Eshetu.

Desta, a woman of the hinterland.

Jass Mofo, leader of the Ashaki set, or gang, of *tsotsi* bandits.

Kimbi, consort of Jass Mofo.

Kalisha, a *tsotsi*, from Jass Mofo's set, who infiltrated the House of Amiyas in the guise of a servant.

Kece, a *tsotsi* of the Ashaki set.

Jumu, a tsotsi of the Ashaki set.

Kutu, a *tsotsi* of the Ashaki set.

Jass Nunu, head of the Hafar set of *tsotsis*, rivals to the Ashaki.

Etiya, a woman of ancient times whose singing first summoned the Jagasti.

Jaussa, the first Matile to makes use of the magic called *ashuma*.

Dardar Issuri, the first Emperor of the Matile Mala.

Dardar Tesfaru, Emperor of the Matile at the time of the Storm Wars.

Dardar Agaw, the Emperor of the Matile at the end of the Storm Wars.

Dardar Birhi, an earlier Emperor of the Matile.

Dardar Shumet, an ancient Empress of the Matile.

Wolde, the drummer during Matile coronation ceremonies.

Yekunu, the greatest of Matile sculptors of earlier times.

Of the Fidi:

Kyroun ni Channar, sorcerer and Seer of the Almovaad faith.

Byallis ni Shalla, an Adept of the Almovaads.

Ulrithana, an Adept of the Almovaads.

Hara, an Adept of the Almovaads.

Eimos, an Acolyte of the Almovaads.

Ruk, an Acolyte of the Almovaads.

Ferroun ni Tamiz, an Almovaad administrator who survived the sinking of the *Swordfish*.

Niall, a survivor of the sinking of the *Swordfish*.

Diamid, a survivor of the sinking of the *Swordfish*.

Aeliel, an Elven woman who survived the sinking of the *Swordfish*.

Pel Muldure, captain of the *White Gull*.

Lyann, first mate of the *White Gull*, and lover of Pel Muldure.

Athir Rin, a rogue sailor on the *White Gull*.

Herrin Junn, a sailor on the *White Gull*.

Hulett Jull, a Fidi merchant who travelled to Abengoni before the Storm Wars.

Channar ni Abdu, father of Kyroun.

Hulm Stonefist, a Fidi Dwarf.

Of the Tokoloshe:

Bulamalayo, the nominal head of the Tokoloshe Embassy in Khambawe.

Rumundulu, the true head of the Tokoloshe Embassy.

Mungulutu, the ruler of the Tokoloshe.

Izindikwa, a Tokoloshe woman.

Chiminuka, an elderly Tokoloshe woman.

Humutungu, the first Tokoloshe child to be born in many years.

Of The Uloans:

Jass Imbiah, ruler of the Uloa Islands

Bujiji, a Uloan warrior.

Awiwi, lover of Bujiji.

Sehaye, a Uloan spy among the Matile in Khambawe.

Jawai, an elder.

Of the Thabas:

Tshakane, a chieftain who is uniting the Thaba tribes and menacing the rural population of the Matile Mala.

RACES AND ETHNICITIES

Matile, the dominant people of the northern part of the continent of Abengoni,
founders of the Matile Mala Empire.

Uloans, people of Matile descent who inhabit a chain of islands of the same name off the
coast of Abengoni. An ancient feud has made the Uloans the arch-enemies of the Matile.

Kipalende, a small-statured, peaceful people who preceded the Uloans in the islands.

Tokoloshe, a secretive, dwarf-like race allied with the Matile.

Thabas, a pastoral, tribal people who dwell in the hill country to the south of the Matile
lands.

Kidogo, a pygmy race that dwells in the forests south of the land of the Thabas.

Bashombe, a full-sized people who live in the same forests as the Kidogo.

Kwa'manga, diminutive, golden-brown desert-dwellers.

Ole-kisongo, nomadic herders who live in the savanna south of the desert.

Wakyambi, an Elven race that dwells in the savanna.

Ikuya, the tall people who live at the southern tip of Abengoni.

Changami, a hybrid people who live in the Gundagumu region in Abengoni's northeast.

Fidi, the people of the far-off continent of Cym Dinath. The name derives from the port
city of Fiadol, from which many voyages to Abengoni set sail in the distant past.

Yaghan, a community of sorcerers who dwell in the Rafja Mountains.

Shadim, a secretive race from the east of Cym Dinath.

Dwarvenkind, a short, stocky, long-lived people.

Elven, an immortal, ethereal, aloof race.

DEITIES AND OTHER SUPERNATURALS

Ateti, a Jagasti, known to the Matile as the Goddess of lakes and rivers.

Akpema, a Jagasti, known to the Matile as the God of the sun.

Alamak, a Jagasti, known to the Matile as the Goddess of the stars.

Chaile, a Jagasti, known to the Matile as the God of fortune both good and ill.

Halasha, a Jagasti, known to the Matile as the God of iron, the blacksmith's craft, and war.

Legaba, a Jagasti, known to the Matile as the God of the Underworld.

Metelit, a Jagasti, known to the Matile as the Goddess of the Afterworld.

Nama-kwah, a Jagasti, known to the Matile as the Goddess of the Sea.

Sama-wai, a Jagasti, known to the Matile as the Goddess of illness and decay.

Ufashwe, a Jagasti, known to the Matile as the God of the wind.

Adwe, a world-spanning serpent that imprisoned the ancient ancestors of the people of Abengoni.

Almovaar, a Fidi deity worshipped by the Almovaads.

PLACES

Abengoni, a vast, tropical continent separated from most of the rest of the known world by huge expanses of ocean, including the Sea of Storms.

Matile Mala Empire, in times past, the mightiest polity ever known on

Abengoni. Now reduced through war and catastrophe to a remnant clinging to its last stronghold on the shores of the Sea of Storms.

Khambawe, the Jewel City, capital of the Matile Mala Empire.

Gebbi Senafa, the royal palace of the Matile Emperors in Khambawe.

Gebbi Zimballa, the Old Palace of the Matile Emperors.

Beit-Amiya, the House of the Vessels of the Jagasti, a temple and dwelling place in
Khambawe.

The Maim, an extremely violent, crime-infested slum in Khambawe.

Imbesh, a Matile hinterland territory recently overrun by the Thabas.

Kembana, a rural territory.

Aglada, a city in the Matile Mala Empire.

Gondaba, a city in the Matile Mala Empire.

Ibela, a city in the Matile Mala Empire.

Jimmar, a city in the Matile Mala Empire.

Tesseni, a city in the Matile Mala Empire.

Nangi Kihunu, a devastated territory east of the Matile Mala, inhabited by beasts fearsomely altered by the uncontrolled sorcery of the Storm Wars.

Uloa Islands, also called The Shattered Isles, an archipelago located to the northwest of the continent of Abengoni.

Jayaya, the largest island of the Uloas.

Ompong, the capital city of Jayaya.

Makula, an island of the Uloas.

Omanee, an island of the Uloas.

Akara, a small island off the southwestern coast of Abengoni, not part of the Shattered Isles.

Khumba Khourou, a desert located to the south of the Thaba country.

Mbali-pana, a savanna south of the Khumba Khourou desert.

Kiti ya Ngai, or Seat of the Gods, a towering mountain in the midst of the savanna.

Mashambani-m'ti, a belt of tropical rain forest that stretches across the middle of Abengoni.

Luango, the greatest river in the Mashambani-m'ti.

Bashoga, a riverine kingdom in the Mashambani-m'ti.

Mukondo, a riverine kingdom in the Mashambani-m'ti.

Nyayembe, a riverine kingdom in the Mashambani-m'ti.

Usisi, a riverine kingdom in the Mashambani-m'ti.

Jhagga, an uninhabited, noxious swampland.

Kashai, a rugged, semi-arid steppe at the southern tip of Abengoni.

Gundagumu, a fertile plateau in the northeast of Abengoni.

Chiminuhwa, a kingdom in the Gundagumu.

Inyangana, a kingdom in the Gundagumu.

Kadishwene, a kingdom in the Gundagumu.

Mbiri, a kingdom in the Gundagumu.

Vengaye, a kingdom in the Gundagumu.

Itsekiri, an island continent of dark-skinned people to the east of Abengoni.

Cym Dinath, a large continent to the far north of Abengoni, beyond the Sea of Storms.

Fiadol, a seafaring nation in Cym Dinath.

Angless, the chief seaport of Fiadol.

Lumaron, an eastern kingdom in Cym Dinath, birthplace of Kyroun ni Channar.

Ul-Enish, a city near Lumaron, birthplace of Byallis ni Shalla.

Vakshma, Cym Dinath's City of Thieves.

Bashoob, a vast desert separating the east and west of Cym Dinath.

Pashtar, an oasis kingdom in the Bashoob.

Rafja Mountains, a distant range in the lands to the east of the Bashoob.

GLOSSARY

abi, a silver rod that focuses the sorcerous power of the High Priest of the Matile.

aderash, estates and mansions that belong to the aristocracy of Khambawe.

Almovaad, a follower of the Seer Kyroun, and Believer in the god Almovaar.

Amiya, a human Vessel, or host, for the magical power channeled by the Jagasti, the pantheon of deities worshipped by the Matile.

ashuma, the power that fuels Matile sorcery, channeled from the deities through the Vessels of the Jagasti.

assegai, the stabbing-spear of the Thaba tribesmen.

blankskin, an Uloan term of derision for the Matile who dwell in the Abengoni Mainland.

chamma, a mantle-like garment worn by Matile men and women.

Degen Jassi, the collective term for the urban aristocracy of the Matile, and also for their formal gatherings.

Dejezmek, the title given to the supreme commander of the Matile military forces.

gede, a sorcerous construct used by Uloan spies to send messages to their island homeland.

gharri, a two-wheeled chariot used by the Matile for transportation and war.

harai, a shoulder-shawl worn by men and women of the outlying, agricultural provinces of the Matile Empire.

huangi, the master sorcerers of the Uloans.

igikoko, eaters of carrion and corpses.

injerra, flat disks of bread that are a staple food of the Matile.

Imba Jassi, the aristocracy of the Matile agrarian hinterland.

imbilta, a type of flute played during the Matiles' First Calling ceremony.

irimu, a legendary supernatural race that can shift shapes between human and animal.

Ishimbi, a group of gigantic statues located at the waterfront of Khambawe.

izingogo, humanoid quadrupeds that hunt in packs and hate all other living beings.

Jagasti, the pantheon of gods and goddesses worshipped by the Matile. The Jagasti dwell in their own Realms: arcane dimensions that are repositories of magical power.

Jass, the Matile equivalent to "Lord" or "Lady," a title held by members of the Matile aristocracy.

jhumbi, a clay-covered, walking Uloan corpse.

kabbar, farmers in the hinterlands of the Imba Jassi.

kef, a red fruit, the seeds of which are brewed into a strong drink of the same name.

khat, a narcotic leaf chewed – and sold – by the *tsotsi* bandits.

Leba, the title of the High Priest of the Matile, the One to Whom All Gods speak.

makishi, malevolent giants that dwell in the most remote, desolate areas of the Nangi Kihunu.

Mesfin, a title used when addressing the Emperor or Empress of the Matile, analogous to "Your Highness" or "Your Majesty."

munkimun, long-tailed lemurs that dwell in the Uloa Islands.

Muvuli, shadow-assassins controlled by the Almovaads.

mwiti, the semi-animate vegetation of the Uloan Islands.

Negarit, an ancient drum used in Matile coronation ceremonies.

quagga, a zebra-like animal used by the Matile as a mount and for pulling wheeled vehicles.

senafil, decorated trousers worn by Matile men.

shamasha, previously a designation for Thabas enslaved by the Matile, now a general term applied to Matile servants.

talla, a grain beer popular among the Matile.

talla-beit, a tavern.

tirss, a spiked, mace-like weapon favored by the *tsotsis*.

tsotsis, gangs of young thieves and brigands who control the less-prosperous sections of Khambawe.

tukul, the round, conical-roofed dwellings of Matile farmers.

wat, an extremely spicy stew eaten by the Matile.

woira, a huge, thick-limbed tree found in the land of the Matile.

MVmedia

For the best in Science Fiction and Fantasy

www.mvmediaatl.com

IMARO
BOOKS ONE THRU FOUR

BY CHARLES R. SAUNDERS

AVAILABLE AT LULU.COM

DOSSOUYE

BOOKS ONE AND TWO

BY CHARLES R. SAUNDERS

AVAILABLE AT LULU.COM